Praise for *Live to Tape*

"Live to Tape, the next Ethan Benson psychological murder mystery unfolds through the investigative journalism process. Utilizing a crack staff at *The Weekly Reporter*, Jeff Diamond's character, Ethan Benson, uncovers the diabolical mind of a murderer through the on camera interview. The attention to detail and the crafting of the story kept me in suspense with many revelations along the way. Unanswered questions, conspiracies, lowlife characters, corruption, and payoffs all come together to weave a page turning novel. Highly recommended."

Michael Pulitzer, Jr.,
retired Broadcast Executive, Hearst Argyle Television

"Jeff Diamond's Live to Tape details the efforts of a dogged television journalist who investigates a lurid crime, discovers a widespread cover-up, and, in the process, puts his career, marriage, and life at risk. Jeff creates, through his forty year career in network television news, a compelling 'I can't put this down' crime novel. The conclusion will leave you breathless."

William Lord,
former ABC News Executive Producer & Vice President

"The suspense sucks you in on the very first page. Ethan Benson—an award-winning TV news producer and crime fighting sleuth—is assigned to a frightening but engrossing murder mystery. We hold our breath as we watch him unravel the dark secret of a terrifying killer, all the while fighting his own personal demons. Ethan may be flawed, stubborn, and irascible, but damn he's good. I couldn't put Live to Tape down until that explosive end."

Bill Ritter,
Anchor, Eyewitness News, WABC-TV

"Jeff Diamond has created a character to rival Hannibal Lechter and a book both chilling and touching. He draws on his extraordinary television experience to give real veracity to every scene and character. As one who has traveled in this world, I am in awe of the research, depth, and detail he brings to his work. A riveting fast-paced read with an unexpectedly poignant and powerful twist, this is what they mean by thriller."

Karen Burnes,
former Co-Anchor CBS Newsmagazine West 57th,
ABC's PrimeTime Live, and Investigative
Correspondent, ABC News

"Only those who have met evil up close and in person can understand how seemingly normal, successful people can sink to shocking levels of depravity. Author Jeffrey L. Diamond, in his decades of work as a journalist, has looked into evil's eyes in the real world, listened to calculated words, and used those memories to create one of the most terrifying killers in fiction, Dr. Rufus Wellington. Live to Tape is a rapid-fire thriller with news producer, Ethan Benson, fighting his own personal demons while digging into what on the surface is the murder of a young girl, but which he eventually comes to realize is much more terrifying. This behind-the-scenes look at the world of television news and its outsized egos is coupled with a smart detective story that will keep you up many a night."

Don Dahler,
correspondent CBS News This Morning,
ABC News 20/20, Good Morning America

LIVE TO TAPE

An Ethan Benson Thriller

by
Jeffrey L. Diamond

PAGE PUBLISHING, INC.
New York, NY

First originally published by Page Publishing, Inc. 2017

ISBN 978-1-63568-621-0 (Paperback)
ISBN 978-1-63568-029-4 (Digital)

Printed in the United States of America

This book is a work of fiction. The characters, places,
businesses, and storyline are solely a product of the author's
imagination. Any resemblance to actual persons, living or
dead, events, locales, or places of employment is completely
unintended and purely coincidental.

PROLOGUE

THE NIGHT WAS WARM AND still, a full moon shimmering brightly in the crystal clear waters of the Quabbin Reservoir as the doctor dragged a fraying garbage bag through the dense forest, bumping the contents over jagged rocks and prickly beds of pine needles. Soaked in sweat, his white shirt stuck to his chest; his khaki pants rode uncomfortably up his calves like an extra layer of skin. He was covered in blood, his hands and face smeared with the congealing liquid, his clothes soaked in a sticky brown paste. Out of breath, he hurried down a narrow footpath and entered a small clearing overgrown with ferns and wild flowers.

He stopped and listened. The melancholy calls of tree frogs echoed in the distance. A swarm of mosquitoes buzzed around his head. He turned and looked back down the trail. Nobody could have followed him here.

Wiping his face with the sleeve of his shirt, he slipped off his heavy canvas backpack and pulled out a shovel, a pickax, and a selection of tools he thought might be useful—lining them up meticulously, by size, in a neat row. Then he started digging, his mind firing in a kaleidoscope of lustful memories. She was a young girl he'd met trolling a red light district in South Boston. He'd seen her standing there on a sleazy street corner, barely

JEFFREY L. DIAMOND

dressed, in her see-through blouse, tight short jeans, her thighs showing, her breasts beckoning, and that's when it started—his hunt, his pursuit, his obsession. Stalking her for days, he watched her hook up with one john after another, before finally getting up the nerve and approaching her for a date. Soon he was seeing her every week, then every day, then every night—wining and dining her at all the best restaurants, showering her with fine diamonds and furs, and sweeping her off in his chauffeured limousine for romantic weekends at his country estate. He began to twitch, his eyes fluttering wildly, as he tried to remember just when he'd fallen in love with her—picturing her silky skin, her sweet-smelling hair, and the delicate features of her face.

He'd longed to spend his life with her.

To cherish her.

To possess her.

"Why had she said *no*?" The words bounced back and forth in his mind like an exploding cannonball. "Why didn't she want me? Why wouldn't she marry me? Why did she make me feel so insignificant, like a speck of dust floating in the wind? I loved her. Loved her. LOVED HER!" he wailed, crestfallen, tears streaming down his cheeks, soaking his collar. He wiped his forehead and continued digging, remembering how she'd sneered contemptuously and how she'd laughed at him. All he'd wanted was to crawl under a rock and make the pain go away.

But that's not what happened.

No.

That's not what he did.

He stopped digging and howled in pain, his tongue darting in and out of his mouth, moistening his dry lips as he obsessed about everything he'd just done to her—the images vivid in his mind—tracking her around his bedroom, naked and screaming, kicking her with his feet, pummeling her with his fists, blackening her eyes, smashing her nose, ruining her beautiful face. She'd crumpled to the floor—blood gushing from her chin and onto her voluptuous breasts—begging, begging him to stop, begging him to forgive her. But she never admitted, not once, that she desired him as much as he desired her. That she wanted to be with him forever. That she wanted to live as man and wife.

"So I couldn't forgive her," he wailed. "Never. Never. NEVER! I had to make her pay for not loving me."

He stopped digging, trying to calm down, his mind a jumble of discordant thoughts as he pictured her crawling on her hands and knees, trying to get away from him—her face bloody with bruises and abrasions. Then he'd kicked her again and again, in her stomach, in her side, between her legs, watching her head seesaw like a pendulum as her eyes rolled back behind her eyelids and she passed into darkness. God had ordained it. She had to disappear before the pain would go away.

He laughed, in a frenzy, as he always did when he was out of control and remembered what he'd done to her next. He'd yanked her out of his bedroom, across the long, twisting hallways, and down the back staircase, her head bumping each step—*thump, thump, thump*—as he dragged her through the living room, the sitting room, the dining room, the kitchen, and down there to his special place, to his secret place, to the place that made him whole, to the place where he became who he was. That's when she'd awakened for the last time, shrieking, promising not to tell anyone about the horrible things he'd just done to her, pleading for her life.

But he didn't listen.

No. No.

Too late for that.

That's where he'd murdered her.

Alone now in the meadow, clouds floating across the sky, blocking the moonlight and casting ominous shadows over the landscape, he finished digging and climbed out of her grave.

"Why did you have to mock me?" he whimpered like a child. "I loved you. Cherished you. Worshipped you with all my heart. Why did you forsake me?"

Then he carefully peeled away the plastic bag and placed her body in a grotesque tableau. Here was that beautiful young woman. Never to smile again. Never to laugh again. Never to bring joy to him or anyone else. His face stiffened into a sneer as he stepped back and admired his handiwork, before quickly filling in the grave, stomping on the loose earth until it was hard and scattering a layer of leaves and tree branches over it. Satisfied, he collected his tools and started back to his house.

He didn't get far.

At the edge of the clearing, a light beam fell on him—and then another. A half dozen policemen were racing up the narrow footpath toward him—weapons drawn. They stopped abruptly, startled, when they recognized him.

"Dr. Wellington," said the sheriff, Eugene McKenzie—a mountain of a man with bulging muscles and a long, thick neck that strained his neatly pressed shirt collar—"we got a 911 call from your neighbor who heard screaming coming from your house. The dispatcher back at the station sent out a code red, but nobody was home when we knocked at the door, so we searched the yard then decided to canvass the rest of your property. Everything okay, Dr. Wellington?" he said suspiciously.

"Everything's just fine, Sheriff," the doctor said truculently.

"What are you doin' all alone out here in the woods in the middle of the night?" the sheriff said, shining his flashlight up and down the doctor's disheveled clothing. "You're covered in mud. You been diggin' somethin'?"

The doctor looked down at his soiled clothes, his body reeking of sweat. "Guess I couldn't sleep. So I went for a long walk in the fresh air and got rid of some garbage from the house," he said. "Now I should ask you the same question, Sheriff. What are you doing trespassing on my property? I suggest you and your men get off my land before I call my lawyer."

"Can't do that, Dr. Wellington," McKenzie said adamantly. "There's blood on your back porch and a trail leading down to the clearing." The sheriff took two steps closer, raising his gun. "Where'd all the blood come from? Did you hurt yourself? Did you hurt somebody else?"

"I have no idea what you're talking about," Dr. Wellington said indignantly. "I live alone, and you and your men all know that. In fact, everybody knows everybody else's business—including mine—here at the Quabbin." His eyes followed the sheriff's deputies fanning out across the meadow, continuing to search, waving their flashlights in small arcs in front of them, inching closer to the makeshift grave site. "It's time for you to go, Eugene. Get off of my land."

"Nope. Not yet," the sheriff said, still pointing his gun. "You still got some explaining to do. See, you're covered in blood too. It's all over your hands and face and on your clothes. How'd it get there?"

The doctor reached up and touched his cheek.

A speck of blood caked under his fingernail.

"Over here," one of the deputies shouted from across the clearing. "I think I found something," he said, shining his flashlight over the fresh mound of earth. "It may be a grave. What do you want us to do?"

"Sift through it carefully," McKenzie said dubiously, "and for Christ's sake, be careful. Step away and wait for forensics if you find anything." The sheriff glared at the doctor. "Turn around, and put your hands behind your back." He snapped on handcuffs. "Now let's go see what's hiding in that hole over there." He grabbed the doctor roughly by his shirt collar and pushed him toward the deputy who was crawling on his hands and knees, gingerly removing loose debris. "What are we gonna find, Dr. Wellington?" he said. "Did you use those tools you're carrying to bury somebody?"

The doctor didn't answer.

"Oh, Lord Jesus, I found something," the deputy said, turning and retching up his dinner.

The sheriff leaned over and stared aghast, then bellowed across the meadow, "Cordon off the entire area, and don't touch anything else. Call the coroner, and get the crime lab down here. We got ourselves a murder, and we got ourselves a prime suspect." He turned to the doctor, "Now lay down, and don't move a muscle, or so help me God, I'll blow your fucking head off."

The doctor began to cackle, the sound of madness echoing across the meadow as he fell to his knees, and collapsed on the ground. After all those years of meticulous execution, he'd finally made a mistake. Now there was no escaping his past. No escaping the truth. A sinister smile broke out on Dr. Rufus Wellington's face as he looked up at the sheriff with hatred in his eyes.

Then his body went limp.

And his mind devolved into a cauldron of chaos.

CHAPTER 1

ETHAN BENSON CLIMBED OFF THE elevator and walked into the waiting room on the management floor of Global Broadcasting's corporate headquarters—the center of power of the most powerful television network in the country. It was his first day in his new job—with all its new responsibilities, with all its uncertainties. He was feeling trepidation as he crossed the room and stopped at the receptionist's desk. Jennifer didn't look up. She was reading e-mail on her computer and making a list of things she had to do for the executives in charge of the award-winning newsmagazine *The Weekly Reporter.*

He cleared his throat. "Jen, do you have the key to my new office?"

"Oh, Ethan, I didn't see you standing there." She didn't move her eyes from the computer screen. Ethan waited as she finished typing a sentence.

"Envelope on the corner of my desk. Your name's on it."

The phone rang, and she picked up. "This is Jennifer. How can I help you?"

Ethan grabbed the envelope and shook out a key, palming it in his hand self-consciously, hoping he was up to the task that lay ahead of him. A big man, standing six feet three and two hundred pounds with sensitive blue eyes and curly black hair—he was approaching his forty-fifth birthday and had just been named senior producer for the show's anchorman, Peter Sampson. They'd recently teamed up on an investigative report about the murder of Cynthia Jameson, the daughter of New York City's deputy mayor. The anchorman had been showered in accolades for getting her father to confess on live television—afterward going to senior management and insisting Ethan be promoted so he could supervise all his other projects. Today Ethan was moving to a large-windowed office right next to Sampson on the eleventh floor.

He should've been happy.

Excited.

Elated.

But all he felt was inadequate.

He placed the key in his pocket and walked over to the door separating the waiting room from the rest of the management floor.

"Would you stop what you're doing and buzz me in, Jennifer? I'm running late."

"Hold on a sec," she said into the telephone before placing her hand over the mouthpiece and looking up at Ethan. "Mr. Sampson's in his office. He wants to see you right away. And let me warn you, he's not in the best of moods." She hit a button under her desk and opened the door.

"Thanks, Jen," he said hesitantly as he pushed his way through and began the long trek down to the anchorman's office—growing more and more self-conscious and out of place. The plush wall-to-wall carpeting, the expensive leather furniture, and the fancy artwork hanging on the walls were a far cry from the utilitarian sparseness one floor below where he shared his old office with the other producers who worked on the show.

He took a calming breath.

His new job was a step up the corporate ladder with a big bump in pay, but deep down, he still wasn't sure he'd made the right decision. Maybe he couldn't handle the pressure of being an executive. Maybe he couldn't take the day-to-day stresses of working with the mercurial anchorman. Maybe he should've walked away from the promotion and remained a producer, reporting on hard-hitting stories.

That was his first love.

That's what he did best.

He proceeded down the hallway and stopped in front of Sampson's office where his pretty Latina assistant, Consuela Santana, was frantically shuffling through documents as she juggled the anchorman's busy schedule of speeches and dinner parties and fund-raisers, searching for any free time so he could actually do some work on the show.

She looked tired.

Stressed.

Would he feel the same way in a couple of weeks?

He shifted his weight from one foot to the next then rapped on the glass partition barricading Sampson from the rest of the floor, "How's it goin', Consuela? Is Peter in?"

"Hey, Ethan. He's on the telephone with Douglas Fitzgerald going over ratings and God knows what else. Take a seat. He doesn't want to be disturbed while he's talking to the president of the News Division. It'll only be a couple more minutes." She looked at her notes then resumed banging away on her computer.

Ethan sat down on a leather couch and leafed through a *Wall Street Journal.* Then a *New York Times.* Then a *Washington*

Post. Growing more and more nervous. More and more impatient. More and more resentful. After waiting for what seemed an eternity, the anchorman finally stormed out of his office.

"You're late," he said, scowling. "My schedule's packed with countless meetings and screenings and telephone calls, and I don't have time to be sitting here, wondering where you are. So let's not get off on the wrong foot on your very first day. You work for me now, and we have a million things to go over. I expect you here every day before I arrive. And don't you forget it."

He turned and briskly walked back into his office.

Ethan could feel his blood boiling. Sampson had a nasty habit of yelling and screaming and pushing his buttons. Now that he'd be spending more time with the anchorman, he had to learn to control his emotions and figure out a way to work with his new boss.

It wouldn't be easy.

After slowly counting to ten, he followed him into his inner sanctuary, sitting down in a satin Queen Anne chair—one of a pair across from Sampson's eighteenth-century Louis XIV desk. Staring at his signature red suspenders and his neatly coiffed white hair, he patiently waited as the anchorman flipped through a stack of documents and answered a series of e-mails.

"I'll be done in a minute," Sampson said harshly. "Just sit there and be quiet." He continued pounding away on his computer, muttering, his eyes glued to the screen. After five exasperating minutes, he turned and barked at Consuela, "Bring coffee for me and Ethan, and use the English china. And where's my itinerary? You're supposed to leave it for me before I get here. How can I plan my day if I don't know my schedule?"

"It's right in front of you on the desk," she said, unfazed by the nasty tone in his voice. "Paul's on line 1. Do you want to take the call?"

"Of course. He's our executive producer. I always take his calls." He straightened his tie and calmly spoke into the phone, "Good morning, Paul, what do you have for me today?"

Ethan wondered if he should get up and leave. Sampson was usually secretive and never wanted anybody listening to his conversations. But today was different. Today he was a senior producer.

Maybe he should stay.

"Yes, Paul, Ethan's sitting right here in my office," Sampson said warmly. "Come join us. I'll make sure he doesn't leave. See you in a few minutes."

"What's going on?" Ethan said, hoping to find his footing with Sampson.

"Paul has a story he wants to discuss with us. He's bringing Dirk Fulton and one of those damn researchers whose name I've already forgotten."

"What's the story?"

"How the hell should I know?" Sampson said, grumbling. "He didn't tell me." He picked up his schedule and began scanning the first page.

Ethan sat fidgeting.

Ready to explode.

He needed a cigarette.

⁓

Ten minutes later, Paul Lang marched into Peter's office followed by Dirk Fulton, the show's editorial producer, and David Livingston, a crackerjack young researcher who'd grown close to Ethan on his last story about the deputy mayor and who knew

Ethan's foibles—both his strengths and weaknesses—much better than most of his other colleagues on the show.

Ethan grinned when they entered the room.

"Welcome to the eleventh floor," Paul said curtly. "Hope you're settling in to your new job with Peter. I know he's not the easiest person to spend time with, but somehow I think you'll manage." Lang was a short, thin man with long blond hair pulled back in a ponytail. He was impeccably dressed in a gray Armani suit, a starched white shirt, and a yellow silk tie. "I don't have a lot of time," he said bluntly. "So enough with the small talk. I have a story I want you to look into for Peter—a story that should help pump up the show's ratings. It's a murder—a rather gruesome murder. Some prominent Boston surgeon killed his girlfriend at his country estate in Massachusetts and buried her in a meadow in back of his house."

"I just did a murder with Ethan," Sampson said, irritated. "Find somebody else for this story."

"Hear me out, Peter," Paul said conciliatorily. "I had the same reaction when Dirk first pitched me the idea, but there's more here than meets the eye." He turned to his editorial producer, "Tell him what you just told me in my office."

Dirk shifted in his chair. An older man in his midsixties, he was the elder statesman on the show with a keen nose for news. "First of all, this is David's story, not mine. He brought it to me and has been working it up the past few weeks. He's already talked to the district attorney and the cops in the town where the murder took place. David, what's the name of the town?"

"Old Salem," David said. "It's a historic village, founded in 1750, so small it doesn't have its own police department. So I've been talking to the sheriff in Athol—a bigger town a couple of miles away. He handled the investigation."

"Anyway," Dirk said, "the murder occurred two summers ago at the weekend home of this heart surgeon who practiced at Mass General in Boston."

"What's his name?" Ethan said.

"Rufus Wellington," Dirk said, checking his notes. "He's fantastically wealthy and a blue blood. His family goes way back in New England society."

Sampson was impatiently tapping his fingers on his desk. "I still don't get it, Paul. Why do you want me to do this story?"

Paul waved him off, "Not finished yet. Go ahead, Dirk."

"The murder was a huge scandal. The victim was a sixteen-year-old hooker named Heather Starr that Wellington picked up on a street corner in one of Boston's 'combat zones.'"

"That's her real name?" Ethan asked, raising an eyebrow.

"Nobody knows for sure," David said, jumping in. "Cops were never able to ID her. Apparently, he fell in love with her and then snapped when she turned down his marriage proposal. So he beat her to death and buried her in a secluded meadow on his property. The cops caught him near her grave covered in her blood."

It sounded like a tabloid story to Ethan. "Why do we care?"

Paul turned to Dirk, "Tell him."

"Wellington was represented by a local attorney—a guy name Bret Davenport, who was a childhood friend," Dirk said, looking from Peter to Ethan. "At the first court hearing, the doc pleaded guilty and waived his right to a trial then refused to say another word to the cops, to the prosecutor, or even to his friend, the attorney."

"So he admitted that he killed her," Ethan said. "Any other proof?"

"Yeah. His DNA was all over her body—and hers was all over his."

"And then, there was his taped confession," David said earnestly.

"Plus that," Dirk said. "There was no doubt he committed the murder. He was sentenced by the judge to thirty years to life."

Ethan weighed the plusses and minuses. "You know, Peter may be right. Seems like a pretty cut-and-dry case. Why should we spend the time and money doing this story? Aren't there other projects—maybe a story about the explosion of heroin addiction in our suburbs or a piece on terrorism—that are more pressing than this one?"

"No."

"But why?"

"Because the guy may get out of jail," Paul said bluntly.

Ethan snapped to attention. "How could that be? He just started his sentence. Only been behind bars a couple of years?"

"A technicality," David said. "Something to do with the chain of evidence. At least, that's what I've been told by an editor at one of the local newspapers."

"What happened?"

"We don't know. The editor said Wellington's attorney—this guy Bret Davenport—is very calculating and hasn't made any public statements about the appeal yet."

Ethan turned to Peter, "Maybe we should check it out? There's more here than I first thought."

"It's still a sordid murder, Ethan," Sampson said stonily. "I'm the anchorman of this show, and this story is beneath me. There's no trial, no visual elements, and just a bunch of talking heads. Give it to another correspondent."

"We can't do that," Paul said.

"Why not? You're the boss. Give it to my coanchor, Julie Piedmont. She does most of our crime stories. She loves them."

"Wellington won't do it with Julie or with any of the show's other correspondents," Paul said pointedly. "He'll only do it with you, Peter...and with Ethan. He watched your last story in his prison cell then contacted his attorney, who called David and told him his client is ready to talk, but only to the two of you." Paul turned to Ethan, "Plus, he's now saying there's more to the murder than anyone can possibly imagine. Much more."

Ethan leaned back in his chair. "Okay, Paul, I get it. He wants to talk but only to us. What's our next move?"

"Wait a minute. I have a say in this, Ethan," Peter said. "You work for me now. Tell them, I don't want to do this story."

Ethan looked at Sampson, uncertain, at a crossroads. The anchorman was testing him, trying to push him around, trying to see how much he could get away with. After weighing his options, he breathed heavily and took control of the meeting.

"Let me check out the story as your senior producer. I'll make a couple of phone calls, talk to the key players, and maybe drive up to Old Salem to do some snooping around. Once I have a better feel for the case, you and I will make a decision and decide if we should put the story into production or kill it. Does that work for you, Peter?"

Sampson hesitated, never changing the stony expression on his face. "Sounds like a plan I can maybe live with." He turned to the executive producer, "Now I remember why I wanted to make him my senior producer. I can let him do all the thinking for me. Okay, Paul, we'll do a little digging then get back to you." He whipped around and stared at Ethan, "But I don't want you spending a lot of time on this. Do the research, and make a decision. You have other responsibilities now that you work for me. That's something we need to talk about in detail—and very soon." He checked his watch. "So is there anything else we have to go over? I'm having lunch with the mayor. Gotta leave in a couple of minutes."

"We're finished," Paul said, standing and gesturing to Ethan, "Come. I need a little time to go over story logistics. Let's talk in my office."

Ethan followed Paul down a long red hallway, past a wall of portraits of the executive producer posing with the rich and famous, Dirk and David tagging along several steps behind them. When they reached his suite of offices, Paul yelled at his number one assistant, "Monica, hold my calls. This shouldn't take long. Let's hope Ethan can handle his new story without too much guidance from me." He sat at his big Florence Knoll glass top desk and turned to Ethan. "So ... what do you need to get started?"

"First, I need David."

"He's all yours," Paul said, nodding at the researcher.

"I'll need him in Massachusetts with me. He knows everybody involved in the story and can make introductions."

"Done."

"And the trip's gonna be expensive."

"Put together a research budget, and e-mail it to me," he said, starting to doodle on a yellow pad. "I'll approve it if it's reasonable."

"And now that I have additional responsibilities working with Peter, I'll need a good associate producer to help me."

"Let me guess. You'd like me to assign Mindy," Paul said, not looking up from his scribblings.

"Perfect," Ethan said, relieved.

Mindy Herman was a first-rate reporter and one of the best associate producers on the show. They shared a very special working relationship, Ethan relying on her editorial judgment and production skills whenever he could swing her as his number two on a story.

"Tell her to call Ethan," Paul said, waving at Dirk Fulton. "Anything else?"

"Just one more thing, Paul. Who do you want me to report to?"

"That should be obvious. You're a senior producer. You report directly to me."

"Not to Dirk or Lenny Franklin or Joyce Cox? Your other senior management?"

"Not to anyone but me. That's how Peter and I want it. From now on, the three of us will work together as a team on all his projects."

"New job. New marching orders," Ethan said, pleased with the unexpected change in his status on the show. "I just wanted to hear it from you."

"Good. Now that we've settled the chain of command, any more questions?"

Everyone shook their head no.

"As soon as you're ready, Ethan, get me your plan to launch the story."

"I will, Paul."

"You do that," he said dismissively. "Now I have work to do."

After saying good-bye, Ethan walked out of Paul's office, buoyed by the first morning in his new job. As he passed Consuela, she looked up from her computer without a second of hesitation.

"I've got your messages, Ethan."

He stopped, perplexed. "What do you mean?"

"Some of Mr. Sampson's producers are looking for you." She handed him a sheet of paper with their names then said timidly, "Mr. Sampson just yelled at me. Said he wants me to help you transition into your new job—now that you're part of his team. Didn't he tell you?"

"So you work for me too?"

"For the time being."

"Cool. I wasn't expecting that."

Then he inserted his new key in the door and fumbled with the lock.

"Let me help you with that," Consuela said, grabbing the key. "Our new security system takes a little getting used to." She unlocked the door effortlessly. "You'll get the hang of it—eventually—like everything else in Mr. Sampson's world."

Would he?

Ethan nodded sheepishly and walked into his office for the first time. A broad grin spread across his face as he peered at the freshly painted walls and new carpeting. He sat in the sleek leather chair at his new executive workstation; dropped his old, beat-up briefcase on the floor; then stared vacantly at the stacks of boxes with all the worldly possessions from his last office. He needed to unpack. Set up his new workspace. Get organized for his new life. But not now. Not today. There'd be plenty of time for that when he was ready. Sighing deeply, he scanned through his messages before picking up the phone and punching in the number at the top of the list.

Time to assume his new responsibilities.

And his role as Sampson's gatekeeper.

CHAPTER 2

ETHAN STEPPED OFF THE MADISON Avenue bus and walked toward Ninety-First Street. He'd been living in the same condominium his entire life, and the neighborhood felt warm and inviting. The unnerving memories of his run-in with the Russian hit man on his last story were fading. Soon they'd dissolve into his distant past. He flipped his cigarette into the gutter and walked into the lobby of his building, said hello to Winston the doorman, and hopped on the elevator.

His Labrador retriever, Holly, was standing at attention, wagging her tail, when he unlocked his front door and pushed into the foyer. He bent over on one knee and gently rubbed her muzzle then left his briefcase on a side table and headed down the center hallway. He found his six-year-old son, Luke, in front of the television in his bedroom.

"Hey, kiddo, what are you watching?" he said lovingly.

"*SpongeBob SquarePants*," Luke said, transfixed by the cartoon.

"What, no Yankees?"

"Dad. Please. The season's been over for a month. You know that."

"Guess I can't outsmart you, can I, little man?" Ethan chuckled. "Where's your mom?"

"In the kitchen, making dinner. I don't wanna talk now. I can't hear the TV."

"Okay. I get it. Television trumps your dear old dad." Ethan paused before leaving. His kid was so damn cute.

Then he headed to the kitchen.

Sarah was standing at the stove, stirring a pot. She was radiantly beautiful, with shiny blue eyes and silky blond hair. There was hardly a wrinkle on her face, her skin soft and creamy, her features alluring. They'd been married for more than a decade, had experienced their ups and downs like most couples, but there was something about her that kept him steady, anchored, and moving forward, that made her his soul mate. Putting his arms around her waist, he kissed the nape of her neck.

"Delicious. Do we have time for a quickie?" he said as she swatted him playfully.

"Sure, right here on the kitchen counter. We won't worry about little Lukie catching us in a compromising position."

They laughed, excited, frustrated. It was more than a routine. They still wanted each other after all these years.

"What's for dinner?"

"Spaghetti and meatballs. Luke's favorite."

"Mine too," he said, inhaling the rich aroma of the marinara sauce. "How was your day, babe?"

Sarah sighed, her mood suddenly changing, darker. "We're still reeling from your special. The DA fired another attorney today who worked the case. Said he was part of the conspiracy that framed that young gang member Pavel Feodor. It was awful. Nobody knows when the purge will end." Sarah was a legal assistant in the Manhattan district attorney's office assigned to white-collar crime. "I'm glad I don't work in homicide, but still, everybody keeps staring at me as if all that's going down is somehow my fault."

"Come on, Sarah, you're imagining things."

"No, I'm not."

"You had nothing to do with my story."

"But my officemates don't see it that way. I'm married to you. Guilt by association." There was a long silence. "Sorry, I didn't mean to jump down your throat, Ethan. I'm just edgy from work. So how was your day? That's what we should be talking about, not me."

Ethan sat down at the table, not knowing where to begin. "First day in a new job is always difficult, you know that."

"I'm sure. Peter Sampson's already called three times, looking for you."

"Oh, God, what can he want now?" Ethan said, startled.

"That bad, huh?"

"Worse. The guy was the consummate professional when we met with Paul this morning. In fact, he was even complimentary at one point. But the rest of the day, he was in my face—calling me on the telephone incessantly, demanding to know what I was doing, who I was meeting with, and which of his stories I was working on. He wanted an accounting of every second of my time."

"Well, you know what Peter's like," Sarah said, an edge in her voice. "We discussed it before you took the job. You've moved up the pecking order of the show, and now you're dealing with the big boys. So you're going to have to adjust to the new work routine, to the new pressures of being management."

"But I don't like it. His micromanaging. Being right next to his office. And I don't like being on the eleventh floor. It cramps my style." He got up and started setting the table. "But our meeting with Paul and his editorial producer, Dirk Fulton, was pretty interesting. We've talked about Dirk before. He's the guy who babysits all the stories for the show."

"So you got your first taste of long-term planning. Of how the show works as a show. That's wonderful, Ethan."

"Well, it wasn't exactly that."

"What do you mean? Isn't that what your new job is all about? The bigger picture—scheduling, story development, staffing decisions?"

"Of course," Ethan said evasively. "That's a big part of it. But this morning, Paul wanted to pitch me and Peter a new story he wants me to work on."

"He wants you to produce a story? While you're learning the ropes of your new job?" she said, growing more incensed. "That's crazy."

Ethan squirmed. He knew what was coming.

"What's the story about?"

"Another murder. And you know how much I like doing crime stories."

"That's not the point—what you like or don't like," she said as she stirred the spaghetti sauce, her voice beginning to tremble. "Now you'll be doing two jobs, not one."

"Come on, babe. That's not fair. We talked about this too. "I'm always going to be a producer, not just a pencil pusher."

"But what about me and Luke? When're you going to have time for us?"

"Not fair, Sarah," Ethan said, trying to control his temper. "Paul wants me to look into this story for Peter. I couldn't say no."

"Is it a big project?"

"Maybe," he said hesitantly. "It's about a sadistic killer named Rufus Wellington. I spent all afternoon reading newspaper stories about the case. The guy's a doctor who's supposed to save people. But he beat a teenage prostitute with his bare hands, some kid he fell in love with then tortured unmercifully before brutally killing her. Made my skin crawl when I read the description of her body."

"Sounds absolutely gruesome, Ethan. Sleazy. Trashy. Tabloidy," she said as she turned the burner to simmer and sat down across from him. "Is it at least a New York story?"

"No," he said quietly. "The murder took place in Massachusetts, which means I'm gonna be away from home a lot. In fact, I'm doing my first survey later in the week. Will probably be gone all weekend."

"That's exactly what I was worried about," Sarah said, abruptly standing. "So you have to travel—on top of adjusting to your new job. Can you handle all the stress? You know what happens when you get stressed."

"Yeah, but—"

"You drink, Ethan. You get drunk."

"Not fair, Sarah," Ethan said, raising his voice. "I'm working on that."

"You won't miss our appointment with Dr. Schwartz, will you?"

"No, babe," Ethan said defensively. "I'm scheduling my trip around him and won't leave until after our session Wednesday morning." Ethan loved Scotch, all kinds of Scotch, and had just entered couple's therapy with a psychiatrist specializing in alcohol and drug abuse and families.

"Good," she said stridently. "You promised to take Dr. Schwartz seriously. You can't handle your liquor anymore. It distorts your judgment. You take risks. And you make bad decisions. Like last summer when you had one too many at that bar,

McGlades—the one near the office—and cracked up the car on your way to my parents on Long Island. You gotta stop, Ethan. Before it kills you. Before it kills us."

Ethan sat there, unnerved, speechless. Then his iPhone pinged, breaking the awkward silence. He picked up on the second ring.

"It's me, Peter. What are you doing?"

"I'm about to have dinner with Sarah and Luke," he said, trying to hide the panic in his voice.

"Well, drop everything," Sampson said robustly. "We have to talk, so you'll eat here with me at my apartment. See you in half an hour. Not a minute later." He hung up without waiting for a response.

"What was that all about?" Sarah asked, vexed.

"Looks like I'm having dinner with Peter."

"You're going out tonight?"

"Peter wants to talk. I gotta run. Sorry, babe."

"So you're not eating with me and Luke?" she said angrily. "First day as a senior producer, and the new reality of our lives begins. Christ, Ethan, just lay off the Scotch, and don't come home drunk."

❧

It was almost eight o'clock when the taxi pulled up to the curb in front of Sampson's building on Park Avenue and Seventieth Street. Ethan hopped out and reached for a Marlboro. He was still reeling from his argument with Sarah, his skin warm and clammy despite the cold chill in the air. Flipping up the collar of his trench coat, he inhaled his cigarette then crushed it out on the sidewalk before approaching the doorman.

"'Evening, I'm Ethan Benson. Peter Sampson's expecting me."

The doorman nodded, escorted him into the building, then picked up the house phone. "There's a Mr. Benson here to see Mr. Sampson." A short pause. "I'll send him right up." He turned to Ethan. "Take the elevator in the back of the lobby. Get off on 14. It's the only residence on the floor."

Ethan had never been to Sampson's apartment before and watched the buttons blink as the elevator rose through the building until the door opened into a large anteroom. There was an expensive Persian rug on the floor and an original Alexander Calder painting hanging on the wall. A short elderly butler named Harrison was standing at attention—dressed in a black suit, white shirt, matching bow tie, and shiny black wingtip shoes.

"Good evening, Mr. Benson," the butler said courteously. "Mr. Sampson's on the telephone. He told me to seat you in the dining room. Please follow me."

Ethan turned and walked briskly down a long hallway lined with photographs of Sampson playing golf with Tiger Woods, Donald Trump, and Barak Obama. There was a pair of Monet landscapes flanking the door leading into a wood-paneled library with a 110-inch Samsung TV and a state-of-the-art Bang and Olaufson sound system and a cavernous living room with a Steinway grand piano and museum-quality antique furniture.

Was it all real?

Must've cost millions.

It made Ethan's apartment feel small and insignificant.

When they reached the formal dining room—with its ornately carved wooden ceiling, crystal chandeliers, and seating for twelve—Harrison paced to the end of the table and pulled out a chair.

"Please take a seat, Mr. Benson. Mr. Sampson should be here shortly. Can I offer you a drink or a glass of wine? He's serving a Lucien Crochet Sancerre with dinner. It's a very good vintage—pungent and quite distinctive—with great depth and texture. Care for a glass?"

Ethan's heart skipped a beat.

He wanted a drink, but not now. Not before Sampson. "A cup of coffee, please," he said reluctantly.

"Of course," Harrison said, adjusting his bow tie. "Is there anything else I can get you while you wait?"

"No. That will be fine, Harrison."

The butler abruptly turned and walked out of the room.

Ethan sighed heavily, wondering if late-night meetings at the anchorman's apartment would now be part of his new reality as Sampson's senior producer. He knew Peter wasn't married, that he often spent his evenings hobnobbing on New York's high-flying social circuit. But did he ever take a night off? Did he work all the time?

Shit, he'd never get used to this disruption in his life.

Either would Sarah.

Reaching for his iPad, he pulled up his travel itinerary and scrolled through the document. He was planning four days on location, bookended by all-day drives to and from Old Salem. The village was quaint and picturesque, one of a handful of sparsely populated communities along the northern tip of the Quabbin Reservoir. It was known as a summer camping destination, and now that the season was over, most tourists had all but packed up and left, leaving the region even more remote and desolate.

Was this why Wellington murdered the girl at his country estate?

Did he think nobody would notice?

Ethan stopped reading, put down his iPad, and peered at his watch. Eight-thirty. Where the hell was Sampson? He shrugged then pulled out his iPhone and called David.

"Hey, pal, I've been going over the itinerary. Is there anything I should know about?"

"Everything's moving along," David said enthusiastically. "Just got off the phone with Bret Davenport. Dinner's set for Wednesday at six-thirty."

"Where're we eating?"

"He's booking a reservation at a steak house in Athol."

"And where're we staying?"

"There's not much to choose from. So I'm looking for a mom-and-pop motel in the area."

Ethan chuckled. "Just make sure it's clean."

"Will do, Ethan."

"And what's the plan for the rest of the week?" Ethan said, scanning the schedule.

"All day with Davenport on Thursday," David said earnestly. "He's taking us to the crime scene at Wellington's estate."

"Can we get into the house?"

"That's a definite yes. He's giving us the grand tour. Then we're headed to his office to go through documents. He says we can take whatever we want."

"Will he give us background on the appeal?"

"That's another yes, Ethan. He's actually written the brief and filed it with the court. He says he's got a copy for us."

"Good. And Friday?"

"Meeting at the Athol sheriff's office in the morning, and then I thought we'd drive around the reservoir and pick shooting locations."

"What about the newspaper editor you talked to—"

"Jonah Wilcox?"

"Yeah."

"He'll meet with us. Just not sure when."

"And do we overnight in Athol on Friday?"

"Yup. We leave for Greenfield at the crack of dawn Saturday and spend the rest of the day at the district attorney's office."

"Who's the ADA who handled the case?" Ethan said, trying to remember if he'd read a name in the newspaper stories.

"Lauren Saperstein."

"Is she going to be there?"

"She's cleared her schedule and is coming in on her day off."

"And what about her documents?"

"Won't be a problem," David said excitedly. "She's giving us everything she has too. The entire court docket—the police reports, crime scene photos, court filings, depositions, and the police videos."

"Why's she being so cooperative?" Ethan said.

"Because she's fighting the appeal tooth and nails. Says Wellington's a stone-cold killer and the facts prove it. Plus, the guy's never told anyone what really happened that night or why he reacted the way he did and killed the girl. And if we can get him to open up, she thinks we'll help sway the judge and keep the guy behind bars."

"Okay, we'll see where this leads us. Nice job, David. You're making this way too easy. Maybe you should produce this story instead of me," Ethan said, chuckling. Then Harrison the butler walked into the room. "Hold on a second."

"Mr. Sampson sent me in to apologize," Harrison said stiffly. "He should be off the phone momentarily." Harrison placed a silver tray of coffee, milk, and sugar in front of Ethan, bowed, and scooted back out of the room.

"Who was that, Ethan?" David said. "It didn't sound like Sarah. Aren't you at home?"

"Believe it or not, I'm sitting in Peter Sampson's dining room, waiting to have dinner with the old boy."

"You gotta be kidding. It's nine o'clock."

"Sucks, doesn't it? I've been waiting for almost an hour." Ethan said, hearing footsteps in the hallway.

It was Sampson.

Finally.

"Gotta go, David. The big man's about to grace my presence. E-mail me updates. We'll talk again in the morning."

He clicked off his iPhone as Peter Sampson strode briskly into the dining room—shoulders back, head held high—and sat down at the long table across from Ethan. "Sorry to keep you waiting. I couldn't get off the damn telephone."

"No problem, Peter," Ethan said pleasantly. "I've been talking to David Livingston and going over the survey for our Wellington story. Shall I fill you in?"

Sampson waved him off. "No. We can talk about Wellington once I decide if it's worth my time."

Harrison walked back into the dining room with the bottle of Sancerre and poured a glass in a crystal goblet for Sampson. "Ah, a very good vintage," he said, swirling the wine and sniffing the bouquet before taking a sip. "Excellent. Just excellent. Crisp and dry." He sniffed the bouquet again. "Care for a glass, Ethan?"

Ethan stared at the bottle. He could almost taste the wine— the pull of alcohol overpowering. He wanted a drink in the worst way to calm his nerves. Get him through the meeting. Get him through Sampson. But then he thought about Sarah—her warning at the kitchen table—and his promise to lay off the booze. So instead, he asked Harrison for another cup of coffee.

"Shall we get down to business," Sampson said, clearing his throat. "You're here, Ethan, so we can chat about your duties as my senior producer. We touched upon them briefly during the day at the office, but Consuela packed my schedule with way too many appointments. She always does that, and it drives me crazy." He swirled the Sancerre and watched it shimmering in the glass. "This is divine. Sure you don't want a glass, Ethan?"

"No. I'm good," Ethan said squeamishly, still trying to control the monkey on his back. "I'll stick to the coffee."

"Suit yourself." He sipped the wine then patted his lips with a lace napkin. "Where should we begin?" he said, rubbing the bridge of his nose. "First off, you'll only produce my big stories. And I do mean, only my big stories. That's why I'm so angry you caved in to Paul and agreed to waste your time on this Wellington murder. I made it clear, several times, that I don't like the story, but no, you didn't listen, did you?"

Ethan didn't react.

"On top of that, you're traveling on that damn survey and will be out of pocket for the rest of the week. How're you gonna manage my other projects? My producers? My schedule?" He glared at Ethan. "Maybe we should call Paul right now and pass on Wellington."

"You're missing the point here, Peter. You promoted me because you trust my judgment. Let me do some digging on location, and then we'll make a decision first thing next week when I'm back. If the story doesn't pan out, we'll go to Paul and tell him there's nothing there. Simple as that."

"I know. I know," Sampson said reluctantly. "That's what you said this morning, but that doesn't mean I'm happy about it." Ethan tried not to watch him sip the Sancerre. "Don't forget that you're not just a producer anymore. You're a manager. My manager. And you need to leave time for your other responsibilities. I'm going to rely on you for editorial advice and counsel, and at the moment, with you gallivanting off to God-knows-where, chasing this Wellington story, I'm not sure you're up to the task. And what if Paul has a conflict this week and I need you to accompany me to some social engagement? How will you do that? You have a proper suit and tie, don't you?"

"I do, Peter," Ethan said, hiding his anger. "Several, in fact. But what does that have to do with anything—"

"Good. So you won't have to go out and buy one," Sampson said, cutting him off as Harrison walked back into the room, placed a fresh cup of coffee on the table, then slipped out again. Sampson continued, "I'm a busy man, Ethan. I work four or five stories at the same time and have a robust social schedule as you're well aware. I expect you to be at my beck and call and drop whatever you're doing when I need you, just like you did tonight. That's how I work with my senior producers. I won't have it any other way. Can you handle it?"

Ethan sipped his coffee and stared at the anchorman. "I know you're demanding, Peter, very demanding, but we agreed when I took this job that along with my new responsibilities, I'd continue producing stories I decided were journalistically important. I'm damn good editorially, and you know that," he said without blinking an eye. "And if that's not the reason you promoted me, you better find somebody else, and I'll go back to being a segment producer. Paul hasn't filled my old job yet. I'm sure he'd give it back to me."

He stood and started to leave.

"Hold on, Ethan, sit down. I haven't changed my mind about you," he said, his hands spread, palms up. "I want you to keep producing your stories, but I also need you to help me manage my life. That's just as important and comes with the territory. So you're gonna have to work a lot harder. That's all I'm saying. Do we have an understanding?"

Ethan thought about Sarah and Luke and family time then pushed it all to the back of his mind before answering, "As long as I can produce, we have an understanding."

"Good. Enough said." Sampson was all business again. "Now, tomorrow morning, we're meeting with three of my producers—at nine o'clock sharp. They all want me on location next week—in three different cities—and that, as you know, is impossible. I need you to decide who I should work with and who I should reschedule. Then we're having lunch with Paul to go over new story ideas. And there's a huge pile of research on my desk you need to go through so you can tell me what to read."

"Sounds like we're gonna be busy," Ethan said. "But let's carve out a little time to talk about Wellington. That's one I want to prioritize."

"All right. As long as you take care of the rest of your responsibilities, you can see about the Wellington story," Sampson said, looking up as Harrison walked back into the room.

"Excuse me, Mr. Sampson, George Pierce is on the telephone."

It was the chairman of the board of Global Broadcasting.

"Jesus. It's ten o'clock. Must be important. I'll take the call, Harrison." He started to leave then stopped at the door. "This might take awhile, Ethan. Don't wait for me. Enjoy dinner, and then go home. I'll see you in the morning."

Flabbergasted, Ethan watched Peter hurry down the hall then packed his iPad into his briefcase, began to get up, then froze. The half-full bottle of Sancerre was sitting in a silver ice bucket. He ran his fingers through his hair and picked up the bottle.

"Sarah's gonna be pissed if she finds out," he whispered to himself. "Fuck it. I've been good all evening, and she's gonna be asleep when I get home."

Then he poured a glass.

The wine tasted warm and comforting as he swirled it in his mouth and swallowed it—all the stresses, all the pressures of his first day in the new job, dissolving into thin air as the alcohol coursed through every cell of his body. He took another long sip, draining the glass, and left it on the table.

No more.

He knew he wouldn't stop.

And didn't want to get drunk.

Not here.

He picked up his briefcase, left his dinner uneaten, and walked out of the room.

❧

It was almost midnight when he opened the front door and entered his apartment. All the lights were turned off, and it was perfectly quiet—the only sound the ticking of a grandfather clock bouncing off the walls in the foyer. Holly came pattering out of Luke's bedroom and rubbed up against his leg. He stroked the top of her head.

"Good girl, sweet girl. Now don't make too much of a fuss. You'll wake up little Lukie."

She sat down on her haunches, her tail thumping the floor, and stared up as if she understood, then scampered back into Luke's bedroom.

Ethan smiled.

Best dog he'd ever had.

He shuffled through a stack of mail on a side table—a couple of bills, a brochure for a timeshare in the Berkshires, and an appeal for a donation from the Democratic National Committee—then left them for the morning and headed straight to his study. There was a bottle of Black Label sitting on his desk. He grabbed it and stared at the luminous gold liquid. He needed another drink. The Sancerre had wet his appetite and the Scotch was calling out to him, beckoning him.

Damn.

He poured a big glass, licked his lips, and drank it all at once. Then he poured a second and drank that one too. Wiping his mouth on his sleeve, he put the glass on his desk as the room began to spin. Staggering, he made his way out of his study and down the hallway to his bedroom. Sarah was lying on her side, snuggled under the covers, her breathing slow and shallow. Ethan slipped out of his clothes and crawled into bed beside her, hoping not to wake her.

"How did it go?" she said suddenly. "You were there a long time."

"You're not sleeping?" he said, startled.

"I decided to wait up for you. See if you lived through your dinner with Sampson."

"I'm okay. Now go to sleep. We can talk about it in the morning."

She rolled over and scooted closer to him, her face just inches from his. "Tell me, Ethan. I've been worried all night. I know how he gets to you."

"I'm okay, babe, really. Like you said, I'm playing with the big boys now and have to get used to him."

Sarah stared into his face, her eyes opening wide. "Ethan, have you been drinking?"

He lay motionless.

"How much, Ethan?" she said, sitting, the covers slipping down to her waist. "I can smell it on your breath. You reek of alcohol."

"Just a glass of wine. Right before I left Sampson's."

"And you didn't sneak a Scotch? I heard you go into your study."

"Well, maybe a couple of small ones," he said defensively.

"Ethan, you promised me you wouldn't drink tonight. We talked about it before you left. Doesn't your word mean anything?" He hesitated, and she continued, angrier, "We've been over this time and time again. You drink too much and try to hide it from me." A single tear dripped down her cheek. "I can't live this way anymore—not knowing when you're gonna come home drunk. You've got to stop."

"I'm trying," he said, sounding insincere even to himself. "That's why we're seeing Dr. Schwartz. So we can work on my problem together, and I'm making progress, really, I am."

"You're just kidding yourself, Ethan. We talk when we're there. Sure, that's what we do. But it's mostly me, not you, doing the talking. So you're not getting better. You're getting worse." She glared then lay back down and rolled away from him.

"Come on, Sarah. I'm doing the best I can."

He waited, but she didn't respond, and after a moment, he slipped onto his back and tried to relax but was too agitated, too stressed, too worked up—even with all the alcohol—and sleep wouldn't come.

CHAPTER 3

THEY SAT QUIETLY, STARING AT the four walls, a frosty silence hanging over them. Ethan wanted to be anywhere else but his psychiatrist's office. He was only there because of Sarah, because she wanted to work on his drinking and what it was doing to their marriage. But he thought the therapy was making things worse, that it was only driving a deeper wedge into their relationship. He glanced down at his watch. Ten o'clock. Christ, he didn't have time for this. He had a long drive up to the Quabbin Reservoir and was eager to get started, to bury himself in his story where he could forget about his problems. He opened and shut his briefcase then stood and paced back and forth across the room, anxious, disoriented.

"I know you don't want to be here, Ethan," she said, flipping through a magazine. "But it's for your own good. You certainly won't listen to me. Maybe you'll listen to the shrink."

An inner door opened, and Dr. Fred Schwartz stepped into the waiting room.

"Good morning, Mr. Benson, Mrs. Benson," he said softly. "Come in and sit down. We have a lot of ground to cover this morning."

He led them into a dimly lit room painted in warm pastel colors and waited for them to get comfortable in two down-filled armchairs. Late sixties, short and heavyset, Dr. Schwartz was wearing gray woolen slacks, a button-down pink shirt, and a red cardigan sweater. He turned on a tape recorder and picked up a pencil and notepad.

"How're you feeling today, Mr. Benson?" he said in a soothing tone. "You look a bit unsettled."

Ethan squirmed. He was used to asking the questions, not answering them, and felt uncomfortable talking about himself. He fixed his gaze on a bookshelf behind the doctor, trying to decide where to begin.

"I'm leaving for Massachusetts later this morning. It's my first day on a new story, and that always makes me feel apprehensive."

"Would you feel more comfortable lying down on the couch?" Dr. Schwartz said, pointing to a sofa. "I'm sure Sarah won't mind."

"I prefer where I am."

"That's fine, Ethan. Whatever helps you relax." Dr. Schwartz adjusted his reading glasses. "So what's your new story about? You didn't mention it during our last session."

"It just came up Monday. It's a high-profile murder involving a doctor and a prostitute."

"Didn't you just finish a project about a murder?" Dr. Schwartz said, checking his notes. "That's what you told me at our last session. Do you always produce stories about violence?"

"No. This is a new genre for me."

"Do you like doing these kinds of stories?"

Ethan hesitated. "Can I smoke a cigarette?"

"Of course. There are no rules about smoking in my office. You know that."

Ethan sighed, pulled out a Marlboro, and took a long drag. "What was your question again?"

"Whether you enjoy producing stories about murders."

Ethan shifted in his chair, shot a quick glance at Sarah, then said, "I prefer doing stories with more substance—about politics, social issues, the environment, consumer fraud. But television news is changing, and crime stories get bigger ratings and bring in more advertising dollars. That's the new reality of television. That's what keeps us on the air."

"Is that why you're feeling *apprehensive*—to use your own word—because you have to work on a story that you don't like, that might be considered tabloid journalism?"

Ethan took a long drag on his cigarette then stared down at the floor.

"Well, Ethan?"

"He's not gonna answer you, Dr. Schwartz," Sarah said, staring at Ethan warily. "It's not just the story that's bothering him. It's much more than that."

Dr. Schwartz shifted his gaze to Sarah. "Tell me, what doesn't Ethan want to talk about? What's he afraid of?"

Sarah slumped in her chair. "Everything. Ethan is obsessing about everything—about his new story, his new job in management, about working with Peter Sampson, and about how I perceive his drinking."

"Is that true, Ethan?" Dr. Schwartz said, jotting a note on his yellow pad.

Ethan sat quietly, stubbed his cigarette in an ashtray, lit another one, and kept his eyes glued to the floor.

"I know this is difficult, for the both you. But if you don't open up, I can't help you. Ethan?"

Still no response.

"Okay, maybe later in our session." He focused on Sarah, "Why won't he talk to me?"

"He's ashamed."

"About what?" Dr. Schwartz said, probing.

"That he's drinking, heavily, and lying to me about it."

"That's not fair, Sarah," Ethan said suddenly. "I tell you."

"Only after I drag it out of you, like you're a twelve-year-old little boy and I'm your mother."

"Is that how you feel, Sarah," Dr. Schwartz said, "like Ethan's mother?"

"Sometimes, like the other night when he worked late at Peter Sampson's apartment."

"He's the anchorman Ethan's now working with. Am I correct?"

"The one and only," Sarah said, grabbing a tissue and blowing her nose. "He came home at midnight, after skipping dinner with me and Luke—who, by the way, he never even said goodbye to before he left."

"And how did that make Luke feel?"

"How do you think?"

"I don't know Sarah, tell me. Tell Ethan."

She turned and stared into Ethan's eyes. "He cried, Ethan. He hadn't seen you all day. So he cried when he realized you'd gone back to work. It broke my heart to see the pain on his face."

"Does this happen often, Sarah?"

"All the time. Ethan always puts work ahead of us."

"That's not true, Sarah. I love you … and Luke. You know that."

"We love you too, Ethan. But it doesn't make it any easier. We feel like we're playing second fiddle to your job."

"But I have to work," Ethan said nervously. "It's what I do. It's how I earn a living for our family. It's what makes me tick as a human being."

43

An uneasy silence filled the room.

Dr. Schwartz waited then said, "And what about Sarah and Luke, they don't make you 'tick' as well?"

"That's not what I said."

"But that's how you act, Ethan," Sarah said, in a small voice. More silence.

"What I'm hearing, Ethan, is that you need to find a better balance between your job and your family. That you need to shift your priorities, maybe just a smidgen, and focus more time on Sarah and Luke and their needs." Then he turned to Sarah and said, "Tell me what else happened that night, when Ethan got home from Mr. Sampson's apartment."

A pall dropped over Sarah's face. "He thought I was asleep. He always thinks I'm asleep when he gets home. And instead of coming to bed, he slinked down to his study where he keeps his liquor and drank himself into oblivion."

"That's not true, Sarah. I only had one, maybe two Scotches. That's all."

"You had much more than that. I checked the bottle. It was a third empty. God, Ethan, you won't even tell me the truth here, when we're sitting with Dr. Schwartz, where we're supposed to be honest with each other."

"What is the truth?" Dr. Schwartz said, gazing at Ethan.

"Well—"

"Look at Sarah. Tell her, not me."

"I guess I drank more than I admitted, and yes, I was drunk when I climbed into bed. Are you happy now, Sarah?"

Another uneasy silence.

"Okay, now that you've been honest about that night, tell me the reason you got drunk after your meeting with Mr. Sampson."

Ethan looked down at the floor again.

"Well, Ethan?"

"He's not going to tell you."

"Why not?"

"He just won't."

"Why do you think he got drunk?" Dr. Schwartz said, shifting his eyes from Ethan to Sarah.

"Lots of reasons."

"How about the main ones."

She shifted in her chair. "Tell him, Ethan. It's your problem. Tell him more about your new boss, Peter Sampson."

"Man, you don't let up, do you, Sarah?"

"Come on, Ethan, that's why we're here. To be honest, remember? Tell him."

Ethan hesitated then said, "He makes my life miserable. He's self-centered, egotistical, and doesn't care about anybody but himself. When I was at his apartment, all he wanted was to beat on me about my responsibilities as his new senior producer. A ten-minute conversation we could have done over the phone—a ten-minute conversation, mind you—that we touched on all day in the office. There was no reason to drag me away from my family."

"And how did that make you feel."

"How do you think?"

"Resentful?"

"Yes."

"Out of control?"

"Yes.

"Insignificant?"

"Yes."

Ethan shrugged. It was all true.

45

Dr. Schwartz glanced at his notes. "Do all people in positions of authority make you feel this way?"

Ethan looked at him, now angry.

"Do they?"

No answer.

"Say something, Ethan," Sarah said pleadingly. "This is good. We're making progress."

Ethan's whole body deflated, then he looked back at Dr. Schwartz and said quietly, "Yes, they do."

"And do they know this about you, Ethan."

"Heavens, no."

"They don't know?"

"I put up a good front. But on the inside, I feel small, incompetent, almost worthless."

"So you drink to feel better?"

"It relaxes me."

"And more in control of your emotions."

"Right on, Dr. Schwartz. Just like the other night," Ethan said heatedly. "After Sampson dismissed me to take a phone call, I drained a full glass of wine as soon as he disappeared down the hall."

"And then more when you got home."

"Much more. And I began to feel better. Stronger."

"That's not what you were doing, Ethan. You were masking your feelings of inadequacy." He turned to Sarah. "Is this Ethan's pattern as you see it? To hide behind alcohol?"

"Ethan drinks to avoid his true feelings about his job, the people he works with, and even me."

"Why you, Sarah?"

"Because he doesn't want to talk about what happened to us."

"What happened to the two of you?" Dr. Schwartz said.

"We're not gonna talk about it," Ethan said, suddenly standing defiantly. "This subject's off-limits, and you know that, Sarah. It's private between you and me." He stared hard at Sarah, trying to remain in control but unable to. "How could you bring this up? You know how it makes me feel. I won't air it in public, especially here with Dr. Schwartz."

He sat back down, his skin vibrating, his blood boiling like a cauldron. He'd just made a scene and hurt Sarah deeply, a scene he couldn't take back. He reached over and tried to hold her hand, hoping to remove the emotional pain he'd just inflicted on her, but instead, she pulled away and refused to look at him.

Dr. Schwartz sat quietly, staring at the two of them. Then he looked at the clock on the wall, turned off his tape recorder, and placed his pencil and paper on the side table next to his chair.

"I'm not sure what just happened, but I sense it's profoundly important, a key to understanding your relationship and possibly the real reason why you, Ethan, can't control your drinking. I'm afraid we're out of time, but I want to pick up right here at our next session. Please talk to each other, and find a way to tell me what the both of you are obviously hiding."

❧

Ethan hardly said a word during the six-hour drive to the Quabbin Reservoir, too upset by his session with the psychiatrist, only breaking his silence to ask David a question or to field a telephone call from Sampson. The rest of the trip, he spent carefully studying the research, jotting down notes in his iPad, and learning as much as he could about Rufus Wellington, Heather Starr, and the murder.

The more he read, the better he felt about the story.

Maybe there was more here than he first thought.

When they got to Amherst, David exited Interstate Ninety-One, a north-south superhighway running through Connecticut and Massachusetts, and turned to Ethan.

"Where to now? You've got the directions, right, Ethan?"

"Yeah, they're here, somewhere." He fumbled through his production notes and found them in the back of his itinerary. "Says to follow Route 202 north to Athol. Another forty miles."

"Want to stop and get a cup of coffee or something to eat? We haven't taken a break since we left New York."

"I can wait until dinner with Davenport," Ethan said, checking his watch. "We should make it in plenty of time if we keep driving."

David gunned the engine of their rental car, a four-wheel drive Jeep Cherokee, and passed a cement truck crawling along the two-lane road.

"Got a question for you, Ethan," David said contemplatively. "I know we just made big news on our last story, but I don't get why Wellington wants to talk to us. Does he think you'll help get him off the hook, like Pavel Feodor?"

"Maybe," Ethan said, lighting a cigarette. "He might think it'll help his appeal, but the guy's a killer, there doesn't seem to be any doubt about that, and if we do the story, we have to be damn careful to stay balanced so we don't sway the judge in one direction or the other. If you ask me, the guy belongs just where he is. Locked up behind bars. The big question isn't his guilt or innocence, but why a prominent heart surgeon with everything going for him would fall in love with a prostitute and then snap and brutally murder her the way he did. It doesn't make sense, does it?"

"Does it ever?"

"I guess not, but if we can answer that question, maybe the story's worth doing."

Then Ethan's iPhone rang.

He braced himself for another call from Sampson but, after checking the LCD screen, relaxed. "Hey, Mindy, what's going on?"

"Jeez, Ethan, no 'hello'? No 'how are you'?" she said half-jokingly. "I've been busy all morning running down experts for our story, and that's all I get?"

Mindy Herman was bright and outgoing, full of confidence, with some of the best law enforcement sources in the business. She was short and slightly overweight, with clipped, mousy, blond hair and lustrous hazel eyes; but somehow, Ethan found her appealing, almost attractive, in a little girl kind of way.

"How's Mr. Anchorman treating you?"

"Just jim-dandy. His usual irascible punctiliousness."

"Sounds like you're having a wonderful time. Can't wait to get into the mix with your new best friend."

Ethan laughed. Mindy always found a way to make him laugh. "Any luck reaching the press office at MCI-Cedar Junction?" he said, getting down to business.

MCI-Cedar Junction was a maximum security prison just outside Boston where Rufus Wellington was housed alongside the most dangerous inmates in the state.

"Sure as shit. I finally got through to the director. Name's Horace Gentry."

"And?"

"And he's got no problem with us coming into the prison and talking to Wellington."

"We can bring our cameras?"

"He thinks so, but he wants to run it by the warden. Says he'll do it today."

"Keep pushing. Sampson's giving me a hard time as it is, and he certainly won't change his mind about the story if all we have is a write-around and no on-camera with Wellington."

"Gotch ya."

"You cleared your schedule?"

"Nothin' else on my plate. I'm on this full time."

"Excellent. We need to have all our ducks in a row when I get back," Ethan said, happy he wouldn't have to share Mindy with another producer. "I need to decide if it's a go or no-go by Monday. Sampson won't give me any more time."

"Hey, Ethan," David said, glancing out the window, checking landmarks, "need you to get off the phone now. We're pulling into Athol. Could use some help finding the motel."

"Gotta go, Mindy. David's lost. Call me after you hear back from Gentry."

⁂

They stopped at a red light in the heart of the business district. Athol was a blue-collar factory town, except now there was no factory. Every other store was boarded up, and those still open for business—a pawnshop, a liquor store, a Laundromat, and a handful of restaurants—all needed a face-lift. Ethan looked out at the desolation and wondered why a heart surgeon with all the money in the world spent his weekends in a place that seemed so depressed.

A piece of the puzzle.

"Next corner is Bearsden Street," he said, checking the directions. "The motel is about a mile up the road."

They hung a left, past the broken-down paper mill and a weedy, old cemetery with cracked headstones. Soon the business district faded from sight, the broken-down stores replaced by broken-down homes. David made another left and pulled into the parking lot of the Shady Rest Motor Lodge, a single-story motel with a neon vacancy sign flashing above the office door.

"Is this the best you could do?" he said, turning to David.

"I checked with the travel department. There's nothing better within fifty miles."

"Where we gonna put Sampson?" Ethan said worriedly. "He won't stay in a place like this."

"Thought about that," David said as he parked and shut off the car engine. "Maybe we can find a private home in Old Salem. There's a bunch of places for rent this time of the year. Bret Davenport says the town is much more upscale than Athol."

"Start checking with real estate agents," Ethan said as he pushed open the door. "Maybe there's a house big enough where all of us can stay. I'm sure Peter will love that, sharing a home with his production crew. Not the kinda crowd he usually hangs out with." He chuckled then stared at the motel. "Let's go check in. We don't have a hell of a lot of time before we have to meet Davenport."

They headed to the lobby, hoping the rooms were clean.

CHAPTER 4

A HALF HOUR LATER, ETHAN walked through the front door of the Quabbin Steakhouse—a small family-owned restaurant at the edge of the business district, about three miles from the motel. On the outside, it resembled all the other shops in Athol. It looked like a spooky set in a Hollywood horror movie. But the inside, to his surprise, had all the amenities of a five-star restaurant: expensive furnishings, a well-stocked wine cellar, and a well-heeled clientele.

He turned to David, "Did we just enter the *Twilight Zone*?"

"Let's see if it's real."

"Is Bret here?"

David scanned the room. There were a handful of young singles working the bar. "I don't think so," he said cautiously. "He told me he'd be wearing a blue pinstripe suit and a white shirt and tie. Nobody here's wearing anything like that."

A pretty young woman in a short dress and open-toe pumps greeted them with a smile, "Can I help you gentleman?"

"We're here to meet Bret Davenport," Ethan said cordially. "There should be a six-thirty reservation for three."

"You must be the producers from *The Weekly Reporter*. Bret told me to expect you. I'm Ginger," she said, her face glowing.

She had long black hair and sparkling green eyes and a smile that could make your heart melt. "He hasn't arrived yet, but I've set aside a table way in the back where you can talk in private. Would you like to be seated while you wait?"

"That would be great," Ethan said.

Ginger led them to a booth set with a white tablecloth, cloth napkins, and crystal wine glasses. The room was paneled in richly stained hardwood and decorated with deer heads and wildlife paintings indigenous to the Quabbin. There wasn't a speck of dust anywhere.

"Can I get you something to drink?" Ginger said as she handed them menus.

"Gin and tonic, twist of lime," David said, smiling at the young woman.

"I'll have a Black Label straight up," Ethan said hesitantly, flashing on Sarah, knowing he shouldn't be drinking.

"Right away," she said, sneaking a smile back at David before heading to the bar to order their drinks.

Ethan grinned at his researcher. "Hang in there, David. I saw the way you looked at that girl. The night's still young. You'll have plenty of time to get to know her better after our meeting is over." He clapped him on the back and laughed out loud then pulled out his iPad. "Tell me what you found out about Davenport before he gets here, beyond what's in the newspapers."

"Well, I've been digging since our meeting with Paul and now know he's far more than just Wellington's attorney," David said, grabbing a research notebook. "Talked this morning to a reporter in Boston who covered the case right after the murder. He told me Davenport is Wellington's closest friend and confidante, that they grew up together not too far from here in a town called Shutesbury, where they went to the same public schools, played on the same sports teams, before attending Harvard together." He paused, flipping through his notes. "According to this reporter, they shared a small apartment in Cambridge that Wellington paid for, and both majored in literature. They apparently were inseparable."

Ethan leaned back in his chair. "Was there anything else going on between them?"

"What do you mean?"

"Come on, David, were they closer than just friends? Maybe lovers?"

"Rumors. All through high school and college, but they were never open about it."

Ethan jotted a note on his iPad. "Okay. We need to do some digging on that, and what about after college?"

"Wellington went to Harvard Medical and Davenport, to Tufts Law School. Then they launched successful careers. One of the reasons Wellington built his weekend retreat in Old Salem was to stay close to Davenport, who got tired of the fast-paced lifestyle in Boston and moved back to Athol to set up his law practice."

"Why in God's name did they put down roots here?" Ethan said. "They could've picked anywhere else in the country. Why the Quabbin? There's nothing here, and I mean nothing—no art, no theatre, no culture, and no nightlife, especially at this time of the year."

"Different strokes for different folks."

"Ah, another reference to their sexual proclivities."

"Just a turn of phrase," David said, handing Ethan a clipping from his notebook. "According to this story the editor of the local paper sent me just after we talked, they shared some great childhood memories at the Quabbin. They both enjoyed hiking the trails, fishing the reservoir, and hunting for deer in the woods. They were like two peas in a pod. Whatever one did, so did the other."

"Maybe that's why they settled here."

"Makes eminent sense."

Ethan scanned the article then said, "And what about Rufus's parents? Do they still live here?"

"Mother's dead, father lives most of the time in Boston. He still owns the same place in Shutesbury where Wellington grew up. Don't forget, the old man is rich. Super rich. He has homes all over the country."

"But they chose to raise Rufus here," Ethan said uncomprehendingly. "Sounds like they could've exposed him to much more in Boston or anywhere else, for that matter."

"Good point. We'll have to ask his father why they chose Shutesbury."

"Is he close to his father?"

"They hate each other."

"Why?"

"Mindy and I haven't figured that out yet."

Ginger returned and set their drinks in front of them.

Ethan looked at his Scotch, felt guilty, and decided drinking might not be such a good idea. He pushed the glass to the corner of the table.

"Changed your mind?" David said, sipping his gin and tonic. "I've never seen you pass up a drink."

"Maybe later. Don't want to hoist one on an empty stomach," he said, reluctant to discuss his alcohol problems with his researcher. "Does Wellington have any brothers or sisters?"

"He's an only child."

"And does he have any friends, besides Davenport?"

"Not that I've been able to track down."

"And what about Davenport? Married?"

"No."

"Siblings?"

"No."

"Parents?"

"Both dead."

"Now things are starting to make more sense," Ethan said. "Wellington moved back here and hired Davenport after the murder, because neither is close to anyone else, and they need each other like brothers. Maybe more. Now that's got interesting possibilities, don't you think?" As Ethan placed his iPad on screen saver, a short, slight man sporting a thick black beard and Coke-bottle eyeglasses walked up to the table.

"Good evening, gentleman, I'm Bret Davenport," he said, a melodic Irish brogue running loosely off his tongue. He thrust out his hand.

"I'm Ethan Benson, and this is David Livingston, but I guess you guys already know each other from the telephone."

"Indeed, we do," Davenport said, turning to David. "But it's a pleasure to finally meet you in person."

"Chardonnay, Mr. Davenport?" Ginger said, opening a menu and placing it in front of him.

"Please. A bottle of Beringer, the 2012 Private Reserve."

Ethan stared at his Scotch, still longing for a taste. "Could you bring me a cup of coffee with a little cream and sugar?"

"Should I take away your drink?" she said, reaching for the glass.

"No. Just leave it where it is. I might want it later."

"No problem. Be right back, gentleman," she said, heading to the wine cellar.

Davenport loosened his tie. "Thanks for making the trip, Mr. Benson. This is very important to Rufus. He's hardly said a word about the murder since he confessed, and as I told David on the telephone, I just filed an appeal to get him out of prison and maybe into a psychiatric hospital where he can get some help. But before I argue the case in front of a judge, I need to know more about what happened that night, what he was thinking and feeling prior to the murder. Maybe he'll tell you. He certainly won't tell me."

"Maybe," Ethan said, peering into Davenport's eyes, trying to read his mind. "But before we talk about the appeal—and I have lots of questions about that—can we start at the beginning? You're his attorney and, as I understand, his best friend. He must've told you something about why he killed Heather Starr?"

A nervous tick surfaced under Davenport's eye. "I'm afraid he hasn't told me anything, and believe me, I try to get him to talk every time I visit him. But he refuses to say a word about the murder or, for that matter, about anything else. He just sits there in the visiting room with this grin on his face, like he knows something none of us will ever understand."

"You sure he did it?"

"Yeah, he's guilty. There's no question about that. The forensics don't lie."

Ethan leaned on the table, watching the tick dance across Davenport's cheek. "Were you present when the sheriff booked him?"

"I got to the police station as soon as I heard about the murder," Davenport said, sighing loudly. "You'll have to excuse me. This is very difficult. Rufus and I go way back. Anyway, I got a call from Sheriff McKenzie, who's also a friend, and he told me to come quick because he'd just arrested Rufus. And from the moment I got there, I knew Rufus was in big trouble. He'd waived his right to an attorney and was singing like a canary, blurting out to everybody and his brother that he'd murdered Heather Starr."

"And the confession's on tape?" Ethan said.

"McKenzie took a formal statement right after I got there," Davenport said, dismayed.

"Were you in the room?"

"No. Rufus wouldn't talk to me until after he confessed on camera."

"Why?"

Davenport shook his head. "Can't answer that. Lawyer-client privilege."

Ethan leaned back in his chair. That's strange. Is he hiding something? "Can I have a copy of the tape?" he said, his mind firing on all cylinders.

"Of course."

"And a transcript?"

"I can give you that too."

"What else can you tell me about that night?"

Ginger walked back to the table with the coffee and the bottle of Chardonnay. She poured a short glass and handed it to Davenport. He swirled the wine and looked at the color, then took a sip, letting the flavor explode in his mouth before swallowing. "Perfect. Just perfect, my dear." He handed her the glass, and she filled it without spilling a drop.

"Are you ready to order?"

"Not yet. Give us a bit more time."

"I'll come back," she said, heading over to another table.

"So where was I?"

"The night of the murder," David said fervently.

"Oh, yes, at the sheriff's office." Davenport continued, "When McKenzie finished his interrogation, I asked him for a private room where I could talk to Rufus."

"And did he say anything to you when you were alone?" Ethan said.

"Nothing, really. Rufus was already climbing into his shell. He just sat there on the floor, arms crossed, and told me to leave. Said he didn't want my help. It was so damn upsetting."

"Did you know Heather Starr?" Ethan said, changing his line of questioning.

"Hell, no. I never met her," Davenport said icily. "I had no idea Rufus was dating. In all the years I'd known him, he never once went out with a woman. So I was absolutely stunned when he was arrested for her murder."

"Was he homosexual?"

"Not that I'm aware of."

"You sure? You just said he never dated women?" Ethan said, pushing a little harder.

"What are you implying, Mr. Benson? That I had some kind of secret relationship with Rufus, because we're such good friends? That's preposterous."

"I just wanted to know if Dr. Wellington liked men."

"Well, he didn't," Davenport snapped back.

"Okay. No offense intended." Ethan waited for Davenport to compose himself. "Did you know Heather Starr was a prostitute?" he said, now realizing with certainty there was, indeed, some weird psychological underpinning to the case.

"No. Not until later when the sheriff identified her."

"Did you know he was planning to marry her?"

"Of course not. I didn't even know she existed until that night."

"Did you question him about her?" David said as he jotted notes on a clean sheet of paper.

"Sure, I asked him. I wanted to know how long they'd been dating. Where they'd met. Why he didn't introduce her to me. And this is where it gets really squirrely. Normally, we talked about everything. And I do mean, everything. But that night, he refused to open up and tell me anything about that woman," Davenport said, banging his fist on the table. "All he'd say was that he'd murdered her and buried her body in the meadow in back of his house."

"And he said nothing else?" Ethan said curiously.

"Just one more thing before he shut down completely," Davenport said, leaning forward.

"And what was that?"

"That he was going to waive his right to a trial so he could spend the rest of his life locked up behind bars."

"That's it?"

"That's it. Then he stopped talking."

"And he didn't offer any explanation?" David said, putting down his pen.

"Nothing," Davenport said, exasperated. "And the next day, at his preliminary hearing, when the judge asked him how he pleaded, he stood there and smiled in this insane way before shaking his head and uttering just one word, 'Guilty.'" Davenport drained his glass and filled it again.

"You know, Bret," Ethan said cryptically, "there's still something I don't understand. Why didn't you fight the murder charge in court? It sounds like Wellington is certifiably crazy and that you could've pleaded insanity right then and there and maybe gotten him committed to an institution for the criminally insane instead of thirty years to life with only a slim chance of parole somewhere way down the road."

"I ask myself that question each and every day. I truly believe Rufus snapped and had no idea what he was doing that night. There's no other way I can explain it. I'm sure I could've pleaded insanity and gotten him into a good hospital and maybe back out when he was healthy, but he wouldn't let me. He just gave up. It makes no sense to me." Davenport's voice trailed off as he stared into the distance.

"You think he's hiding something?" Ethan asked. "Maybe something else he didn't want to come out in a trial?"

"What could that be?"

"You tell me."

"I don't have any idea, not one in a million," he said, seemingly upset. "That's why I'm so happy he wants to talk to you and Mr. Sampson. Maybe we'll get some answers that'll help my appeal so I can get him out of that fucking shithole at MCI-Cedar Junction."

Ethan was stunned at the vitriol in his voice. "Why do you hate the prison so much?"

"Because it creeps me out. You'll see when you go meet Rufus."

"Any idea when can I do that?"

"Not sure yet. I'm working on a date with the warden."

"Think he'll let us bring in our cameras?"

"I'm hopeful," Davenport said thoughtfully. "Cedar Junction houses the state's most violent criminals, and Warden Dunkirk is worried your cameras might incite the inmates and cause an incident that would reflect poorly on him and the institution. The guy's all about good impression, hates negative publicity. So all I can say is, I'm working on it and should have an answer in a couple of days."

"Fair enough," Ethan said respectfully. "I've also got my associate producer, Mindy Herman, making calls. Maybe between the two of you, we can get him to commit." Ethan paused a moment. "Look, Bret, I'm still a little confused. Rufus Wellington has already come clean and made a full confession. So what are we looking at here? He won't talk to you. He won't talk to anybody at the prison. Why does he want to talk to me and my anchorman, Peter Sampson?"

"Only Rufus can answer that," he said, emptying the bottle of Chardonnay in his glass. "All I want is to understand what happened to my friend. And all I know is, Rufus called me out of the blue after watching your special and told me to set up an interview with you and Mr. Sampson. He must have his reasons, but he certainly won't tell me. I'm just hoping, as I said, that your interview will help my appeal and get Rufus out of that damn prison and into a place that will give him the care he needs." Davenport wiped his brow then said nervously, "After everything I've just told you, do you still want to move forward with your story?"

"Let's take it one step at a time," Ethan said, "see what the prison says about our cameras and whether Wellington really comes back to life. Now, before we order dinner, Bret, tell me a little about the appeal." But before Davenport could answer, Ethan's iPhone buzzed. He looked at the LCD screen, and his whole body tensed. "I've got to take this," he said flatly before hitting *Accept*. "Hey, Peter, wasn't expecting to hear from you again today. Is there a problem?" He paused and listened. "Yes. I'm in a meeting with the defense attorney." He paused again. "It can't wait until the morning?" Another long pause. "Okay. I'll call him right away." He put the phone in the crook of his ear, grabbed David's pen and paper, and jotted down a telephone number. "I'll drop what I'm doing and take care of it right away."

The telephone went dead.

"What's going on?" David said with alacrity.

"Sampson wants me to talk to one of his producers about a location problem."

"Who?"

"Not important. I just have to do it right away." He turned to Davenport, "Guess we'll have to talk about the appeal tomorrow. The two of you enjoy dinner. I have to head back to the motel." He stood, reached for his cup of coffee, stopped, and grabbed the Scotch.

He needed a drink.

A real drink.

Then he drained the glass all at once.

CHAPTER 5

ETHAN WAS RIDING IN THE passenger seat of Bret Davenport's Audi S5 Cabriolet as it snaked its way through the thick woods along Route 202 and down the western shore of the Quabbin. The man-made reservoir was built in the 1930s as the main source of drinking water for the Boston metropolitan area. The watershed looked much the same as it did back then, a wild and pristine wilderness, with few homes dotting the landscape and fewer cars traveling the back roads. Ethan stared out the window—tired and hungover from all the Scotch he'd consumed while reworking Sampson's production schedule—and peered at the fall colors, brilliant reds, oranges, and yellows bursting in the sunshine.

"How much further until we get there?" he said, glancing at Davenport.

"Maybe another ten minutes," Bret said. "I think you'll find Rufus's estate quite unusual." Davenport had been chatting away ever since he'd picked up Ethan and David at the motel—recalling one childhood memory after another, trying to humanize his friend. "Rufus and I liked to hike through these woods after dark," he said, dispirited. "We'd sneak out of our bedrooms, take our bikes to the north gate, then make our way through the forest until we got to the reservoir. Sometimes we'd stay out all night, camping along the shore and staring up at the stars. Rufus loved to fish in the moonlight, even though it was forbidden at night. He'd catch a few bass, maybe a trout or two, then gut them and cook 'em up right away. Damn, we would've been whooped by our parents if we'd ever been caught by the cops." Davenport laughed at the memory. "He wasn't a bad kid, you know. He had a wild streak, but I never saw any signs of violence or cruelty in him. Never. He just liked to have fun. I don't understand what happened. It's all so puzzling." His voice trailed off, and there was silence, just the sound of the car cruising along the roadway.

"This has been very tough on you, hasn't it?" Ethan said sympathetically.

Davenport's voice quivered, "Something must've happened to Rufus that night. Something inside his head. I hope you can get some answers when you talk to him." Davenport slowed down and stopped. "This is the turn off to Old Salem. We'll be at his estate in a couple of minutes."

He waited for a pickup truck to drive by then turned left onto a potholed dirt road, driving past a sign welcoming visitors to *Historic Old Salem,* and through a town square straight out of a Norman Rockwell painting in the *Saturday Evening Post.* There were white clapboard houses, a country store, a town hall, library, and an old church with a weathered bell tower. Sitting behind a stone wall was an ancient cemetery filled with tombstones dating back to the American Revolution.

"Don't let all this charm fool you," Davenport said, matter-of-factly. "It looks like a quaint New England village, but everything's gonna change once we get down to the reservoir. Lots of very rich people have built huge estates there, so Rufus, in his own strange way, fit right in here."

"Can we stop a few minutes?" Ethan said. "I'd like to get out and take a look around."

"No problem," Davenport said. "Take as much time as you need."

They hopped out of the car and walked back to the town square—a grassy mall lined with park benches and old oak trees.

"David, snap some pictures," Ethan said, gesturing at the bucolic surroundings. "I want to show Sampson what this place looks like. Maybe it'll help give him a feel for the story."

"Sure thing, Ethan," David said, pulling out a Nikon D3200 camera and heading over to the cemetery.

Ethan stood there, looking around the village, and noticed the haunting silence. There were no dogs barking. No kids playing on the streets. And no cars—anywhere. He turned to Davenport, baffled, and said, "Where is everybody? It looks like a ghost town in a Stephen King novel."

Davenport grinned. "You aren't used to small towns, are you, Ethan? It's always like this in Old Salem. The population is less than a thousand, and it's the middle of the week. So the weekenders are all off living their other lives, and the locals, well, they stay to themselves mostly. They don't like strangers."

Ethan stared from one house to the next. He had an unsettling feeling he was missing something, something in Old Salem that Bret Davenport wasn't telling him—that maybe the townsfolk were watching from behind curtained windows, afraid to come out and talk to him.

"Bret, do you know anybody who lives here year round?"

"I know a few people, Rufus's neighbor for one, a woman named Mary Murphy. Why do you ask?"

"I'd like to meet her and see if she can give me background on Dr. Wellington, maybe tell me what he was like as a neighbor and how he spent his time when he was here. It would be great for my story to get a local's perspective on him."

"I'll call and see if she's willing to talk to you."

"Can you try for tomorrow afternoon? I'm free except for a site survey after I meet with the sheriff."

"Let me see what I can do," Davenport said, looking at storm clouds gathering on the horizon. "There's a front approaching. We should head to the house before the rain comes."

"Sure thing," Ethan said, turning and waving to David. "You got everything we need?"

"All finished. Shot plenty to show Peter."

"Good. Time to look at the crime scene."

They drove to the outskirts of town, where the forest was thicker, where large weekend homes were discreetly tucked away under the foliage. Davenport hung a quick right when the road dead-ended at a stone wall and passed a lily pond straight out of a Claude Monet landscape. A dense canopy of sugar maples blocked out the sunlight, casting everything in dark, dappled shadows.

"No more houses," Ethan said, peering through the windshield.

Davenport grinned broadly. "Rufus's estate is way off in the woods. He's got over three hundred acres. The nearest property is a quarter of a mile away. He was a very private person, always complaining that he spent too much time with people at the hospital and that he wanted a quieter life when he was here." He pointed to an overgrown driveway. "That's it on the left. Pretty imposing, don't you think?" He stopped in front of a wrought iron gate flanked by two eight-foot high stone pillars marking the entrance to the property. A big sign out front warned strangers to keep out, and a chain-link fence topped with razor wire ran around the perimeter of the property as far as the eye could see.

Davenport climbed out of the car, unlocked the gate, then drove down a poorly maintained dirt road as it snaked through the woods—crossing a small wooden bridge over a stream and swerving around a large stone outcropping. Then he pulled through an imposing granite archway and into a broad circular driveway and turned off the car.

Ethan stared wide-eyed at a massive gothic structure—three stories in height—that was sitting at the center of a compound of outbuildings. It looked like a medieval castle—with turrets and gargoyles, massive oak doors, and stained glass windows. It could've been straight out of a *Grimm's Fairy Tale*.

"I'm not sure what I imagined, but this certainly wasn't it."

"Rufus's vision of paradise," Davenport said as he opened his car door, "where he could hide from the outside world. Only a handful of people have seen the inside. And fewer have ever stayed here."

"Were you ever his houseguest?"

"Of course. Many times. I was his best friend."

Ethan filed that in the back of his mind then said, "Why is it so big? A person could get lost in all these buildings."

"Everything had to be big and ostentatious. That's how Rufus lived his life—very grand and all alone. Pretty sad, don't you think?"

"Sounds like it," Ethan said, scanning the huge property.

"Where do you wanna begin?" Davenport said, glancing from Ethan to David. "There are lots of things I can show you."

"Can we go inside?" Ethan said, checking the sky. The rain was still off in the distance.

"Sure thing. Let's go around back. That's where the sheriff entered the house the night of the murder."

Ethan turned to David, who was already snapping pictures, then followed Davenport to the foot of a stone staircase leading up to a porch that stretched the entire length of the first floor.

"The sheriff found drops of blood on the steps and trailing to the door," he said, pointing. "He knew something was wrong and immediately began searching the property." Davenport pulled out a key chain and unlocked the door. "Let's head to the master bedroom where Rufus lost it and began beating Heather before he killed her."

They proceeded into a stale-smelling mudroom. A thick layer of dust covered the furniture; cobwebs hung from one wall to the next; and mouse droppings littered the floor. Ethan figured the house had been closed tight since the night of the murder. Making their way through a maze of passageways, they hiked up a back staircase and down a long hallway. The ceilings had leaked, and water had cascaded down the walls, staining the wood floors.

"Did Wellington maintain this place when he lived here?" Ethan asked, touching a water-logged sofa sitting under a bay window.

"Of course. The guy was a surgeon. Everything had to be immaculate. He never would've let this place fall into ruin like this. Never. The sheriff says it's still a crime scene and won't let anybody in to clean or make repairs."

That's strange, Ethan thought to himself. *Are the police still searching the house? Looking for evidence? Don't they know what happened?* He started to ask Davenport why the case was still open but caught himself at the last moment, deciding it would be better to ask the sheriff instead. "If this is still a crime scene, how'd we get permission to look at it?"

"Because I went to the sheriff, told him I needed to show you—give you the big picture—so you'd understand what Rufus did to Ms. Starr."

"And he agreed?"

"Took a bit of persuasion, but he finally saw the light."

"Okay, so where's Wellington's bedroom?" Ethan finally said.

"Just down the next hallway," Davenport said, leading Ethan around another bend and stopping in front of a door sealed with yellow police tape.

"Can we take a look?"

"I don't see why not," he said, removing the tape.

They followed Davenport into a sitting room, David capturing the scene with his Nikon, then pushed into the master bedroom. "This is where Rufus did most of the damage before he killed Heather, and as you can see, little has been disturbed since the murder."

Ethan pivoted, making a complete circle.

There was dried blood splattered on the bed, smeared on the carpeting, and staining the wallpaper. The sheets and blankets were strewn haphazardly on the floor, and the furniture was overturned. A bra and lace panties were hanging over the back of a chair, and a pair of men's socks and boxer shorts lay crumpled on the top of an oak dresser.

"Don't touch anything," Davenport said fervently. "I promised the sheriff we'd leave the room exactly as we found it. That was a condition for getting access." He walked over to a king-size bed sitting under a mirrored ceiling. "The crime scene guys think Rufus started pummeling Heather as she lay naked on the bed. That's why there's so much blood on the mattress. Then they think he dragged her across the bedroom and into the sitting room, striking her over and over again. That explains the streaks of blood on the carpet and the wallpaper. Come, I'll show you what the sheriff thinks he did next."

They headed through the sitting room, down the winding hallway and back staircase, Davenport pointing out more blood splatter that Ethan hadn't noticed on their way to the bedroom. When they reached the back door, Davenport stopped and pointed to a rocking chair overturned on the porch. It too was lying in a pool of caked blood.

"Was Heather still alive when they got here?" Ethan said, horrified.

"That's what the sheriff thinks," Davenport said.

"So he didn't kill her in the bedroom?" David said, making a series of pictures. "The newspapers implied that's where the murder took place."

"The newspapers missed most of the story. After Rufus pleaded guilty, the big papers pulled out and relied on local coverage for their headlines. And the local paper, *The Athol Gazette*, well, let's just say it's not the best."

"So where did he kill her?" Ethan said.

"That's the million-dollar question."

"What do you mean?" Ethan said, aghast.

"Nobody knows. The sheriff and his deputies searched for days but never found the kill site."

"How's that possible?" David said skeptically. "The cops must've pored over every square inch of the property."

"They did, with a fine toothcomb," Davenport said. "So did the forensic guys. They looked in every room, in the garage, in the guesthouse, and in all the other outbuildings, even searched the woods down to the reservoir with dogs—the best in the county—but they never found the kill site. But based on the condition of Heather Starr's body when they found her, the cops are pretty damn sure he didn't murder her in the bedroom. Nonetheless, they've never been able to pinpoint the exact spot where Rufus beat that poor girl to death."

Ethan was puzzled. This seemed like a big, unanswered question. "We didn't get into it last night, Bret, because I had to leave so abruptly, but is this one of the arguments in your appeal? That the cops never found the kill site? So they don't know exactly how Heather Star was murdered? Is that enough to overturn the court's sentence and spring Dr. Wellington from jail? Doesn't seem like enough to me, based on everything I know about the case."

"No, it probably isn't, but it's part of a pattern," Davenport said evasively. "There's much more to the appeal than just the sheriff's failure to unearth the exact location of the murder. It'll all become clear once I give you the documents."

"Later today?"

"Later today."

Ethan peered up at the sky, where clouds were thickening, the storm drawing closer. Something about the house and the murder wasn't making sense. Was it the missing evidence, something Davenport knew but wasn't telling him? He had more questions than answers, and discovering the truth was growing into an obsession.

"Bret, show me where Wellington buried the body before it starts to rain."

"This way," Davenport said, locking the door then walking down the porch steps, across the lawn—now overgrown with weeds and small saplings—and over to a narrow footpath cutting through the forest. "One of the deputies spotted a huge depression in the underbrush over here and thought something heavy might've been dragged along the ground. Of course, they didn't know at the time, but it was Heather Starr's body." Davenport knelt, flattened the tall grass with his hand, and stared up at Ethan. "So the deputy shone his flashlight down the path, noticed droplets of blood, and yelled for the sheriff. Then they followed the blood trail until they got to the clearing. That's where they found Rufus standing like a phantom."

"And where did they find the grave?" Ethan said.

"Lemme show you." Davenport trudged down the path, through the woods and into a large meadow. "They found it right over there," he said, heading to the far side near a line of trees still circled with strips of torn police tape. "Her body was neatly arranged right here, with her arms sticking out and the palms of her hands facing straight up. I've seen the crime scene photos. Rufus posed her so she looked like an angel."

"God Almighty," Ethan said stoically, "I'll need to see those photos."

"They're all yours," Davenport said, shaken. "If I never see them again, it'll be too soon." He paused as the first raindrops splattered the ground. "Is there anything else you wanna see? We should head back to the car before we get soaked."

"I'm good," Ethan said. "Do you need to shoot any more pictures, David?"

"Got enough for Sampson."

"Then let's get the hell out of here," Bret said, hustling across the clearing.

They reached the car five minutes later.

And hopped into the Audi.

Just before the heavens exploded and the rain began pelting the hood of the car.

CHAPTER 6

THEY ALL HAD LUNCH AT Nell's Café in Athol—a greasy spoon that served hamburgers and hot dogs and not much else—then split up: David taking the rental car and peeling off for a meeting with the editor-in-chief of *The Athol Gazette*; while Ethan followed Davenport to his law office in a nondescript redbrick building on Main Street. After climbing a flight of stairs, they stopped at the last door at the end of a short hallway. Stenciled proudly in big gold letters with black edging was the name of the law firm: *Bret Davenport LLP, Attorney-At-Law.*

Davenport opened the door and motioned Ethan into his suite of offices. The waiting room smelled of new money—the walls painted a fresh linen white, the floors covered in thick blue carpeting, and the furniture all new and ultramodern. Sitting at a sleek desk with a state-of-the-art IBM computer with enough memory to run a Fortune 500 company was an elderly woman with cheap-dye red hair that matched her fake nails—a look that was further bogged down with tortoise-shell reading glasses hanging from a string and costume jewelry dangling off her scrawny neck and wrists.

"Ethan, this is my girl Friday, Ms. Landau," Davenport said with a big smile. "Grace runs my office like a maestro conducting an orchestra." He chuckled at his feeble attempt at humor. "She knows where I am, what I'm doing—"

"And what you should be doing," cracked Ms. Landau.

"See? Anyway, you need me, she'll track me down and put you straight through."

Ms. Landau stood and thrust out her hand. "Pleased to meet you, Mr. Benson." She handed Ethan her business card and sat back down at her desk.

Davenport patted her shoulder then pushed through a door leading to another hallway. "I've organized everything in here," he said, leading Ethan through a well-stocked legal library and into his large, very posh office. He pointed to an expensive Italian couch sitting across from an equally expensive mahogany desk and told Ethan to take a seat. Ethan peered around the room. Real Tiffany lamps, an original Jackson Pollack painting, and a Frederick Remington bronze horse and rider perched on an antique coffee table.

Where did all the money come from?

He had to be loaded.

Ethan made a mental note to check Davenport's finances.

"Mind if I smoke?"

"Be my guest," Davenport said, motioning to a handmade porcelain ashtray sitting on his desk.

Ethan flipped open a pack of Marlboros, watching Davenport. "Looks like you're doing quite well, Bret. I've been to a lot of Fifth Avenue law offices that aren't nearly as fancy as yours. How do you pay for all this in a small town like Athol? The area seems pretty depressed to me."

Davenport didn't mind answering, "I represent a select few high rollers."

"Like Dr. Wellington?"

"Like Rufus," Davenport said proudly. "I've been his lawyer for years."

"Do you still represent him?"

"Of course," Davenport said. "After he was sentenced, he told me to continue managing his vast portfolio of investments, which I've been doing as I work on getting him released from prison."

"So he talks to you about his finances but not the murder?" Ethan said, wondering again if Davenport was hiding something. "I thought he wasn't talking to anybody about anything. That's what you told us at dinner last night."

"Well, you must've misunderstood me, Ethan," he said, not losing his cool. "Rufus has refused to talk about the murder ever since that fateful night, and that's why I'm happy he's reached out to you. But he's never stopped talking to me about his stock portfolio or his real estate holdings. He's a very wealthy man who comes from a very wealthy family. He learned at a very young age that he had to watch out for his money."

"So you're in communication with him about his estate?"

"Yes."

"But not the specifics of the murder."

"No. Never."

"And what about his appeal?"

"Of course. We talk about that all the time. How else can I get him out?"

Ethan hesitated a moment. "I'm confused, Bret. I thought Wellington wanted to go to prison, and that's why he pleaded guilty to the murder," he said, tilting his head. "And he committed a pretty heinous crime. Can't imagine the state of Massachusetts will ever put him back on the street."

"Stranger things have happened," Davenport said, twirling his hand in the air. "This was Rufus's first brush with the law. Granted, it's not your run-of-the-mill speeding ticket, but he's a prominent heart surgeon from a prominent New England family that goes all the way back to the American Revolution. So I'm exploring his options. And as I told you, maybe he just needs a little time to get well in a psychiatric hospital. With proper treatment, he stands a good chance to be released back into society."

"So as you work on his appeal, you manage his personal wealth."

"That's right."

"How much is he worth?"

"That's lawyer-client privilege. I can't tell you that."

"And how much does he pay you?"

"Can't tell you that either, Ethan."

"Fair enough, but you must make a ton of money to pay for all this," Ethan said, glancing around the room.

"Rufus can more than afford it," Davenport said, smiling. "And don't forget, I have other clients too."

"Okay, I get it, but is Wellington trying to buy his way out of prison?" Ethan said, pushing his buttons.

"Of course not," Davenport said curtly. "There are enough holes in the chain of evidence—beyond the sheriff's inability to locate the kill site—for me to file an appeal and for the judge to overturn his sentence and remand him to a psychiatric facility where he can get some help."

Ethan leaned back on the couch. "What holes?"

"Can't give you details, Ethan, not yet. I haven't argued the case before a judge and can't risk any leaks before he makes his decision. But I can tell you, the sheriff and his deputies failed to properly catalogue much of the forensic evidence after the murder and before the sentencing. So the court failed to properly weigh the extenuating circumstances when it sentenced him to thirty years to life. That's all I'm gonna say at the moment."

"Okay, Bret. I respect your decision to keep the appeal close to the vest," Ethan said, discomfited. "But you promised me documents. Can I at least have a copy of your motion to appeal?"

"I know that's what I told you," Davenport said cagily. "But upon reflection, I've decided it's just too risky for my case. So at the moment, you can't have it."

Ethan stared quietly at Davenport. His eye was twitching again. "So what can I have?"

"I've made copies of most of the court docket," Davenport said. He buzzed Ms. Landau on an intercom. "Grace, two cups of coffee. And bring Mr. Benson another ashtray. He's a chain-smoker like me, and my ashtray's filled to the brim." Then he pointed to a table covered with a stack of thin file folders. "All the documents are over there. I'd start with the police reports and work my way down to Rufus's confession."

"Is there a copy of the confession video?"

"On a disk in the marked folder."

Ms. Landau walked into the room with the coffee and handed Ethan another handmade porcelain ashtray. "Use this, Mr. Benson, and don't drop ashes on the new carpeting. I just had it installed." She turned abruptly, pushed her glasses up her nose, and hurried back to her desk.

Ethan stared at the file folders.

Along with the police reports, there were a handful of depositions, several motions filed by Davenport and the district attorney, a forensic report, the transcript of the confession, and several video disks.

"Doesn't seem like much. And this is everything?"

"Everything I saved," Davenport said, twirling a silver pen. "Remember, there was no trial. So there's not a lot of paperwork."

"What about crime scene photos?" Ethan asked, lighting another cigarette.

"JPEGs are on a disk in the same folder as the confession video."

"Is there a police tape?" Ethan had found it very useful on his last story.

"There is, but I can't seem to put my hands on it," Davenport said apologetically. "Grace went through everything, searched my computer for hours, but she couldn't find it on the hard drive either."

"Kind of an important piece of evidence to be missing," Ethan said sarcastically.

"I had it when I needed it. Shit happens. Why don't you ask the sheriff or the district attorney for a copy? They should have it."

Ethan thought this was odd, since everything else seemed to be carefully saved and stored.

Was Davenport maneuvering him?

Maybe.

After peering at the file folders one last time, he looked up at Davenport. "I'm gonna take everything back to my room and spend the rest of the day reading. If I have any questions, can I call you?"

"You know where to reach me," he said. "Come on. I'll give you a ride back to the motel."

⋘⋙

Ethan unlocked the door and walked into his room. It was four o'clock, and the maid still hadn't cleaned. Frustrated, he picked up the phone and called the front desk but after ten rings, got no answer. Dropping the receiver into the cradle, he cursed out loud then breathed deeply, trying to calm down. He arranged the file folders on the unmade bed before grabbing the police reports and sitting in a stained wing chair that was worn in the seat and torn in the back.

The first document, written by Sheriff Eugene McKenzie, was dated two years earlier on August 11—the day of the murder—ten single-spaced pages recounting every detail the sheriff had witnessed at the crime scene. Ethan began reading, pausing at a description of Wellington's state of mind when the police found him stumbling across the meadow. He marked the page with a yellow Post-It, walked to his bedside table, and poured an inch of Black Label into a dirty glass that he tried to rub clean on the bedsheet.

Fuck it, he thought, *Sarah's not here to yell at me. It'll clear my head.* He drank the Scotch then walked back to the wing chair and read:

> He was acting strange when we approached. His hair was standing in every direction; he was sweating profusely; and his clothes were torn and covered in mud and what appeared to be blood. He was holding a shovel and a backpack and identified himself as Rufus Wellington. Then he began laughing hysterically. I took a step back and unholstered my firearm. When I asked him why he was in the meadow at three o'clock in the morning, he shrieked and said he was burying garbage. After telling me we were trespassing on his property, he ordered me to

leave. He began to shake uncontrollably and rant and rave. I thought he was crazy. That's when Deputy Wilkerson yelled across the clearing he'd found something.

Ethan stared at the passage and underlined the words, *I thought he was crazy*, turned on his iPad, and made a note to ask the sheriff what he meant when they met the following day. Then he scanned through the rest of the document and shuddered as he read a graphic description of Heather Starr's body on the final page:

A naked woman was lying in a half-filled grave. The forensic team carefully removed the loose dirt from around the body. We saw she'd been beaten savagely. Her face had swelled up the size of a basketball; her eyes were black-and-blue and puffed up like balloons; and her teeth were broken out. Deep stab cuts ran up and down her arms and legs. Her hands and ankles were twisted and probably broken. The body was covered with blood. While forensics was taking pictures, I watched Dr. Wellington. He was staring at them with a grin that seemed like the devil's—as if he was more than just proud of what he'd done.

Ethan pressed his fingers to his forehead. A headache was coming on. *Shit. I need to find a good forensic psychiatrist*, he thought as he jotted himself a reminder in his iPad, *someone who can tell me what would drive a prominent doctor like Rufus Wellington to commit a crime like this.* Then he drained his Scotch, poured another two inches, and picked up another police report. A knock on the door interrupted him.

"Ethan, it's me, David."

He opened the door. "I've been going through Davenport's stuff. You gotta take a look at what I found. The police reports are giving me some interesting insights into Wellington's psyche." He took a long pull on the Scotch. "Want one?" he said, holding out the bottle.

"Hell, no, Ethan. Way too early in the day for me," he said, concerned. "You're hitting that stuff pretty hard. Watched you down your drink in one swill last night before you left the restaurant. Thought it was odd. You okay?"

"Just having a taste."

"While you're going through documents? It's gonna distort your judgment, cause you to make mistakes. Come on, Ethan, something's bothering you. What's wrong?"

"Christ, you sound just like Sarah. I can handle it," he said, brushing him off, not wanting to talk about his drinking. He abruptly changed the subject. "What did you learn at the newspaper?"

David stared long and hard at the bottle until Ethan put it down then said, "Had a long talk with the editor-in-chief, Jonah Wilcox. He wasn't too sharp on details like Davenport said. Maybe that's why he runs a small-town newspaper. He made me copies of all their stories on the murder. It was front-page news for a couple of days, but as soon as Wellington pleaded guilty, it faded from the headlines. There were no in-depth features on Wellington or the police investigation or the court proceedings. No back-of-the-book reporting. The coverage was basically over before it got started."

Ethan slugged back his Scotch and shot David a look. "Am I the only one thinking this case went by at light speed?"

"It's a country courthouse. Not much on the docket to slow it down," David said thoughtfully.

"That's true. But by pleading guilty immediately and remaining silent, Wellington avoided any digging into his background. Maybe he didn't want anybody looking into his past."

"Come on, Ethan, you have no proof of that. He was probably insane. Doesn't seem like he was thinking with any clarity—either during the murder or after. I don't think he's covering up anything."

"Maybe, but most of what we know about Wellington comes from Davenport or from the society columns in the Boston papers, and most of it is gossip from before the murder," Ethan said, beginning to slur his words.

"I don't know, Ethan. The alcohol is clouding your judgment."

There was an uneasy silence. "I don't think so, David."

"Maybe we can press Davenport to fill in some of the blanks?" David said, trying to smooth over the awkward moment.

Ethan sipped his Scotch then said, distracted, "I've got that feeling, again, that maybe Davenport..."

"What?"

"Has a real twisted relationship with Wellington, dating all the way back to their childhood."

"We discussed this at dinner. Then you asked Davenport after he arrived, and I still don't see it. Are we reading something into this that isn't there?"

"Could be, but we know they're more than just good friends, and Wellington's paying him a shitload of money to manage his personal affairs. You should see the art in his office. You have to wonder what he's got at home. Let's run a background check, get our hands on his financial records."

"How we gonna do that?"

"Maybe we can't, but Lloyd can."

Lloyd Howard was a private detective and former New York City police officer whom Ethan had hired as a consultant on his last story.

"He's damn expensive."

"Paul made it clear he likes this story. I'll get him to pull the money from the show's research budget."

"And I'll see if Lloyd has time to work with us." David picked up the folder with the disks. "Did you screen these?"

"Not yet. I was about to look when you knocked. Hand me the disk that says *Crime Scene Photos*." Ethan popped the disk into his computer, and nothing happened. It was blank.

"Here," said David, handing him the one labeled *Wellington's Confession*, "try this one."

Ethan loaded the second disk into the computer, but it too was blank.

"Should I call Davenport?" David said, fumbling for his cell phone. "Ask him to make us new copies?"

Ethan tried both disks one more time but didn't answer.

"No?" David said, looking at him. "You think he did it on purpose?"

Ethan poured another drink. The alcohol was now raging through his body. "Let's talk about it at dinner."

"Ethan, put down the glass. You're drunk."

"No, just pleasantly buzzed." Then he downed the Scotch and said, "Let's go. I'm suddenly starved."

CHAPTER 7

ETHAN LEFT DAVID CATALOGUING DOCUMENTS at the motel and drove the three miles to the sheriff's office. There wasn't a cloud in the early-morning sky, the sun peeking over the horizon as he passed the overgrown cemetery and the derelict factory—the roof caved in and the windows smashed—made a right turn onto Main Street, and cruised through the center of town. He stopped at a red light. An old woman hobbling with a cane slowly limped across the street, and a teenage mother—not more than a day over sixteen—pushed a screaming baby in a stroller as she hauled a bagful of groceries into a crumbling apartment building. The light changed, and Ethan hung a left onto Exchange Road and pulled into a parking lot in front of the Franklyn County Sheriff's Department. It was a two-story cement structure with bars on the windows and a ten-foot high chain-link fence blocking the entrance to a lockup in the back. Like every other building in Athol, the walls were crumbling and the paint, peeling.

Ethan grabbed his briefcase and got out of the car.

He passed a line of police cruisers angled along the road and approached a small group of deputies smoking cigarettes and drinking coffee in Styrofoam cups. A big man wearing a dirty uniform, scuffed black shoes, and wraparound sunglasses perched on top of a balding head stepped in front of him. Ethan was momentarily cautious.

"Morning, I'm Ethan Benson from *The Weekly Reporter*. I'm here to see Sheriff McKenzie."

The deputy looked Ethan up and down and sipped his coffee, not cracking a smile. "Up the steps, first door on your right, but he's busy."

"I was told he'd see me this morning."

"Up the steps. First door on the right. Don't you listen, motherfucker?"

Ethan glared contemptuously at the deputy then said harshly, "Got a bug up your ass, deputy? You should treat guests in your town with a little more respect, don't you think?" He glanced at the deputy's name tag—Percy Wilkerson—before staring into his eyes and slowly moving past him into the building.

Cocksucker.

Making his way through the waiting room, he was stopped by a female deputy named Elizabeth, who was sitting behind a large desk, reading a printout on a clipboard. "Can I help you?" she said, sliding her reading glasses down her nose.

"I have an appointment with the sheriff."

"Name?"

"Ethan Benson."

She ran her finger down the printout then peered up at his face. "Yup, your name's right here," she said officiously. "Please put your briefcase on the counter. I need to take a look. Standard procedure. But I'm sure you already know that." The deputy eyeballed the contents, closed his briefcase, then scrutinized the photo ID in his wallet before handing him back his belongings. With an impenetrable expression, she said, "Everything seems to be in order, Mr. Benson. Please take a seat. The sheriff will be with you in a moment."

Ethan sat on a wooden bench and waited.

Five minutes.

Ten minutes.

Then he stood and approached the deputy. "Does the sheriff know I'm here?"

"Patience. Mr. McKenzie's a very busy man." She pushed her reading glasses back up her nose and began typing on her computer.

Ethan sat down again, growing more agitated. Why was he so stressed? The sheriff wasn't that late. Was it the story? Was it the hangover from all the Scotch he'd belted down the night before? Man, he had to ease off the bottle. At least for a little while. Then he said testily, "Are you sure he knows I'm here? He was supposed to see me fifteen minutes ago."

The deputy removed her reading glasses. "He's on an important telephone call. You just have to wait."

"Really?" he said and, without hesitation, strode past her desk and through the door to the sheriff's office, leaving her staring in disbelief.

"You can't go in there," she said hastily.

"The hell I can't."

"That's all right, Elizabeth," the sheriff said, waving her off. "I was just about ready to see him." Eugene McKenzie was hunched over a cluttered table in the middle of the room, eating his breakfast and drinking a black coffee. He looked at Ethan then wiped his mouth on a checkered cloth napkin. Standing, he said, "You must be Ethan Benson. Hope I didn't keep you waiting too long." He stuck out his hand. It looked as large as a baseball glove. "Call me Gene. Everybody calls me Gene."

Fully six feet five and three hundred pounds, with a big potbelly—he wore a neatly trimmed mustache, slicked-back black hair, and well-manicured fingernails. His light-brown sheriff's uniform was immaculate and neatly pressed, his shoes polished to perfection, and his tie fastened adroitly to his shirt by a solid gold tie clip. He looked more like a Wall Street businessman than a country sheriff. "So what can I do for you, Mr. Benson?" he said politely as he offered Ethan a chair.

"I'm working up a story on Rufus Wellington."

"Yes. I know. Your assistant, David Livingston, told me on the telephone."

"And I spent most of yesterday with Bret Davenport at Dr. Wellington's estate. Thanks for giving us permission to look at the crime scene."

"My pleasure, Mr. Benson."

"Call me Ethan."

The sheriff nodded.

Ethan decided enough with the pleasantries. "Bret showed me the bedroom where Wellington beat Heather Starr and the meadow behind his house where he buried her body. The only thing he didn't show me was where Rufus Wellington actually murdered the girl. I understand you searched the property with your men but never found the kill site."

"Nope, never found it," McKenzie said. "Me and my boys and the Feds spent days lookin' with the best dogs in the county. Every square inch of the house and up and down every trail in the forest. None of us have any idea where he killed the girl."

"You brought in the Feds?" Ethan said, surprised. "That's the first I've heard of the Feds' involvement."

"Yup. Called them because they've got more expertise than we have in this kind of thing."

"And they couldn't find the kill site either?"

"Nope. Had no better luck than we did."

"Are you still looking?"

"It's still an active investigation, but it's costin' us taxpayer dollars we just don't have."

"Isn't the kill site a pretty big loose end, Sheriff?"

"You might think so," McKenzie said, lighting a cigarette. "But we got our man, and he's locked up in jail, probably for the rest of his life. Don't see how it matters anymore, do you? We got a full confession after catching him red-handed committing the crime."

"But if you found the kill site," Ethan said, flippantly, "that might help explain why Dr. Wellington murdered the girl. That seems to be an unanswered question everybody's still asking."

"He killed her because he's a pervert, don't you think? He fell in love with a kid prostitute he picked up on a street corner, and when she refused to marry him, he lost it and beat her to death. What exactly are you asking for?"

"The crime scene details aren't clear," Ethan said, coming at it from a different angle.

"How so?"

"You haven't found the murder weapon, for one."

"That's a whole other story," McKenzie said, his eyes glowing. "Forensic experts say he clubbed her to death with a blunt instrument. Could've been a hammer or a baseball bat, but whatever, her skull was bashed in and unrecognizable. You can rule out doing that with his fists."

"I still don't get it," he said, boring into the sheriff's eyes. "You arrested him within minutes of her death. How could he hide the murder weapon or the kill site that you and your deputies and the Feds and the search dogs haven't found them after all this time?"

"We looked, Mr. Benson—"

"Ethan."

The sheriff frowned. "Everywhere and real hard, even with the dogs, and that's what they're trained to do," McKenzie said, "his house, garage, outbuildings. Nothin' was found."

"I assume you asked Wellington," Ethan said tetchily.

"Of course, but I'm sure you know, once he admitted to the murder, he clammed up. It's all there on the confession tape."

"Which brings me to the tape and crime scene photos. The disks I received from Bret Davenport were blank. I thought I might get them from you."

"Afraid not," McKenzie said, blowing a smoke ring.

"Surely you kept them?"

"No reason to keep that stuff," McKenzie said, lowering his eyes. "Gave my copies to the district attorney after I carted Wellington off to the joint. You'll have to get the video and the pictures from Lauren Saperstein."

First Davenport.

Now McKenzie.

Would the district attorney's office give him a runaround too?

"I just have one more question, Sheriff. In your police report, you said Rufus Wellington looked 'crazy' when you found him in the meadow. What did you mean by that?"

McKenzie squirmed in his chair. "Well, that was kinda figure of speech. Why else would he do somethin' like that to the girl? Doesn't make sense, does it?" He leaned across the table and stared fiercely into Ethan's eyes. "I'm a lawman, not a shrink, Ethan. But if you want my opinion, I don't think he's crazy at all.

He's probably as sane as you and me and belongs just where the court put him, in prison for murder."

Ethan watched the sheriff, wondering about the kill site and the murder weapon and whether McKenzie was being honest with him, then pushed back his chair and stood. "I'll be in touch if I have any more questions. Thanks for your time."

"Sure thing."

When he reached the door, he stopped and said, "By the way, you don't have a problem telling me all this on camera, do you, Sheriff?"

McKenzie grinned. "Sounds like a heap of fun. Maybe you can shoot pictures of me and my deputies showin' you around Wellington's property. We can take the dogs. That would make me look real good in your story," McKenzie said before returning to his coffee.

"I'll be in touch," Ethan said, grinning back.

The sheriff was a bigger buffoon than he thought.

꽃

Eugene McKenzie waited for Ethan to exit the building, dabbed his mouth with his napkin, then closed the door and shuffled over to his desk, dropping into a well-worn armchair facing the front window. He opened the top drawer and pulled out a cell phone then punched in a number.

"Hey, it's me, Gene."

"You on a burner?"

"Yeah. The call can't be traced."

"So?"

"Just gettin' into his car now. Grilled me for an hour about Rufus and the murder."

"And?" the man said, annoyed.

"I said what you told me to," the sheriff said, feeling a sharp pain in his chest. He waited for the throbbing to subside then lit another cigarette. "But the guy kept pushin', askin' me more questions. He was really hung up on why we didn't find the kill site and the fucking murder weapon."

"What did you tell him?"

"That we mostly stopped after Wellington got shipped off to prison."

"And his reaction?"

The sheriff rubbed his chest. It still hurt. He was going to have to lay off the greasy food and all the cigarettes, maybe see a doctor and get some pills. "Nothin' much. But what could he say? He couldn't say we didn't try."

"You think so?" The man was still irritated. "Anything else?"

"I may have said somethin' I shouldn't have," the sheriff said sheepishly.

"What the fuck does that mean?"

"I slipped. I said we brought in the Feds to help search for the kill site."

"Goddamn it, Gene, you're an idiot," the man exploded. "What happens if he calls and checks? How am I gonna handle the mess that'll create?"

The sheriff inhaled his cigarette, ignoring the ache in his chest. "I don't know. You'll have to think of somethin'."

"Did you say anything else stupid?"

"That was my only fuckup."

"And what about the confession tape?"

"I told him I didn't have it or the crime scene photos," the sheriff said. "Told him Lauren had everything and to go to her."

"Good. I'll take care of Lauren. Anything else you need to tell me?" the man said harshly.

"One more thing."

The sheriff paused.

"And what's that?"

"I want more money," McKenzie said pointedly.

"How much?"

The sheriff did a rough calculation in his head. "Another ten thousand should keep my lips sealed."

"Done. I'll leave it in the usual place. And, Gene, if you fuck things up again, I guarantee you, Rufus won't be happy."

The sheriff blinked and puffed away on his cigarette. "Don't you worry about me. Just get me the cash."

He waited for a response.

But the phone went dead.

McKenzie smiled, pleased with himself. "Money in the bank." He stood, hiked his pants up, and placed a call to his first deputy. "Percy, he just left. Take an unmarked car—one of the Crown Victoria's—and get after him. Put on an overcoat so he doesn't figure out you're a cop. And for Pete's sake, don't let him out of your sight."

"Ten-four, boss," the deputy said.

"Cut the shit, and keep me informed."

The sheriff clicked off and dropped the burner back in his desk. Everything was under control, but the pain in his chest was beginning to alarm him.

CHAPTER 8

AFTER PICKING UP DAVID AT the motel and grabbing coffee at Nell's Café, Ethan drove south on Route 202, beginning the half-hour trip to Old Salem. He'd just gotten off the phone with Bret Davenport, who'd arranged a three o'clock meeting with Wellington's neighbor at the library in the town square. If they hurried, they'd make it just in time. As they cruised down the county highway, Ethan cracked open his window. The air was damp and sticky, the trees in the dense forest swaying in the wind. Another storm was approaching, and Ethan could feel the chill in the air. Soon fall would turn to winter, and the rain would turn to snow. He hated the cold weather and longed for the warmth of the summer.

"Did you check with Mindy?" he asked David.

"She's working the phones. Nobody in Boston seems to remember Heather Starr."

Ethan had called Mindy earlier that morning and told her to begin digging into the hooker's background. The Boston media had mostly focused on Wellington after the murder, the blue blood and hotshot heart surgeon. Heather had been a foot-note, a troubled young woman who'd hooked up with the wrong john and paid with her life. Ethan thought it strange and wondered why no one seemed interested in her backstory—a loose end. Did they even try to notify her family?

"Next week," David said, pulling up a preliminary schedule on his iPhone.

"What?" he said, confused.

"Your survey. You leave for Boston Wednesday afternoon and come back either Friday or Saturday, depending on how many people Mindy lines up for you to meet."

"Who's booked so far?"

"Just Kirk Fulbright, a heart surgeon who worked with Wellington at Mass General. He's on Thursday, and she also has calls into his father, Virgil Wellington, at his apartment in the Back Bay. He'd be on Saturday if she can locate him."

"What's on Friday?"

"Mindy was still working on that when I talked to her this morning."

"Call her. Let's see if she's lined up anything else." David dialed her on his cell phone. "Put her on speaker," Ethan said, frustrated by a slower-moving USPS truck hogging the road in front of him.

She picked up on the fourth ring.

"Mindy, it's me, Ethan. David's got you on speakerphone."

"Jeez, the two wayward travelers, both at the same time," she said jestingly. "Where you guys headed?"

"To talk to one of Wellington's neighbors."

"Feeling better, Ethan?"

"What do you mean?" he said carefully.

"David told me about last night. Said you really hung a lollapalooza."

Ethan shot David a quick, angry glance then said. "I had a few to unwind, maybe one too many. Nothing more than that."

"Just don't tell Sarah. She'll have your ass."

"Very funny," he said, wondering if everybody knew he and Sarah were arguing over his drinking. "What do you have for me next Friday in Boston?" he said abruptly.

"Thought we'd head down to Dorchester," she said, sounds of papers rustling on the speakerphone. "That's one of the new combat zones on the south side, just outside the city center."

"Are we sure that's where Heather met Wellington?"

"Nope. Nobody's sure. But I've been checking all the big online sex sites and call girl services. Hang on. Let me find my list. Got it. I've talked to The Sophisticated Gentleman, Night on the Town, Beautiful Escorts, Girls for an Evening. Like the names? No question what services they provide."

"You're a barrel of laughs this morning, Mindy. Any others?"

"Maybe another ten places, and believe me, there's plenty more, and so far, they all told me the same thing—no underage kids and nobody named Heather Starr."

"Do you believe them?" David said dryly.

"They could be feeding me a line, but I don't think so."

"So that's why you think Heather was a street hooker?" Ethan said, breaking for the USPS truck then checking for landmarks.

"That's the gist of it. Plus, I got a tip from one of my cop sources in the sex crimes unit at the Boston PD, who said Heather may have worked in Dorchester. That's where most teenage prostitutes hook for johns."

"So that's where we start."

"Probably our best bet."

Ethan picked up speed and passed the delivery truck as it turned onto a side road. "You coming to Boston with me?"

"Joyce approved my travel." Joyce Cox was the senior producer on *The Weekly Reporter* responsible for assigning personnel and running the day-to-day operations of the broadcast. "She grumbled about the money," Mindy said, "so we went to Paul, who said he wants a decision as soon as possible, but you already know that, and if this is what you need to make it, I should go."

"I need you. We don't have enough to convince Peter—or me, for that matter—and if I don't give him something solid and soon, beyond the basics of the murder, he's gonna pull the plug and make me move on to another project."

"Done."

He checked the mileage on the odometer.

They were getting close.

"I assume you haven't heard back from Wellington's father?"

"Not yet."

"Keep trying, and don't stop checking the call girl services."

"Wasn't planning to."

"And one more thing, Mindy," Ethan said. "Call your sources in Washington and see if the Feds were involved in the search for the kill site. McKenzie mentioned it to me offhandedly at our meeting this morning. See what you can find out."

"Roger and out."

"Making progress," Ethan said as David punched off the speakerphone. Then his own iPhone pinged.

He checked the screen.

It was Sarah.

Shit.

"Gotta take this, David," he said, beginning to perspire. "Hey, babe, how are you?" he tried to sound cheerful.

"Haven't heard from you, Ethan, in almost two days. I was getting worried."

"I'm okay. How's Lukie?"

"He's fine. We're both fine. But we miss you. Luke wants to know when you're coming home."

There was a long pause.

"Did you tell him I'm back on Saturday?"

"I told him, but he wants to hear it from you." Another long pause. "Can you talk to him now?"

"I'm on my way to Old Salem for a meeting. Maybe at dinnertime."

Her voice hardened, "Okay. I'll tell him you'll call later, but you need to talk to him today. Don't forget."

"I won't, Sarah," his promise sounding hollow.

"How's the story going?"

"Got some good leads, but not enough to push it into production."

"Is Peter giving you a hard time?"

He hesitated, remembering the barrage of daily phone calls. "Just the constant stream of bullshit."

"Are you drinking?"

"No."

"I don't believe you. How much?"

Ethan could hear the tension in her voice. "Don't wanna talk now, babe. David's in the car."

"So when?"

"Maybe when I call Luke?"

"You always push it off until later, Ethan," she said, her voice beginning to quiver. "And you never give me a straight answer. I know you're drinking. I wanna know how much."

"Come on, Sarah."

"No. We need to talk."

"But, babe—"

She hung up the phone.

"Everything okay at home?" David said timidly.

Ethan didn't respond.

"Did she ask about your drinking?"

"Yeah," he said, deflated.

"Why didn't you own up to last night?"

"Didn't have to. Sounds like you told her, like you told Mindy."

"Well, you were pretty smashed when we got back to the motel after dinner," David said, uncomfortable. "And we're all worried. So when she called me this morning, it kinda slipped out."

"Why'd she call you?"

"Because she hadn't heard from you." There was deafening silence, then David said, "Something's obviously eating at you. You need to talk to her."

"Yeah. Yeah, I will, but now we gotta focus on our story. That's what we gotta do. Focus on our story."

⁓

Percy Wilkerson dropped back a little farther, hoping not to be noticed. Adjusting his sunglasses, he continued to follow Ethan as he approached the turn off to Old Salem, made a sharp left, and headed down Main Street—past the cemetery, the fire department, the town hall, and the church. He looked at the sky. It was growing darker—the wind picking up, the trees straining—as he eased off the road and pulled into an alley across the street from the library. Percy had seen this kind of storm sweep across the Quabbin many times. One minute the weather seemed calm, almost serene; then in an instant, all hell would break loose. This front had all the earmarks of a doozy. Grabbing a pair of binoculars he'd stashed in the glove compartment, he got out of the car and hid behind a dense row of blue spruce. After focusing on Ethan, he reached for his burner.

"Gene, it's me. He's about to go into the village library," Wilkerson said as he moved the binoculars to a window in the front door. "There's a guy with him. Never seen him before. They must be meeting someone, yeah, now I can see her. It's some old lady. She's sitting in the back of the room."

He panned back and forth but couldn't see her face.

"Who is it?"

"Her back's to the camera. What should I do?"

"Keep watching, and for Christ's sake, Percy, make sure he doesn't see you."

"Gene, I'm gonna get soaked," he said as big drops began smashing the top of his bald head.

"Stop bitchin'. You been wet before. Just do what I say."

Percy could hear the sheriff wheezing in the background.

"Look, I gotta make a call, see if the big boss knows about the meeting."

"Gene. Gene?"

He'd hung up.

Percy tucked the burner into his pocket and continued peering through the binoculars.

❧

Ethan hurried into the foyer just as the sky opened and rain began falling in earnest. He shook off his trench coat as David closed the door and peered around a quaint New England–style reading room that was lined with floor-to-ceiling bookshelves containing hundreds of old leather-bound books covered in a thin layer of dust. Sitting at a table, thumbing briskly through an old newspaper, was Mary Murphy—a small, stern-looking woman with deep age lines on her face and graying hair pulled back in a bun. She was wearing a threadbare cotton blouse that matched the chalky-white color of her skin, a green-and-red checkered skirt, and a pale-blue cashmere sweater. He slowly approached, the old floorboards creaking with each step, and waved his hand to greet her. There was a moment of strained silence.

"May we sit?" he said, gesturing to David.

She nodded almost dismissively.

They pulled out two chairs and sat down.

"Thanks for meeting with us," Ethan said, trying to cut through the chill in the air. "I hope this isn't an inconvenience."

"Of course, it's an inconvenience," she said bluntly, the corners of her mouth bending down in a scowl. "So how can I help you, Mr. Benson? I don't have a lot of time."

Ethan smiled to himself. All the old gal had, it seemed to him, was time. There wasn't much else to do in this sleepy little town.

"May I call you Mary?"

"Suit yourself."

"How well did you know, Dr. Wellington, Mary?"

"I'm his next-door neighbor down by the reservoir," she said flatly. "I assume that's the reason you're speaking to me."

"Were you friendly?"

"Hardly."

"Did you socialize?"

"I'd see him drive by my house every now and then, and I'd call him every so often to turn down his damn music, if you call that socializing."

Ethan paused a moment, trying to recall if he'd seen her house when he'd surveyed the crime scene with Davenport, but all he could remember was the thick forest and the underbrush and the Quabbin off in the distance. "I'm surprised you could hear his music," he said softly. "Wellington's house is a long way from you."

"The sound carries in the woods, Mr. Benson. Some nights I could hear his damn rock music like it was playing right there on a stereo in my parlor. The man was downright rude and a scoundrel who moved into our peaceful town and built that monstrosity at the end of the road."

Ethan wondered if he'd get the same reaction from Wellington's other neighbors in Old Salem.

"Didn't like him from the moment I met him," Mary Murphy said, her eyes scrunching into thin slits. "I tolerated him because I had to. He was my neighbor, and he wasn't going away."

"Was anybody friendly with him?" David said.

"Nope. And we kept well away from him," Mary Murphy said. "Gave everybody the creeps, especially me."

"How'd he do that if you never socialized with him?" Ethan said.

"He and I had somewhat of a history."

"What kinda history?"

"We grew up together in Shutesbury," she said, finally easing into the conversation. "We were classmates in the public schools. I met him when my family moved here in the third grade."

"Mind if I take notes?" Ethan said, pulling out his iPad.

"Be my guest," Mary Murphy said impatiently.

"So what was he like as a kid, Mary?"

"Very strange."

"In what way?"

"He was the richest kid in the county," she said, pulling a piece of lint off her sweater. "So he was aloof, standoffish. His parents wouldn't let him hang out with any of us common folk— only his friend, Bret."

"You knew Bret Davenport as a kid? What was he like?"

She ignored the question.

Ethan wondered why.

"None of us knew Rufus real well. Not a one of us, especially the girls. Even back then, we thought he was a wack job. We knew there was something genuinely wrong in his head. So we all stayed away from him."

Ethan remembered how different Davenport's description had been, how he'd insisted Wellington was just a normal kid who liked to have fun. "What was wrong with him?" Ethan asked.

"Even as a ten year old, he'd stare at us, ogle us, try to look up our dresses. He thought we didn't notice, but we did. He had this look on his face, like he always wanted to touch us and maybe do something bad to us. None of us girls wanted to be alone with him, not one of us."

"Did he ever do anything to you?"

"Nope. Never let him come near me."

"Did he date…any of the girls?" Ethan said, staring in amazement.

"Hell, no," Mary Murphy said, horrified. "He was sick, real sick."

"And what about the boys?" David asked as bowled over as Ethan.

"No boyfriends either, except Bret," she said, emphasizing each word. "What does that say about the two of them?" She pressed on, "The boys teased him mercilessly, called him a sissy, and beat up on him from time to time. He was bullied all through grade school and middle school and even in high school. They made his life miserable."

"And his parents did nothing?" David said.

"Apparently not."

Ethan finished typing a note and paused before asking his next question. "Mary, what happened the night of the murder?"

"I heard that poor girl screaming from my porch. It was bloodcurdling, but not surprising. This was just the thing we thought he might do one day."

Ethan leaned back, watching her. "You thought he might kill somebody?"

"That's what I'm saying."

"Did you ever go to the police and tell them you thought he was capable of violence," David asked, glancing sideways at Ethan, "before the murder?"

"Of course. But the sheriff thought I was just some wacko. Didn't believe me—not until the night Heather died. Poor girl. As a matter of fact, when McKenzie interviewed me after the murder, I reminded him about what I'd told him. That Rufus was a damn sick pervert. But it was too late by then. Rufus had done the deed, and McKenzie had his confession, so he wasn't interested in listening to me, not one bit."

Ethan tried to remember if he'd read any references to Mary Murphy in the sheriff's police report or in any of the other police reports, for that matter. But McKenzie and his deputies had never mentioned speaking to her and only briefly referred to her 911 call. "How do you feel that the sheriff didn't heed your warning?"

"Madder than a hive of riled-up hornets," she said bitterly. "Might've saved that poor girl's life if he'd just listened to me."

"And how do you feel," Ethan said, turning off his iPad, "that the sheriff didn't care the murder seemed to fit a pattern, that Wellington had a long history of harassing young girls like you?"

Mary Murphy's faced contorted into fury. "How do you think I feel?" she said, looking from Ethan to David and then back to Ethan. "Haven't you been listenin' to me at all? I'm suspicious. I'm downright angry. I think there's somethin' else goin' on big time—that the sheriff doesn't want to hear the truth about Rufus, that nobody wants to hear the truth about Rufus. Good. Now I've said it. Been eatin' up my insides for near on two years now. There's been a big cover-up goin' on by the sheriff's office and by all those other people involved in this damn case. I'm sure of it. And I ain't gonna say no more."

CHAPTER 9

Percy Wilkerson was soaked to the skin when Ethan and David left the library and dashed to their Jeep Cherokee. Hustling through the alley and back to his car, he jumped into the driver's seat and started the engine but before pulling out dialed the sheriff.

"They just left," he said. "They met with Mary Murphy, the lady who called 911."

"Fuck," the sheriff said bluntly. "She's a nosy bitch. What'd you hear?"

"Hear? How could I hear anything?" Percy said angrily. "They were in the library, and I was stuck outside in the rain. Shit, you could wring me out in a clothes dryer, and I'd still be soaking wet."

"Stop bellyaching. Follow them."

Percy stepped on the gas.

"Where're they heading?" the sheriff said, screaming into the telephone.

"How the hell should I know?" Percy said sharply. "They just turned right onto Route 202. Maybe they're heading back to Athol?"

"You call me if they stop, if they make one little turn."

"Count on it."

"And, Percy, I'll hang you up by your ears if they spot you."

Percy dropped his burner onto the passenger seat and banged his fist on the steering wheel. "What does that asshole take me for, a fool? Don't I know how to tail somebody? I've been doin' it for him since I joined his goddamn sheriff's department. Fuck him." Then he raced down Main Street, looked both ways at the intersection, and slipped onto Route 202, keeping a safe distance behind.

Ethan glanced into his rearview mirror and saw the Crown Victoria. It had just turned out of Old Salem and settled in behind them. He eased off the gas pedal and watched as it slowed down and matched his speed. "Back again."

"The same guy you spotted at the library?"

"Same guy. Percy Wilkerson. I recognize the big bald head and sunglasses," Ethan said slyly. "He's the deputy I had the run-in with this morning before meeting the sheriff. The jerk's wearing an overcoat. Must think we wouldn't notice he was a cop."

"Think the sheriff sent him?"

"Maybe."

Ethan checked the rearview mirror and stepped on the gas. The Crown Victoria picked up speed, continuing to keep pace. So now he'd have a tail for the rest of the survey. All he had to do was figure out why.

"You're smiling, Ethan," David said, looking at him coyly. "You enjoying this?"

"Makes life a bit more interesting."

They both laughed.

But neither felt happy.

They were tailed for most of the rest of the day as they drove through the handful of small towns dotting the watershed, stopping to survey Wellington's childhood home, his schoolhouse in Shutesbury, the church where he went to Sunday school, before looping through Athol and back to Old Salem. The sheriff's deputy was never too far behind—hovering back a safe distance, hiding in side streets when they stopped to block shooting locations, and then pulling into the far corner of the parking lot when they broke for dinner at the steak house. Ethan didn't lose him until the end of the evening when he drove back to the motel and the deputy figured he was done for the night.

"Long day planned for tomorrow, Ethan," David said as he got out of the car. "You headed back to your room?"

Ethan peered at his wristwatch.

Ten o'clock.

Still early.

"Need to pick up cigarettes. All out."

"Well, don't stop for a nightcap. You had enough at dinner, and it's wheels up at nine o'clock tomorrow morning. Gotta drive almost a hundred miles for our meeting with Lauren Saperstein in Greenfield."

"I'm a big boy, David," Ethan said, smiling. "Be there right on time." He waved good night and accelerated out of the parking lot, burning rubber as he tore down the street. Checking to make sure the deputy was truly gone, he drove a circuitous route back to the steak house, angling into a space next to the front door, and walked into the bar. The restaurant was virtually empty, the bartender cleaning glasses with a dishtowel, a busboy setting tables with flatware, while the manager was going through the evening's take in the cash register. Ethan sat at a table in the corner, spotted Ginger the hostess, and waved her over.

"Back again," she said, feigning surprise.

"Thought I'd grab a quick one before calling it a night."

"And where's your friend?"

"David? Already turned in."

"Smart boy. Want the usual?"

"Black Label, and make it a double."

"Only if you let me join you," she said, offering him a quick smile.

"Be my guest."

Five minutes later, she was back at the table with a Scotch for him and a diet Coke for herself. "That all you drinking?" he said, furrowing his brow.

"Bit of a teetotaler," she said, "and by the looks of what I served you tonight, you should be one too."

Ethan smiled knowingly then sipped his Scotch.

She shuffled nervously in her chair. "Mr. Benson, I'm actually glad you stopped back tonight. There's something I've been meaning to tell you, and now that you're alone, I think it's the right time."

Ethan took another sip of Scotch, listening.

"Okay, here goes," she said, running her thumb around the rim of her glass. "I know you're working on this Rufus Wellington story. Everybody in Athol knows about it. Lots of small-town gossip." She paused, trying to compose herself, then took a deep breath. "I had an awful experience with Rufus Wellington before he murdered that hooker—a real bad experience," she said, flummoxed.

Ethan straightened in his chair and waved to the bartender for another Scotch. "What happened?" he said quietly.

There was a difficult pause.

Ethan could see a pained expression on her face.

"He tried to rape me," she finally said, looking up from the table and staring into his eyes.

"What?"

"He tried to rape me, here at the restaurant, in the parking lot."

"Okay, slow down," he said as the bartender placed his drink in front of him. "Start from the beginning."

She took another deep breath. "He used to come into the steak house every Saturday night like clockwork. Always ate by himself. That was his routine. He'd look at the menu, order dinner, but after that, there was never any small talk. He'd just stare at me—hauntingly—all through the meal, and the way he looked at me always made me uncomfortable. Then one night, maybe a month before the murder, I was the last to leave. It was like three in the morning, and I had to lock up by myself. As I was heading to my car in the parking lot, I saw him standing in the shadows under the big maple tree."

"What was he doing?"

"Just waiting."

"For you?"

She nodded and licked her lips. "At first I felt startled, thought maybe I was being silly. He was this rich doctor, yeah, a little eccentric, but well known in the community. But he kept staring at me in this crazy way—like he did in the restaurant—and I got scared, really scared, and ran for my car. But I didn't make it. He grabbed me before I could open the door and assaulted me—pulled down my pants, ripped my blouse, fondled my breasts, tried to shove his hand between my legs. So I screamed, real loud, and he threw me to the ground and climbed on top of me."

She paused.

Shaking.

And Ethan took her hand.

"How'd you get away?"

"A car stopped for a red light, and he covered my mouth with his hand and told me to shut up. Then when the light turned green and the car didn't move, he got scared. Thought, maybe they'd seen us and called the cops, 'cause he kicked me a couple of times real hard—oh, it hurt so much—then said he'd kill me if I ever told anyone, and hightailed it outta there."

"So you never told the sheriff?"

She shook her head. "I was too afraid, then when I read about Heather Starr in the newspapers and the awful things he did to her, I vowed never to say a word to anybody—ever."

Ethan drained the rest of his Scotch and said, "Why are you telling me now?"

"Because you're doing a story about that man, and everybody needs to know the truth."

"Will you tell me on camera?"

"No," she said. "Never. If he ever gets out and finds out I talked, he'll come after me and kill me, just like that girl." She pushed away from the table, tears in her eyes. "This was a mistake. I shouldn't have said anything."

"Look, Ginger," Ethan said, reaching across the table, "I won't tell anybody."

"Promise?"

"Cross my heart. This is between you and me. I won't say a word unless you change your mind and say it's okay." He rubbed her arm gently, trying to soothe her, then turned and searched for the bartender. "One more Scotch for the road, and make that another double."

CHAPTER 10

ETHAN WOKE UP TO THE sound of ringing in his head, over and over like an alarm clock. But that wasn't it. No. It was his iPhone. Stumbling out of bed, he knocked over an empty Johnny Walker bottle and stared at the clock in his motel room. It was almost nine o'clock. Shit. He'd overslept and had a hangover. A big one. How many Scotches? Too many. He needed to get control, or he'd blow something important. He checked the display on his cell phone, hoping it was a call he could let bounce to voice mail. But not this one. It was his boss. Paul Lang. He lit a Marlboro and answered, his voice raspy, "'Morning, Paul."

"Wow, big boy, sounds like you're just waking up," Monica said cynically. "Party hearty last night?"

"Cut the crap, it's Saturday."

"That's no excuse to tie one on. Pull yourself together. Paul's got Peter on the line. He wants to conference you in. Hold on a second."

Ethan inhaled his cigarette, three quick puffs, and chewed two Motrin.

Now what?

"Where the hell've you been, Ethan?" Paul asked, yelling into the phone, his voice bouncing around Ethan's head. "I haven't heard from you since you left on Wednesday. I can't run my show like this, and I certainly can't help Peter plan his schedule without you."

"Listen to the man. You're my senior producer, or have you forgotten?" Sampson jumped right in. "Martin Humphrey wants me in LA on Monday to interview Jennifer Lawrence, and Sharon Rumpling needs me in Atlanta the following day to work on her diet story. I can't rocket back and forth across the country willy-nilly like that. What should I do?"

Ethan closed his eyes.

He'd had enough of Sampson's sarcasm.

"Look, I know all about your shooting schedule. Consuela's been e-mailing me your itinerary every morning, and if you check your messages, you'll see I sent the two of you a detailed e-mail last night about both stories."

"Hold on, lemme look," Paul said quietly. "Yes, here it is. I must've missed it."

"You missed it too, Peter," Ethan said, stubbing out his cigarette and lighting another one. "I talked to both producers and made a decision. You need to go to LA. Jennifer Lawrence is a big star. She'll cancel on us if you don't sit down with her yourself. All Sharon has is an interview with a nutritionist at the CDC and some cover footage. She doesn't need you for any of that. I told her to set up two cameras—a tight shot on the doctor's face and a medium shot of his profile. Then she can edit the interview without needing you for a cutaway. She thanked me and said she'd call you first thing this morning. So both producers know what to do. I took care of it."

"Okay, okay," Peter said, "I should've read my messages before calling Paul and complaining. But I prefer telephone calls, not e-mails. You should know that by now. Then nothing falls through the cracks."

"Come on, this didn't fall through the cracks. I could've called and harassed you at the governor's dinner party last night. That's where you were according to the schedule. But I don't think that would've made you too happy, would it?"

"Enough, Ethan," Paul said, refereeing. "You've made your point and quite clearly. So what's happening with Wellington? You're on location, spending my research budget. Have you made a decision? Should we put the story into production?"

"I can't answer that yet."

"Why not?"

"Still too many loose ends," Ethan said honestly. "I've met with the defense attorney, the sheriff, and one of Wellington's neighbors, and I've got another meeting in about two hours with Lauren Saperstein, the ADA who handled the case."

"Will you know then?" Paul asked.

"Maybe," Ethan said.

"Just maybe?" Peter was pissed. "How can I plan my life?"

Ethan kept his cool. "I should have an answer soon, but I still don't know whether we have a story that's worth doing. You're a journalist, Peter. So you should know I can't just snap my fingers and make a decision. There's definitely something going on here—something his friends are hiding about him—but is it a story we want to pursue? I'll tell you when I have enough to go on, and right now, I don't."

"When?" Paul asked.

"After I find out about Heather Starr."

"Why's that important?"

"Gut feeling. Rufus Wellington was rich and famous and a player in Boston, and I wanna know why he fell in love with a prostitute. From what I've learned, he had real problems relating to women—other women beyond Heather Starr. Maybe

114

that's the answer, maybe part of the answer, but I need to nail it down, and so far, I haven't dug up anything on the hooker. The authorities know zip, because nobody bothered to investigate her. They just seemed to slow walk through the evidence. And when I asked the sheriff about her, he didn't give me an answer. He just shrugged his shoulders like he didn't care. That's why I gotta go to Boston. Need to find out more about their relationship."

"Okay, Ethan," Paul said, pausing. "You've got one more week, then we put the story into production, or we kill it."

"I'll know after Boston."

"Good. Check in with me after your meeting with the ADA."

They all hung up.

Ethan had just dodged a bullet.

❧

By ten o'clock, Ethan was speeding down Highway Two—a scenic two-lane road that weaved through the rolling mountains west of the Quabbin—heading to the Franklin County district attorney's office in Greenfield. Puffy white clouds floated aimlessly in the sky as a red-tailed hawk circled in the distance. Ethan was having trouble concentrating as he watched the majestic bird make one final pass over a farmhouse then swoop down and disappear behind a stand of trees. He lowered his window, needing fresh air to help clear his head.

"What happened this morning?" David said, peering acidly at Ethan. "We're an hour late."

"Must've overslept."

"I tried calling, but you didn't pick up. Then I banged on your door, but you didn't answer. What's going on, Ethan?"

Ethan remained quiet.

"I'll tell you what happened," David said, not letting up. "You drank too much at dinner and couldn't get outta bed."

Ethan stared at the road, afraid to tell him he'd gone back to the steak house, afraid he'd break his promise to Ginger.

"Talk to me, Ethan. What's wrong with you? I had to get on the horn with Lauren Saperstein's paralegal and make excuses for us."

"We got a problem?" he said, alarmed.

"No. I sweet-talked the guy, and they're waiting for us."

Ethan nodded, embarrassed.

"So you're not gonna tell me."

"No."

"That's it?"

"Yup," he said, passing an eighteen-wheeler at seventy miles an hour. "Did the paralegal say anything else?"

"Plenty," David said, finally easing up on Ethan as he glanced down at his notes.

"What's his name again?"

"Ryan Thomas. Sounds like a kid who just got out of high school," he said, shaking his head. "He's got a real squeaky voice, kinda funny on the phone. Anyway, he's made us copies of everything. The entire docket, even Saperstein's personal handwritten notes."

"When do we get the crime scene photos and the videos?"

"Today. He's got them too."

"Did you ask him why we didn't get them in Athol?"

"He seemed surprised when I told him. Both Davenport and McKenzie are supposed to keep all the evidence in a murder case. They should've given us the crime scene stuff, the still pictures and the video, along with the confession. Thomas said it's all public record."

"Any thought they might be holding out on us?"

"He got very quiet when I asked him that question then said he didn't know. Kid's straight by the book."

"We'll run it by Saperstein," Ethan said. "I didn't buy their excuses, not for a minute. Did Mindy check with her sources about the Feds?"

"Talked to her while I was waiting for you," David said, flipping through his notes. "She reached guys at both the FBI and the Justice Department."

"And?"

"Never helped the sheriff search for the kill site. Never got a call from anybody up in Athol."

"So that asshole lied to me. What else is he lying about?" Ethan said pensively. "More grist for a cover-up. This story looks better all the time."

⁊⸿

The district attorney's office was tucked away in the Franklin County superior court building in the heart of downtown Greenfield, right across the street from the public library and the post office. It was a monolithic redbrick structure with neatly trimmed lawns, manicured flower beds, an American flag fluttering proudly in the wind, and a Vietnam War Memorial sitting out front. Ethan parked a short distance down the block and grabbed his briefcase.

"A bit different from Athol, don't you think?"

"Couple of notches up the economic ladder," David said, looking down Main Street. There're restaurants, la-di-da boutiques, even a Starbucks on the next corner. "Maybe we can find a four-star hotel here for Sampson?"

"Yeah, and we bring him in and out every day by chopper. I like your Old Salem idea better. Can't wait to see Peter's face when he finds out he's staying in the same house with the rest of us peons," he said, grinning from ear to ear.

As they came through the front door, a short, balding man dressed in khaki pants, button-down shirt, and a clip-on bow tie was standing in the near-empty lobby. "One of you guys David Livingston?"

"That's me, and this is Ethan Benson." David looked at Ethan, startled. "Ryan Thomas?" He certainly wasn't a kid, had to be over fifty.

"Pleasure to meet you," he said, thrusting out his hand. "And it's a pleasure to meet you too, Mr. Benson." He checked his watch. "We're running very late. Gotta get a move on it. Ms. Saperstein hates to be kept waiting. Shall we head upstairs, gentleman?"

They followed him through the lobby, up a broad marble staircase with an intricate wrought-iron railing adorned with bald eagles, and through a glass door leading into a bullpen. There were rows of cluttered cubicles, dozens of rooms lining the walls, and a law library filled with old, tattered books. Most of the work space sat empty, only a handful of wayward secretaries working the phones or typing away on computers.

"Ms. Saperstein's office is way in the back, next to the district attorney," Ryan said, pointing across the room.

"Is he here today?"

"Hunter Newman is in an emergency budget meeting with the mayor."

"Is that why there's hardly a soul here?" Ethan said, glancing around.

"Well, it is Saturday, and most of the staff is off for the weekend, but the city downsized after the fiscal crises a few years back, and since the economy is just beginning to recover here in Greenfield, we're still somewhat shorthanded. It's a real problem. Sometimes things, important things, fall through the cracks."

Maybe that's why the district attorney's office accepted Wellington's guilty plea without so much as a whisper, Ethan surmised. Not enough money to do a proper investigation.

"Lauren is the next office," Thomas said excitedly. "Come, I'll introduce you."

They followed the paralegal into a small vestibule where a high-powered secretary was sitting at her desk, stacking documents in short piles. She smiled at Ethan, her shiny white teeth filling her face.

"Hi, Ryan. Are these the producers from *The Weekly Reporter*?"

"Yup, Patty, this is them. Is Lauren ready for us?"

"She's been ready for hours. Lemme buzz her." She picked up the phone. "The producers are here, Ms. Saperstein. Okay, I'll send them right in."

Lauren Saperstein was sitting at an old metal desk, cluttered with papers and file folders, thumbing through a legal brief. A robust woman with brown eyes and jet-black hair, she had an oval-shaped face, white porcelain skin, and a small bump on the bridge of her nose. She was wearing a new Stella McCartney blue suit, a pale-yellow silk shirt, black high-heeled shoes, and reading glasses perched on top of her head. "Mr. Benson, you finally made it. Please take a seat. I'd like to get started so I can spend the afternoon at home with my family." She pointed to a small table in the corner. "Can I get you anything?" she asked. "Water? Coffee? Maybe tea?"

"Coffee would be great," Ethan said.

David nodded, him too.

Patty stuck her head in, "I heard. Coming up."

Saperstein turned to Ryan, "Did you give Mr. Benson the court docket?"

"Not yet." He opened a folder, slid out a disk, and pushed it across the table.

"Ryan and I spent most of last night organizing the documents on that disk," Saperstein said authoritatively. "It contains every piece of evidence in the case file."

"Does it include the confession tape?" Ethan said pointedly.

"Didn't Bret give it to you?" she said, surprised. "He told me he made you a copy."

"He did, and he didn't," Ethan said. "He gave me a disk, but it was blank. So was the disk with the crime scene photos. On top of that, he couldn't find the police video."

"Typical," Saperstein muttered, frowning. "He's so fucking careless."

"I also asked the sheriff," Ethan added, "but he told me he shipped all his files back to you after the sentencing."

She turned to her paralegal. "Did the sheriff ship us his copy of the evidence?"

"Not that I know of."

"Check on that for me. He's supposed to keep a record at his office. That's standard operating procedure. Give Mr. Benson the photos and the videos."

The paralegal pulled a disk from another folder and handed it to Ethan. "This is all the stuff shot at the crime scene, the pictures and the police tape. I'll need to make you a copy of the confession video."

"Shouldn't take too long. As I said, we thought Bret was giving you the confession. That's why we don't have it at the moment." Saperstein leaned forward. "You know, I'm not supposed to tell you this, but the district attorney wasn't planning to give you any of the evidence. Davenport called and tried to convince him to seal the entire court docket because of the appeal. He argued it might compromise his case and influence the judge's decision if we gave it to you. Hunter didn't give me the final go-ahead until late yesterday afternoon."

"So how'd you get the district attorney to change his mind?" Ethan said, looking from the disks to the ADA.

"I didn't. Hunter heard from the warden at Cedar Junction who said Wellington was insisting we give you everything. Usually, the attorneys make the decision on what to make public, but in this case, Wellington went around Davenport."

"But Bret told us Wellington wasn't talking to anybody about the murder," Ethan said, surprised.

"I guess he made an exception."

"So is he opening up to everyone now?" David said, worried about the exclusivity of their interview.

"No, of course not. He only wants to talk to you, Ethan, and Peter Sampson about what happened that night. Nobody else."

"But I still don't get it," Ethan said. "Why did Wellington insist on giving me the entire court docket, including the videos? Why didn't he listen to his attorney?" He picked up the disks. "Is he that confident in the appeal that he doesn't have to worry about any of this evidence? What's he got up his sleeve?"

"No idea what he's thinking. Nobody does. The man is bewildering," Saperstein said. "But as far as I'm concerned, Wellington has no case. There's nothing on those disks that would give the judge any ammunition to overturn his sentence. And my job is to fight tooth and nail to make sure he stays right where he is, locked up behind bars. That's why I'm glad we're giving you everything."

"Care to enlighten me with your strategy?" Ethan said probingly.

"Can't do that, Ethan."

"How about copies of your court filings?"

"Can't do that either. The appeal hasn't been argued yet. So nothing—and I mean, nothing—can be released until after the judge hears arguments and makes his decision. You should know that, Ethan."

Ethan smiled. "Davenport told me the same thing, but you can't fault a guy for trying."

"Touché," she said, nodding. "Looks like Bret and I are on the same side, at least on this issue. Now is there anything specific you want to talk about, now that you've got the docket?"

Ethan stared at the disks. "I've read the handful of police reports Bret copied for me and been out to Wellington's estate. I'd like to start by looking at the JPEGs of the crime scene photos you just gave me."

"Grab the box in the corner," she said, turning to her paralegal. "I made hard copies. Thought they'd be easier to look at."

Thomas handed the ADA a file folder, and she dropped three pictures on the table. "I gotta warn you. These are pretty gruesome."

"I've seen crime scene photos before," Ethan said confidently.

"Not like these," Saperstein said, pushing the pictures across the table. "These'll give you a good idea of just how sick a bastard Rufus Wellington really is."

Ethan lined up the photos one next to the other and, in spite of himself, gasped.

They were color images of the grave site, taken from different angles. The first—a wide shot showing the sheriff standing next to two crime scene investigators in masks and white jump-suits. Flood lamps had been set up around the perimeter of the site, making it look more like the middle of the day than the dead of night. Ethan picked up the photo and stared at the eerie scene. When he finished examining every sordid detail, he handed it to David and reached for the second photo.

It was a medium shot of Heather's body. She was lying face up, her arms spread to her sides, her legs bent at right angles, her toes splayed. She was naked, half buried, and covered in blood. That's when it hit home. The body was sectioned into pieces and carefully put back together in a macabre tableau. He closed his eyes, then opened them, and turned to Saperstein.

"Wellington cut her into pieces before he buried her?"

"You didn't know?" the ADA said.

"This is the first I'm hearing of it."

"We kept it out of the newspapers after the murder. Thought it was unnecessary to alarm the public. Bret didn't tell you?"

"No, he didn't, neither did the sheriff," Ethan said, baffled. "Seems like a pretty important part of the case to be hiding from me and the public, don't you think?"

"Well, I guess we could've been more candid, but when the case ended and Wellington was shipped off to Cedar Junction and the press dropped the story, we decided not to release the gory details. That's one of the reasons I'm giving you the pictures, so you have all the facts."

Ethan stared at the ADA, probing, trying to decide if she too was hiding something. Then he handed the second photo to David, before picking up the third and last one: a tight shot of Heather's hand. Her fingers had been sliced apart at the joints and her nails ripped from her fingertips. "Christ, he really butchered that poor girl, didn't he?" Ethan said, dropping the picture on the table and looking up at the ADA.

"It's pretty frightening, isn't it?" Saperstein said coldly.

"Where's her thumb?" Ethan said, glancing back at the photo.

"Never found it."

"That's curious, don't you think?"

"The CSI thought so," Saperstein said, staring at Ethan. "But they often can't find all the evidence at a crime scene, and once they finished searching the meadow with a fine-toothed comb, we figured we had plenty to nail the son of a bitch. So we stopped worrying about it."

"Are there other photos like these?"

"Dozens on your disk—more of the body, of the grave site, the bedroom, and the sheriff and his deputies searching the property. I'm also giving you this." She slid another file across the table. "It contains a disk with the autopsy findings. Read the coroner's report before you look at the photos. It's the only way to fully appreciate just how much Heather Starr must've suffered before she died."

Ethan stared at the folder then placed it into his briefcase, rattled. "I could really use a cigarette. Mind if I smoke?"

"There's no smoking in the building. But I know how disturbing these pictures are, so I'm gonna let it slide, just this once."

Ethan lit up and waited for the nicotine to course through his body. "Do you have a picture of Wellington from the night of the murder?"

"I thought you might want to see what he looked like," Saperstein said. "Ryan, give Ethan the photo."

Thomas dropped it on the table. "There are dozens more like this one on the disk with the other crime scene photos."

Ethan peered down at the picture. Wellington was standing between two deputies with his hands cuffed behind his back. He was wearing a torn white shirt and khaki pants, his arms covered in blood, his hair matted with dirt. But it was the expression on his face that gave Ethan the shudders. The distinguished surgeon was hiding somewhere in the picture, but his countenance was distorted, his eyes cold, distant, almost menacing, his mouth turned up at the corners in a frightening sneer.

"What do you think?" Saperstein said.

"He looks absolutely insane," Ethan said, staring vacantly at the picture.

"I thought so too, especially when I first looked at it," Saperstein said.

"You don't think so now?"

"No. And either does the court-appointed psychiatrist who examined him. We wanted to make sure Wellington belonged in prison and not locked up in a hospital for the criminally insane. The DA had a lot of doubts, and so did I. We thought he might be crazy, a real homicidal maniac. Why else would he do all those things to that girl? So we had a shrink study him for several days before sentencing, and in his written report, he concluded that even though Rufus might've been temporarily insane when he murdered Heather Starr, he knew exactly what he was doing and clearly understood the difference between right and wrong. That's why he's in a maximum security cell at MCI-Cedar Junction and not at Bridgewater State Hospital. There's a copy of the report on the disk with the other documents. You can read it for yourself."

"And you agree with the shrink's diagnosis?" David said, perplexed.

"I only met Rufus a couple of times, and frankly, he barely said a word to me. Just sat there and smiled as if he knew something I didn't. It was really creepy. But the psychiatrist is one of the best in the business. We use him all the time to evaluate suspects before they go to trial or after they've begin convicted and before sentencing. He knows what he's doing and spent plenty of time studying Wellington before recommending to the court that he belonged behind bars."

"What's the shrink's name?" Ethan said as the ADA pushed her chair away from the table and stood up.

"Walter Hosenfeld." She turned to Ryan Thomas, "Give Ethan his contact information, and let him know Ethan will be calling." She handed Ethan her business card. "You can reach me at these numbers if you have any more questions. Now I have one last question for you. Are you planning to interview me for your story?"

"That's my plan," Ethan said, packing the rest of the file folders into his briefcase. "Once we decide it's a go, I'll be in touch, and we'll set up a shooting schedule." He thrust out his hand. "Thanks for meeting us on a Saturday, Ms. Saperstein. I know it's your day off."

"My pleasure, Mr. Benson," she said, smiling. "Time to take my little girl to the movies. Call if you need anything."

❧

Fifteen minutes later, they were cruising down Interstate Ninety-One at seventy miles an hour. Traffic was light, and with some luck, Ethan hoped to make it back to New York in time for dinner with Sarah and Luke. "So what do you think, David? Should we do the story?"

"Above my pay grade," he said, accelerating around a line of slower-moving vehicles. "I really can't answer that question."

"Thanks for your input," Ethan said jovially.

David laughed grimly. "You're going to do it, aren't you?"

"Yes. Even without knowing anything about Heather Starr, there are unanswered questions about the crime, unanswered questions about Wellington, and unanswered questions about the investigation. No one really knows what happened that night."

"And you think you can find out?"

"Yes."

"And you think that's enough to make a story?"

"Don't you?"

"Honestly, I don't know what we've got here."

"Well, I think we've got exactly the kind of story Paul likes to program. So let's keep pushing. While Mindy and I are in Boston next week looking for background on Heather Starr, I want you to track down the psychiatrist so we can find out what makes Wellington tick. Then I want you to pick up Mindy's contacts and work with Davenport to make sure we get our cameras into Cedar Junction. That's the only thing that can torpedo our project."

"I'll get on it first thing Monday morning."

"Good. That's what I wanted to hear, a little enthusiasm. Now it's been a long week, and I'm wrung out, so I'm gonna try to get some sleep." He reclined his seat and closed his eyes, pleased he'd finally made the decision. He might be a manager, but he was still thinking like a producer. If he could get Peter to buy into the story, he could balance both worlds.

CHAPTER 11

BRET DAVENPORT TOOK A DEEP breath, slipped through the door, and walked into the waiting room at MCI-Cedar Junction, the last place in the world he wanted to be. A maximum-security lockup, the prison housed the most violent rapists, child molesters, cutthroats, and murderers in the state—maybe in the country—and was once home to such notorious deviants as Richard Wilding, "The Masked Rapist"; Joseph Druce, "The Priest Killer"; and Albert DeSalvo, "The Boston Strangler." Davenport knew the prison's reputation for mayhem and madness and always felt a moment of abject fear before meeting with Rufus. Steeling himself, he waded through a crowd of people and stopped in front of a bulletproof glass enclosure in the back of the room. An emaciated security guard named Frederick—sporting a buzz cut, a Fuller Brush mustache, and fingernails bitten to the quick—looked up from his computer and stared into his eyes as he slid open a three-by-eight-inch portal in the glass.

"Name?"

"Bret Davenport."

"Purpose of your visit?"

"I'm here to see Rufus Wellington."

The security guard closed the portal, pulled up a screen on his computer, and peered down at a list of names. Then he gazed back at Davenport, grabbed a telephone, and tapped in a number. "He's here."

A moment of silence.

"Yes, sir. I'll tell him you're on your way." The guard slid open the portal a second time. "Warden's gonna take you down to the visitors' room. He'll be along in a few minutes."

Davenport nodded then sat on a plastic chair next to a crusty, old biker dressed in black leather and covered in tattoos over every square inch of his body. He stared at the man nervously, his Adam's apple bobbing up and down. The biker stared back and shot him a sinister smile. Davenport swallowed deeply and looked away, terrified.

✐

Rufus Wellington was perched on a perfectly made bed with hospital corners in an eight-by-twelve-foot cell on block 10 of the C building. Known as the Segregation Unit, it housed a world of misfits—criminals too incorrigible to mingle in the general population and too explosive to be given any but the most basic of freedoms. A cement corridor ran down the center of the cellblock, patrolled by well-armed security guards dressed in riot gear and carrying two foot-long nightsticks they constantly wrapped on the bars. Every thirty feet, a computer-controlled steel gate divided the cellblock into sections, so inmates causing a disturbance could be isolated before being beaten and dragged to their cells.

On block 10, that happened almost every day.

Suspended from the ceiling were three heavily fortified modules, manned by prison guards with bullhorns and long guns. Wellington's cell was next to an observation room filled with computers and TV screens that recorded the output of dozens of cameras strategically placed to monitor every square inch of the cellblock. Sitting at a desk, scanning from one screen to the next, was the commanding officer who was keeping a vigilant eye on the inmates.

Big brother was watching.

Always watching.

Wellington slid out an unfiltered Camel from a pack of cigarettes and struck it with a match. He took a long drag then stood and paced around his cell, never taking his eyes off the security guards hovering in the bubble just above him. A tall, thin man, standing six feet one and weighing a hundred and eighty pounds, his hair was a rusty shade of orange, his eyes a deep pool of black, his hands small and delicate, and his fingernails perfectly manicured—he looked more like a surgeon ready for the operating room than a convicted sicko confined to a cage.

He snuffed out his cigarette in an ashtray and sat down on his bed as the commanding officer opened the steel door next to his cell. Two burly prison guards walked onto block 10, one holding a set of handcuffs and leg restraints and the other a Ruger Mini-14 automatic rifle. Rattling the chains, the first guard grinned. His name was Ralph, and he was missing his front teeth.

"So, Rufus'p, you ready for your big meeting?" he said with a lisp.

Wellington lit another cigarette and stared back at the guard. He took a long puff then blew one smoke ring after another, careful to remain silent and not to make a sudden move. The second guard, a tiny man named Lionel, pointed his rifle and tapped the bars with the end of his nightstick.

"Let's go asshole, your attorney's headed to the visitors' room. Put out the cigarette, and assume the position."

Wellington didn't move.

"What's the matter, fuck-face'p," the first guard asked, "cat got your tongue?"

The second guard looked at him petulantly. "You gonna give your attorney the silent treatment too?"

Wellington still didn't move.

The mood abruptly changed. "Let's go, ass'phole!" Ralph said, screaming. "You don't want to keep your attorney waiting, do you?" He lifted the chains and rattled them then spit a ball of phlegm into the cell and onto Wellington's shoes.

Wellington peered at the glob of spittle, took a drag on his Camel, and walked over to the steel toilet at the far end of his cell. He turned and faced the two prison guards, dropped his trousers, and sat down.

"What the hell's wrong with you?" Lionel said, echoing his partner. "Finish up. We don't have all day."

Five minutes passed. Then five more, the guards growing more and more impatient. Then Wellington stood, pulled up his pants, and flushed the toilet. After washing his hands and drying them on a clean towel, he tucked in his shirt and walked to the front of his cell, never taking his eyes off the two guards.

"About time, ass'phole," Ralph said, holding up the chains. "Now turn around and put your hands'p behind your back, and be quick about it."

The second guard motioned to the CO in the command center who released the locking mechanism to Wellington's cell. The door creaked open, and the first guard walked in. Wellington slowly turned and faced him, his hands opening and closing into fists, his face taught, his eyes menacing. Ralph stopped dead in his tracks and motioned to the other guards perched overhead. They all raised their rifles and pointed them at Wellington.

"Turn back around, Rufus'p. I don't want any trouble," he said fearfully. "Do what I say. I'm not going to tell you again."

He waited—the cellblock growing quiet with the tension—then began to back out of the cell, never taking his eyes off Wellington. Seconds passed. It felt like hours... before Wellington suddenly smiled, dropped his hands behind his back, and faced the back wall. Ralph exploded in rage, humiliated, and shoved Wellington up against the bars, locking the chains tightly around his hands and feet.

"You fuck-face'p. Should have shot you dead then and there. Would have put all of us'p out of our misery."

Wellington didn't react. He turned to the two guards and stared silently, his face expressionless, his eyes piercing like icicles.

"Let's go, Mr. Shithead," Ralph said, laughing nervously. "I like that name better than fuck-face'p. Mr. Shithead. That's what I'm gonna call you from now on. Nice'p ring to it. Mr. Shithead."

The two guards yanked him out of his cell, still unsettled, through the security checkpoint, and out of the cellblock— Wellington shuffling along, his chains rattling, his mind fantasizing about how he would've butchered them right there on the spot if they'd only given him the chance.

Ah, all the blood.

So much fun.

He could almost taste it.

❧

Davenport waited, watching the room crowd with the kind of people who made his skin crawl: a greaser with slicked-back hair, chains hanging from his clothes and piercings on his face; a hooker wearing a miniskirt, her lipstick smeared, her eyeliner dripping; and a tough-looking gangbanger standing in the corner with a jagged scar running from his forehead to his chin and a huge swastika tattooed on his cheek.

Davenport could feel perspiration on the back of his neck.

He had to get out of there.

Then Philip Dunkirk strode into the room and not a minute too soon—a short man dressed in a gray pinstripe suit, a white shirt, and a blue polka-dot tie; his blond hair was parted on the side and neatly combed, not a hair out of place. He had small soulful eyes, deep lines on his face, and puffy jowls under his chin. Davenport thought he looked beaten down, a man on the precipice weighed by the responsibilities of his job.

"Bret, it's been a while," Dunkirk said as they shook hands. "Sorry to keep you waiting. It took us longer than we thought to bring Wellington down to the visitors' room and restrain him in his chair. The guards said he had to finish some unpleasant personal business then became confrontational before they got him out of his cell. You know how he gets."

"I can just imagine. It's all part of a mind game he likes to play. He's never gonna change."

"Yeah, a real piece of work. Shall we go and say hello?"

"Is he talking today?" Davenport said, already knowing the answer.

"Not yet. Maybe he'll change his tune when he sees you. But I have my doubts."

The warden motioned to Frederick, the guard who opened the steel door and ushered them through to a second security checkpoint. Davenport emptied his pockets and put his briefcase into a plastic bucket before walking through an X-ray machine.

Then he followed the warden down a dilapidated corridor, fixated on the fading yellow floor tiles and the bright fluorescent lightbulbs. The crumbling infrastructure made him feel more uneasy. At a third security checkpoint, they went through a sliding steel door leading to a long underground passageway running the full length of the prison. Every hundred or so feet, there was a dank hallway branching off to one of the cellblocks. Block 10 was all the way down at the end.

Davenport followed the warden, water dripping from a crack in the ceiling, the sound of their footsteps bouncing off the walls. He felt claustrophobic as he ventured deeper into the prison and closer to Wellington, dreading the meeting with his friend.

Sweat soaked his clothes.

All he wanted was to get out of there.

He followed Dunkirk down another long hallway. Inmates were yelling and screaming, angry and hostile, ready to tear each other apart. The warden pulled out a walkie-talkie when they reached the final checkpoint.

"Is he secure?"

A burst of static.

"He's locked into the restraints," a voice boomed out of the speaker.

"Let us in," Dunkirk said forcefully.

Then a steel barrier slid open, and they walked into the visitors' room.

Davenport straightened his tie.

Time to see Rufus.

And his skin began to crawl.

❧

Rufus Wellington was strapped into a steel chair in the middle of the room, his hands and feet chained to eyebolts anchored to the floor, his body secured in a leather harness so he couldn't move either left or right. Davenport took a deep, gloomy breath and entered the room, taking a seat across from his friend.

"Is this really necessary, Phillip?" he said, turning to the warden.

"You know the rules, Bret," Dunkirk said. He nodded, and the guards left the room. "We'll be watching through the window. Wave to us if you need anything." He glanced at Wellington and then back to Davenport. "You've got an hour."

Then the warden strode out, the steel door locking in place behind him.

Davenport looked up at his friend. "Rufus, are you all right? Are they treating you okay?"

Not a blink.

"Do you need anything? Extra clothes? Books? Cigarettes?"

Still no response.

"Look, Rufus, I know you don't want to see me. I know you're waiting to meet with Ethan Benson," he said, deflated. "But I've spent some time with the guy, and so has Gene. I think you're making a mistake. He's the last person in the world you want to talk to. He's digging deep into the murder, asking lots of questions. He wants answers. And I'm worried he's gonna figure out what's going on."

Davenport waited, but there was no change, Wellington staring straight ahead, expressionless.

"Please, Rufus, talk to me," he said pleadingly.

Nothing.

"Okay, Rufus. We'll talk about Benson when you're ready. I guess today's not the day. I'll come back." He stood up to go.

"Sit down, Bret," Wellington said, hissing. "And light me a cigarette. There's a pack in my shirt pocket. Then we'll talk."

Davenport sat back down, fumbling with the Camels. He put a cigarette into Rufus's mouth and lit it.

Wellington took a long drag and blew the smoke out his nose. "My only vice in this hellhole," he said, "that is, except for 'aiding and abetting a known felon.'" He grinned precariously at Davenport, who had no idea what he meant. "Confused, Bret?" he cackled. "I like to masturbate. Do it eight or ten times a day. It's even more exciting in here because I know certain guards are watching."

Davenport blinked.

His friend was sinking deeper.

"Rufus, we gotta talk about Benson. He's got the docket and the crime scene photos and the police video. What did you do?"

"I instructed the district attorney to give Benson everything."

"I can't see what purpose—"

"Because I wanted him to see what I did to sweet Heather in all its glory."

Davenport couldn't think of what to say next.

"See if he can figure out what really happened." He inhaled his cigarette. "But he won't. Can't be smart enough. Anything else I should know?"

"He spoke to your neighbor, Mary Murphy. That was my mistake. I'd forgotten how much she hates you."

"And what did she tell him?" Wellington said, now rolling his cigarette around in his mouth.

"I don't know, Rufus."

"Well, Bret, I'm sure it wasn't complimentary. And what about you? Did you tell him about me? Does he know?"

"No. No, Rufus. I'm your friend. I'd never tell him anything," he said, squirming in his seat.

"What about Gene? Can we trust him with our secret?"

"Yes."

"Are you sure?" Wellington said, squinting, as he spit the cigarette on the floor.

"I paid him more money to keep quiet," Davenport said, trying to regain his composure.

"Sounds like you have everything under control." Wellington was looking at him closely. "Your tic is back."

"What?"

"Your tic. It's bouncing up and down. Telltale sign you're scared."

"Listen," Davenport said forcefully, "I'm not scared. I'm just worried you're taking an unnecessary risk."

Wellington smiled, "Well, I won't tell him if you don't."

"Look, Rufus, stop joking. I'm your lawyer as well as your friend. Ethan Benson is a serious threat, and I strongly advise you not to talk to him."

"That's what makes it interesting, don't you think, Bret? A little risk."

"You don't care."

"No, Bret. I want to talk to Ethan Benson, and I want you to make sure the warden lets him in with his cameras."

"I'm working on it, but I'm not sure he's going to allow it."

"MAKE IT HAPPEN. Or I'm gonna get mad. Real mad. And you know what happens then, don't you, Bret?"

"Okay. Okay. But—"

Wellington leaned forward, pressing against the body restraint. "Don't argue with me. I wanna meet Benson and his pompous anchorman, Peter Sampson, and the sooner, the better.

So talk to the warden. I don't want to have to tell you again, and if I do, I might just have to find another lawyer, and that means I'll stop paying you all that money. You like my money, don't you?"

Davenport swallowed reflexively.

"And, Bret, I don't have to spell out what else I'll do to you. You know it won't be pleasant."

"All right, Rufus, I'll make sure Benson gets in with his cameras."

"I thought you'd listen to reason. Now, when are you going to get me out of here?" Wellington said emphatically.

"I filed the appeal. The judge is going to hear arguments in a couple of weeks, shortly after your interview with Benson, that's why—"

"Don't go there again, Bret. I'm finished discussing it. I'm doing the interview. Now, just get me out. I'm tired of living in a cage and need my freedom to go hunting so I can satisfy my itch."

Davenport slumped in his chair. "I can't make any promises, Rufus."

"I don't want promises. I want a date, and I want it soon. Convince the judge and GET ME OUT OF HERE!" Wellington lurched forward. "Now go. I don't wanna talk anymore." Then his body went limp, and his eyes glazed over as he crawled back into his head.

Davenport peered at his childhood friend then stood, walked over to the observation window, and waved to the warden.

It was time to leave.

Time to get out of there.

CHAPTER 12

ETHAN OPENED HIS EYES AND stared at the alarm clock. Four o'clock. Too early to get up. He draped an arm over his eyes and tried to sleep but was too wired, too stressed, too worried about his story. He rolled over on his side and stared at Sarah curled up under the covers, her long blond hair spilling over her pillow, her body pressing up against him. She'd barely said a word since he returned from the Quabbin, angry he hadn't called, angry he'd been drinking. Kissing her tenderly up and down her back, he slipped out of bed, reached for his bathrobe, and padded down the hall to check on Luke sleeping soundly, Holly lying beside him on the floor. He adjusted the covers, petted Holly behind her ears, and made his way to the kitchen to make a pot of coffee. Then he headed to his study, trying to shake that nagging feeling he was overlooking something obvious about Rufus Wellington. What was he missing? He wracked his brain but couldn't find it. Grabbing a pack of Marlboros, he lit his first cigarette of the day.

The sudden burst of nicotine jarred him awake.

He stared at a hard copy of the court docket David had shipped to his apartment. It was much bigger than he'd first thought and much more detailed. He inhaled his cigarette deeply and swept the contents of an overstuffed ashtray into the garbage.

That was better.

Now he could fill it up again.

He thumbed through a stack of file folders, searching for Dr. Walter Hosenfeld's psychiatric report. The court-appointed psychiatrist had spent multiple sessions over several days evaluating Wellington, and if anyone could make sense of what drove him to kill, it was Hosenfeld. He ran his finger down the table of contents. The shrink had organized his findings into three main categories: the facts of the case, the transcript of the interviews, and his conclusions. Each category was broken down into subcategories so information could be easily accessed. Ethan checked the time. Almost four thirty. Three hours before he had to leave for the office. He poured a cup of coffee and flipped to page 10—a detailed description of the beating:

> Dr. Wellington states that when Ms. Starr first spurned his proposal of marriage, he felt a deep sense of rejection and sat down on the end of the bed, hoping if he told her just how much he loved her, she'd reconsider. He says he remembers holding her hand and stroking her face and telling her that he was rich and powerful and would provide her with all the material pleasures she desired. He remembers her sitting there naked, cupping her small breasts in her hands, offering to have sex with him. That's when he told her that his feelings were deeper and that he wanted to take her away from a life of prostitution and make her his wife. He says she laughed and taunted him and told him she

didn't love him, that she only cared about his money and the presents he gave her.

At this point, Dr. Wellington paused, asked me for a cigarette, and began sobbing. I told him to take a moment and collect his thoughts. Then he wiped his eyes and said he was ready to go on. That's when it all spilled out of him. He said his deep sense of sadness slowly turned to anger and rage as Ms. Starr continued laughing and mocking him and touching herself like the "disgusting whore" that she was. He said he remembers climbing off the bed and pacing back and forth across the room, trying to control his temper but growing more and more agitated. Then he says he was overcome by an uncontrolled urge to punish her for rebuking him. So he began striking her face repeatedly with his fist, breaking her nose, splitting her lip, blood spraying on the walls and the bedsheets. When I asked him if he realized what he was doing to her, he paused and stared at me, then said in a clear and even voice, "Of course. I wanted to hurt her. Make her pay for what she did to me."

I asked him what happened next, and he laughed and said he just beat her, over and over, striking and kicking her. So I asked him if he knew he was killing her, and he laughed again and said, "I wanted to kill her. The urge to snuff out her life was raging through my body. It just overpowered me." Then he calmly asked

me for another cigarette, showing no signs of
guilt or remorse.

Ethan turned to the police reports and found the document signed by Sheriff McKenzie. He quickly flipped through
the pages until he got to a passage highlighted with a yellow
marker that described the bedroom. The references to the blood
on the walls and on the bedsheets supported Wellington's account
of the beating in the psych evaluation. So did his memory of the
bedroom from the survey with Bret Davenport. But what did it
mean? Was the blood a sign of something deeper than uncontrolled rage? Was it a sign of Wellington's madness?

He grabbed another cigarette and checked his watch. Six
o'clock. Luke would be waking soon. Not enough time to read
the whole document. So he turned to the interviews and started
skimming the pages. When he got to a section where the psychiatrist asked Wellington about the grave site, he took a last drag on
his cigarette, crushed it out in the ashtray, and carefully read the
passage. The exchange was chilling:

> **Hosenfeld:** So you dragged the plastic garbage
> bag into the meadow and dug a shallow
> grave. What did you do next?
>
> **Wellington:** I began removing the body parts.
>
> **Hosenfeld:** Do you remember what you
> grabbed first?
>
> **Wellington**: Of course. What kind of question
> is that? Are you a moron or something?
>
> **Hosenfeld:** Why are you so hostile, Rufus?
> What are you feeling?
>
> **Wellington:** Anger. Because it should be obvi-
> ous. I needed her head. Her beautiful face.

Her lustrous eyes. So brilliant. So sensual. So lustful. I could see right into her very soul through those portals into her mind. I kissed each eye one more time before placing her head in the grave to symbolize my deep feelings for my sweet departed Heather.

Hosenfeld: But she was dead, Rufus? You'd killed her.

Wellington: Only her body. Her spirit was still alive, like all the others that came before her.

Hosenfeld: What do you mean, "all the others?"

Wellington: All the other prostitutes that I loved and cherished.

Hosenfeld: There were others?

Wellington: There were many other sweet girls I loved before Heather.

Hosenfeld: But you murdered Heather?

Wellington: Yes, I did. That was unfortunate. But it couldn't be helped. She made fun of me.

Hosenfeld: Is that why you murdered her? Because she made you feel inadequate?

Wellington: I don't see any reason to go through my feelings again. I've already told you several times why I had to kill her.

Hosenfeld: Did you kill the other prostitutes too?

Wellington: A very good question, Dr. Hosenfeld. They were all punished in their own way, but Heather, my dear Heather, she was special. So she deserved a special punishment.

Hosenfeld: So you won't tell me about the other girls?

Wellington: I just told you they weren't special. So there's no need to talk about them. And besides, the subject of this session is Heather, my sweet Heather.

Hosenfeld: Okay. Maybe we'll come back to the other girls. So tell me what you did after you placed Heather's head in the grave?

Wellington: I finished rebuilding her body. She had to be whole for her spirit to be accepted by God in heaven. So I grabbed her torso and placed it just beneath her head. Then I put her arms and hands and fingers where they belonged. I couldn't find one of her thumbs or most of her fingernails. Such a pity.

Hosenfeld: Did that upset you?

Wellington: No. No. A few missing pieces hardly mattered.

Hosenfeld: Then what, Rufus?

Wellington: I reassembled her legs and feet. She had beautiful feet. I didn't cut off her toes. So she had all ten of them. Her feet were perfect.

Hosenfeld: And then?

Wellington: Then I was finished. My beautiful Heather was whole again. Ready to be received by the Almighty. I was sending her off to a better life.

Hosenfeld: And what did you do next before you filled in the grave?

Wellington: I masturbated on what was left of her body. I took off all my clothes and stood there in the starlight. I was so excited looking at my Heather, naked as a baby in her final resting place, ready to be accepted by the Lord our God. My last gesture of love to the woman I wanted for eternity.

Hosenfeld: Rufus, you're smiling.

Wellington: Yes, of course, I'm smiling. She was a vision of loveliness.

Hosenfeld: But she was dead, Rufus. She was gone forever.

Wellington: Only her body was gone, not her spirit. It still lives on in my soul just as if she was real and here with me. I still love her with all my heart.

Hosenfeld: But you murdered her.

Wellington: Yes, I did. She deserved it. She never loved me. She just used me for my money. She had to die. That was her fate. It was God's will.

Ethan stopped reading. Rufus Wellington was a full-blown lunatic. He'd actually become sexually aroused at the sight of Heather Starr's butchered body. That wasn't normal. Why didn't Walter Hosenfeld see that? He poured another cup of coffee and carefully reread the passage, highlighting it with a yellow marker. Then he flipped on his laptop and began writing a list of questions he wanted to ask the court-appointed psychiatrist. What does the act of masturbation say about Wellington? Did he believe God was telling him to murder Heather Starr? And why didn't Hosenfeld push harder when Wellington told him about the other prostitutes he'd punished before Heather? He underlined that question then turned to the last page of the document and Hosenfeld's recommendation to the judge:

> After spending the better part of three days evaluating Dr. Wellington's state of mind, I find that he exhibits a clear understanding of his actions the night he murdered Heather Starr. While he was driven by anger, stemming from a sense of deep-seated rejection, Dr. Wellington certainly knew he was inflicting bodily harm on Ms. Starr that culminated in her death. There were moments during the course of the interviews when the doctor did, indeed, manifest deviant sexual and religious fantasies triggered during the murder, but overall, I find that his psychiatric and emotional health falls well within the acceptable range of sanity as defined by the American Psychiatric Association and the laws of this land. As a result, I believe Dr. Wellington does not need to be institutionalized in a psychiatric facility for the criminally insane and can be remanded by the court to a maximum-security prison as stipulated by the penal codes of the State of Massachusetts.

Ethan finished reading and jotted one final note on his laptop: "Double-check the psych report. Find an independent forensic psychiatrist—a national expert. Give him or her Walter Iosenfeld's evaluation, and get a second opinion."

As he was turning off his computer, Sarah walked into his study in her nightgown, holding a cup of tea, her feet bare, her hair tussled, still sleepy. She made her way over to the couch and sat down. No hello. No kiss good morning. No chitchat.

"How long have you been sitting here?" she said accusatorially.

"A couple of hours," Ethan said offhandedly. "Are we talking?"

"What do you think?"

"Sounds like we're talking."

"Very funny." She pointed at the bottle of Black Label sitting on his desk. "You been drinking?" she said, staring bullets.

Ethan lifted his cup. "Coffee."

"That's it?"

"That's it." He stood and walked over to the couch and sat beside her. "How about a truce?"

"How about we talk about it first," she said, never taking her hard gaze off Ethan.

"My drinking?"

"No. The reason you're killing yourself with alcohol."

"Come on, Sarah. You're being dramatic. It's just a temporary relapse. The pressure of my new job, Peter, my story. I'll get it under control."

"You're kidding yourself, Ethan. Work isn't the real reason you can't stop drinking."

Ethan stood and paced. He lit another cigarette, filled his lungs, blowing out smoke as he said, "We've been over this. I don't want to talk about it." His body grew rigid, his shoulders slumped.

He looked small.

Distraught.

Devastated.

"We have to talk about it, Ethan. It's always there, hovering around us, eating away at you, eating away at me."

"No, Sarah. It's part of our past, long dead and buried."

She stood and slowly walked across the room, until she was standing face-to-face with him. On her tippy-toes, she draped her arms around his neck and looked deeply into his eyes. "We can't avoid this any longer, Ethan. We have to talk. It's the only way you'll stop, the only way you can save yourself, the only way we can save each other." She ran her fingers through his hair then touched his cheek.

"God, Sarah. I'm hurting," he said, burying his face on her shoulder, the scent of her hair filling his lungs. "Let's go back to bed. I need to be close to you. I need to love you. Is there time? Before Luke wakes up?"

She looked into his eyes and nodded then kissed him gently on the mouth as Luke slipped into the room clutching his teddy bear, the moment vanishing as quickly as it had overpowered them. She turned and smiled at the little boy, "Good morning, Luke. How'd you sleep?"

"Good, Mom. I'm hungry."

"Should I fix you some breakfast?" He shook his head, still not fully awake. "And how about you, Ethan? Want some eggs?"

"Maybe later, babe. I still have work to do," he said quietly.

"Well, I've got an hour before I take Luke to school and head to the office. Maybe we can talk before I leave."

"Maybe."

Then he watched her head to the kitchen holding Luke's hand, the teddy bear dragging along the ground.

His heart was breaking.

His world falling apart.

CHAPTER 13

At nine o'clock, Ethan made his way down the hall, past rows of empty desks and closed doors. Consuela was waiting when he reached his office, typing a memo, her eyes focused on her computer screen. She didn't miss a beat as Ethan waved good morning, handing him a copy of Sampson's schedule and a list of meetings he had to attend.

"Is he here?" Ethan said hurriedly.

"Not yet," Consuela said, still concentrating on the memo. "He's at a breakfast meeting with Douglas Fitzgerald in the executive dining room. He's due back in a little while."

"Breakfast with the president of the News Division. Guess we know who's got the real power around here. Buzz me when he's back," Ethan said as he walked into his office and closed the door. His office had all the trappings befitting a senior producer: a Coaster Pergola pedestal desk with felt lined drawers, a Dell Precision 5810 desktop computer, an Eames Time-Life executive chair, and a solid oak conference room table for meetings. It was definitely impressive, but somehow cold and sterile, much like the rest of his life. There were no knickknacks sitting on the bookshelves, no family pictures on the counters, and dozens of unpacked boxes. Still disquieted from his conversation with Sarah, he stood and frantically ripped open one box after another until he found his Emmy Award for investigative reporting on political corruption in Washington. He carefully removed it, spilling crumpled newspapers on the floor, and placed it on an oak credenza opposite his desk.

There, he thought, *now at least I'll remember who I am.*

Then Mindy Herman pushed into his office, unannounced, and sprawled out on the couch with a full cup of coffee. "What is this, a stock room? Are you ever gonna unpack?"

"I'll get around to it one of these days."

"Let's hope so," she said flippantly. "Have you gone over my schedule for Boston?"

"David walked me through it when we were up at the Quabbin." He pulled up the itinerary on his computer screen and scrolled down the first page. "Nothing much has changed. Just the doctor at Mass General on Thursday and looking for leads on Heather in Dorchester on Friday. Still pretty thin."

"Got a few more days of digging before we leave."

"Are you still checking the online sex sites?" he said, turning to Mindy.

"Don't hold your breath. We're not gonna find her at one of those call girl services."

"So all signs point to Dorchester."

"Yup. That's where she hooked, and that's one of the last places you can still find girls working the streets."

"What're the odds we'll find somebody who knew her?"

"Probably not good, but it's the best I can do at the moment."

"Why's the father still tentative on Saturday?" he said eagerly.

"Because I haven't found him yet. His secretary said he's traveling in Southeast Asia and can't be reached. I'll keep trying."

"And the court-appointed psychiatrist, where's he?"

"Jeez, Ethan. You just e-mailed me about that guy this morning. A little patience. I've left him a long message. He'll get back to me."

"Book him for Friday if you can."

"Will do," she said, swinging her feet off the couch. "I took the liberty and asked the engineers in the tech department to rig a hidden camera in a shoulder bag. Might come in handy when we're looking for hookers."

"I hope it's a shitty-looking bag."

"I told the guys what we'd be using it for, and they said no worries. They had just the right setup for us."

"Well, if we see any streetwalkers to point the camera at," Ethan said halfheartedly, "they won't be looking at our bag. You can bank on that."

Mindy laughed. "Right on. When's your meeting with Sampson?"

"Ten o'clock," Ethan said, checking the anchorman's schedule. "Rest of the morning, I'm with Peter's producers. Four of them. After that, he leaves for LA and his interview with Jennifer Lawrence. Won't be back until Wednesday, as we head off to Boston." He grinned. "Good scheduling."

"I do my best."

Mindy finished her coffee and got up. "I'll ring you later." As she disappeared down the hall, Consuela popped into his office.

"Peter just arrived and went straight to see Paul. He's hopping mad about something."

"So what makes this day different from any other?" Ethan said, still trying to keep it light. Then he picked up his briefcase and headed to the executive producer's suite of offices. Time for fun and games.

Ethan straightened his tie, buttoned his sports coat, and pushed into the conference room. "Gentleman, good morning. Hope you haven't been waiting for too long." He walked to the end of the table and sat down, clicked open his briefcase, and spread his notes in front of him as he waited for the anchorman's opening salvo.

It didn't take long.

"You're late again, like usual," Sampson said gruffly. "And you know how much I hate that."

Ethan calmly looked at his watch. "I'm actually five minutes early, Peter, according to the schedule Consuela handed me this morning."

"I don't care what the schedule says, you're late."

"No, I'm not," Ethan said testily. "And I'm getting tired of you always beating on me. Is this a game you like to play with everyone who works for you, or is it a game you reserve just for me?"

"Gentleman, take it down a notch," Paul said diplomatically. "'I'm tired of always playing matchmaker." He turned to Peter, "He's not really late. We've been discussing other business and are just now ready for him." He turned back to Ethan. "So where do we stand on Wellington? Do you like the story any better since you met with the prosecutor at the district attorney's office?"

Ethan poured a cup of coffee from a thermal pot, trying to get control of his emotions, then looked from Paul to Peter.

"We should do the story," he said, anticipating the anchorman's reaction.

Sampson hissed out a long sigh. "Why, Ethan?" he said languidly. "What's changed? It's still just a sleazy murder. I don't understand why you want to waste any more time on it. There are lots of other stories more important."

"Take a minute, and read this," Ethan said, sliding a file folder across the table. "It's an outline of what I've got so far—the evidence, the people who've agreed to go on camera, and everything else I expect to nail down. I also want you to look at the pictures of the crime scene that David shot while we were on location."

"Is this really necessary?" Peter said, still objecting.

"It'll only take a moment, and it'll save a lot of time so you and I can go meet with the producers on your schedule before you leave for the airport."

"I'll look, but let me be perfectly clear, Ethan, this isn't going to change my mind," he said, waving the folder.

Ethan leaned back in his chair and counted to ten.

Peter pulled out the photos and lined them up in front of him, slowly scanning from one to the next. "Well, it's a quaint little town, Old Salem, pretty little houses and picture-perfect country stores, and Wellington's estate looks like a fortress in the woods." He continued staring at the pictures. "And these bloody bedroom photos—is that where he killed the hooker, Heather Starr?"

"That's where he beat her before he murdered her."

Sampson continued staring at the photos. "Well, these photos don't prove anything. This still isn't enough."

"And there's nothing new in your memo since we last talked," Paul said staunchly as he flipped through the pages.

"Why the sudden change of heart? You know I like the story, but have you heard from the warden at MCI-Cedar Junction? Do we have permission to bring in our cameras?"

"Not yet."

"So how am I gonna do an interview with Wellington?" Peter said stubbornly. "We don't have a story without him."

"We'll get into the prison," Ethan said. "Everybody and his brother want us to do the interview—his attorney, the ADA, the sheriff, and Wellington himself. The warden will agree."

"What makes you so sure he'll talk to me?"

"Bret Davenport reached out to us and said his client is ready to open up, remember? That's the reason we're looking at the story in the first place, to get the exclusive." He stared across the table. "And now that I've done some digging, I'm convinced both Davenport and the sheriff, Eugene McKenzie, are hiding something."

"What proof do you have?" Paul said irritably. "There's no reference to a conspiracy or a cover-up in your memo."

"Nothing solid, but lots of strange things happened last week up at the Quabbin that I haven't told you about," Ethan said mysteriously.

"Like what?" Paul said.

Ethan smiled, knowing he'd just captured the boss's attention. He raised a finger. "One, both Davenport and McKenzie conveniently misplaced key evidence they promised to give me." He raised a second finger, "And two, Rufus Wellington butchered Heather Starr's body before he buried her."

"What?" Paul said, repulsed. "Where'd you learn that?"

"From the prosecutor, Lauren Saperstein. The DA's office never released that particular piece of information to the public. We're the first to know."

"So he's sadistic as well as a killer," Paul turned to the anchorman, "changes things a bit, right, Peter?"

Peter didn't answer. He just tapped his fingers on the table impatiently.

"Anything else?"

Ethan shuffled the documents he was holding. "Wellington's next-door neighbor—a woman named Mary Murphy—told me he sexually intimidated her when she was a kid, and this may be the most important thing I learned, from a woman who will remain unnamed at the moment. She told me Rufus Wellington tried to rape her right before the murder."

Paul looked over at him. "So Wellington has a history of sexually abusing women?"

"Looks that way," Ethan said bluntly.

"Will this 'unnamed' woman tell us her story on camera?" Peter was suddenly interested.

"Not yet. She's a confidential source. I'm the only person who knows, other than the two of you."

"Get her to agree to an interview," Paul said.

"I'll see what I can do."

"And what about the appeal?" Paul said, starting to doodle, distracted again. "Does his attorney really think he can get him out?"

"He says he can, and the ADA is definitely worried about it."

Paul hesitated, thinking, "There's a lot here, Ethan. I can see why you want to push the story into production."

"So let's cut to the chase," Peter said emphatically. "Here's my bottom line. I'll do this story if—and only if—we get into the prison and I can interview Wellington."

Before Ethan could respond, his iPhone buzzed.

"Hang on a sec. It's David." A moment of silence. "Who told you?" Ethan listened intently for another moment. "When?" He looked at Peter and smiled. "Perfect timing, David. Thanks for the heads-up." He clicked off the phone. "David just had a conference call with Bret Davenport and Phillip Dunkirk, the warden at Cedar Junction. The interview's been approved by everybody, including the district attorney. We're scheduled to shoot two weeks from Friday. Plenty of time to get ready."

"Perfect," Paul said, pounding on the table. "The story goes into production right away. Peter?"

"If you think it's a good story, Paul, I'll do it."

"Then it's settled." He turned to Ethan, "When can I see a budget and a shooting schedule?"

"The end of next week," Ethan said.

"You still need to go to Boston?"

"It's critical. Only way I'll find out about Heather Starr." He reached for his briefcase. "And I'll need to take Lloyd Howard with me, along with Mindy. He's got better access than us to the police and their records."

"Hire him," Paul said, "I like Lloyd."

"And there's one more thing, Paul. I was followed most of the week at the Quabbin."

"Followed?"

"By a sheriff's deputy."

"Are you sure?" Peter said, jumping in.

"Positive," Ethan said.

"Why?" Paul said, stunned.

"Can't answer that, but there's something really evil about Rufus Wellington, and it scares the shit out of everybody around him, including me."

CHAPTER 14

ETHAN WAS SITTING IN THE waiting room with Sarah, studying Rufus Wellington's psych report, still trying to make sense of the findings. Wellington was clearly brilliant, a genius, maybe even a prodigy, yet his ramblings during his sessions with Dr. Hosenfeld struck Ethan in a strange way, as if every word was carefully rehearsed. What was he missing? What was Wellington trying to hide? He felt a thread of understanding coiling in the back of his mind, but then it slipped away, lost in a thicket of troubling thoughts.

"Ethan, put that away," Sarah said, fidgeting with the hem of her skirt. "You'll have plenty of time to work on your story in Boston. "We're here to work on your drinking. To work on us." She picked up his hand and kissed it softly.

Ethan brushed a lock of hair from her face then placed the transcript into his briefcase as the door opened and Dr. Schwartz called them in. He led Sarah over to the now-familiar armchairs and sat down next to her, Dr. Schwartz taking the seat across from them and turning on his tape recorder.

"So how are you feeling, Mr. Benson?"

"You really want to know?" Ethan said, tensing. "I'm paranoid."

"Because of your story?"

"It's not just Rufus Wellington. It's everything."

"Care to explain?"

Ethan grew silent and lit a Marlboro.

"Not talking again today?"

Ethan stared at his lap and puffed on his cigarette, remaining silent.

Dr. Schwartz turned to Sarah. "Do you know what else is upsetting him?"

Sarah nodded. "Lots of things, but one in particular. He was followed by a cop during his survey up at the Quabbin."

"Ethan?"

No response.

"You can't just sit there, Ethan," Sarah said, now incensed. "You wanted to start with your story, and that's okay, but you know that's not what I really wanna talk about. So tell Dr. Schwartz why you're feeling paranoid so we can move on."

Ethan blinked and sucked in a mouthful of cigarette smoke. "This isn't the first time I've been harassed on a story. I was tailed on my last project by a Russian hit man who worked for the syndicate in Brooklyn. And I was scared, but maybe not enough. Then one day he came out of nowhere and beat me. He could've killed me if that's what his handlers had wanted, but they were expecting me to back off my story."

"Did you?" Dr. Schwartz said.

"No."

"And what does this have to do with what you're feeling now?"

"He's worried the same thing's gonna happen again," Sarah said, not waiting for Ethan to answer.

"And this is making you feel unsettled?" Dr. Schwartz said, jotting a note on his yellow pad.

Ethan stubbed out his cigarette. "All those feelings have flooded back. Paranoia. Fear. Anxiety. I've been looking over my shoulder, worried the guy's still out there, hiding in the shadows. And of course, *that* guy is not out there."

"But the new guy is now haunting you.

"Yes.

"And you're worried he's gonna hurt you like the last time."

"Yes."

"And somehow hurt Sarah."

"Yes."

"And Luke."

"Yes."

"Are you worried?" he said, shifting his gaze to Sarah.

"Maybe a little. But I'm mostly worried about Ethan."

"Because it's making him drink more?"

She shook her head up and down.

"Is this contributing to your drinking?" Dr. Schwartz said, peering intently at Ethan.

Ethan started to stand, wanting to bolt from the room, then sat back down. "Yeah, that's it, and for all the other reasons we've been beating to death—my new story, my new job, working with Peter Sampson, my career. All that shit."

"How much are you drinking?"

"A lot."

"Every day?"

"Never miss one."

"He's out of control, Dr. Schwartz. And they're starting to figure it out at the office. I got a call last week from the researcher working on his story. He told me what was going on at the Quabbin."

"Ethan?"

He shrugged.

"I could prescribe medication to help smooth you out, maybe alleviate your paranoia. A small dose of Klonopin or Zoloft might help."

"No drugs."

"Preferable to alcohol."

"No."

"Okay," Dr. Schwartz said. "No tranquilizers." He checked his notes, paused, then looked up at Ethan. "Sarah mentioned at our last session there's something else, much deeper, that's troubling you, something we haven't talked about yet."

A hushed silence filled the room.

"I've hit a nerve, haven't I?" he said. "Are you ready to tell me?"

"There's nothing," Ethan said harshly.

"Sarah?"

She looked at Ethan, hesitated. "I'll tell you, Dr. Schwartz."

"No," Ethan said, jumping out of his chair. "Not another word."

"But we have to, Ethan, don't you see—"

"I won't. We buried it, and it's gonna stay buried, at least with me. I've got a story to produce. I'm outta here."

"Ethan, don't go. We've got to discuss this with Dr. Schwartz. It's the only way we can help you," Sarah said as he wrenched his briefcase off the floor and tore out of the room, slamming the door behind him.

She burst into tears.

"Take a moment, Sarah," Dr. Schwartz said gently, handing her a box of tissues.

She wiped her eyes.

"Are you all right?"

"This is so difficult, Dr. Schwartz. I still love him and always will, but I'm worried I've lost him. He's all tied up in knots and won't talk to me. He ignores Luke, comes home late, and drinks in his study—one Scotch after another—and he won't even try to stop."

Dr. Schwartz waited for Sarah to compose herself then said, "Tell me what Ethan is so afraid of."

She grabbed another tissue. "We lost a baby, a couple of years before Luke, and Ethan blames himself."

"What happened?"

"I was in my eighth month, and I was home alone. It was the middle of the night, and Ethan was off in an editing room, finishing a story. I started having contractions and knew the baby was coming. So I called him, over and over, but couldn't reach him. He thought I was okay, that there was another month before the baby was due." She paused, unnerved. "This is very hard, Dr. Schwartz."

"Take your time, Sarah, we're in no rush."

She shuddered then said, "I started to panic because the contractions were coming faster, and before I realized what was happening, I was giving birth, to a little girl." A tear dripped down her cheek. "I know I should've called somebody else—my sister, my mother, a friend—but it all happened so fast. I had the baby on the floor in our living room."

She wiped her eyes.

"Go on, Sarah."

"The baby was stillborn."

"And Ethan found you when he got home."

"Yes."

"And he's been unable to forgive himself."

"He just fell apart." She blew her nose again. "We had a small funeral. Our families came and stayed with us, and he took a month off from work. That helped for a while. He seemed to be okay, but then he started to go downhill—a slow, steady decline. At first I didn't notice. He'd have a drink at dinner, not every day, then one in the afternoon, and another before bed. It kept building, slowly, until he couldn't stop."

"Do Peter Sampson and Paul Lang know?"

"He's very discreet around them. I think only his researcher, David Livingston. And maybe Mindy Herman."

"Does anyone know about the baby?"

"Probably not. It happened almost ten years ago, and Ethan wasn't working for *The Weekly Reporter* back then."

"And he's been burying the pain in alcohol ever since."

"Yes.

"And refusing to face the loss."

"And it's tearing him apart bit by bit."

Dr. Schwartz nodded then checked the time. "I've got another patient, Sarah." He put down his yellow pad and turned off his tape recorder. "I'm worried Ethan may be on the verge of a breakdown. Can you convince him to come back next week?"

"I don't know. He's gonna be angry when he finds out I told you."

"You have to convince him, Sarah. It's the only way we can help him. We've got to do this together."

CHAPTER 15

TWO HOURS LATER, ETHAN GOT out of a taxi in downtown Brooklyn, toting a small suitcase. He was still furious about his session with the psychiatrist—angry at Sarah, angry at himself for storming out, angry at the world. Midday traffic was bumper to bumper, the streets packed with people scurrying in and out of stores and heading to lunch. As he entered Dexter's Diner, a heavy odor of grease hit him in the face. He scanned the room for Mindy, but all he could see was filth—dirty dishes stacked on tables, bits of food covering the counters, crumpled napkins littering the floor.

A hand touched him on the shoulder.

Ethan spun around to find Mindy next to him. "Jeez, Ethan, didn't you see me waving when you walked in?"

"I couldn't see over the dirty dishes."

She stared into his face. "What's wrong? You look like you've seen a ghost."

"Nothing. I haven't been sleeping."

"Sure?"

"It's nothing, really," he lied. "Lloyd here?"

"We've been bullshitting in the back. He's already signed the consulting contract and is way ahead of us. He's dug up some interesting stuff on Davenport."

They pushed their way through the crowd to the back of the restaurant, Ethan sliding into a banquette across from Lloyd. "So we meet again, my friend, in your favorite restaurant. What's up?"

"A little of this and a little of that," Lloyd said, grinning. "How's the new job?"

"Loads of laughs."

"And the story?"

"I bet Mindy's given you the lowdown."

"That she has. Said you're heading to Boston after lunch."

"When can you join us, Lloyd?"

"Got a few things to take care of, so not until tomorrow."

Mindy passed them the latest version of the schedule.

"I'm bringing my surveillance van," Lloyd said keenly. "Might come in handy when we're looking for street hookers who knew Heather Starr."

"What's that gonna cost me?"

"I'll cut you a fair price. But you're gonna need it, along with the hidden camera Mindy's bringing, for backup. And my surveillance cameras, as you know from our last story, are the best in the business."

Ethan playfully smacked the air. "Guess I'll bury the cost."

"Shouldn't be a problem for a new senior producer."

Mindy smiled at the two of them then scanned down her notes. "I reached out to a woman named Janice O'Brien. Got her name from a source in the Boston PD who said she might've come across Heather in the work she does. She's a former nun who operates a runaway girl's shelter called The House of Hope—just off Route 93 in Dorchester. We meet her after the doctor tomorrow afternoon. O'Brien promised to talk to her girls. See if any of them knew Heather."

"So you've filled in more of our schedule," Ethan said. "Why can't we talk to the girls ourselves?"

"Because they're all underage kids—sex workers with drug habits—that O'Brien's trying to keep off the street. She's adamant about protecting their anonymity, so she's not exposing them to any publicity. They're all hiding from something or somebody."

"So what do we do if O'Brien doesn't come through for us?"

Mindy pointed to the schedule. "Two nights of cruising in Dorchester looking for anyone who might've worked with Heather. How's that sound, Ethan?"

"Doesn't sound like much."

"No, it's not," said Mindy, frustrated. "But it's the best I can do at the moment."

"So we'll put my surveillance van to good use," Lloyd said, cupping his hands and panning back and forth across the table as if he was peering through a camera lens. "I can picture it now as I follow you up close—the two of you trolling down the street, talking to the girls in their short skirts, see-through blouses, and fishnet stockings, searching for leads, looking for background on Ms. Starr. It'll make quite the sequence."

"All kidding aside," Ethan said, worried, "we're leaving too much to chance."

"And the alternative is?" Mindy said.

Ethan turned to Lloyd, "What about your pals in the vice squad? Can they help us?"

"Not likely. It's been two years since the murder. The leads aren't just cold, they're nonexistent. Remember this thing went from confession to conviction to jail in about ten seconds. There were no leads even back then."

"I know. I know," Ethan said, dismayed. "We'll have to wait and see what happens when we get to Boston. Let's order lunch.

You can catch me up on Bret Davenport while we eat." Ethan waved to a young waitress dressed in a white cotton blouse, a plaid wool skirt that fell below her knees, white calf-length tube socks, and simple brown loafers. She looked like a parochial school student. "Cheese sandwiches, French fries, and coffee for the table."

"Anything else?" she said, smacking her chewing gum.

"Not at the moment," Ethan said, handing her the menus.

Lloyd snapped open a canvas briefcase and pulled out a stack of file folders. "So here's Davenport, compliments of a buddy of mine at the IRS." He slid the file over to Ethan who looked at it, then at Lloyd, incredulously.

"You got his income tax filings for the three years prior to the murder?"

"And Rufus Wellington's." He grinned and pushed that file across the table to Mindy.

"Jeez, can Lloyd deliver? Yes, he can," she chuckled at Lloyd's efficiency, snapping her fingers to an imaginary beat, then thumbed through Wellington's records. "He made a shitload of money, and I mean, a shitload, over ten million dollars each year, and paid the IRS everything he owed them."

"Where'd the money come from?" Ethan said, staring over her shoulder.

"From stocks, real estate investments, and his family trust," Lloyd said, "as well as his surgical fees from Mass General, where he made out like a bandit. But there's nothing unusual here. He's a heart surgeon who's paid handsomely for his special skills, and he's clean. Never been audited."

"What about Davenport?" Mindy asked.

"He made a lot less," Ethan said, scanning through the sets of forms. But there's nothing unusual here either." Then he looked up at Lloyd, who was grinning wryly. "What's so funny?"

Lloyd took the files and arranged the two sets of tax returns next to each other. "Now go through them both page by page."

Ethan got through five pages and gave up.

Mindy gave up too, perplexed. "What are we looking for?"

Lloyd returned their stares calmly. He circled a figure on Wellington's most recent return.

They both looked.

"Wellington claimed an expense, here, for a half million dollars in legal fees."

"And?" Ethan said.

"Go back to Davenport's return. Look at his 1099."

They looked, still not getting it.

"It's the exact same amount of money."

Mindy looked again at the figures. "So? Wellington's a kazillionaire and Davenport's his attorney. He needs tons of legal advice, right?"

"Absolutely," Lloyd said casually.

"But that five hundred thousand dollars Wellington wrote off for legal expenses represents Davenport's entire net income for the year. That's why this is important," Ethan said, suddenly realizing. He peered up at Lloyd. "Each tax filing the same?"

"Yup," Lloyd said. "Rufus Wellington was Bret Davenport's sole source of income in each of the three years we can document."

"But Davenport told me he had clients other than Wellington. That's how he got the money to pay for all the expensive artwork in his office. And unless he's hiding money under the table—that he's not reporting to the IRS—his one and only paying client is his good friend Rufus Wellington. The bastard lied to me."

"He certainly did," Lloyd said.

"What about since the murder?"

"My guy at the IRS couldn't give me those documents but did confirm nothing has changed. The only difference now—according to my source—is that Wellington is paying Davenport much more money to watch his properties and manage his investments."

"And to do his appeal," Ethan said harshly. "How much more is he paying him?"

"Why's that important?" Mindy wondered out loud.

"Because if he cuts off the money, Davenport goes belly-up," Lloyd said, connecting the dots.

"Think he's paying off anyone else?" Ethan said.

"Like who?" Mindy asked.

"Maybe Sheriff McKenzie."

"But why?"

"To keep him quiet too." Ethan turned to Lloyd Howard. "We need to find out how much Wellington is coughing up and whether it's hush money. Then we'll have a motive for a cover-up."

The waitress arrived with their fries and cheese sandwiches.

And they ate their lunch in silence.

❧

By midafternoon, they were driving up Interstate Ninety-Five through New Haven, Connecticut, in a rental car. Mindy leaned on the horn, impatiently, crawling along at ten miles an hour in bumper-to-bumper traffic. Ethan was sitting in the passenger seat, eyes closed, running through their three days on location. He turned to Mindy.

"Mind if I smoke?"

"No. Just crank down the window so I don't asphyxiate."

He reached for a pack of Marlboro's and slipped a cigarette into his mouth then grabbed his iPhone and punched in a number. "David, it's me."

"Was about to call you," David said, the sound of video fast-forwarding in the background. "I'm in an Avid room, logging the JPEGs and the crime scene video the ADA gave us. There are dozens of images you haven't seen yet, each one more horrible than the next."

Ethan thought about Heather Starr, lying in her grave—broken and butchered—and cringed. "When you finish in the edit room, David, I want you to check with your contacts in Athol, see what they say about Davenport's spending habits."

"What am I looking for?"

"His bank accounts, homes, cars, what he does on vacation, stuff like that."

"Why?"

"Because I think he's paying for everything with dirty money. Lloyd Howard just gave me his tax returns. He's declaring half a million in income a year, all from Wellington. That's a lot, but I think he's living much larger than that. I need proof."

"Should I check out the sheriff?"

"Run background on him too. I wanna see if there's anything that connects him to Davenport or Wellington."

"Maybe I'll start with the editor at *The Athol Gazette*. See if he knows anything."

"If he's reluctant, offer him an exclusive, a chance to break part of our story," Ethan said, wheeling and dealing. "Maybe that'll stir his journalistic juices and help pry away any documents he's sitting on. And, David, first thing Saturday morning, meet me back at the Quabbin. We're gonna take another look at Wellington's estate, without Davenport."

"But that's trespassing, Ethan."

"Let me worry about that," Ethan said, cutting him off. "Find us a motel in Belchertown, on the southern tip of the reservoir. We'll be a good forty miles from Athol. I don't want anybody to know we're snooping around."

"Hope you know what you're doing."

"Just do it."

Ethan disconnected the phone.

"Want me to go with you?" Mindy asked.

"I need you back in New York to work up the logistics for the Wellington interview and to carefully finish double-checking the court docket. See if we missed anything that might connect Wellington to Davenport or the sheriff's office."

"Like what?"

"Go over the transcript of Wellington's confession and the tax returns with our lawyers. See what they can flag. Maybe McKenzie's line of questioning. Or Wellington's responses. Or Davenport's absence. Then check with your sources at the NYPD, and find a good forensic consultant to mock up a possible scenario where investigators wouldn't be able to find the kill site. My bet is, they won't be able to do it."

"What's that gonna prove?"

"That McKenzie is either a fool or he's hiding something."

"Okay, but—"

Ethan's cell phone pinged. "Got to take this. Hey, Lauren, what's up?" There was a pause. "When did you talk to him?" Another pause. "And what was his excuse?" Ethan pulled out his iPad and started taking notes. "Well, the plot thickens. Thanks for the heads-up." He clicked off his cell phone.

Mindy waited for him.

"Saperstein had her paralegal check if the sheriff ever sent them his Wellington evidence," Ethan said quietly.

"Surprise me."

"He never did. So she called McKenzie and confronted him, and he told her that I must've misunderstood him, that he's got everything in storage and all I had to do was ask and he would've given us anything we wanted."

"Son of a bitch, he lied."

"Yes, he did. Seems like everyone's been lying to me."

༄

They checked into the Marriot Copley Place in downtown Boston at nine o'clock, made a plan to meet in the lobby at eight the next morning, and said their good nights—Ethan heading straight to the bar for a Scotch. He was sitting alone, lost in thought, on a tall high-back stool, under a series of spotlights glowing softly over the countertop. He was working on his third drink, sipping it slowly, feeling the warmth pulsing through his body. He looked at his iPhone. Sarah had called three times since he'd stormed out of the shrink's office, but he'd let the calls bounce to voice mail, not wanting to know if she'd told Dr. Schwartz. Then he played them back—Sarah angry, worried, scared—but no mention of the baby. He stared at the phone, knowing he should call her, but instead tucked it into his pocket.

He finished his Scotch in one swell swoop, banged his shot glass on the bar, and yelled loudly for another drink. The people around him stopped talking—dead silence—and stared open-mouthed as if he was a sideshow freak. The bartender walked over—a white dish towel draped over his shoulder—asked him to settle down, then poured him another Black Label.

He stared blankly at the Scotch, wondering if Mindy had any idea he was down in the bar, drinking himself into oblivion. He laughed out loud then sighed. Somehow he had to pull himself together. He had a story to produce. A reputation to maintain.

But instead he felt lost.

Rudderless.

Alone.

He thought about calling Sarah and apologizing for his bad behavior that morning, but he couldn't face another argument. Not tonight. Not tomorrow. Maybe not until he got home. Wobbling, he pulled a fifty out of his wallet and dropped it on the bar.

"Keep the change," he said, slurring his words.

Then he staggered out of the bar and into the lobby, where his cell phone rang. All the color drained from his face as he braced for a call from his wife. But it wasn't Sarah. It was Martin Humphrey in Los Angeles.

"What's up, Martin?" he said, trying to sound sober.

"I just had a big disaster with Peter."

CHAPTER 16

Massachusetts General Hospital was a sprawling complex of buildings connected by crisscrossing glass corridors linking one shiny pavilion to the next. The main entrance led into a massive stone lobby jammed with visitors and patients looking for world-class doctors specializing in every ailment known to man. The Corrigan Minehan Heart Center was one of the best in the country—a Mecca for cardiac arrhythmia, hypertrophic cardiomyopathy, coronary heart disease, valve replacement, and heart transplant surgery. Before the murder, Rufus Wellington was its most famous practitioner—a heart surgeon with a national following and an international reputation.

Ethan pushed his way through a revolving door and down a long corridor to the elevators in the Gray Bigelow Building. "Shit. We should've left earlier. We're gonna be late."

"Calm, calm," Mindy said soothingly. "What's upsetting you?"

"Martin Humphrey called me at midnight last night. Of course, it was only nine o'clock in Los Angeles. He had a meltdown with Peter, who was more than an hour late for their interview with Jennifer Lawrence. She got pissed and only gave them thirty minutes before storming off the set."

"Did they finish?"

"Only got through about half the questions."

"What about visuals?"

"She wouldn't even stick around for a walking sequence," Ethan said dejectedly. "So we have nothing to cover the narration except still pictures, news footage, and her damn movies."

"Is there enough to make a story?"

"Humphrey was in an absolute tizzy when he called."

"So what are you gonna do?" she said, pressing.

"It'll have to wait until I'm back in the office and see if I can make something out of the mess."

"When do you have time to do that?"

Ethan wasn't sure. Between the Wellington story, managing the myriad of projects on Sampson's plate, and juggling his insane schedule, there was no time for Ethan. No time to eat or sleep or smooth out his problems with Sarah. Something had to give, but he didn't know what.

"Things will ease up," Mindy said, trying to sound positive, "once you get into your new routine with Peter."

"Let's hope so, or I'm gonna fall apart."

There was no mention of his drinking.

Or the bar the night before.

The elevator opened on the eighth floor, and they passed through double doors to the main desk at cardiology.

"I'm Ethan Benson with *The Weekly Reporter*, and this is my associate producer, Mindy Herman. We're here to see Dr. Rasmussen."

An African American receptionist with piercing black eyes and tight cornrows checked their names on her computer. "I'll let Dr. Rasmussen know you're here. Please take a seat."

Five minutes later, a tall thin man hurried into the room, stopped briefly at the nurse's station, before making his way over to the two of them. Dr. Rasmussen was fiftyish, with long black hair sprinkled with streaks of gray. He had deep blue eyes, a pointed nose, and a strong square chin. Impeccably dressed, he was wearing a starched white lab coat, dark-blue flannel pants, a pale-yellow button-down shirt, and a red-and-black striped tie.

"Mr. Benson. Ms. Herman. I'm Dr. Jerome Rasmussen," he said, with a slight British accent. "Pleasure to meet you."

They shook hands then proceeded down a narrow corridor and into a bright, cheery office, where they sat in slightly threadbare furniture under a wall of windows facing the Prudential Center.

"I'm not sure I know much more about Rufus Wellington than was written in the newspapers," he said, rather formally. "I haven't seen or talked to him since he was arrested two years ago."

"Nobody's really talked to him," Ethan said casually. "He's pretty much shut down since the murder—at least that's what we've been led to believe."

"So you wanted to ask me a few questions about him?"

"Yes, because you were a friend and colleague here at Mass General."

"I wouldn't call him a friend, but I was certainly his colleague."

"And you worked closely with him?" Ethan said, taking notes on his iPad.

"All the time," Dr. Rasmussen said. "His office was down the hall from me. So we routinely consulted on tricky cases. His mind was sharp, precise, quick, encyclopedic. He always knew the latest techniques—stent graphs for thoracic aneurisms, endoscopic vein harvesting, transcather aortic valve replacement, and all kinds of minimally invasive cardiovascular surgeries. He came to life in an operating room, like a CEO running a multibillion-dollar corporation. It's not the same around here since he left. He was a prodigious mentor and a terrific colleague. I can't reconcile what I know of him as a surgeon and what he did to that girl as a killer. It just doesn't make sense."

"Do the other surgeons feel the same way?" Mindy said, surprised.

"All of us do," Dr. Rasmussen said, loosening his tie. "Everybody went to Rufus, and he always seemed to have just the right answer to help us in an operating room. He may have been a little aloof, a little formal in his demeanor, especially since he came from such a lofty position in Boston society, but he was a regular guy, nothing out of the norm." He sighed deeply then continued, "You know, Mr. Benson, none of us saw it coming. The brutality hit us all like a ton of bricks."

Ethan hesitated, trying to decide what to ask next. Rasmussen's impression of Wellington was far from the sadistic butcher who'd murdered Heather Starr. He sounded more like Bret Davenport than either Ginger or Mary Murphy. Would the real Rufus Wellington please stand up? "Did the police ask you about Dr. Wellington after the murder?"

"Not me. Not anyone here at the hospital that I know of."

"What about a Sheriff Eugene McKenzie?"

"He the guy that ran the case up at the Quabbin?"

"That's the guy."

"Nope. Never met him either. Guess that's because Rufus pleaded guilty."

"So nobody came here looking for background on Dr. Wellington?"

Dr. Rasmussen paused for a split second. "Well, not back then, but I just had a long meeting with his attorney, Bret Davenport. He asked me a lot of the same questions you've been asking. He wants me to testify as a character witness for Rufus at his appeal hearing. Wants me to tell the judge what it was like working with him, about his reputation here at the hospital."

"And you've agreed?" Mindy said rigidly.

"Of course. Why not?"

Ethan stared into Rasmussen's eyes, trying to take measure of the man. "Do you know anything about Rufus Wellington's private life?"

Rasmussen shuffled uneasily in his seat. "Not really. I just knew him as a surgeon, and as I said, he was a damn good heart surgeon at that."

"How did he interact with the women at the hospital?" Ethan asked.

"You know, that's a good question," Dr. Rasmussen said, placing a finger on his chin as if a lightbulb was going off in his head. "Some of my female colleagues thought he was a bit inept socially. He put up walls to intimacy, that's true, but most of us have to create a distance when treating patients. So I never saw it as abnormal."

"Did you ever wonder if it was something else, though," Mindy said, "something more than social awkwardness?"

"Not really, but maybe I was just used to him as a surgeon. It was difficult to get to know him on a personal level, and certainly for the women on the staff. I don't remember Rufus ever attending an office party or going out for a drink after work. In fact, I don't think I ever saw the man on a date."

"No girlfriend?" Mindy said.

Rasmussen chuckled nervously. "I never really thought much about it until just this minute."

"What about a boyfriend?"

"Heavens, no. Not Rufus."

"So he didn't have a love life?"

"Not that I know of. What makes you ask?"

Ethan leaned forward. "A neighbor of his up at the Quabbin where Wellington owns a country estate said she'd known him since they were kids and that he made her feel very uneasy when they were growing up. She caught him many times looking down her blouse and peeking up her skirt, like he was undressing her in his mind. She was afraid to be alone with him because she worried if she gave him even the slightest opening, he'd be all over her in seconds—pawing her, fondling her, and who knows what else. She said all the girls felt the same way, that he was a sexual powder keg."

"God, I had no idea he had a weird history with women," Rasmussen said, visibly uncomfortable. "I never saw any signs of sexual perversion in Dr. Wellington. Never."

"And when you heard about the murder? That didn't trigger any questions about his 'social ineptitude' here at the hospital?" Ethan said probingly.

He stood and paced in front of the window, uncomfortable. "No. I was absolutely stunned. All of us were stunned. We worked with him every day. We lived with him here at the heart center. We never imagined he was capable of doing such horrible things to a young woman. He was a surgeon who saved lives, not an animal who took them."

"Do you think he's psychotic?" Ethan said bluntly.

"I don't know."

"A pedophile?"

Rasmussen sat back down.

"His victim, Heather Starr, was only sixteen."

Rasmussen sighed. "I was bowled over when I heard. Not only was Rufus a killer, but he was into children. My God, that's sick, isn't it?"

"And you had no idea?" Ethan said, sensing the surgeon's discomfort.

Rasmussen didn't answer.

Ethan waited then said pointedly, "This never hit the newspapers, Dr. Rasmussen, but do you know what Dr. Wellington did to Heather Starr after he murdered her?" Rasmussen shook his head no. "And Bret Davenport didn't tell you when he was here talking about the appeal?"

He shook his head no.

"Well, he didn't tell me either, but I've seen the crime scene photos, and they're gruesome. He dissected her. Cut her into small pieces. There wasn't much left before he buried her. And you had no inkling, working alongside this man, that he was capable of such horrors?"

Rasmussen slumped into his chair. "I had no idea that's what he did to that poor girl. For the love of God, none of us at the hospital knew he did that. He never once showed any signs of abhorrent behavior while practicing heart surgery here at Mass General." He tapped his finger on his wristwatch. "I'm sorry, Mr. Benson, but I'm out of time. I've got a bypass procedure scheduled in two hours and need to go check on my patient. Is there anything else I can help you with?"

"Just one more thing. Maybe you can recommend a psychiatrist here at the hospital who knew Dr. Wellington, to go over the psych evaluation the judge ordered before sentencing and explain what might've triggered the violence in his personality that led to the murder."

"Let me make some calls."

Ethan gave him his business card.

Then they shook hands and said their good-byes.

CHAPTER 17

THEY WERE DRIVING SOUTH ON Highway Ninety-Three, heading to their meeting at The House of Hope. Mindy was speeding, weaving from one lane to the next, accelerating around slower-moving cars and trucks.

"Slow down, please."

"Relax, you're getting worked up for no reason."

"Slow down."

She grinned, hit the brakes, and pulled behind a Greyhound bus. "Better?" she said, trying to get a rise out of him.

Ethan looked at his notes and frowned.

"Davenport's going to use Rasmussen as a character witness," he said, "unless he has a change of heart based on what we just told him, and we, on the other hand, know nothing about the appeal. What if Davenport succeeds, gets the judge to overturn the sentence and sets Wellington free?"

"Jeez, Ethan, one step at a time. We still haven't talked to everybody involved in the case. Done any real digging on the appeal. That's what we need to do. Then we'll know whether there's even the slightest chance the judge is gonna set him free."

"I think we know more than enough now to say that should never happen," Ethan said, focusing on his notes. "Look, stay on

Rasmussen until he finds us a respectable psychiatrist at the hospital. That's critical. We need a second opinion about Wellington and whether there's any chance he could kill again if he's put back on the streets."

"Is that the reason you've been so jumpy this morning? You're worried he might get out of jail?"

"Yes."

"Why you worrying about that? Do you think the guy may come after you?"

He licked his lips. "Not just me. Anybody."

"Jeez, Ethan, your hands are trembling," she said, looking long and hard at him. "What else is bothering you? Can't just be Wellington."

Ethan began to crawl into his shell.

"Ethan. It's me. Mindy. Open up."

"It's nothing, really."

"Not true. I know somethin's eating you," she said sharply. "I've been talking to David, remember? He told me you were drinking hard up at the Quabbin. Is that why you're trembling? Did you drink last night?"

"Mindy, please—"

"Not gonna back down, Ethan. I think you're hungover."

"I'm just strung out from the story."

"Deny. Deny. Deny," she said rapid-fire. "Have you talked to Sarah?"

"Of course."

"Not true. You ducked her calls all day yesterday. You didn't think I noticed, but I did. And David said you were ducking her calls last week too."

"We're going through a tough patch," he said, avoiding her stare.

"Look, Ethan," she said, softening, "we've been friends a long time, and I see signs you're in trouble. You can open up to me. Anytime. I just wanna help." She checked the GPS on the dashboard. "We're almost there, but I'm not finished with you, not by a long shot. We'll talk more later. Bank on it."

❧

She pulled off the highway into Dorchester, an industrial community on the outskirts of the city. They drove past a Burger King, a seedy Dominican restaurant named Las Palmas, a hardware store, and a series of old man bars. Sprinkled amongst factories and abandoned warehouses were single-family homes, many with boarded up windows and rotting wood siding. First generation immigrants—Chinese, Vietnamese, Hispanic, Irish, and Italian—trudged up and down the littered streets, many dressed in ethnic clothing and speaking their native languages. Mindy hung a left onto Freeport Avenue and weaved through a maze of side streets, past a Walgreens, Jinx's Tattoo Parlor, and a sleazy sex shop. The streets were growing seedier, groups of teenagers hanging on the corners selling drugs as small children rode their bicycles and played touch football, oblivious to the trafficking going on all around them.

"There it is," Mindy said, pointing, "number 77, the next house on the left."

The House of Hope was a two-story redbrick building, dating back to the 1930s, which had seen better days. There was a torn awning over the front door, a crumbling porch littered with broken furniture, and rain gutters hanging from the roof. It was sandwiched between an Easy Dollar Pawnbrokers and a Little Wing's Convenience Store with girlie magazines displayed in the windows. She pulled up to the curb in front of the building.

"You together enough to do this, Ethan?"

"I'm fine, Mindy, really."

"Let's hope so."

They exited the rental car, pushed through a broken gate, and up the front steps. The buzzer didn't work, so Ethan banged a rusted doorknocker until a waif of a girl, wearing a miniskirt and a tank top with no bra, pulled open the door.

Blocking their entrance with an icy stare, she said, "Who're you?"

"Ethan Benson. This is Mindy Herman."

"Cops?"

"We work for a TV show called *The Weekly Reporter.*"

"What do you want?" she said, twitching, as she leaned up against the doorframe.

"To see Ms. O'Brien," Ethan said, noticing track marks running up and down the girl's arms.

"Why?"

Mindy rolled her eyes at Ethan.

"She's expecting us," he said calmly.

"Well, she's not here. Come back later," the girl said, starting to slam the door.

"Hold on, Sugar. That's no way to treat guests. I thought I was teaching you manners." A woman put her arm around the young girl, whispered something in her ear, and waved her down the hall. "I'm Janice O'Brien. Been expectin' you," she said. "Sorry about Sugar. She don't trust strangers much. She was a mess of cuts and bruises and cigarette burns when she first got here, and I guess you'd say, she's still pretty rough around the edges. She's still shootin' that smack and is gettin' ready to run. I can feel it in my bones. Hopefully, God will show her the way when she's back on the streets. Oh, look at me cackling away while you're standing outside in the cold. Come on in. I've got coffee and homemade cookies in the kitchen."

Janice O'Brien was tiny, no more than five feet tall, with dark-brown hair styled in a crown braid and skin as smooth and wrinkle-free as a baby's. Pushing her late forties, her posture was as straight as an arrow, her hands delicate, her fingernails perfectly shaped and painted a lustrous red. She was wearing a pleated black skirt, a pink chiffon blouse, black suede Nina Kymari boots, and a flowered silk shawl draped over her shoulders.

Ethan was immediately on guard.

Her appearance didn't fit her blue-collar slang.

Nor that of a former nun running a home for wayward girls.

They followed her down a long hallway, past the sitting room where Sugar lay on a couch, to the kitchen way in the back. O'Brien closed the door for privacy and poured three cups of coffee then placed a tray of oatmeal cookies on the table.

"How many girls are here, Ms. O'Brien?"

"Fourteen, Mr. Benson. I've had as many as twenty-five. Needless to say, that stretches our resources to the breaking point."

"All the girls are runaways?"

"Most," O'Brien said, making the sign of the cross.

"From what you told me on the telephone," Mindy added, "they're sex workers, and most of them drug users."

"They come here looking for hope and salvation. I can save some of them, but not all."

"Mindy tells me you were once a Catholic nun," Ethan said. "Why'd you leave the church?"

"Because this is the life God chose for me," she said, her face soulful as if she was talking to Jesus himself. "He didn't want me sittin' in a church prayin' all the time. He wanted me out in the community, workin' directly, helpin' these young girls livin' on the street who have no family and no place to go."

"How long have you been here?" Mindy asked.

"Eight years," O'Brien said proudly.

"And who pays for it?"

"We're a nonprofit, Ms. Herman, funded by private donations. Can't divulge who my supporters are. Most of 'em want to remain anonymous." She paused before shifting the conversation, "So you came to talk about poor Heather?"

"Yes," Ethan said objectively. "There's very little written about her in the newspapers. But you were one of the few people who came forward and talked to the press about her."

"Well, I felt it was my duty. She was such a pretty little thing—auburn hair, fair skin, and bright azure eyes. She claimed to be sixteen, but I think she was more like thirteen or fourteen, if you want my opinion."

Ethan glanced at Mindy. "When was Heather a resident here?"

"Can't remember exactly. She must've got here in late May or early June before the murder. Yup. That seems about right. Anyway, she'd been on the street for quite some time when she arrived, working for this black pimp named Lewis. Slick guy. Always well dressed in expensive handmade designer suits. Must've run a pretty big harem of hookers to afford all the rich stuff that he owned."

"Know his last name?" Mindy asked, opening a pad to take notes.

"Don't matter no more. He's dead. Killed in a shoot-out with the cops about a year ago. Where was I? Oh, yeah, I was telling you about Heather and when she got here," O'Brien rambled on, talking a mile a minute. "She was pretty strung out, shootin' all that meth all the time. I took her in, cleaned her up, and got her away from that nasty pimp, at least for a little while."

"Why didn't she stay?" Ethan said, cocking his head.

"She needed her drugs. So she started sneaking out late at night, hitting the streets, turning tricks, shootin' up. It was a vicious cycle, day in and day out. I tried reasoning with her, praying for her, but it did no damn good. Then one night she went out and never came back."

She crossed herself again.

"Did you notify the authorities?"

"I called the cops right away and told them she was a missin', but Lord knows, she was a runaway, a street person. So the cops didn't care. I spent a few nights searchin' on my own down there in the Mattapan District where she liked to proposition johns."

"But you never found her."

"Nope. Never did. And I had a houseful of other kids to look after, so I prayed to sweet Jesus and asked him to look after her. But then I read about the murder and knew God had finally taken his child up to heaven."

"Ms. O'Brien, did you ever see Heather with Rufus Wellington?"

"Never knew the man until I read his name in the papers."

"She never talked to you about him?" Ethan said delicately.

"Nope. Not to me."

"Did she confide in any of her friends?" he said, thinking he might've reached a dead end. "Any girls who might still be living here?"

"I asked around like I said I would, but there ain't no girls here today who were here back then. Hmm," she picked up a cookie and waved it in front of them, "might've told some of her friends who are still hooking up in Mattapan."

"Do you happen to know their names?" Mindy said propitiously.

"One was African American—very black skin—her name, I think, was Queen Chekilla. She had a streak of white runnin' through her hair, if my memory serves me right. The other was Asian. Big eyes. Very pretty. Everybody called her Lotus. They might know about Rufus Wellington. More than that, I can't help."

Ethan gave Mindy a nod, and they stood up. "Thanks for your time, Ms. O'Brien. We might check back with you, if that's okay."

"I hope you find what you're lookin' for," she said, pushing away from the table. "Anythin' else before you leave?"

"Do you have a picture of Heather? All I've got is a mug shot the district attorney's office gave me, and it's not very good."

"Give me a second." She straightened her skirt and pulled her shawl tighter around her shoulders then scurried out of the room, past a skinny girl with a deep red scar running down the side of her face, who was hiding in the stairwell staring at Ethan. Without uttering a word, the girl waited for Ms. O'Brien to disappear down the hall, before rushing into the kitchen, handing him a crumpled slip of paper, and dashing out and up the stairs.

"What did she give you?" Mindy said, surprised.

"Looks like a telephone number."

"Think it's hers?"

"No idea," Ethan said, stuffing the paper into his pocket. "She certainly didn't want O'Brien to see. We'll try calling later."

Then Janice O'Brien walked back into the kitchen and handed Ethan a set of pictures. "I took these while Heather was stayin' with me. Like I said, pretty girl, don't you think?"

"A real beauty," Ethan said, studying the photos. "Can we keep them? I'd like to use them in my story, if that's okay with you, Ms. O'Brien?"

"They're all yours, Mr. Benson. I don't need them anymore. Will you be coming back with your cameras?"

"Absolutely. You're okay with sitting for a formal interview?"

"Of course. Anything I can do to help," she said enthusiastically. "Maybe her family will see your story. We never found them, and I'm sure they'd like to know what happened to their little girl."

"Thank you, Ms. O'Brien. You've been more than generous with your time."

"My pleasure. Hope I was helpful."

Ms. O'Brien peered through a slit in the curtains as they got into their rental car and drove off. She went back to the kitchen, shut the door, unlocked a cabinet, and pulled out a cell phone.

"Gotta get a new one of these and soon. Almost out of time." Then she tapped a number into the burner. It rang three times. "It's Janice."

"What happened?" a man asked.

"They were here. Just left," she said, dropping her fake accent.

"And?"

"They asked me all the questions you said they would."

"What did you tell them?"

"What do you think? Just what you told me," O'Brien said assuredly.

"Did they ask for the pictures?"

"Yes. They wanted to see what she looked like. I'm still not sure that was such a good idea."

"Why?"

"Because they're smart and seem to know a lot about Heather and the murder," she said. "What if they show them to some of the girls on the street and somebody remembers?"

"That's a possibility," the man said, backpedaling slightly. "But I warned Rufus, and he didn't care. He insisted we give the pictures to Benson. It's all part of the sick game he's playing."

"But what if they put two and two together and figure out about me?" O'Brien said urgently. "That'll be a problem."

"Well, we can't let that happen, can we, Janice?"

O'Brien chose her words carefully. "But Rufus is playing with fire. Benson is going to figure it out and bring us all down. You've got to go back to the prison and tell Rufus to back off."

"I've tried, but he thinks he can outsmart Benson and wants to do the interview. I can't get him to change his mind."

"Well, I want no part of this. I'm gonna wash my hands of the whole thing."

"I wouldn't cross Rufus, Janice. He doesn't like that."

"What's he gonna do? Kill me from prison?" she said haughtily.

"Just a warning," he replied bluntly, "I'm gonna get him out of prison, and when I do, you don't want him coming after you. That might get rather nasty. Maybe you should think about it."

O'Brien was thinking about it.

"You know what needs to be done," the man said testily. "Call your guy. Tell him we'll pay, and have him get rid of Benson. That'll take care of our problem."

"And I'll get my cut too?"

"What do you think, bitch?"

The line went dead.

And O'Brien shuddered.

She was in too deep to get out.

After locking the burner back in the cabinet, she put her lips to her Bible then carried it with her into the sitting room. Throwing her arms in the air, she rolled her eyes into the back of her head and wailed like the Messiah, "The Lord our God is our savior, our Rock and our Redeemer. He giveth us his plenty. Then taketh away. Oh, Sweet Jesus. Sweet Jesus. We place our hearts and souls in your hands. Halleluiah! Halleluiah! Halleluiah!"

The girls shrank back, and she began to preach like an apostle.

CHAPTER 18

It was almost ten o'clock when Ethan pulled into a Dunkin Donuts on Dorchester Avenue, slid into an empty space near the door, and killed the engine. Lloyd Howard's white surveillance van was already parked in the lot, and the PI was perched in a window with coffee and cream donuts. "Bring the hidden camera, Mindy. It'll be easier to set up in the restaurant than outside on the street."

"What about the Panasonic two-chip?"

"Bring that too."

Mindy grabbed the camera bags and followed him to Lloyd's table. "When did you get here?" Ethan said as they sat down across from him.

"About three," Lloyd said, wiping a crumb from the corner of his mouth. "Met with a couple of my cop buddies who gave me the lay of the land." He waved at the waitress. "Bring my friends coffee and some of those cream donuts. That okay with you, guys?"

"That's fine, Lloyd," Ethan said brusquely. "What did they tell you?"

"They said the hookers usually work in groups of twos and threes."

"I didn't see any on the way over from the hotel," Mindy said as she began setting up the electronics on the back of the two-chip.

"Don't forget to white balance."

"Jeez, this isn't the first time I've worked with a handheld camera."

Ethan ignored her comment. "Think we'll find any girls?"

"If we're patient," Lloyd said, reaching for another donut. "Most of the hookers in this neighborhood are street kids—runaways—who hide in the alleys between buildings so the cops won't spot them. They only come out when they see a mark. Then they're all over the place. The hard-core prostitutes are more brazen because they've been working the streets for years. We'll just have to wait and see what happens."

Ethan tapped his fingers on the table. So far, he'd learned little more about Heather Starr than he'd read in the newspapers. Not enough to fill in the blanks and flush out his story. She was still a mystery—a name without a pedigree, a girl without a history, a victim without a soul. He needed answers and was running out of time before his interview with Wellington.

"We need to focus on the older prostitutes," Ethan said, sipping his coffee. "The nun at the halfway house told us the kids won't know Heather. She's been dead for too long."

"She's not a nun anymore," Mindy said, peering through the camera lens.

"Yeah. Yeah. Yeah."

"Are we looking for anyone in particular?" Lloyd said, crinkling his forehead.

"O'Brien mentioned a black girl named Queen Chekilla and an Asian girl named Lotus."

"It's gonna be a stretch to find them."

"It's our only lead."

"Do you have a plan?"

"Heather used to hang out a couple of miles south of here at a place called Mattapan," Mindy said, opening the shoulder bag with the hidden camera. "Maybe that's a good place to start."

"My cop friends told me there's a derelict railroad bridge in that part of town—at James E. Oxley Square—that's usually crawling with girls turning tricks, along with lots of other lowlife. They warned me to be careful if we go there. Said they'd rob us blind if we give 'em a chance."

"They'd rob us blind anywhere around here," Ethan said. "Are you finished tweaking the cameras, Mindy?"

"Just need five more minutes."

"I brought a Nikon D600 digital camera with a 300-mm lens as well as my Sony DV Cam. I'll lock the Sony on a master shot of the intersection and snap a bunch of tight shots with the Nikon."

"Should work," Ethan said as he turned to Mindy. "You've got the hard job. Are you still cool with our plan?"

"I've got nerves of steel, Ethan. You know me."

"What's she gonna do?" Howard said, raising an eyebrow.

"She's gonna troll the streets with the hidden camera, try to see if any of the girls know Heather. She's got a much better chance of getting them to talk than I do. All they'll do if I'm out there is hit on me for a trick."

"That thing's got sound?" Howard said, glancing at the tiny camera.

"Not great but okay. There's a mic in the pocket of the shoulder bag," Mindy said, pointing to a small hole in the front flap. "It's wired to a small recorder buried in the bottom of the bag."

"Clever," Lloyd said. "What's the two-chip for?"

"Brought the bigger handheld camera in case we land an interview. The image will look and sound better. But that's probably a long shot."

Howard leaned back. "And you sure you're cool with this plan, Mindy?"

"I'm fine, Lloyd, relax, already."

"Pimps might have something to say about it," he said, turning to Ethan.

"I'll be sitting in the rental car, watching her carefully," he said haltingly as he began to worry about the deputy sheriff and the hit man who'd beaten him on his last story. Was he making the same mistake again? Was the alcohol clouding his judgment? "I'll be close enough in case there's a problem." He turned to Mindy, "There's still time to change your mind. We can call it off and try something different tomorrow night."

"No way, Ethan. I'm as ready as I'll ever be," she said, a glint in her eye.

"Okay. We'll take the rental car, and, Lloyd, you take your van. Time to rock and roll."

❧

They pulled single file into James E. Oxley Square and cased out the intersection. The street was deserted and mostly dark, illuminated by a solitary streetlamp. There was a liquor store next to a 7-Eleven, a Mobil gas station, a Wendy's fast-food restaurant, and a pharmacy that had been shuttered for years. Overhead was the railroad bridge, rusting and derelict and decayed. They circled the block, not once, but twice, before Ethan picked up his iPhone and called Lloyd.

"Why don't you park in the gas station? It's closed, and your van won't look too out of place sitting next to all those other cars. Can you get off a clean shot of Mindy?"

"Won't be a problem as long as she stays in the light," Howard said, "but if she walks under the tracks, I'll lose her. It's way too dark for my cameras."

"Got it. I'm gonna park a half block away in front of the Wendy's. I can see everything from there and should be close enough to Mindy in case something happens. Hang on, Lloyd. I'm putting you on speaker." He placed his cell phone in the cup holder, squeezed into a parking space, then turned to Mindy, "You sure the hidden camera's working?"

"All systems go."

"Hand me the two-chip," Ethan said, lighting a cigarette. "I wanna be ready with the second camera if you get lucky and land a hooker for an interview. Now, hop out of the car."

Then they waited—the intersection mostly quiet except for a teenage tough guy who walked by hooting a catcall at Mindy, a drunk who wobbled down the street drinking a beer wrapped in a brown paper bag, and a businessman who cruised by trolling for a trick. But there were no hookers.

A half hour passed.

"How you holding up, Mindy?" Ethan said, lighting another cigarette.

"I'm fine, but it's fucking cold out here. You sure we're in the right place?"

"This is Mattapan, where O'Brien told us to go. And this is where the cops told Lloyd we'd find the hookers. It's our best shot at tracking down somebody who might've known Heather."

"Just bitchin', Ethan."

Another fifteen minutes.

Still nothing.

"How much longer we gonna give it?" Lloyd said, his voice booming out of the speaker. "It's well after midnight. Maybe somebody tipped off the girls we'd be out here."

Ethan scanned the block. There was still an occasional john looking for sex, but for the most part, the neighborhood was quiet. "Another hour," Ethan said, trying to boost morale. "The girls must be turning tricks somewhere."

A patrol car slowed to a crawl and stopped in front of them, two uniformed cops from the vice squad giving them a long look before hitting the gas and speeding away. Mindy poked her head through the window. "That's the third time those guys have passed by. I'm not sure we can hang here much longer. The police know we're up to something."

"She's right, Ethan," Howard said, chiming in. "It's only a matter of time before they ask us what we're doing and make trouble for us."

"Can you call your friends at headquarters and tell them to call off the dogs?"

"I'll call, Ethan. But I'm not sure what good it'll do. These cops work for a precinct where I don't have a lot of pull. They'll be back, and the next time, we're gonna have some explainin' to do."

"I don't care. We're gonna hang a bit longer," Ethan said firmly. "Something's bound to happen soon."

Ten more minutes.

Then Howard whispered in a steely voice, "Get Mindy ready. Two girls heading your way. I can see them through the lens of my Nikon. They should be under the light in a minute."

Ethan waved at Mindy. "Did you hear, Lloyd?"

"Just rolled the hidden camera."

"Do you have the pictures of Heather?"

"Got 'em."

"Only use them if you have to. Don't want to risk losing them."

"Should I go?" Mindy whispered, adrenaline pumping.

"Wait until they reach the railroad tracks, then head to the nearside of the underpass, and don't forget, stay in the light so we can see you."

"Go, go," Lloyd said urgently, "they're moving faster."

Ethan watched her hustle across the street, the camera hidden in her shoulder bag, a chill running up his spine. What if he hadn't thought this through carefully enough? What if something bad happens to her? He'd never forgive himself. Just like the baby.

❧

Mindy took a deep breath. The two prostitutes were fifty feet away and passing into the darkness under the tracks. When she reached the intersection, she stopped in the pool of light and aimed the camera at the hookers. Then she was spotted, and the bigger woman—a heavyset African American wearing a red wig and heavy makeup—broke out in a cautious smile.

"Well, well. What's this? A new girl muscling in on our territory? Don't look like a ho to me, girl. Who you workin' for? Can't be my man. He wouldn't put a ho on the street lookin' like you."

"I don't have a pimp," Mindy said, worried they'd spot the camera.

"No pimp?" the second hooker said ominously, advancing a few steps closer. She was a petite Asian woman, her skin as pasty as a ghost, her face covered in rivulets of sweat. "So who the hell are you, bitch? Tell us."

"I work for *The Weekly Reporter*. Can I ask you a few questions?"

"We don't talk to no reporters," the Asian girl said.

They started to walk off.

"It's about a girl who got murdered, she used to work the streets here. Her name's Heather Starr. I've got her picture—"

The hookers kept walking.

Mindy got out the pictures, trying to keep up. "I promise this won't take long. She was young, pretty, and involved with a rich doctor who murdered her. We're trying to find out what happened."

"You know what happened?" the Asian hooker said.

"I know what happened," the black hooker said, adjusting her wig. "All the girls walking the street know what happened to that pretty little thing."

"So you knew her?"

"Yeah, we knew her."

"Did she ever tell you about the doctor?"

"Hell, yes," the black girl said angrily. "All the girls talk about the rich guys they date. But why should we tell you anything else about Heather? She's long dead."

"Maybe it's to help someone like you."

"You don't want to help someone like me," the Asian hooker said hostilely, her nose beginning to run. "That's bullshit. Maybe you really a cop. Not no reporter."

"You a cop?" the black hooker said threateningly.

"No. No. I—"

She took a few steps closer to Mindy, stopping in the middle of the streetlight. "Our man ain't gonna like it if he finds out you been asking us about that dead ho."

Mindy jammed Heather's pictures back in her pocket and began backing up as the hooker continued advancing, "What you got in that shoulder bag?"

"Maybe it's a gun?" the Asian girl said, shrieking.

"Give it over here," the black girl said, reaching for the hidden camera bag.

Then all hell broke loose. She was on top of Mindy, violently shoving her, ripping the collar off her coat as she struggled to pull the bag from her shoulder.

"Get off me," Mindy said, screaming as she twisted away, clutching the camera bag with both arms. "Help me, Ethan, now."

In a flash, it all became a blur, the screams unintelligible, as Mindy pitched backward and hit the ground, the big black prostitute hovering over her, pulling at the shoulder bag.

❧

Ethan watched—momentarily paralyzed—as Mindy, flat on her back, wrestled with the hooker, trying to break free.

"Lloyd, she's in trouble," he said, panic in his voice.

"I'm on a tight shot with my Nikon," Lloyd said, screaming through the speaker. "I can't hear what they're saying, but the hooker's pissed, and Mindy's scared out of her mind. Get your ass over there before the bitch hurts her real bad."

Ethan dropped the digital camera on the passenger seat, jumped out of the car, and began running, arms pumping, feet flying, streaking toward the underpass. Waving frantically, he tried getting the hooker's attention, "Stop. Stop. Don't hurt her! She's not doing anything wrong. Just give us a minute, and we'll be outta here."

But the hooker ignored him and continued clawing for the shoulder bag.

Christ, he wasn't going to make it.

She was going to kill Mindy.

And it would be all his fault.

As he darted through the intersection, he suddenly felt a searing pain ripping through the back of his head, like a sledgehammer pounding a brick wall. He crashed face-first, smashing his forehead on the blacktop, opening a big gash, blood running into his eyes. Rolling over with a groan, he looked up, his vision blurred. A big, muscled man stood over him, about to hit him again. He was holding a blackjack covered in blood—his blood.

Shit.

Must be the hookers' pimp.

Then he heard Mindy screaming, screaming, screaming, and everything went dark.

❧

Lloyd was out of his van in a flash, running, his Beretta 9-mm handgun drawn from a shoulder holster. As the pimp raised the blackjack to strike Ethan again, he knelt on one knee and leveled his gun at the man.

"So help me God, if you move another inch, motherfucker, I'll blow your fucking head off."

"Lewis, he's got a gun," the Asian girl said, wailing in alarm as she turned to the black hooker. "Forget the bag, and get off the fuckin' girl. The guy's gonna shoot us."

The pimp's swing stalled in midair when he saw the Beretta. Slowly, he backed away, flashed a gold toothy smile at Lloyd, signaled the two hookers, and took off with them down the block—through a littered alley and around the back of a boarded-up building.

Lloyd lowered his handgun and ran to Ethan, who was slumped on all fours, blood pouring onto the pavement.

"Christ, there's blood everywhere," he said, alarmed.

Ethan tried to speak but only managed to moan.

"Hold this on your forehead." He gave Ethan a handkerchief.

"Jeez, Ethan, you okay?" Mindy said, racing over, out of breath.

Ethan stared up at her, his eyes flat and unseeing, then collapsed down on his back.

"Is it bad?"

"I dunno, maybe," Lloyd said, kneeling next to Ethan, trying to stem the flow of blood. "What happened back there, Mindy? One minute you were talking to that hooker, and the next, she was all over you like a bat outta hell. What did you say to her?"

But Mindy was speechless, shaking all over, her eyes fixed on Ethan.

Lloyd looked at her. Was she going into shock? "Snap out of it, Mindy. You hurt?"

She continued staring at Ethan, at all the blood pooling around him. "I'm fine, Lloyd. A bit roughed up, but okay."

Lloyd looked back at Ethan and dialed 911. "I need an ambulance at James E. Oxley Square in Mattapan. There's a man down who needs to go to the emergency room. Hurry. He's bleeding bad from a head wound."

❧

A paramedic was shining a flashlight in Ethan's eyes, checking to see if he could follow the beam of light moving back and forth. She'd already cleaned up the abrasion on his forehead, checked the laceration on the back of his head, and stopped all the bleeding. She was now worrying about a possible concussion.

"You need to go to the hospital, Mr. Benson," the paramedic said, still staring into his eyes. "You may need stitches."

"No, not goin' to the emergency room," Ethan mumbled. "It's just a bump and a little cut. I'll be okay."

"You really need to be examined by a doctor, but I can't force you," she said, flipping off the flashlight and hastily handing him a clipboard. "Sign here where it says you're refusing treatment." He scrawled his John Hancock on the document. "If you're smart, you'll take it easy for a few days and go to the emergency room if your headache gets worse. Questions?"

Ethan shook his head no.

She stared into his eyes one last time then got into the ambulance alongside her partner, fired up the engine, and roared down the street. Shakily, Ethan climbed to his feet, steadied himself, then turned to Mindy, who was hovering like a mother hen.

"Are the cops here?"

"Lloyd's giving them a statement. Should be done in a minute."

"What about local news?"

"No cameras. Cops are keeping it quiet for us. Thank God for Lloyd. We owe him big time. You okay, Ethan?"

Ethan touched his forehead where he'd hit the pavement. Pain radiated through his head. "A little sore," he said stubbornly, "but I'll be good as new in the morning."

"Doubt that."

"And what about you?"

"Unhinged, but no worse for wear."

"Thank God. I really thought I'd gotten you killed. Scared the livin' shit out of me."

"Oh, you were worried about little old me. How nice. Well, that fuckin' bitch didn't get the camera."

"Were you rolling?"

"Jeez, I forgot to check." She ripped the bag off her shoulder, unzipped the cover, and peered inside. The red light was flashing. "Still recording," she said, turning it off.

"Did you get the whole scene? The hookers? The pimp? Me going down?"

"I'm sure I got parts of it, Ethan, but can't it wait until tomorrow? We gotta get you back to the hotel. It's almost 3:00 a.m. You're not gonna be able to move in the morning."

Ethan's head was pounding, his eyes watering from the pain, as he wondered how he'd break the news to Sarah. Maybe he'd tell her he walked into a door or fell down a flight of stairs. He grimaced. No way she'd believe any of that. She'd know he fucked up. And she'd know it was the alcohol. Then the world began to spin, and he turned back to Mindy, "You may be right. I'll screen the footage in the morning. I gotta lay down and get some sleep."

CHAPTER 19

Four hours later, Ethan opened his eyes, reached over, and grabbed a cigarette, then stumbled into the bathroom. After turning on the overhead light, he carefully removed the bandages and stared at his face in the mirror. His forehead was black-and-blue with a nasty cut over his right eye, and there was a lump on the back of his head where he'd been struck with the blackjack. He blinked several times, trying to clear his blurred vision and will away the pain.

It didn't work.

Then he took three quick puffs on his cigarette and dropped it in the toilet.

Turning on the shower, he let the warm water cascade over his body, soothing the aches and pains and washing away clumps of dried blood on his face. Did he need to see a doctor? Probably. But there wasn't time. He had to keep working. So he pushed the thought to the back of his mind, and after toweling himself off, shaving, and gingerly combing his hair, he took one last look in the mirror and sighed.

Sarah's going to be furious he didn't go to the hospital.

And more furious he didn't call her.

He headed back to the bedroom, got dressed in gray slacks, a white shirt, and blue blazer, then sat down and booted up his computer. Mindy had uploaded the hidden camera video, along with the still pictures and the surveillance footage Lloyd had shot. He was itching to take a look before heading to his first meeting with the court-appointed psychiatrist.

He reached for a bottle of Black Label.

And poured a short glass.

Maybe that would dull the pain in his head.

After lighting another cigarette, he imported everything into his Final Cut Pro editing program, cued the hidden camera footage to the top, and fast-forwarded to the confrontation. He leaned forward and watched the video. The image was crystal clear, but the sound was muffled, almost inaudible.

Damn, he could barely make out what they were saying.

The two hookers seemed to know Heather Starr, and he thought the small Asian girl might've described a rich john, maybe a doctor, who could've been Rufus Wellington. But did that prove anything? Probably not. He couldn't tell if the hooker used his name, so he was no closer to learning how they had met. Sipping the Scotch, he jotted himself a note to ask Wellington's father if his son routinely cruised the streets looking for sex—that's if Mindy ever found him.

Then he watched the sequence a second time from the top—the two hookers coming through the underpass, the Asian girl hovering in the background, the big African American marching up to Mindy, gesturing wildly then demanding to know who she was. The video shook wildly as both hookers got aggressive, their faces contorted in rage, their voices shrieking. At one point, the black hooker bumped Mindy, then shoved her, before backing off and screaming again. Then, without warning, she leaped forward and reached for the shoulder bag, the shot panning wildly—a blur—as they struggled before Mindy fell to the ground. Ethan stopped the video and took a deep breath. The scene looked frightening through the lens of the hidden camera. Mindy must've been terrified.

He stared at the bottle of Black Label sitting on the desk. He wanted another drink to steady his nerves, but his head was aching, and it was nine in the morning, so he buried the urge.

Racking the video back, he played it a third time, filtering the sound to enhance what Mindy and the two hookers were saying. The African American standing in front seemed to accuse her of being a cop, but he could only make out parts of what the smaller Asian hooker was saying in the background. She was too far away from the microphone. He adjusted the levels again, minimizing the extraneous sounds and boosting the dialogue. Then he listened again and wrote down as much as he could understand:

> Beat down on —— bitch. She ain't no cop. She's the girl —— O'Brien —— The House of Hope —— workin' with that producer we —— warned about —— must be —— here —— somewhere. Get the bag —— Mess her up real good —— drive 'em out —— here."

Then there was only screaming. He paused the video. Somehow the hookers had known they'd visited The House of Hope. How was that possible? Who had told them? He pulled up the video Lloyd Howard had shot from the surveillance van and hit *Play*. The image was a locked-down wide shot of the entire intersection, Mindy and the two hookers standing in the road in front of the railroad bridge. He watched the entire sequence, this time the confrontation unfolding from an outsider's perspective. It was even more surreal than the point-of-view shot from the hidden camera. As the black hooker knocked Mindy to the ground, he suddenly noticed a flash of light in the background. What the hell was that? He rolled back fifteen seconds and played it again, pausing just as the flash filled the screen. After carefully zooming in and adjusting the contrast, he saw a small woman standing in the underpass. The electronics had flared, bringing her into focus for just a split second. Ethan zoomed in closer and stared at the woman's face. Reaching for a fresh pack of Marlboros, there was a rap on the door. His eyes still glued to the computer, he walked across the room and unchained the door.

"Mindy, hey, am I running late?"

"No. But I was worried. Wanted to make sure you were okay." She peered at his face then gently touched the bruise on his forehead. "Ethan, the wound hasn't closed. You need to see a doctor."

"It's okay, it's healing," he said, grimacing.

"Now."

"Later."

"Jeez, Ethan, you never listen—to anyone."

He pointed at his computer screen. "Do you remember seeing a fourth person under the railroad tracks?"

"Nope, just the two hookers, then the pimp who clocked you."

"Check it out. There's someone in the background, hiding in the underpass."

Mindy sat next to him and looked at the screen. "I can't see anybody. What caused the flash?"

"Not sure." He racked back the image a couple of seconds and played it back frame by frame. "There. A woman. And she just lit a cigarette. That's why we can see her."

"Can you make out who it is?" Mindy said, leaning closer to the screen.

Ethan advanced the video and stopped on the frame where the woman's face was the clearest. "Well?"

"No way," Mindy said, looking up at Ethan. "It's fucking Ms. O'Brien. What was she doing there?"

"Following us, like the deputy in Athol."

"But how'd she know we'd go to the railroad underpass?"

"She told us where Heather looked for johns, Mattapan. The two hookers that confronted you, the big black one and the Asian girl, have to be the same two prostitutes she told us about when we met with her—Queen Chekilla and Lotus. She knew where to find them…"

Mindy finished his thought, "And used their story to lure us into a trap."

"And set me up for a beating."

"Lewis. The Asian hooker called him Lewis. Think it's the same guy who ran Heather?"

"Maybe he isn't dead?"

"But why would O'Brien come after us with the three of them?"

Ethan stared at the computer screen. "To scare us away from the truth."

"Why would she do that?"

"I have no idea."

"Maybe the girl who gave you the telephone number knows?"

"Shit. Forgot all about her," Ethan said, reaching for the crumpled piece of paper he'd tossed on the dresser the night before. He picked up his cell phone and called the number. "No answer."

"Let it ring."

He waited—seven, eight, nine—then on the tenth ring, a girl answered with a whisper, "Hello?"

"This is Ethan Benson," he said carefully. "I'm the guy who was at The House of Hope yesterday. Did you give me this telephone number?"

A long silence.

"Are you still there?" Ethan said, hoping she hadn't hung up.

"I'm here," she said timidly. "And it was me."

"What's your name?"

"No name. If Ms. O'Brien finds out I talked to you, they'll kill me."

There was another long silence.

"Maybe I made a mistake. Maybe I should hang up the phone."

"No, no, don't do that," Ethan said kindly. "You can trust me."

"Why should I?"

"I won't do anything to put your life in danger. Are you in a safe place?"

"I'm alone. Nobody can hear me."

Ethan put his hand over the mouthpiece, "She's gonna talk." He continued patiently, "Why'd you give me your telephone number?"

"Because I knew Heather," the girl said uneasily.

"How?"

"We bunked in the same room at The House of Hope. We were trying to get clean and outta the business."

Ethan turned to Mindy, whispered, "She was friends with Heather."

"Ask her what she was like," Mindy said rapidly. "Keep her talking."

Ethan cleared his throat. His headache was getting worse. "Can you describe her?"

"I loved her like a sister. Now she's dead," the girl began whimpering.

"C'mon, tell me the good things you remember about her."

She sniffled, "There weren't any good things. She ran away from home. She hated her parents. She just thought she'd be better off on her own in Boston. But life sucks. Some guy got her hooked on meth and then started her turning tricks to pay for her habit."

"Do you know where she came from?" Ethan said, pumping for background.

"It always made her cry when I asked. So I stopped. I only knew her a couple of months before she was murdered."

Mindy jotted a question on a piece of paper and handed it to Ethan. He read the prompt then said gingerly, "Did you and Heather work the same street corner in Mattapan?"

"I don't do tricks anymore."

"This is important. Did Heather ever tell you about the guys she dated?"

"She told me some of them."

"Did she tell you about the doctor, Rufus Wellington?"

"All the time," she said, her voice turning vicious.

Ethan covered the phone and turned to Mindy, "She knows about Wellington."

"What was he like?" he said softly.

"I don't want to talk about him."

Ethan paused, carefully choosing his words, "Look, honey, you don't have to tell me if you don't want to, but I promise, nobody will ever find out you talked to me."

He waited, listening, hoping she'd overcome her fear.

Then she said hesitantly, "He got rough during sex. Liked to slap her, beat her with a belt, hold a knife to her throat when he was fucking her. That was the only way he could get hard and come, when he physically abused her. He scared the shit out of her, real bad."

"Why'd she go with him if he frightened her so much?"

"Because he was rich and gave her pretty gifts and lots of money," the girl said enviously. "Thousands of dollars for a single night of sex."

"Did you ever meet him?" Ethan said, holding his breath.

"Just once."

"On a street corner in Mattapan?"

"No."

"Then where?"

"At The House of Hope."

Ethan leaned back and stared at Mindy, his eyes like saucers. "You met Rufus Wellington at The House of Hope?"

"Ms. O'Brien set them up on their first date."

"I don't understand," he said, trying to be persuasive. "I thought Ms. O'Brien was helping you girls."

"She's a phony, a liar," the girl said frantically. "That's why I gave you my cell phone number, to warn you about her." There was another long pause. The girl was suddenly terrified. "Somebody's coming. I gotta go."

"Hold on. Hold on. Let me help you—"

The telephone went dead.

"Shit." He looked at Mindy, worried. "She heard somebody coming and hung up."

"So what should we do now, Ethan?"

"Tell Lloyd to call his contacts at the Boston PD and do a background check on O'Brien. See if she has a rap sheet. Then maybe we can double source if she knows Wellington … and if she's tied to Heather's murder." He closed his eyes. His head was throbbing. "What time's our meeting with Dr. Hosenfeld?"

"Noon. You sure you're okay? You look flushed to me."

Ethan nodded, his headache pounding furiously.

"You sure, Ethan?"

"I'm sure. Let's head to the shrink's."

"Well, go brush your teeth first. I can smell the alcohol on your breath."

✥

Janice O'Brien was sitting in the kitchen, drinking hot coffee. The door was closed and the curtains drawn, the room cast in a myriad of shadows from an overhead fluorescent lightbulb. She was searching the *Boston Globe* for a story about Ethan Benson and his run-in with Lewis the pimp.

So far, nothing.

Smiling, she closed her laptop and was about to head to her morning prayer meeting when her burner buzzed. She unlocked the cabinet over the sink, grabbed the cell phone, and checked the number. She paused then answered, "It's done."

"What happened?" the man said acidly.

"I called Lewis, and we went down to Mattapan, the place I told Benson about, and waited for him just like you told me."

"And?"

"I signaled Lewis to get him when he jumped out of his car and ran to help his assistant, after my girls started messing with that bitch. Lewis clocked him on the head real good with a blackjack."

"Is he in the hospital?"

O'Brien hesitated, "A third guy sitting in a white van I didn't notice came after us with a gun. We ran as quick as we could."

"What happened to Benson?" the man was angry.

"Look, the guy was gonna shoot Lewis," O'Brien said firmly.

"So you didn't scare him off? He might still be working the story?"

"Might be—"

The man cut her off. "I want Benson out of the picture. Not tomorrow. Not the next day. Today. I don't want him digging into Rufus's past. I don't want him talking to any of the girls. And I don't want him finding out about me. It's too risky for all of us."

"But you told me Wellington ordered you to bring Benson into the game, that he wants to do the interview with *The Weekly Reporter*, that this is all his idea."

"It is, but sometimes Rufus is his own worst enemy. And part of my job—our job—is to protect him from himself. So I don't care how you do it, but figure out a way to stop Benson." There was chilling silence. "And, Janice, what about the girl who slipped Benson the note?"

"You mean Sylvia?"

"I don't care what her name is. Did she talk to him?" he said abruptly.

"A little while ago."

"And what did she tell him?"

"Just heard bits and pieces outside her door," O'Brien said begrudgingly.

"Shit, Janice, did she blow our cover?" he said, now screaming like a banshee. "Did she tell him about you and Rufus? Did she tell him about me?"

"I don't know," O'Brien said, articulating each word. "Weren't you listening? I just told you, I didn't hear much of what she said."

"Well, get rid of her too. I don't want her talking to Benson again."

"Don't worry," she said, cackling, "she won't be a problem."

"She better not. Everything's starting to unravel, and I can't have that," he said, slamming down the phone.

O'Brien sat quietly.

Thinking.

Bret Davenport was a fool.

She'd call Lewis right after her morning sermon—another big payday for both of them. She slipped the burner into her pocket, picked up her Bible, and headed to the parlor—bursting into the room, waving her arms wildly, all fire and brimstone, the girls shrinking farther and farther back with every word, cowering in fear.

CHAPTER 20

DR. HOSENFELD'S YOUNG SECRETARY WAS applying her lipstick, getting ready to head to lunch when Ethan arrived. Startled by the nasty gash on his forehead, she fumbled her lipstick and dropped it in her lap. "I'm sorry... Mr. Benson? I'm Constance, Dr. Hosenfeld's assistant." She got up awkwardly. "He told me to send you and Ms. Herman right in. Is there anything I can get you? Coffee? Tea?"

"I'm good," Ethan said,

"Does it hurt?"

"Only when I laugh," he said, in no mood for small talk.

She opened the door for them, and they walked into his office.

"Dr. Hosenfeld? Ethan Benson. This is Mindy Herman, my associate producer."

The doctor stood up to welcome them. "Come in, and have a seat."

Ethan and Mindy sat in two upright chairs across from his desk.

"I go from one case to the next like a ping-pong ball," he said, scooping up a stack of documents and placing them next to his computer, "rarely have time to come up for air. He cracked his knuckles and sat back down. "May I ask you what happened to your forehead, Mr. Benson?"

"I ran into someone's pimp."

Hosenfeld looked at him for a moment, startled. "Well, I think we'll leave it at that," he said, changing the subject. "Shall we discuss Dr. Wellington?"

"Might be a good idea, Dr. Hosenfeld," Mindy said politely. "I think Ethan's a little short-winded this morning."

"Fine, fine. Not a problem. So ... Rufus Wellington. A big-time heart surgeon murdered a teenage prostitute he wanted to marry. Now, that kind of love affair doesn't happen all that often, does it?" he said, staring from Mindy to Ethan.

"Guess not," Ethan said, surprised by the psychiatrist's flippant comment. "We're interviewing him in a couple of weeks, and I'm trying to figure out the best way to build a set of questions for my anchorman, Peter Sampson. It would be very helpful if you could begin by telling me what he's like."

"First off, let me say, the man is a killer and belongs just where he is—locked up behind bars for the murder of Heather Starr. That was my recommendation to the court back then, and I stand by that decision today. Now, Dr. Wellington," Hosenfeld said, picking up his psych report and leafing through the pages, "I spent three days examining him at the Franklin County Jail in Greenfield shortly after he pleaded guilty. The judge needed an evaluation before sentencing, and I must say, I had a rather difficult time diagnosing him. He didn't talk very much—just sat there during most of our sessions, staring vacantly and nodding short responses to my questions. But he told me just enough for me to draw my conclusions."

"You didn't find him mentally unstable?" Ethan asked. "The ADA gave me pictures of Wellington taken at the crime scene by the sheriff's department. He was standing like a statue next to the grave, covered in blood, his hair flying in every direction. He looked downright crazy, if you ask me."

"Looks can be deceiving," the psychiatrist said casually, "especially after someone's committed such a horrific crime. It can throw them for a loop, alter their psyche, push them into a completely unnatural state of mind. In Wellington's case, it was just temporary. When I met him, he appeared quite polished, sophisticated, and immaculately groomed—not a hair out of place. And from my experience handling cases like Rufus Wellington's, he may have appeared crazy after the murder, but he was perfectly rational and totally in control of his feelings when he was sitting in front of me."

"So how'd you figure him out?" Mindy said taciturnly. "Killing someone and carving them into pieces isn't normal, everyday behavior, is it, Dr. Hosenfeld?"

"Of course not. Most people can control their actions when they're feeling anger or rage, but Dr. Wellington couldn't and certainly didn't. He was probably insane when he committed the crime."

"So doesn't he belong in a mental institution and not a state prison?" Ethan said questioningly.

"It could be viewed that way, Mr. Benson, but you have to remember—and this is clearly noted in my report—that Dr. Wellington may have been out of his mind at the very moment he committed the murder, but in the hours leading up to the crime, he knew exactly what he was doing and why he was doing it. See, he carefully planned to murder Ms. Starr if she spurned his proposal—and when she did, well, we all know what happened, don't we? And when I asked him if he understood the consequences of his actions, he repeatedly said yes, that he'd made a conscious decision to beat her to death if she refused his hand in marriage."

"And there's no question in your mind that's what happened," Ethan said, "notwithstanding everything else he did to her?"

"None whatsoever. The murder was premeditated. Rufus Wellington had a plan that kicked in the moment Heather Starr said no."

"That wasn't in your report," Ethan said, eyeballing the doctor.

"That's because Wellington never articulated that thought in those exact words. As I noted, he's incapable of expressing his feelings. So I had to base my evaluation not only from what he said but from his body language and how he appeared before me."

"So you determined he's sane and not totally psychotic?" Mindy said, reading her notes.

"Ms. Herman, I'm trained to evaluate violent behavior in individuals like Rufus Wellington. He definitely reacted in a psychotic manner. He lost control of his emotions and acted against the norms of society. But he definitely knew what he was doing and was fully aware of the consequences. He wanted to kill Heather Starr."

"But how do you explain his decision to cut up her body?" Ethan said. "No rational human being would ever do something that gruesome, would they, Dr. Hosenfeld?"

"Well, if the average person dismembered somebody they'd murdered and buried them in such a ritualistic manner, I'd have no doubts they suffered from some deep-seated psychosis. But in Dr. Wellington's case, I had to factor in that he's a surgeon—a heart surgeon—who cut up people for a living. He did it almost every day of his working life. And when I weighed that fact into the equation, his actions didn't seem quite so abnormal or psychotic or insane to me."

"That's what one of his colleagues at Mass General inferred to us," Ethan said, the room suddenly beginning to spin. "But if I remember correctly, you wrote in your psych report that Dr. Wellington kept referencing God and the need to cleanse Heather's soul as reasons for his actions. Sounds like the ravings of a madman to me, Dr. Hosenfeld."

Mindy interrupted. "Ethan, you're slurring your words. Are you all right?"

"I'm fine, Mindy," he said, pinching the bridge of his nose, trying to focus. "It's just my headache."

"Would you like a glass of water?" Dr. Hosenfeld said.

"I'm okay, really. So let me summarize," Ethan said, still sounding shaky, "based on your experience as a court-appointed psychiatrist and on the three days you spent analyzing Dr. Wellington, you believe he belongs right where he is—in prison and not in an institution for the criminally insane. Is that correct, Dr. Hosenfeld?"

"I'm perfectly comfortable with that decision."

But something still wasn't adding up. Everything Ethan had learned so far about Rufus Wellington—his propensity to abuse his female classmates, his strange social behavior at the hospital, and his attack on Ginger the waitress—pointed to a pattern of sexual dysfunction that culminated in the murder of Heather Starr. Could he do it again?

"Hypothetically," Ethan said, wondering out loud, "if Rufus Wellington's sentence is overturned—and an appeal has been filed asking the court to make that happen—do you think he's capable of committing another murder like this one if he's released back into society?"

"Funny you should bring that up," Hosenfeld said, straightening a stack of papers on his desk. "His attorney was just here and asked me the same question."

"Bret Davenport?"

"Yes, Mr. Davenport."

"Is that ethical, Dr. Hosenfeld, for you to talk to Rufus Wellington's attorney before an appeal hearing?"

"Of course. He was just asking my opinion."

"And what did you tell him?" Ethan said, pushing.

"I said, in some cases, I would definitely say yes, but based on my personal observations and the fact that Dr. Wellington has no record of violence in his past, I have no reason to suspect he'd do it again."

"Would you testify to that in court?" Mindy said, shocked.

"Rest assured, Ms. Herman, the court made the right decision locking him up at MCI-Cedar Junction. He committed murder and belongs behind bars for a very long time."

"But what if he wins his appeal and the court releases him on some technicality," Ethan said, still not satisfied with Hosenfeld's answer, "you're positive he wouldn't kill again?"

"You can't ever be positive about anything, Mr. Benson. But if the court sets him free, I highly doubt he'd kill again. I'd stake my reputation on that."

Ethan watched the doctor for a moment. "You've been very generous with your time." Then he stood, and as he grabbed his briefcase, the pain in his head snowballed into a firestorm. So he reached out to steady himself, and the last thing he heard was Mindy's screams echoing into the distance as he crashed headfirst to the floor into darkness.

Ethan stirred, a blinding light in his eyes, and tried to sit up. "What's goin' on?" he said, confused, as two strong hands pushed him down on his back.

"You're in the emergency room at Mass General. I'm Dr. Siegel. Try not to move just yet," he said soothingly. "I'm stitching your forehead." He adjusted a clean white sheet draped over the lower half of Ethan's face. "It's infected," Siegel continued, concentrating. "You could've avoided a lot of problems by coming in last night. We'll have to keep you a day or two for observation."

"Not possible," Ethan said stubbornly. "I'm a producer. I'm working on a story. I have a full schedule of meetings. I can't delay them."

"I'm afraid you have no choice. On top of your injuries, you're intoxicated. Your blood alcohol level is .09 percent. That's above the legal limit, Mr. Benson. Have you been drinking in the past twenty-four hours?"

Ethan closed his eyes.

"I thought so. We can't send you home."

"But—"

"Jeez, Ethan, listen to the doctor," Mindy said from the corner of the room. "I've already canceled everything. You're not leaving the hospital until Dr. Siegel gives you the all clear."

Ethan started to protest again but stopped, his ears ringing.

A male nurse in hospital scrubs walked into the exam room, wheeling a portable EKG machine and carrying a metal tray loaded with bandages, ointments, and medical instruments. He hooked a dozen electrodes to Ethan's arms and legs and chest and waited for the machine to spit out a trail of squiggly lines on a long sheet of paper. Dr. Siegel examined the readout.

"Heart rhythms appear normal, but the contusion on the back of your head worries me." He moved his hand in front of

Ethan's face, watching his eyes as they mirrored the motions. "Can you sit up?"

"I think so."

Dr. Siegel placed an arm around Ethan's back and slowly lifted him. He felt weak, but the dizziness had passed. After gently probing the back of his head, Siegel said confidently, "There's some blood matted in your hair that we'll need to clean up, but the wound doesn't look all that bad. No sutures back there. Does it hurt when I touch it?"

"Not really."

"Is that an honest answer, Ethan?" Mindy said. "Tell him the truth."

"It hurts, but not bad, really. I'll live."

Dr. Siegel continued pressing his fingers around the abrasion then listened to his heart through a stethoscope one last time. "I think you probably escaped a concussion," he said, "but after I admit you to the hospital, I'm gonna run a couple more tests—including an MRI—to make sure there isn't a blood clot hiding in your head. We can probably get you outta here first thing tomorrow morning, if everything shows up normal."

"Is this really necessary?"

"Yes. Now lie down, Mr. Benson, and try to be patient while I find you a bed." He stepped out, and Mindy came up to Ethan.

"You scared the hell out of me. Why didn't you tell me you were feeling so shitty? We could've gone straight to the hospital this morning." Ethan lay back down on the gurney, Mindy pulling up the covers and adjusting his pillow. "Better?"

"Thanks."

"Look, I called Paul and told him."

"And?"

"What do you think? He was furious. I explained what happened and what we captured on the hidden camera video. That got him to calm down. Now he's just worried about you like I am."

"Peter?"

"Paul told him," Mindy said, sighing heavily. "And what about Sarah?"

"I didn't call her," he said sheepishly.

"I knew you hadn't. So I did, as soon as we got here. She said you haven't called since you left on Wednesday. What's goin' on with the two of you?"

Ethan shrugged.

"I told her what happened and to come, that you were in bad shape. But she said, 'No, you take care of him. I can't leave Luke.' Ethan, she's really pissed. You need to talk to her."

"Oh, boy."

"I told her you'd call, like, now."

She punched in Ethan's home number and handed him the phone. Sarah answered immediately.

"I don't want to talk 'til you get home," she said, her voice hovering between anger and fear. "Are you okay?"

"Still in the emergency room, babe."

But there was only silence, Ethan feeling the anxiety on the other end of the line So he drew a deep breath and told her everything—about being beaten by the pimp, passing out in the psychiatrist's office, and about all his drinking.

❧

Ethan was lying in bed in a private room on the fifth floor of the hospital, still worrying about Sarah, a heart monitor hooked up to his chest and saline solution running into his arm from an IV drip propped next to the nightstand. A pretty nurse named Gladys—with brown eyes, black hair, and a dimple on her chin—hurried into the room. She didn't say a word as she pulled out a syringe and injected the contents into his IV—a heavy-duty antibiotic called Ampicillin—to combat the infection on his forehead. Walking to the foot of his bed, she noted the time on his chart, then took his temperature and blood pressure, listened to his pulse, and hurried out of the room.

Ethan stared at his iPad, trying to read his notes, struggling to concentrate, the words dancing on the screen. He looked up as the door opened, and Mindy came in, accompanied by a distinguished-looking older woman.

"How're you feeling?" she said. "Any better?"

Ethan shrugged.

"This is Dr. Althea Oliphant. She's a friend of Dr. Rasmussen and the head of psychiatry here at Mass General. She's agreed to help us with our story. Up for a short conversation?"

"Sure," he said, sitting up. "I'm afraid I can't shake hands. I'm hooked to all these damn wires and tubes. Bit of a nuisance, don't you think, Dr. Oliphant?"

"Mindy warned me you'd make light of what happened. The doctors want you to rest, so I'm only gonna sneak a quick chat, and call me Althea, please."

Dr. Oliphant was a thin woman with short gray hair cut in a pageboy hairstyle, gold wire-rim glasses, and not a stitch of makeup on her face. Her eyes were crimson blue and her fingernails short and well groomed.

"Dr. Rasmussen mentioned you needed a second opinion about Dr. Wellington. I knew him quite well professionally. We attended medical conferences together and often met at faculty meetings, even though I never really had much conversation with him."

"Anything you might say now that sticks out, looking back?"

"The times we chatted, he seemed very guarded. If I had to guess, I'd say he seemed closed off to other people, but that's not unusual for a heart surgeon, as I'm sure you know. From what I've heard, he did things by the book, and he did them well."

"But this is a guy who committed murder. You didn't pick up on anything strange in the years he was here?"

"Did he have psychological problems?" she said thought-fully. "Might've. Was he psychotic? Well, I can't answer that. I never treated him, so I don't really know."

Ethan looked at her, stumped. "So can you help us?"

Gladys the nurse poked her head into the room. "Mr. Benson needs to rest now."

"Just another minute," Mindy said, handing Dr. Oliphant a file with Hosenfeld's psych evaluation.

"I'm gonna carefully study this psych report," she said, smiling. "Maybe discuss it with some of my colleagues. Then we'll talk. Feel better, Mr. Benson."

CHAPTER 21

IT WAS TWO IN THE morning when Lewis the pimp slipped into The House of Hope through the kitchen door. He opened the refrigerator, grabbed a bottle of Bud, and sat down. A big man with a barrel chest, an Afro, and a sneer on his face—he lit a cigarette and began rapping his fingers impatiently on the kitchen table as he blew out a smoke ring.

A few minutes later, Janice O'Brien came in, poured herself a cup of coffee, and sat down across from him. "Do you have a plan?" she asked, making herself comfortable.

"Where's your little snitch?"

"Upstairs, asleep."

"And the other girls?"

"All asleep too. Won't be a problem if we're quiet."

"That's what this is for," he said as he reached into his coat pocket and removed a handkerchief and a bottle of clear liquid."

O'Brien looked at it, not sure what it was.

"Chloroform," he said. "This'll quiet her down, until we're ready for her."

O'Brien slid a fat envelope across the table. "Ten thousand in cash—all small bills—just like I promised."

Lewis picked up the envelope, peered inside, then stuffed it into his pants pocket.

"Aren't you gonna count it?" she said, leering.

"Lewis trusts you," he said, stomping out his cigarette on the floor, indifferent to the burn mark it made in the linoleum. "And Lewis says, let's take care of the bitch right now."

O'Brien quietly led him up the carpeted steps and tiptoed to the last room at the end of the hall. Pausing to make sure no one had stirred, she opened the door and peeked at the girl with the jagged scar on her face, lying on her back, the covers kicked to the foot of the bed, her nightgown hiked to her waist. She motioned to the pimp to follow and entered the room, glaring as she watched him leer at the half-naked girl.

"Stop licking your lips," she whispered into his ear. "No time for thoughts of sex. Not now. Just do it."

Lewis emptied the contents of the bottle onto the handkerchief, leaned over, and pressed it tightly over the girl's nose and mouth. Her eyes flew open as she writhed on the bed, frantically pulling at his hands, trying to push the cloth with the sweet-smelling liquid away from her face. After struggling a few seconds, her eyes gently closed, her body went limp, and her breathing grew heavy.

Lewis smiled and ran his big hand up her thigh. "Sylvia was once so beautiful. So fine," he said, continuing to lick his lips, "until she disobeyed her Lewis, and he was forced to mess up her pretty face to teach her a lesson."

O'Brien pulled at his hand. "Stop touching her, you fool. Not here. Just keep your dick in your pants. You'll wake the other girls."

"Always time for a little pleasure," he said, chuckling. He ran his hands over her breasts, before lifting her off the bed and carrying her to the door.

"Don't move," O'Brien said, sweat pooling under her arms. She listened a few seconds and when she was sure everyone was still sleeping, motioned to the pimp to follow—across the hall, down the stairs, into the kitchen, and out the door. Once outside, she made him stop as she looked back up at the windows—all dark.

Good.

No one awake.

"Where you parked?" she whispered.

"Lewis is parked down the block," he said, throwing Sylvia over his shoulder.

"Keep your voice down, you fool. Somebody'll hear us. Let's go."

Lewis picked his way around the garbage in the back alley, past a derelict warehouse, and through a jagged hole in a chain-link fence. After hurrying down the street and crossing to the near corner, he abruptly stopped and turned to O'Brien, "That's Lewis's car, the big black Cadillac. A real beauty, ain't she? Key's in my coat pocket."

O'Brien fumbled until she found them and clicked open the trunk. "Get her in, Lewis. Hurry up."

He dropped the girl on the tire jack, cracking open her forehead. "Aw, look what Lewis did. What a shame. Messed her face a little more." Aroused as blood trickled down her cheek, he leaned over and touched her between the legs.

"Cut the crap, Lewis," O'Brien said, anger in her voice. "If she comes to, she'll scream and wake the neighborhood."

"Not gonna happen," he said, slamming the trunk. "Lewis give her a big enough dose to knock out an army."

"Where we going?" O'Brien asked, peering over her shoulder nervously, still worrying someone might see them, before getting into the car.

"Lewis has a secret place not too far where cops never go," he said, pulling out of the space and heading down the block. "Just chill. Lewis take care of everything."

After weaving through the empty streets for fifteen minutes, he drove into a neighborhood that looked more like a war zone than a once-thriving industrial park. There was a shuttered gas station on the corner, a cluster of abandoned warehouses, and a row of condemned single-family homes pock marking the side streets. A rat scurried in front of his Cadillac as he slowly passed a stripped-down car sitting under a solitary streetlamp. He cut his head-lights and drove through a broken gate and around an abandoned factory on Savin Hill Avenue, checking his rearview mirror before stopping next to a loading dock. The factory doors and windows were all boarded up tight.

"Here?" she asked.

Lewis didn't need to answer her. He got out and looked around.

"Lewis uses it all the time when he needs to dump some-thin'." He popped the trunk and stared at the half-naked girl. "Well, looky here, the little bitch is awake and kicking."

Terrified, Sylvia stared up at the pimp, whimpering for her life, "Please, lemme go. I didn't do anything, Ms. O'Brien."

"What did you tell Ethan Benson? I was outside your door the whole time you were talking to him but could only make out bits and pieces of what you said. Now tell your mama everything."

"Please, I didn't tell him anything."

"Not sure I believe you," she said sweetly. Then she nodded at Lewis.

He slapped Sylvia hard, tears and blood flying. "Now Lewis wants to know. What did you tell that reporter?" he said, squeezing her nipple, her face contorting in pain.

"Nothing, I swear."

"You're lying. What did you say to Benson?" O'Brien said. "You don't want Lewis to hurt you anymore, do you?"

Sylvia began wailing. "Nothing. Nothing. I didn't say a word about Heather."

"Liar," O'Brien said, bellowing. She leaned over and burned a hole in the girl's face with her cigarette. Sylvia screamed. "You told him about Heather and Wellington, didn't you? Tell me the truth, and maybe I'll let you go."

Pleading, Sylvia said, "I didn't tell him, Ms. O'Brien. Please believe me."

"Lewis thinks this pretty little thing needs to be taught a big lesson," the pimp said, removing his overcoat and neatly placing it on the hood of the car.

O'Brien nodded her head.

He smiled, then grabbed Sylvia by a clump of hair, and pummeled her with his blackjack, shredding her nose and shattering her teeth.

More blood.

Everywhere.

"What did you tell that reporter?" Ms. O'Brien said, shrieking.

Sylvia didn't answer, her eyes blank.

O'Brien signaled Lewis again.

Still smiling, he wrapped his hands around her neck and squeezed—five seconds, ten seconds, fifteen seconds—her eyes bulging, her lips turning blue. "Talk, bitch. Tell Ms. O'Brien what she wants to know." He punched her hard—one, two, three times—her face swelling, her eyes puffing shut.

"Stop. Please stop," Sylvia whispered, blood gurgling in her throat. "I told him I knew Heather was dating Dr. Wellington, that he was paying her lots of money for sex, that he was probably in love with her." She paused, gasping for air. "That's all. I didn't tell him anything else. I swear." Blood bubbled down her chin. "Don't hurt me anymore. Please."

Ms. O'Brien nodded to Lewis.

He hit her again with his blackjack, breaking her jaw.

"Did you tell him about me?" O'Brien said, peering into her eyes, trying to decide if she was telling the truth.

Sylvia tried to answer but couldn't open her mouth and nodded her head yes instead.

"You told him about me and Wellington?"

She nodded yes again.

"You bitch, after all I've done for you, you ungrateful cunt." She bent over right in front of Sylvia's face. "You had to go and open your big mouth and tell that fucking reporter everything. Now he's gonna come snoopin' around again, trying to figure out what else you know." She turned to Lewis, seething, "Do it. Now!"

Lewis's tongue darted in and out of his mouth like a snake. "Tasty. Tasty. Tasty. You sweet little thing."

Sylvia's eyes bulged as he yanked her out of the car, dragged her across the parking lot and into the factory—the skin on her back shredding on the asphalt and the broken glass littering the floor. He tossed her onto a dirty mattress and waited a moment as she lay there moaning. He knelt next to her, pulled out a combat blade strapped to his calf, and slit her throat from ear to ear. Blood spurted across the floor as she clutched her neck, drowning in her own blood, her eyes rolling into the back of her head.

Lewis stood up and watched her final gasps.

Leering.

O'Brien yelled, "C'mon. Let's get outta here."

"Patience. Lewis always likes to enjoy the finale. Makes him tingle all over."

O'Brien peered down at Sylvia, then up at the dark sky, the moon shining through a massive hole in the roof, and started to pray, "The good Lord takes care of those he loves. This is all part of his master plan for me, his beloved servant. He's taken the dear departed Ms. Sylvia into his arms. Now she's his problem and not mine."

She heard Lewis start the car engine and hurried out of the factory to catch up to him.

❧

O'Brien looked at the wall clock in her office: 6:00 a.m.—early, but not too early. She picked up her cell phone, dialed his number, and waited. After five rings, Bret Davenport answered.

"It's done," she said nonchalantly.

"Lewis took care of her?"

"Yes."

"Any trouble?"

"No."

"Where'd you leave the body?" he said, the relief in his voice palpable.

"That's for me to know and not you." O'Brien waited silently, puffing away on her cigarette, trying to gauge his reaction.

"Did she tell you anything?"

"Nothing, really," she said, deciding not to mention that Sylvia had blown their cover. The less he knew, the better.

"You're sure, Janice?"

"We're safe," O'Brien said, hesitating, "at least, if you believe that little bitch. So there's no reason to panic."

"Where's Benson now?" Davenport said irritably.

"In Mass General. He collapsed yesterday afternoon, and paramedics rushed him to the emergency room. Lewis did a better job on him than we first thought."

"Get the hell over there," he said, ranting. "I wanna know when he gets out and where he goes next. And take Lewis with you."

"Sure that's a good idea?"

"If the opportunity arises, I want you to finish the job."

Davenport clicked off.

O'Brien lit another cigarette and started pacing. This wasn't going to be easy. Benson was smart, and he and his assistant might recognize her if she wasn't careful. She paused at her desk. Fuck his plan. She couldn't risk being connected to Lewis. She wasn't going to take him. Then she stared down at her cell phone. Shit. It wasn't the burner. She'd used the wrong phone—a mistake, maybe a big one. Now what should she do?

She reached for her Bible and kissed it.

God would give her a sign.

He always did.

CHAPTER 22

ETHAN WAS ANGRY, FRUSTRATED. A slew of doctors had paraded through his room—a neurologist, a cardiologist, a hematologist, a wound specialist—poking and prodding, testing and retesting, consulting and reconsulting, trying to decide if he was healthy enough to be sent on his way. Tired of watching the clock, he threw off the covers and got dressed. A few minutes later, Mindy and Lloyd pushed through the door.

Mindy looked at him, irritated, "What're you doing? You should be in bed."

Lloyd pointed to Ethan's head, "How's that workin'?"

Ethan tenderly rubbed his forehead, "Sore, but the headache's gone."

"Lloyd's got some news," Mindy said, still annoyed. "Your hunch about Janice O'Brien was right on the money. She's not who she says she is."

Ethan looked back at Lloyd.

"Dorchester vice squad tells me O'Brien may've been a nun once, but she didn't leave the church for any higher calling like she says. She was dismissed by a bishop after he discovered that she'd embezzled close to a quarter of a million dollars from the church's operating fund. The diocese didn't prosecute because they also found out she was sexually molesting a fourteen-year-old altar boy and that she'd been doing it for years. The church didn't want to risk another big scandal, so it was swept under the rug."

"Did it make the newspapers?" Ethan said, sitting down on the bed.

"The church managed to keep it quiet. The cops think they paid off the kid's parents quite handsomely. Sound familiar?"

"Tell him the rest," Mindy said hurriedly. "We haven't gotten to the juicy part yet."

"There's more?"

Lloyd chuckled, "O'Brien's really quite the piece of work. My sources slipped me her rap sheet." He passed Ethan a thick notebook. "You'll find it interesting. Since leaving the church, she's been arrested for indecent exposure, assault and battery, robbery, and working for a high-end call girl service—several of them, in fact."

"So she was a hooker," Ethan said, flipping through the book, "a flying nun hooker."

"Notorious in her day," Lloyd said, chuckling out loud. "When she got too old to walk the streets, she became a madam, running her own house of prostitution. She was busted ten years ago, another big scandal, and spent three years in the slammer."

"And that's still not all of it," Mindy said impatiently. "Get to the point, Lloyd."

Lloyd pressed on, "She's been running The House of Hope since she got out. There's a parade of runaways going in and out all the time. Cops watch the place. They think she uses them to service a high-end clientele of sickos who are into young kids."

"One of them being Wellington," Ethan said. "How does she get away with it?"

"Not enough evidence to bust her, not yet," Lloyd said. "But the vice squad says they're getting close to shutting her down."

Ethan stood and started pacing. "I need to talk to that girl. See what else she knows about O'Brien."

"The girl who gave you her phone number?" Lloyd asked.

"Mindy told you about her?"

"And everything she said about Heather and Wellington."

"I'll call her as soon as I'm outta here," Ethan said, glancing at the time. "What's taking so long? They just need to fill out paperwork."

"Easy does it," Mindy said. "The doctors will spring you soon enough. Anything else we should worry about?"

"Find out where O'Brien gets her money," he said, turning to Lloyd, his mind firing on overdrive. "She told us The House of Hope is a nonprofit funded by wealthy do-gooders. I don't believe her. See if you can dig up paperwork on her finances. Let's see if there's any connection to Wellington. That would help prove what the girl told me."

"Might take a couple of days. I'm on the clock."

"I don't care. We need to know. Let's run with it. And, Mindy, what's going on with Wellington's father?" Ethan said, slumping in an empty chair, his head woozy. "Any luck finding him? We've got all morning with nothing to do before I leave for the Quabbin."

"Still nowhere," she said. "I checked back with his secretary then rang his apartment in the Back Bay, even left messages at his homes in New York and LA and in Shutesbury. But all his assistants—and let me tell you, there are lots of them—say they have no idea where he is. I'm starting to think he doesn't want to talk to us."

"Keep trying," he said impatiently. "I need to find out what Wellington was really like as a kid."

❧

Janice O'Brien slumped in the front seat of a Dodge minivan as they walked through the revolving door and chatted a moment in front of the hospital, then watched as Mindy broke away and disappeared into a crowd of people congregating on Cambridge Street. She grabbed a new burner from her purse, dialed Bret Davenport, and waited, never taking her eyes off Ethan.

"He's leaving the hospital," she said soberly.

"Is he alone?"

"He was with Mindy Herman, but she just left. That gunslinger from the other night peeled outta here an hour ago."

"Any idea who he is?"

"Nope. All I know is he's packing and not scared of nobody."

"Well, find out. I'm talking to Rufus later today, and he's gonna want to know."

"Don't shit your shorts," O'Brien snapped back. "I'm doin' my best to find out."

"What's Benson up to now?"

"He's tipping the valet and getting into his car."

"Has he seen you?"

"Hell, no, I'm way across the street. He has no reason to suspect."

"Don't underestimate him, Janice," Davenport said harshly. "The guy's getting very close to figuring out what we're doing. We gotta finish the job we started the other night. Let me talk to Lewis."

"No can do," Janice said with a snigger. "He ain't with me."

"But I told you—"

"Don't care what you told me. I thought it was too risky."

"Listen, Janice. We have to work together, or everything we've built is going to fall apart."

"We are working together," she fired back. "But sometimes you have to listen to me. I'm on the ground here, and you're not. It's the wrong time to take the guy out. Hold on. Benson's getting into his car."

"Stay on the phone with me," the man said hastily. "Rufus wants to know everything he's doing."

O'Brien shifted the car into drive, followed Ethan as he exited the hospital, and turned onto Charles Street, hanging back several car lengths, trying not to be noticed. "Shit, I think he's making his way to Highway Two, maybe heading back to the Quabbin."

"Why's he coming here?"

"You should know better than me," she said, dropping back farther.

"Zip it, Janice. I need a moment to think."

"No time to think. What do you want me to do?"

"Stay with him. I need something I can use to persuade Rufus to back out of the interview. Benson won't stop. And if we let Rufus run wild, we're all gonna spend the rest of our lives in the slammer, just like him. Keep me posted."

O'Brien clicked off and tossed the burner onto the passenger seat. If only Lewis had killed Benson like he was supposed to. If only…

She took a deep breath.

Maybe it was time to cut her losses and get out.

Ethan headed west on Highway Two, happy to be out of the hospital and on his way to Old Salem. Tonight was a big night, a chance to do a bit of snooping at Wellington's estate and see if he could find anything Davenport or McKenzie might be hiding that would prove there was a cover-up. The answer was somewhere in that house. He could feel it in his bones. Reaching for his iPhone, he dialed David Livingston.

"Where are you?"

"Waiting for you at the Sunnyside Lodge in Belchertown. That's where we're staying tonight. It's far enough away from Wellington's that nobody will find us."

"Is it better than the place we stayed in the last time we were here?"

"Much better. It's small but clean. You'll like it."

"I hope so, 'cause I need to lie down when I get there. I'm logy from all the painkillers the docs gave me."

"Mindy was pissed you didn't take her with you, said you're in no shape to be driving a car."

"Too much to do. I needed her back in New York to work the loose ends. We can't find Wellington's father, and there's a shitload to get ready for the shoot. Gotta make a budget, book crews, order equipment, work up an itinerary—"

"Slow down, Ethan. I got it. What about Lloyd? Why isn't he driving you?"

"He's doing a background check on Janice O'Brien, looking for a money trail connecting her to Wellington. We're running out of time—"

"Ethan, you sound frazzled. Are you sure you're up for tonight?"

"Look, David, I need to search Wellington's compound, and I don't want Davenport or McKenzie or anybody else to know we're doing it. There's no better time than tonight. We're going in."

"And you're not drinking?"

"Come on, David, I just got out of the hospital."

"But—"

"Okay, I got it. No alcohol. Did you meet Jonah Wilcox at the *Gazette*?"

"Yup."

"Was he helpful?"

"Yes and no. He didn't have anything useful on either Davenport or McKenzie, but after I told him what we were looking for, he put me in touch with a banker in Athol—a guy with a longtime grudge against the sheriff—who was more than happy to help us once I promised we wouldn't say where we got the information."

"So he's a confidential source?"

"That's what I promised. Can't even tell you who he is."

"I don't wanna know," Ethan said emphatically. "So what did he give you?"

"He took me into a backroom at the bank, the Athol Savings and Loan on Main Street, and downloaded a truckload of shit for us—investment reports, real estate holdings, more tax information, and bank statements on both of them—a complete picture of their net worth."

"And he gave you copies of everything?"

"Everything."

"So what do we know?" Ethan said eagerly. "Start with the sheriff."

"His base salary is seventy-five thousand, but he lives much larger than that," David said. "He owns a Porsche, a fishing boat, an RV, and a new house on the reservoir. Hang on, I'll tell you what it cost." Ethan listened as David shuffled through documents. "Here it is. McKenzie paid three quarters of a million and put down half in cash."

"Where'd he get that kind of money?" Ethan said, stunned but not surprised.

"Good question. It certainly didn't come from his base pay."

"And Davenport?" Ethan said brusquely.

"Don't drive off the road, but he's making a lot more than he's claiming in his tax returns—just like we thought. He's worth close to twenty million dollars."

"How's that possible?" Ethan said, stupefied.

"Wellington must be slipping him tons of money under the table."

"You can bet your ass on that. Think Wellington is paying off McKenzie too?"

"That's another good question."

"Find out," Ethan said, barking into the phone. "We need proof."

"On it, Ethan."

"And one more thing, call your source back and ask him if there's anything in the bank's database about Janice O'Brien. Lloyd's checking with his contacts at the Boston PD, but I wanna know if she's connected to Davenport or McKenzie and if they're all working together for Wellington. I'll call you back when I get closer to Belchertown."

Ethan clicked off then pulled out the scrap of paper and dialed the girl at The House of Hope. He let it ring. Three times. Four times. Five times. "Come on. Come on, pick up," he whispered out loud. "Damn, where the hell are you?" He gave up and tossed his phone onto the passenger seat then glanced into his rearview mirror.

Janice O'Brien flipped her blinker and followed Ethan down the Highway Two off-ramp and onto Route 202. The country road running along the west shore of the Quabbin was nearly deserted, no cars or trucks to hide behind, so she dropped back a quarter of a mile and picked up her phone.

"Heading south on 202," she said into the burner. "He's coming up to Athol. Can't tail him much longer. He's gonna spot me."

"What's he driving?"

"A green Ford Fusion."

"Okay. We'll take it from here," Davenport said bluntly. "McKenzie's got a bunch of deputies positioned along the highway. I'll make sure he knows Benson's headed his way."

"And, Bret, where's my money?"

"Is that all you care about? Your fucking money? Swing by my office on your way back. I've got the cash."

"All fifty thousand?" O'Brien said eagerly.

"It's all here."

"Don't go anywhere. I'm on my way." She hung up the phone and pounded on the steering wheel, smacking her lips. "Thank you, Lord Jesus, I'm gonna be rich."

Ethan watched as the Dodge minivan exited onto Route 32A and headed toward Athol. He turned and caught a glimpse of the driver. It was Janice O'Brien. Why had she tailed him all the way here? And where was she going now? Reaching for his cell phone, he called Lloyd, "Have you learned anything about O'Brien?"

"Still digging."

"Well, here's a lead. She's been following me since I left the hospital and just peeled off for Athol. Can you ask your cop friends if they can link her to Davenport or McKenzie? David's also trying with a source in Athol."

"You think she's working for them?"

"Yeah, and the money's coming from Wellington," Ethan filled him in on everything David had learned from the banker and how it confirmed what they'd learned from the tax returns. "I just tried reaching the girl at The House of Hope. I was hoping she could somehow connect them as well. But she's not answering her phone."

"I may have bad news, Ethan. A couple of kids riding their bikes found a body in a deserted warehouse this morning and called the cops. It's a teenage girl, a runaway. Maybe fifteen years old. She was badly beaten, cigarette burns. They think some crazy john got pissed off about something and disposed the body like a piece of trash."

"Any idea who it is?"

"The cops ID'd her from her dental records. Her name's Sylvia Anderson, and they're pretty sure she lived at The House of Hope."

Ethan began shaking, the color draining from his face. "Man, I hope it's not the same girl."

"Don't jump to conclusions. I've got somebody sending me a photo, but I'm not sure it's gonna help much. The rats ate most of her face."

"I may've gotten the girl killed, Lloyd. She was worried they'd find out she was talking to me."

"One step at a time, Ethan. Cops just started their investigation."

"Keep me posted," he said, hanging up abruptly. "Shit. Shit. Shit." He pounded on the steering wheel. "She's dead because of me. I just know it. It's happening all over again. The baby. The baby. The baby."

He pulled off the road, clicked open his briefcase, and stared at the bottle of Scotch, every fiber of his body craving a drink—to settle his nerves, to help him forget. He closed his eyes, trying to calm down, then slammed shut the briefcase, gunned the engine in frustration, and tore down the highway—his very being wracked by anxiety and fear.

When he reached the turnoff to Old Salem, he spotted a brown Crown Victoria easing onto the highway right behind him and recognized the bald head and aviator sunglasses.

Percy Wilkerson.

They were still following him.

He gripped the steering wheel and hit the gas pedal harder, hoping to lose him.

But Wilkerson sped up and settled in just inches behind him.

Ethan pushed the Ford Fusion to 60—the deputy keeping pace, roaring along, riding his tail. He hit 70, then 80, but couldn't shake him on the straightaway. When they reached a looping curve in the road, Ethan slowed, and Wilkerson bumped his fender, trying to push him into a ditch—the two cars fishtailing, skidding sideways. Now terrified, he managed to avoid crashing into a guardrail then crossed into oncoming traffic, swerving around a propane gas truck, almost colliding head-on with a Volkswagen Beetle. He checked his rearview mirror, sweat pouring down his forehead. But the Crown Victoria was still back there, its front end crumpled, Wilkerson accelerating, gaining on him. Ethan raced to 90, driving like a maniac, honking his horn as he zoomed past one car after another. When he reached the city limits of Belchertown, he eased off the gas and quickly glanced over his shoulder; the Crown Victoria was now half a mile back, stuck in slower-moving traffic. He drove several more blocks, through a red light, and skidded into the motel parking lot.

Making an instant decision, he speed-dialed David, "What room are you in?"

"Huh? Two-eleven."

"I'll be there in a minute." He grabbed his briefcase, and as he got out of his car, he spotted the Crown Victoria pulling up to the curb half a block from the motel—Wilkerson calmly smoking a cigarette, watching him through his aviator sunglasses. Racing into the lobby, he approached the front desk. A teenager, bored out of her mind, was perched on a chair, absentmindedly leafing through a copy of *Vanity Fair*.

"'Help you?" she said, looking up over the top of the magazine.

"Room 211?" he said, out of breath.

"Up the stairs and down the hall on the left. That's Mr. Livingston's room. I'll call to let him know you're here?"

"He's expecting me," Ethan said, fleeing up the stairs and knocking on the door.

David threw the dead bolt, and Ethan hurried in.

"What's goin' on, Ethan? You look out of it."

"There's been somebody tailing me ever since I left Boston—first Janice O'Brien, now the deputy sheriff, Percy Wilkerson. And he's been fucking aggressive, just tried to run me off the road."

"What?"

"Shut the lights off, and look for yourself."

They hurried to the window and pulled the curtain back just enough to see. "He's staring up at our window," David said, puzzled. "Doesn't care that we're looking back at him."

"He's a cop. He's doesn't have to care. He can do and say anything he wants."

"So what are we gonna do? He knows we're here."

"Don't know yet," Ethan said, trying to catch his breath.

David handed him a page from a file, "I found this in the *Gazette* articles Jonah Wilcox gave me before I went to see the banker. Your pal down there has a record. Was arrested in high school for assault and battery. Was jailed for two months for punching out a classmate in a drunken bar fight. He's a real piece of work."

"And he's working for the sheriff."

"The whole department must be corrupt. Look, Ethan, he's not gonna back off. No way."

Ethan sat on the end of the bed and massaged his temples. The gash on his forehead was throbbing.

"We gotta call off tonight," David said pleadingly.

There was no response.

"They know we're here."

There was still no response.

"Ethan, what the hell are you thinking?"

Ethan looked up, now perfectly calm, then walked back to the window and peeked out at Wilkerson. "We need to lose that asshole and get back to Old Salem."

CHAPTER 23

THEY MADE THEIR WAY DOWN to the lobby, and as David checked out, Ethan walked into the parking lot and over to his Ford Fusion, the back end totaled beyond repair from the collision. He glanced at the deputy, still sitting in the front seat of his car, wearing his sunglasses. After five minutes, David exited the motel, Ethan following his movements, constantly checking on Wilkerson, as David opened the driver's door of his rental car and sat down behind the wheel. He waited thirty seconds then called him. "Think he saw you?"

"Never turned and looked at me once."

"Good. Sit tight. I'm gonna take 202 south toward Holyoke, like I'm making my way back to New York. Don't follow me. I'll call as soon as the coast is clear. Then we'll find a place to link up."

"Watch yourself, Ethan. You don't want to end up back in the hospital."

Ethan quivered. "No way. There should be lots of traffic. So the asshole won't be able to play bumper cars again." Then he put the Fusion into drive and pulled onto the street. He checked his side-view mirror. The deputy had eased in right behind him.

❧

Percy Wilkerson stayed on his tail, matching his speed. Keeping his eye on Benson, he slugged down a Miller Light, wiped his mouth on his sleeve, squished the can, and dropped it on the floor next to the rest of an empty six-pack. They headed south past the tip of the reservoir then west on Route 202.

Where the hell's he goin'? he thought, fixing on Ethan's taillights. Then he called McKenzie's cell phone. "It's me, Percy."

"What's he doing?" the sheriff said bleakly.

"Back in his car."

"He didn't check into the motel?"

"Nope," Wilkerson said, easing up right behind Ethan's bumper. "Didn't bring in a bag, just his briefcase."

"Did he meet up with anybody?"

"Not sure. Caught him peeking out a window, may have been somebody else there, but I couldn't tell. All I know is he went in alone and came out alone."

"Where's he goin' now?" McKenzie said, worried.

"Seems to be heading toward I-91. Maybe he's hightailing it back to the city? What do you want me to do, Gene? Could try to run him off the road again," he said, savoring the thought. "That'll finish the job Janice fucked up."

"No. Change of plans. The cops in Boston found the hooker's body in a fucking warehouse. Bret is freaking out. Thinks they'll track the murder back to Janice and then to us. Everything's a big mess."

"So you don't want me to try to kill him?"

"No."

"So what should I do?"

"Just follow him. See where he goes. If he gets on the interstate, hang with him, and if you're sure he's heading back to New York, peel off and meet me back at the office."

"I ain't gonna do that, Gene. It's gonna be the middle of the night."

"I don't give a shit what time it is," McKenzie said, cutting him off. "We need to regroup and plan our next move. Keep calling me."

⁓

Ethan never took his eyes off the Crown Victoria, maintaining a constant pace just under the speed limit, until he got to Holyoke—a small college town just a few miles from the interstate—where he stopped for a red light and dialed David. "The asshole's still behind me, but he hasn't tried anything funny. Too many cars, like I thought. But he isn't backing off."

"Where are you?"

"Stuck at a traffic light in Holyoke."

"What are you gonna do?"

"Lose him when I get to I-91."

"Think he'll take the bait?"

"Let's hope so." The light turned green, and Ethan pulled through the intersection, the deputy following like a bloodhound.

"What do you want me to do?" David said urgently.

"I just passed a Starbucks, maybe a mile back, left-hand side of the road, across the street from the hospital. Start driving. It's gonna take you awhile to get there. I'll meet you after I shake him." Ethan tucked his iPhone in his coat pocket, gripped the steering wheel with both hands, then counted to ten. "Time to lose you, douche bag," he blurted to himself, before pushing his foot to the floor and tearing down the two-lane highway.

❧

Percy was growing impatient, hungry for a confrontation, when Benson suddenly streaked ahead like a bat out of hell. "Shit, what the fuck's he doin' now?" he screamed, leaning on the horn and swerving recklessly around a FedEx truck, trying to keep pace. "Goddamn it. Can't let him get away. Gotta know where he's goin'." Banging on the steering wheel, he crossed the white line and passed a long line of cars one at a time, avoiding the oncoming traffic. "Fuck. Fuck. Fuck. The cocksucker's gonna get me killed." He pushed the accelerator to the floor and started to relax as he closed the distance and pulled up right behind him. Then, without warning, Benson hung a sharp left, and the Fusion skidded across the road, tires smoking, and sped up the entrance ramp to the interstate.

Panicking, Percy stomped on the breaks, but the car didn't stop in time. "Jesus, I'm gonna lose the motherfucker," he wailed to himself as he fishtailed a hundred feet, flashing his lights, blasting his horn, before forcing an oncoming car off the road. Then he hung a U-turn, retracing his steps, trying to catch up to Benson. "Man, I gotta find him. McKenzie's gonna be pissed if I don't. Where the fuck is he?"

❧

Ethan pulled into traffic on the interstate, his adrenaline pumping—pushing the rental car to seventy, eighty, ninety miles an hour—his skin clammy, his palms prickly, his fingers gripping the steering wheel like a vise. He checked his rearview mirror—no headlights behind him coming down the ramp. Buoyed, he pressed his foot to the floor and hit 100, ripping into the left lane around a caravan of long-haul truckers. One mile. Two miles. Three miles. Still no sign of the deputy's Crown Victoria. Beginning to relax, he let off the gas as he approached the exit to the Hampshire Mall and steered off the highway, pulling to a stop at the intersection. He turned and quickly looked back. No Percy Wilkerson. Wiping his brow, he hung a left and drifted under the overpass, killing his lights and parking in the high grass along the road. He lit a Marlboro, gulping down the nicotine, and waited. One minute. Two minutes. Five minutes. Still no sign of the Crown Victoria. Smiling, he flipped the cigarette out the window, waited for an opening in the traffic, and pulled onto the interstate, heading back toward Old Salem.

❧

Percy roared down the ramp, a sea of taillights in front him, staring in disbelief. "Fuck. Fuck. Fuck. I ain't gonna find him. What the hell am I gonna tell Gene? Think, man, think," he moaned as he cruised down the interstate, hoping beyond hope he'd catch a glimpse of the Ford Fusion. "Shit. I lost him. Shit. Shit. Shit! He's gone." He kept driving, past the Mass Pike, past the Sheraton Hotel in Springfield, and as he approached the turnoff to Bradley International Airport, reached for his cell phone. "Hey, it's me, Percy."

"What happened?" McKenzie said, breathing heavily into the phone.

Percy cringed anxiously then lied, "He's on Interstate Ninety-One, heading south. Been following him for about fifty miles. Just approaching Hartford, Connecticut. Looks like he's goin' back to New York." He waited for a reaction but didn't get one. "So what do you think, Gene? Should I keep after him?"

There was an agonizing pause. Percy could hear the sheriff striking a match and lighting a cigarette. "Another ten miles or so. And if you're sure he's not gonna double back, come to the station house."

Percy gulped. "Ten-four. Be there in about two hours."

"And, Percy, get rid of the burner. You've been on it all night."

Then the connection went dead.

Percy rolled down the window and tossed the burner into traffic then began looking for an exit. *Hope that asshole doesn't make trouble for me*, he thought as he peered down the highway one last time, searching for the Fusion. Sighing, he hit the blinker and pulled off the interstate.

❧

Ethan was leaning against the car window, his head throbbing, sipping from his bottle of Scotch, when David drove into the Starbucks and parked in the space next to him.

"No sign of the deputy. Lost him on the entrance ramp to I-91 just as we planned," he said before climbing out of the Fusion and slipping into the passenger seat next to David.

"You okay, Ethan?"

"Little weary, but okay. Been a long day."

"You smell like a brewery. How much?"

"Just one pull. That's all."

"Are you sober?"

"Cut the shit, David, I'm fine."

"So you still wanna go through with it?"

"After all I've just been through shaking that guy, bet your ass we're goin' through with it," he said, chewing three Motrin and grimacing at the bitter taste. "We'll leave my car here and pick it up later on our way back to the city. With a little luck, we'll slip into Wellington's, poke around a bit, and make our escape."

"I'm with you, Ethan, but I gotta say this one more time—we're breaking the law the moment we sneak onto his property, and if we get caught, we're gonna be fucked."

"I'll take that chance," he said. "We need to search his house by ourselves without somebody giving us the grand tour. They're hiding something in there, and I wanna know what it is."

"What happens if the sheriff figures out you came back?"

"Stop sweating it," Ethan said confidently. "I'm sure they bought my ruse and think I'm gone. Now, let's get going. We've got a long night ahead of us."

CHAPTER 24

It was well after midnight when they pulled off Route 202 and slipped into Old Salem. The streets were quiet, the town closed up for the night.

"Cut the headlights," Ethan said, peering through the moonlight. "No reason to announce we're here."

David slowed to a crawl, easing the car down Main Street, past the general store, the cemetery, the fire department, the library, and the old church with its oversized bell tower. A dog suddenly began barking somewhere in the distance, breaking the haunting silence. When they reached the edge of town, the road narrowed and the forest thickened. Ethan checked the GPS.

"Take the left up ahead," he said, pointing to a turnoff. "It circles around and bypasses Mary Murphy's house. Don't wanna risk her hearing us." They drove another five minutes, then Ethan spotted Wellington's driveway mostly hidden in the underbrush. Motioning to the dirt road down to the reservoir, Ethan said, "I'll unhook the chain. Drive the car a little ways down, and hide it in the bushes."

When they regrouped, he handed David the small two-chip digital camera Mindy had brought to Boston and quickly scanned through the still pictures David had shot on their survey then put his phone into a backpack. "Can't get through the gate. It's locked," he said, whispering. "Let's walk around the property and see if there's a hole in the fence." He checked his watch—one o'clock. "We've got an hour. Then we're outta here."

They quickly picked their way through the underbrush, Ethan eyeballing every square inch of the eight-foot-tall chain-link fence, until he found what he was looking for. "This way. There's a gap over here," he said as he slipped through the opening onto Wellington's property. David followed, and they crept down a narrow footpath covered in pine needles until it broke into a clearing. Ethan gazed across the meadow to where Wellington's house stood like a fortress backlit by the moonlight. "Start shooting," he said, pointing at the structure. "I want pictures of everything we see tonight."

David began rolling as they passed Heather's grave site, grabbing a shot of the yellow police tape, still visible, even now, two years after the murder. He knelt on one knee and panned across the meadow then made a point-of-view shot of the path where the sheriff had picked up the blood trail. When they reached the porch at the back of the house, he stopped and focused a big, wide shot, capturing the turrets and gargoyles, then followed Ethan as he went up the steps to the back door.

"What are we looking for?" David said, pausing to check the video on the tiny screen on top of the camera. It was dark and grainy but would clean up nicely in the editing room.

"I'll know when I see it," Ethan said as he rattled the door. "Wellington must've used surgical knives and saws to cut through the bones when he mutilated Heather's body, so he must've had a place to do it. It makes no sense that the sheriff couldn't find the kill site."

"Is it locked?"

"Won't budge."

"Now what?" David said, adjusting the camera settings and shooting Ethan checking the windows then hopping off the porch and heading around the side of the house, pausing to frame a shot as Ethan began searching the overgrown flower beds.

"What are you doing?" David said, alarmed, as Ethan picked up a small rock.

"I'm gonna break a window so we can get in."

"What if Mary Murphy hears and calls the cops?"

"Stop worrying. She won't hear us, and I'll make sure we're in and out of here quickly." He dropped into a window well and heaved the rock through the glass with a crash then unhooked the latch and slipped into the basement. David handed him the camera and jumped into the darkness.

"This is crazy, Ethan. We're gonna get caught."

Ethan ignored him, pulled a small flashlight out of his back-pack, and strafed the room with a beam of light. It was twenty feet square, covered in cobwebs, with old furniture hidden underneath soiled bedsheets and rotting wooden crates stacked from the floor to the ceiling. In the center of each wall, there was a massive oak door. Ethan opened the first one and peered into a small empty room. He tried the second—another empty room. Then the third, where he found a stairwell leading up to the main floor.

"This way," he said, "and keep rolling." He climbed the steps two at a time and pushed into a large country kitchen, David right behind him, following the beam of the flashlight with the camera.

They passed through the kitchen and into the mud room.

"Here's the door to the back porch where Davenport brought us in," Ethan said. The flashlight moved back and forth in a steady arc as they went up the staircase and stopped at a landing. "Time check, David."

"One twenty-five."

"Let's keep moving."

They crept down the winding hallway, past the dusty furniture and water stains dripping down the walls, and into the master bedroom—stopping to shoot the dried blood on the carpeting. The furniture was still overturned and the duvet cover still bunched at the foot of the bed. David grabbed Ethan's shoulder.

"We've already seen this. Why are we up here?"

Ethan didn't respond, continuing to wander around the room, then said, "Okay, back downstairs."

They retraced their steps—along the littered hallway, down the creaky staircase, through the kitchen with dirty dishes in the sink and mouse droppings on the counters, and back into the basement—David rolling a series of images each step of the way. Ethan opened the two oak doors again and checked the empty rooms, carefully running his flashlight up and down the walls, across the ceiling, and along the floorboards.

Nothing.

A dead end.

What was he missing?

He circled the basement, lifting the sheets off the furniture, poking around the stacks of wooden crates, crawling on his hands and knees, looking for anything out of the norm. He stood, puzzled, then fixed his eyes on the fourth and last door.

"Ethan, it's two o'clock. Let's get the hell outta here."

"Give me a second," he said, walking over and twisting the knob. Locked. Why was that? All the other doors were open. Taking a step back, he raised his foot and kicked as hard as he could. The frame splintered, but the door didn't budge.

He kicked again, harder, and this time, the frame shattered and the door flew open with a bang—revealing a small landing and another set of stairs leading down to a subbasement. "Now, what do we have here?" he said, smiling at David.

"Are you gonna go down?"

"I'm game if you're game," he said, swiping with his hands to clear a path through the cobwebs and slowly descending a narrow staircase that spilled into a room filled with thousands of books.

"What the fuck? A library?" David said, astonished, as he walked behind Ethan, his eyes glued to the screen on his camera.

Ethan ran the light over to a cluttered desk then back to the floor-to-ceiling bookshelves. The books were mostly bound in leather, some dating back decades, all neatly arranged by subject matter. He pulled out a volume—a copy of Schwartz's *Principles of Surgery*—and skimmed through the yellowing pages. Then he dropped the book on the desk. "They're all textbooks on surgical procedures," he said, turning to David. "Many on the science of human dissection—hands, feet, eyes, skin, arteries, bones—you name it, Wellington's got it."

"Why dissection?" David said, panning his camera lens across the titles. "The guy's a heart surgeon."

"The guy's also a butcher. This is where he learned to section the human body. This is where he learned to cut up Heather."

"Two fifteen, Ethan. We're pushing our luck."

"Just a few more minutes."

David put a fresh disk into the camera and began shooting a series of medium shots, as Ethan moved about the room, then lowered the camera. "Think this room leads anywhere?"

"Doesn't appear to," Ethan said as he pulled out another thick volume, entitled *Shearer's Manual on Human Anatomy.* As he flipped through the pages, he abruptly stopped. There was a cutout in the middle of the book, concealing a small spiral notebook. David approached and looked over his shoulder as he thumbed through one page at a time. There were lifelike drawings of human body parts—a head, an arm, a leg, a foot—and unrecognizable notations in the margins.

"Odd, it's some kind of code."

"What does it mean?"

"I don't know, David," he said, going through the pages one last time, before slipping the spiral notebook into his coat pocket. Then he began probing the room—checking behind each book, running his hands up and down the walls, eyeballing each crevice. As he swept his hand along the top of the last bookshelf, he stumbled across what felt like a small rectangular box. Curious, he pulled over a chair, climbed up, and shone the flashlight on the object.

"What is it?" David said, focusing the camera on Ethan.

"Not sure, but it appears to house a small lever." He studied the lever then said, "Stand back, David." He pulled, and the entire wall of books slowly swung open. Ethan jumped off the chair and pointed the flashlight.

Another door.

A steel door.

"It's locked," he said as he ran his hands over the shiny surface, "and there's no knob, just a dead bolt." He tried pushing, then kicking the door several times. But it wouldn't budge. Not an inch. He took a step back and stared, wondering, "What the fuck's in there?"

"Quiet, Ethan."

"What?"

"Listen."

Off in the distance, a wail of sirens was approaching. "Shit," Ethan said, frustrated, "somebody called the cops."

"Mary Murphy?"

"Who else? Let's go. Quickly."

They retreated up the stairs, through the basement, and out of the house through the broken window, hustling across the backyard, out the hole in the fence, through the woods, and into the car. The sirens were closer. Much closer.

"Get us outta here, David. And no headlights."

"But it's pitch-black. I can't see."

"Don't care. Just drive."

They slowly pulled down the dirt road and around a bend, past Mary Murphy's house—all the lights shining brightly. David suddenly hit the brakes and stopped.

"Headlights coming our way."

"I see them, for Christ's sake, don't panic. They can't see us." Ethan leaned forward and searched the forest, straining in the darkness, then pointing. "Over there, an opening big enough for the car. Pull in and cut the engine. Hurry."

David dropped into reverse and backed in. Then they waited in silence as two patrol cars—lights flashing, sirens blaring—peeled past them and disappeared around the bend.

"That was the sheriff and Percy Wilkerson. The asshole's still in the same smashed-up Crown Vic he was driving when he tried to run me off the road," Ethan said breathlessly. "They're heading to Wellington's. We don't wanna be anywhere near here when they figure out there's been a break-in."

Ten minutes later, they were streaking down Route 202.

Away from Old Salem.

To pick up Ethan's car.

And make their way back to New York.

CHAPTER 25

ETHAN UNLOCKED HIS FRONT DOOR and slipped into his apartment—hungry, tired, and emotionally drained after driving all night. He tossed his backpack on the floor in the foyer and made his way down to the bedroom, looking for Sarah. She was sitting in a Queen Anne chair, a cup of coffee untouched on a side table, an unread book sitting in her lap. She stood and slowly walked across the room, reaching for his hand, kissing him on the lips. Then she backed away and stared at the mess on his forehead.

"Ouch. Looks painful," she said, gently probing the skin around the wound.

"Hurts, but feels better than yesterday," he said, dropping his suitcase at the foot of the bed. "Where's Luke?"

"I dropped him at his friend Henry's. Thought we needed time to talk uninterrupted and alone," she said, withdrawing and sitting back down, her mood suddenly growing sullen. "I'm at the end, Ethan. I can't take it anymore—your disappearing on the road, your recklessness, your shutting me out, and your lying about your drinking. I don't want to live this way anymore."

Ethan began to protest but then stopped, not knowing how to respond.

"You have nothing to say?"

"Babe, you know I love you."

"And I love you too," she said, her voice flat. "But there's a void in our lives, and it's growing into a chasm."

"I'm trying, Sarah," he said, now desperate.

"So why did you walk out on me at Dr. Schwartz's?"

"You know why. Did you tell him?"

She nodded.

"So he knows about the baby."

A tear dripped down her cheek. "But he doesn't understand why you won't talk about it. Or why it's making you drink."

"But—"

"No more buts, Ethan."

He sat on the end of the bed and stared blankly, his mind torn by conflicting emotions.

"I tried to explain about the baby," she said, "but he wants to hear it from you."

"Sarah, please," he said, begging, "it's just too hard. I can't face talking to him about it."

"Like you can't face talking to me?"

"That's not fair."

"No. But it's the truth. Do you talk to Mindy about it?"

"What?"

"You certainly spend enough time with her."

"This is insane, Sarah."

"Are you having an affair with her?"

Ethan turned ashen gray. "What are you talking about?"

"Tell me."

"Of course not. I'm in love with you."

"Well, I wonder about the two of you. Always together. Alone on the road." She stood and faced the window overlooking

Ninety-First Street, her back to Ethan. "So are you going to see Dr. Schwartz with me?"

"Sarah, please—"

"You've got to tell him. It's the only way."

"But—"

"Otherwise, I'm gonna take Luke and leave you."

Ethan hurried into his office at the Broadcast Center, reeling from his conversation with Sarah. He hadn't showered, shaved, or changed his clothes, needing to get out of his apartment—and away from everything Sarah had just told him. He felt alone and scared. He unlocked the door and flipped on the lights, maneuvering around the stacks of boxes, settling into the big leather chair, and reaching for the pint bottle of Black Label hidden in his desk. He took a healthy swig, dulling the pain, then reached for his briefcase.

Work.

He'd bury himself in his story.

It would help him forget.

Shuffling through the contents, he grabbed the spiral notebook and opened it to the first page. The detailed drawing he'd first seen in Wellington's library was a woman's head—sketched with great precision, the eyes, nose, and mouth highlighted down to the last detail. He looked at the notations in the margins. Other than a handful of meaningless medical terms, there was little else he could make out. But at the top of the page, there was a handwritten number: "5-7-9-1."

He looked at it, puzzled.

What did it mean?

He flipped through the rest of the notebook—twenty-two pages—all numbered and containing lifelike sketches of random female body parts, marked with the same cryptic scribblings.

What in God's name did it mean?

Ethan put the notebook back into his briefcase and flipped on his computer. As he waited for it to boot up, his iPhone pinged. A text from Lloyd.

"Was this the girl who handed you the telephone number at The House of Hope?"

He opened the attachment and stared at the JPEG. The girl's face was bruised and disfigured from the rats, but there was no mistaking the jagged scar that ran down her cheek.

Sylvia Anderson.

It was definitely her.

Shaken, he took another pull on the Scotch and punched in Lloyd's number. "It's the girl. Have the cops identified the killer?"

"Homicide guys don't have anything solid yet."

"Did they speak to Janice O'Brien?"

"They're bringing her in this afternoon for questioning," Lloyd said. "All they know is that Anderson lived at The House of Hope."

"Is O'Brien a suspect?"

"Person of interest, but not at the top of their list. They're pulling her telephone records and credit card receipts, hoping to track her movements the past couple of days."

"Can you get a copy from your sources?"

"I'll see what I can do."

"Thanks, Lloyd. You're a hell of a PI."

"No, I'm just a cop at heart."

Ethan hung up then stared at the photo of the dead girl. After clicking off the image and dropping his cell phone, he buried his face in his hands and started to sob. All the emotions he'd hidden deep inside were rushing through him like a freight train. The drinking. His career. Sarah. And the baby. It was the baby all over again. He'd killed the girl. His fault. Grabbing the bottle, he drained it, then wiped his mouth on his sleeve.

He stood and paced the room.

His head pounding.

The sutures on his forehead on fire.

"You're falling apart, Ethan," he thought out loud. "Get a grip on yourself." He wiped away the tears and calmed his breathing. "Gotta work. Gotta work," he repeated those words over and over like a mantra. Then he spotted the crime scene video from Lauren Saperstein sitting on the corner of his desk.

He grabbed the disk and loaded it into his computer then hit *Play*. A grainy image of the meadow, lit by huge flood lamps, rolled across the screen. A half dozen sheriff's deputies came and went in the foreground as crime scene investigators in white protective clothing sifted through the grave site. The camera zoomed in just as a deputy turned away and retched up what was left of his dinner. Then the camera bounced uncontrollably, the image flaring as the electronics adjusted to the flood lamps then settled on a tight shot of a CSI in latex gloves picking up a severed leg covered in flakes of dirt and crusted blood. Panning, the camera followed the CSI as he placed the leg in a clear evidence bag, lining it up next to a row of other body parts. After momentarily losing focus, the operator found the right exposure and zoomed into a tight shot of Heather's foot then slowly tipped the camera from one body part to the next—a finger, a forearm, an ankle, a mutilated breast. Ethan paused the video and wiped his brow. He'd have to make magic in the edit room if he used the sequence in his story.

He thought about Sylvia Anderson.

Then pushed her to the back of his mind.

Keep working.

He racked back the video and rescreened it from the top, this time taking notes on his iPad as he carefully studied each shot. When he was nearly at the end, the camera panned over to Sheriff McKenzie huddled next to Rufus Wellington a short distance from the grave site. The sheriff was rubbing his back and whispering in his ear, Wellington smiling and nodding in affirmation. Ethan rolled back, adjusted the sound levels, and listened again. But the sound was too distorted, and he couldn't make out what they were saying. Pulling the disk, he headed down to the screening room next to Paul's office, where there was a better sound mixing board. After powering up the Avid Pro Tools audio deck, he inserted the disk, boosted the voice levels, and softened the background sound, then hit *Play*. The sheriff was still muffled, but Ethan could hear snatches of the conversation. He wrote it down on his iPad:

> Rufus, I —— couldn't ignore a 911 call. Everyone heard —— the dispatcher —— my deputies —— bad —— real bad —— called Bret —— gonna meet us —— said —— don't utter a word —— figure it out.

Ethan paused the video and reread the passage, underlining, "I —— couldn't ignore the 911 call." What the hell did that mean? Had McKenzie buried other 911 calls involving Rufus Wellington? And why did he call Davenport? It wasn't his job to call a defense attorney, was it? More proof they were all working together. He made a mental note to keep digging and pulled out the disk as his cell phone pinged—a text from Sarah:

"Are you coming home? You haven't seen Luke in a week. He wants to know where you are. Call me."

Shit. It was eight o'clock.

He'd forgotten about Sunday dinner.

He needed to go home, see his son, and face the music with Sarah.

⁓

Ethan climbed off the bus and headed down the block to his building. He waved hello to Winston the doorman without stopping, hurried through the lobby, and took the elevator up to his apartment. When he opened the door, Luke flew into his arms.

"Dad, you're home! Finally!" Then Luke noticed the cut on his forehead. "What happened to your face?"

Ethan put Luke on the floor and knelt down across from him. "Daddy got into a fight with some very bad people."

"Does it hurt?"

"A little."

"Did you beat up the bad guys?"

"Something like that, kiddo. Where's Mom?"

"You missed dinner, Dad. Mom left a plate in the oven."

"Where is she?"

"In bed, reading."

"Is she mad at me?"

"A little."

"Shall we go say hello to her?"

"Not me. I already said hello today, and the commercial's gonna be over soon. Gotta go back and watch my TV show." He dashed down the hallway and into the living room, Holly trailing faithfully behind him.

Ethan braced himself and headed to the bedroom.

Sarah was lying on a comforter, dressed in a bathrobe. She didn't say a word, her mood cold and distant. Ethan bent over and kissed the top of her head.

"Still mad?"

"What do you think?"

"You didn't really mean what you said this morning."

"I don't know what I mean anymore, Ethan. Will you talk to Dr. Schwartz?"

"Let's not fight about this again," he said, sitting on the edge of the bed.

"Will you do it, for me?" she said, her voice pleading.

Ethan looked into her eyes, once again wracked by insecurity and self-doubt. Standing, he kissed her again, walked out of the room without answering, and headed to read Luke a bedtime story.

After eating dinner alone, Ethan retrieved his briefcase and headed to his study. He cleared a space for his laptop, walked to the wet bar, and poured a glass of Black Label. Then he sat down and began making a list of people he was planning to interview for his story. At the very top was Rufus Wellington. Then—in no particular order—Bret Davenport, Eugene McKenzie, Janice O'Brien, Lauren Saperstein, Dr. Jerome Hosenfeld, and Mary Murphy. He looked at the list—too many characters for a fifteen-minute segment. Was the story worth more airtime? Maybe. He'd have to think about that.

He roughed out a shooting budget and began preparing a production schedule. He decided to split the field work into three trips—one to the Quabbin, one to Boston, and the last one to the state prison in Cedar Junction to interview Wellington. He'd let Mindy shoot Boston, and he'd produce everything else. That would give him plenty of time to write a script, launch the edit, and work with Peter on his other projects.

Satisfied, he attached the documents to an e-mail, wrote Paul a quick message explaining his thinking, copied Peter, Mindy, and David, and fired it off. Then he lifted the Scotch to his mouth and stopped. No more. I've had enough today. Shutting his eyes, he placed the glass on his desk and tried to concentrate. There was a long list of unread messages. One marked urgent from Mindy that had just landed in his mailbox:

"Spent the last hour going through the autopsy report. You need to read it. VERY important."

Lauren Saperstein had also said it was important at their meeting. But why?

He searched through several stacks of documents scattered on the floor, found the folder, sat back down at his desk, and pulled out a handful of photos. The top one was a tight shot of Heather's face. Her hair had been slicked back, and what was left of her skin had been washed of all the dirt and debris. Wellington had surgically removed her teeth and sliced off her nose, ears, lips, and eyelids. Her right eye appeared fixed and dead to the world, and her left eye had been gouged out, leaving a glutinous black hole. Ethan felt his insides tighten then flipped through the rest of the photos—all as disturbing as the first one. He turned them facedown on his desk and noticed a handwritten note from the ADA attached to the front page of the report:

> Read page 4. The coroner says Wellington injected Heather with a powerful anesthetic

called Vecuronium, which brings on paralysis but keeps a patient fully awake. He says she was probably alive and aware of everything he was doing when he cut her into pieces.

Ethan read the passage several times. The guy was more than a monster. He was the devil incarnate. After taking one final peek at the pictures and leafing through the rest of the report, he locked everything in his desk so Luke wouldn't find it then poured his Scotch down the drain in the wet bar, pleased he'd controlled the craving, and headed to the bedroom—stripping out of his clothes and climbing into bed next to Sarah.

She rustled under the covers.

"I don't want you sleeping in here tonight."

"But I didn't drink anything."

"That's not the point. You know what you need to do. Just leave."

CHAPTER 26

ETHAN BLINKED AT THE CLOCK. It was 6:00 a.m. and still dark. Where was he? Where was Sarah? Then he remembered. They'd argued; she'd kicked him out of the bedroom; and he was in his study, sleeping on the couch, still in the same clothes from the day before. He sat up and swung his feet onto the floor, wasted. He grabbed a cigarette, looked at the bottle of Black Label, then quietly slipped out of the room, past Luke's bedroom—Holly following him down the hall with her eyes—and into his bedroom. Staring long and hard at Sarah, he wondered if they'd ever patch their lives back together—or if it was already too late—then headed to the bathroom and stripped out of his clothes. After splashing cold water on his face, he looked in the mirror. The gash on his forehead was beginning to heal, but the wound was still raw and angry. He'd have a scar—a reminder of his night on the town with the hookers and the pimp and the blackjack.

He quickly shaved and showered and put on a bandage, then dressed and made his way down to the kitchen, where he brewed a pot of coffee and checked his e-mail. Another message from Mindy:

"Talked to Althea Oliphant. Call her first thing in the morning. Only available between six and nine. Call me after."

Ethan fired back a thank-you and headed to his study—Holly following him, wagging her tail, curling up at his feet. He stroked her head then pulled out Wellington's psych report and clicked the shrink's number on his iPhone. "Dr. Oliphant. It's Ethan Benson."

"Ah, Ethan. Mindy said you were an early riser. How are you feeling? Better, I hope?"

"Getting there. This a good time to talk?"

"Yes. Give me a second to find the document." Ethan listened as she rifled through a stack of papers. "I need to preface this by saying, once again, that I only know Dr. Wellington as a colleague and never treated him. Having said that, I've spent my entire career studying people like him."

"Mindy gave me your CV, Dr. Oliphant. Quite impressive."

There was a short pause. "I think Dr. Hosenfeld made a grievous mistake in his recommendation to the court. Rufus Wellington belongs in a state institution for the criminally insane and not a state prison. He's a very sick man, delusional and psychotic."

"Care to elaborate?"

"He's the classic example of a both a sociopath and a psychopath. Dr. Wellington is a danger to himself and to everybody around him and needs to be treated by doctors in a psychiatric facility."

"That's quite different from what Hosenfeld concluded in his psych report." Ethan turned to the last page of the document. "He says, and I quote, 'I find that his psychiatric and emotional health fall within the acceptable range of sanity and believe that Dr. Wellington can be remanded by the court to a maximum security prison.' End quote. He goes on to say that Wellington knew exactly what he was doing and was fully aware of his actions when he murdered Heather Starr. Was he wrong, Dr. Oliphant?"

"Yes and no."

"That's not really an answer."

"In Dr. Wellington's case, it is."

"I still don't understand," Ethan said. "Is it because you believe he's both a sociopath and a psychopath?"

"That sums it up, Mr. Benson," she said succinctly. "Let me explain. Sociopaths are individuals who function in the social world in what appears to be a normal and acceptable pattern. To his peers, Dr. Wellington was a respected surgeon—successful and confident. In an operating room, he was fully in control of his environment, everybody around him, and of himself."

"So that's why his colleagues at Mass General were stunned by the murder," Ethan said, remembering his conversation with Jerome Rasmussen.

"Exactly. But what makes him a sociopath is that he hides his inner self from everybody around him. The real Dr. Wellington has a total disregard for other people and only cares about himself. Plus, he blames them for everything that's wrong in his life."

"A lot of people think that way."

"But in Wellington's case, he uses violence as a means to get even. He has no sense of right and wrong and enjoys hurting people."

"So when Heather Starr spurned his marriage proposal," Ethan said, "he murdered her? Just like that?"

"Yes," Dr. Oliphant said.

"And he saw nothing wrong with it?" Ethan said intensely.

"Nope."

"But from the crime scene photos and video I've screened, Dr. Wellington appeared totally out of his mind after the mur-der—a lunatic—covered in mud and blood, his clothes ripped and disheveled. That doesn't sound like a cold and calculating killer, somebody who's in control of his actions."

"It doesn't, and that's why he's also a psychopath," Dr. Oliphant said candidly. "Psychopaths exhibit many of the same behavioral traits as sociopaths, but they're also erratic, excessive risk-takers, and don't retain their cloak of respectability. When the trigger is pulled, they lose control, become explosive, violent, and deadly—without worrying about what other people might think of them."

"So that's why he appeared the way he did the night of the murder?" Ethan said, beginning to understand.

"That's one way to look at it," she said. "But there is one more thing that makes him a classic psychopath. I read in the psych report that Dr. Wellington cut Heather Starr into pieces then reassembled her body parts in her grave. That's a red flag, Ethan. Psychopaths often mutilate their victims in bizarre rituals and get great pleasure out of doing it. When you put that together with the fact that he functions in the real world as a prominent heart surgeon, it adds to my hypothetical diagnosis. Rufus Wellington is a rare combination of a psychopath and a sociopath, who shows the worst tendencies of both, and that's why he belongs in a hospital for the criminally insane and not a prison. The guy's a ticking time bomb."

Ethan sat quietly, reflecting, then said, "Can he ever be cured?"

"Probably not."

"Should he ever be released back into society?"

"Heavens, no."

"Are you aware his attorney is trying to do just that?"

"That would be a disaster."

Ethan paused then said, "I'd like you to sit down for an on-camera interview with my anchorman, Peter Sampson, and tell him what you just told me."

"I'll make the time, Mr. Benson."

"Thanks, Dr. Oliphant."

Ethan hung up and checked his watch—7:00 a.m. He had to get out of the apartment before Sarah woke up. He couldn't face another scene before heading to work. But as he started shutting down his laptop, his cell phone rang. What now? He checked the LCD screen and was startled by the caller ID. It was Ginger the hostess—from the steak house in Athol.

❧

Monica was filing documents as Ethan rushed to her desk.

"He's prepping for this week's show and doesn't want to be disturbed."

"I'm sorry, this is too important," Ethan said, pushing his way around her.

"Don't go in there—"

Ethan ignored her.

Paul looked up, startled, then waved off Monica, placed the script he was reading into a folder, and said, "What's so urgent, Ethan, that you have to barge into my office unannounced?"

"You get my e-mails?"

He picked up a printout. "Another memo, a proposed shooting schedule, and the budget for Wellington. Your story seems solid, well organized. Has something changed?"

"I've had a busy morning. This story just got really big. There's enough here to produce a full hour of programming."

Paul dropped the memos on his desk and stared at Ethan. "Is that the reason you barged in here. To tell me you need more airtime for your story?"

"Always need more airtime," Ethan said, half-joking.

"Don't I know it," Paul said. "Hold on. Lemme get Peter. He's not gonna want to hear this." He stood, walked to the door, and barked at Monica. "Call Peter, and tell him I'm meeting with Ethan and need him right away. And bring us a pot of coffee. We're gonna be here for a while."

Five minutes later, Peter arrived. "I don't have a Wellington meeting on my schedule this morning. Why am I here?" He dropped a copy of his itinerary on Paul's desk and eased onto the couch.

"Ethan's proposing we turn the story into a special edition of *The Weekly Reporter*," Paul said.

"An hour of airtime for a convicted killer?" Peter said skeptically. "What's the twist in the story I'm not seeing?"

"Did you read the new memos?"

"Was about to go through my e-mail when I got your call," he said, waving his hand dismissively.

Monica walked in with a tray of coffee and placed it on Paul's desk.

"Well, I've read everything," he said, turning to Ethan, "and didn't see anything new warranting an hour of airtime. It's a solid story—a sensational murder, with a high-profile doctor/killer, big-time payoffs to people who work for him, and a possible conspiracy and cover-up—plenty for a solid two-, maybe a three-parter, but not a full hour of programming. Not by a long shot."

Ethan leaned forward in his chair. "What if I was to tell you I have a source—a roommate of Heather Starr's at The House of Hope—who told me how Wellington was a sicko who got off torturing her while they were having sex."

"What's the girl's name?" Paul said sharply.

"Sylvia Anderson."

"Will she go on camera?"

Ethan swallowed, visibly upset. "She can't. She was murdered shortly after she talked to me."

There was silence in the room.

"What happened?" Peter said quietly.

"The cops are still investigating, but Lloyd Howard's sources are telling him all the evidence points to Janice O'Brien."

"The woman who set up Wellington and Starr?" Paul said.

Ethan nodded.

"But why would she murder the girl?"

"My theory? She was probably ordered by either Davenport or McKenzie to get rid of her to protect Wellington."

"But you can't prove that."

"No, Paul, not yet, I'm still digging."

"So we think there might've been a murder to cover up Wellington's sexual perversions with the hooker," Peter said. "Still not enough to bump the story to a special. Anything else?"

"I just talked to the girl Rufus Wellington tried to rape," Ethan said, not missing a beat.

"The girl you told us about?" Paul said.

"Her name's Ginger Morrow, and she's agreed to go on camera." Ethan waited to make sure he had their full attention then said, "She's scared but thought long and hard and decided she'd tell us everything Wellington did to her—as long as we don't use her name in our story, we distort her voice, and shoot her in shadow."

"Everything?" Peter said inquisitively.

"Everything."

"Well, that's an element I wasn't expecting," he said. "So now we have a character who'll sit down for an interview and give us a blow-by-blow of how Wellington stalked and sexually brutalized her. Now, that's good television."

"There's more," Ethan said, feeling he was close to landing his hour of airtime. "I also talked to a prominent shrink this morning—Dr. Althea Oliphant, head of the department of psychiatry at Mass General."

"Respected in the field?"

"One of the best."

"And what does she add to the story?" Peter asked.

"She says Rufus Wellington is highly unstable, a classic psychopath and sociopath—a rare combination of killer—and if the court, after hearing his appeal, puts him back on the street, he's more than likely to kill again."

"Does Wellington have a case?" Paul said ardently.

"Don't know. Neither Davenport nor the prosecutor will give me the documents. But the judge's ruling won't consider his guilt or innocence. It'll hinge solely on whether there's a problem with the chain of evidence."

"So he could get out?"

"It's definitely a possibility.

"Is there a date for the appeal?"

"Exactly two weeks to the day after our interview with Wellington."

"Well, this certainly ratchets up the story, Ethan," Paul said, turning to Peter. "I'm inclined to give him the hour. Thoughts?"

"Agreed."

"Can you make an airdate before the hearing?"

"Our interview with Wellington is next week. We'll need to shoot everything else before we go to the prison." He turned Peter, "I'm gonna move around a couple of things in your schedule."

"Not possible. You know that." Then he paused abruptly and said, "And I won't move my weekend with Rush Limbaugh in Palm Beach. I'm not gonna miss that party. Everyone's gonna be there."

⁓

"So what are you gonna do?" David wondered. "We need Sampson in the field most of the week."

Ethan had brought his team together for a scheduling meeting in the conference room on the tenth floor—away from Sampson and his bitching and moaning.

"Not sure yet."

"He's refusing to travel to the Quabbin or to Boston?" Mindy said, appalled.

"He's only agreed to make the trip to Cedar-Junction to interview Wellington, and that's not gonna work," he said, distributing copies of the production schedule. "Here's the plan. Mindy, you produce the interviews in Boston with Peter. He's gotta do all of them—the heart surgeon, the court-appointed psychiatrist, the ADA, and Dr. Oliphant from Mass General. Where do we stand with Rufus's father?"

"Still AWOL."

"Keep trying."

"What about Janice O'Brien?"

"She's not gonna play ball with us now that she's a suspect in a murder investigation," Ethan said. "We'll have to ambush her on the street. We can at least get pictures if she won't talk."

"Want me to do that one too?"

"I'll do O'Brien myself. Get Lloyd to figure out the best time to jump her." He whipped around to David, "You line up the interviews at the Quabbin. Pencil in Ginger and Mary Murphy on Tuesday. We'll do them while Peter's shooting with

Mindy in Boston. Then schedule all the pickup shots including Wellington's estate on Wednesday. See if the sheriff and his deputies will show us the crime scene. He suggested that would make a good visual. Let's take him up on his offer."

"Think he'll sit down for an interview?"

"Yeah, the guy's got a big ego," Ethan said, pointing to the schedule. "Set him up for Thursday morning and Davenport that afternoon."

"With Sampson?"

"He's gotta do both interviews. They're confrontational. And, David, we need two camera crews. So book Herb Glickstein and Bobby Raffalo. Sampson likes working with both of them."

"What about a lighting director?"

"Rudy Finch," Ethan said. "And a grip truck with extra lighting equipment."

"Rent a house for everyone in Old Salem?"

"Bingo. We'll arrive on Monday, and Consuela will book travel for Sampson from Boston to the Quabbin Wednesday evening after he's finished with Mindy. Then we'll caravan to the prison on Friday morning to interview Wellington."

"Jeez, Ethan, anything else?" Mindy said, rolling her eyes.

"One more thing," he said, turning to David, "we still don't have the confession video. I need to screen it before we start shooting. It's important."

"I'll check back with the DA's office. They keep promising to send it, but they don't."

"Well, hound Saperstein. I want that video," Ethan said, pushing his chair back from the table. "Everybody knows what to do. Now I gotta go battle with Sampson. Tell him he's got to do most of the interviews and cancel his weekend with Rush Lambaugh. Wish me luck. I'm gonna need it."

CHAPTER 27

Rufus Wellington sat motionless, strapped into the steel chair in the middle of the room, surrounded by a half dozen correction officers—a cigarette dangling from his mouth. He took a long drag, held the smoke in his lungs, and exhaled a slow stream through his nose that wafted to the ceiling, hanging there like a cloud, before vanishing into the stale air. His mind was fantasizing, hungering, obsessing—with sweet memories of that marvelous night when he'd dispatched dear Heather off to heaven. At first, the memories were short flashes, then vivid daydreams, and now a constant flow of high-speed ravings—building like a volcano, reaching a crescendo, threatening to push him over the deep end. He puffed on his cigarette, a smile on his face.

He needed his freedom.

He needed to hunt.

He needed Bret.

***

Five minutes later, the security door eased open—creaking on old, rusted tracks—and Davenport eased into the room. The first thing he noticed was his friend sitting in a trance, statuesque, as he dropped awkwardly into a chair directly in front of him. All the signs were there—his affect, his distant gaze, his body language, the lustful look in his eyes. Rufus was teetering on the edge, his time quickly approaching, his appetite building, and he knew there was no way to stop it. He turned to the warden, who was standing by the door.

"I'd like to be alone with him, Phillip."

The warden nodded and led the guards out of the room.

Davenport sighed deeply and said, "Rufus, how are you?"

No answer.

"Do you need anything?"

No answer.

"Another cigarette?"

No answer.

Davenport stood, then sat back down, impatient. "Rufus, listen to me. Ethan Benson keeps digging. He's unearthing information on you and me and Gene, and maybe even Janice. I haven't figured out a way to stop him."

He waited and, when there was no response, pushed a little harder.

"The sheriff's been tracking him all over the Quabbin. He met with Mary Murphy, but maybe I already told you that, and Janice O'Brien who played dumb, but then he talked to one of her hookers, who told him about you and Heather. He knows, Rufus. About you. About me. About all of us. I just don't know how much." Davenport paused and stared at his friend then leaned over, waved his hand in front of his face, and got no response.

Rufus watched, taking in every word. Bret was scared, terrified, of Ethan Benson. He'd always known he was weak—a coward, unable to handle pressure. Just look at him, sitting there sweating, fidgeting, his eyes twitching. *If I didn't need him, I would've gotten rid of him a long time ago. But now, he's my only link to the outside world, my only chance to take care of business and get out of this hellhole.*

"What's eating you, Bret?" he said without warning.

Davenport jumped in his seat, startled. "You were listening, Rufus?"

"I heard every word. Light me another cigarette."

Davenport fumbled with a pack of Camels, pulled out a smoke, and put it into Wellington's mouth.

"Do you have news, Bret?" he asked. "Anything to make my day a little more pleasurable?"

"We don't think you should do the interview. All of us agree. It's too dangerous."

"That certainly doesn't make me happy. Why, Bret?"

"Isn't it obvious?"

"Should it be? I don't see any risk," he said calmly.

"But he knows."

"Knows what? The specifics about Heather and the murder? I wanted him to know. I was the one who told you to set up the interview with my dear old friend, Mary Murphy, and with sweet Janice. I instructed you to give him the evidence—my confession, all those wonderful police photos, and that video of the crime scene. Ah, the video. So vivid, enlightening, so special. You did all that, right, Bret?"

"He's got everything, Rufus, except the confession video."

"Why hold that back? It's all part of what he needs to know."

"But the appeal?"

"Ah, my appeal. Don't want to hurt my appeal. Tsk. Tsk. Tsk. How about my house? Did you give him a tour of my house?"

Davenport squirmed. "Of course, and he wants to come back and tape it."

"Good. Good. He can show all the people in his audience my beautiful home in the woods—where the real Rufus Wellington comes to life. What about my secret room?" he said, relishing the thought.

"God, no. Nobody's seen the room but you and me and the sheriff."

"Maybe we should show him. That's all he's missing. Then he could tell the world the whole wonderful story." Wellington took one last pull and spit his cigarette across the room. "Light me another one, Bret. The smoke feels invigorating in my lungs. Makes me strong and powerful and ALIVE."

Davenport reared back, stunned by the evil on his friend's face, then carefully grabbed another Camel and placed it in his mouth. "Listen to me, Rufus. You can't talk to that TV show."

"You don't think I can handle Benson and his silly anchorman, Peter Sampson? You know me better than that. I hacked into Benson's computer—and you know how good I am with computers—from that little laptop I had you sneak into the prison with all the software you acquired from our special friend, the one I hide behind the loose cinder block in my cell, the one the stupid guards haven't found yet." He leered and blew another smoke ring, proud of himself. "And guess what, you're right, Bret, he knows all about you and McKenzie and everybody else in our little family. Isn't that fun? He knows. But I know something curious about him as well, something he tries to hide from everybody—something I'm sure you haven't figured out—that he may be smart in some ways, but also weak in others. VERY WEAK. Like you, Bret."

"What are you talking about, Rufus?"

"A glorious revelation I can use against him," Wellington said, the corners of his mouth drooping in a scowl. "He's a drunk. An ALCOHOLIC. There are references to his drinking in his e-mails. Subtle exchanges between Benson and his wife, the lovely Ms. Sarah. Isn't that a beautiful name? Their marriage is shaky. Very shaky. About to go poof in the wind. Now that's a tidbit I can exploit during the interview, don't you think? Just like I exploited sweet Heather in my bedroom."

"But—"

"But what, Bret?" he said tauntingly.

"What if it doesn't work, and he finds out the rest?"

"Is that what you're worried about?" Wellington strained against the restraints, his face suddenly a mask of fury. "Pull yourself together. I'm not worried about Ethan Benson or Peter Sampson. I'm more than up to the task. But the question is, are you, Bret? I'm paying you lots of money to manage Benson. Are you doing your job?"

"I've done what you've told me to do."

"Then go back, and make sure that fat fuck Eugene McKenzie and that dried-up old prune Janice O'Brien do their jobs too. Otherwise, I'll cut off the money, and after you win my appeal and I get out of here, well, you know what'll happen, and none of you will like that very much, will you, Bret?"

Davenport was silent.

"So when is my hearing?" Wellington said smoothly. "The itch is unbearable. I need my freedom."

"I'm working on it, Rufus, a couple of weeks after the interview."

"Not good enough. Work harder. I can't hold on much longer. The hunger is growing."

"But, Rufus, I can't—"

"But you can," Wellington said, rocking back and forth. "Get me the fuck out of here. And do it RIGHT AWAY!"

❧

Davenport began shaking as Rufus screamed, trying to break free. The warden, who'd been watching from the observation window, rushed in, accompanied by the heavily armed security guards.

"What did you say to him?"

"Nothing." He tried to compose himself as Wellington thrashed against the restraints. "We were just talking about the interview and the TV show," he said. "I have no idea what triggered it."

The warden looked from Davenport to Wellington and then back to Davenport. "I think he's had enough for today. I'm taking him back to his cell."

Bret nodded and stared at his friend, who had suddenly stopped struggling. "I'll be back before the interview, Rufus, so we can talk one more time," he said, trying to sound reassuring. "Is there anything I can bring you?"

"How about a woman? I could really use a beautiful woman. I could really use a little PUSSY. Can you take care of that for me, Bret? I would like that more than you can possibly IMAGINE."

CHAPTER 28

Davenport rounded the corner and headed down Main Street toward Nell's Diner. The weather was misty, a dense fog blanketing the landscape, the city a ghost town. It was four o'clock. He'd just make it if he hurried. Wrapping a scarf around his neck to ward off the chill, he hustled past Lucy's Appliances, Otto's Barber Shop, Downtown Wine and Spirits, and a half dozen boarded-up storefronts—the desolation all around him mirroring his mood.

Rufus was out of control.

Off the deep end.

And he was in trouble.

They were all in trouble.

He pushed into the restaurant. It was almost empty. Nell was standing at the grill in a white apron, reading a newspaper. She barely looked up.

"Afternoon, Bret. What can I fix you?"

"Cup of coffee. Maybe a couple pieces of dry toast. That's it."

"Like always, sugar," she said, gesturing to the back of the room. "He's in the corner booth. Been sitting there quite some time, stuffing his face." She twisted her mouth and laughed hysterically.

288

Sheriff McKenzie was hunched over the table—a double cheeseburger, a plate of home fries, coleslaw, and macaroni salad spread out in front of him. A paper napkin was tucked into his shirt, protecting his neatly starched uniform.

"Where's Janice?" Davenport said, scanning the room.

"Stuck in traffic on Highway Two. She should be here in a few minutes." He took a bite of his cheeseburger, careful not to smear grease on his fingers.

"Hear from Benson?"

"Late yesterday evening. He wants to shoot my interview on Thursday. And you?"

"Same day, in the afternoon. And what's this I hear about you and your deputies taking him to the crime scene? He told me you're going to reenact for his cameras how you searched for the kill site."

"That's the plan," McKenzie said as he continued devouring his food.

"Shit, Gene, don't you think that's a bit risky? I thought we were gonna get him in and out quickly. Keep it simple."

"Not anymore," the sheriff said, staring up from his plate, visibly irritated, "I'm givin' him the full tour. Should be good publicity for me and my boys."

"I don't like it."

"You have no choice in the matter. I'm doin' it."

Nell brought Davenport's coffee and toast, and as she placed his order on the table, the front door swung open, and Janice O'Brien walked in—wearing full makeup, a gray silk shirt, a Ralph Lauren navy-blue suit, and a matching hat and coat.

"Now, don't we look pretty," McKenzie said cynically, "and rich, very rich."

"Cut the shit, Gene," she said, sitting down next to him. She swiveled and stared at Davenport, "Why the fuck did you call a last-minute meeting? Had to blow off my afternoon and drive like hell down that fucking two-lane highway and still couldn't make it on time. Lord Jesus, you know how much I hate bein' late." Nell brought her a cup of black coffee. "What's so important it couldn't wait?" she said, sipping the hot liquid.

"Wellington. That's what. I met with him this morning," Davenport said tetchily.

"That's your job," McKenzie said, "to run when he calls. Keep the money flowing. Tell us what to do."

"Was he in his right mind? Or was he in one of his cuckoo phases?" O'Brien said truculently.

"He's dissembling," Davenport said. "He can't control his urges much longer. It's eating him alive."

"God's talking to him again," O'Brien said. "That little voice in his head is about to send him into a frenzy. What about Benson and that television show? Doesn't sound like Rufus is gonna be sane enough to talk to them."

"He's hell-bent on going through with it," Davenport said, dismayed. "I tried to reason with him, but he wants to meet Peter Sampson. Thinks he can outsmart him."

"What if we just tell him he can't do it," McKenzie said, finishing his cheeseburger and delicately wiping his mouth on his napkin. "He's in there, and we're out here. He can't get to us."

"Not at the moment," Davenport said, checking to make sure nobody was in earshot of their conversation. "But when I argue his appeal before the judge—"

"You gonna get him out?" McKenzie said cautiously.

"Looks that way, unless Rufus somehow blows it during the interview. Lauren Saperstein's freaking out that the blood DNA evidence is missing—thanks to your deputy, Percy Wilkerson. I'm gonna argue there's been a breach in the chain of evidence, and that there's no real proof Rufus is the killer, other than his confession. And I'm getting that thrown out too, saying he was under duress when he confessed and that he's now denying he had anything to do with Heather Starr's murder."

"Think it'll work?" O'Brien said.

"It'll work. I greased the judge just to make sure. Rufus is going to get out."

"Shit," she said gloomily. "So that means we have to do everything he says, or we risk facing the wrath of the monster when he back's with us."

"That's what he's threatening," Davenport said.

There was silence around the table as O'Brien pulled out a cigarette.

"You can't smoke in here," McKenzie said. "You know that."

"Fuck the law. I need a cigarette." She took a long drag and blew the smoke in his face. "So Wellington says we gotta go through with the television show. Well, I'm not gonna do the interview."

"You have to do it, Janice," Davenport said forcefully. "Wellington wants all of us to be part of his story, including you."

"Well, I'm dealing with another problem at the moment—a much bigger problem than Rufus Wellington," O'Brien said icily. "The cops are looking at me for Sylvia's murder."

"I told you to reign in the pimp, to be careful about how you got rid of that bitch and where you dumped the body," McKenzie said, enraged. "Can't you hang the murder on Lewis?"

"Sure," she said sarcastically. "Then he'll come and slit my throat before the cops have a chance to arrest him."

"The cops don't change nothin'," the sheriff said, enraged. "You still have to do the interview. I need Wellington's money. I got bills to pay. Call Benson back, and tell him you'll do it." He rubbed his chest and groaned.

"What's wrong, Gene?" she said, smirking. "Worryin' you'll lose all those nice things Wellington's paid for?"

"Cut the shit, Janice. I got heartburn."

"Enough," Davenport said. "We gotta do damage control." He turned to O'Brien, "Tell me more about the cops."

"They know Sylvia was one of my girls and wanna know what she was doin' the night she was murdered."

"And what did you tell them?"

"What do you think? I played dumb, said she was doin' real good—no tricks, no drugs—and that I had no idea what happened to her."

"Did they believe you?"

"Who the fuck knows."

"And what about Lewis? Do they know about him?" Davenport said caustically.

O'Brien smiled maniacally. "Not yet. He's a sly mother-fucker. Kinda does his thing then hangs in the shadows."

"What do you mean?"

"He helps me clean up the garbage, but he's careful, cunning, and never leaves evidence behind," O'Brien said, stubbing out her cigarette. "Cops ain't gonna connect him to the murder, and as I just said, I ain't gonna help them figure it out."

Davenport stared into her eyes contemptuously. "Do the cops know that you're working for me and Rufus?"

"Maybe."

"What do you mean, 'Maybe.'"

"Well, I may've fucked up once or twice and not used my burner when we talked."

Wellington pounded on the table. "And they pulled your phone records?"

"Probably."

"So they can connect us."

"Mor'n likely."

"Does Benson have them?"

"If he doesn't yet, he's gonna get them soon. His bodyguard friend's been hanging out with the Boston PD. You can bet your ass he's already asked for them."

"So what are we going to do, Janice?" Davenport said, ready to explode.

"I don't know about you, but if the cops keep snoopin', and I get wind they're sniffin' up my ass, then I'm gonna make my escape out of Boston before the noose tightens around my neck so I can protect you and my good friend, the sheriff here, and of course, our fearless leader, who's the reason we're all in this big mess."

"But you gotta stay and do the interview first," McKenzie said, rubbing his chest again. "Or I'm gonna go broke and lose everything."

"I don't give a shit about your money problems, Gene," O'Brien said. "Money ain't gonna do me no good if I'm rottin' in jail. I'm outta here as soon as the cops try to finger me for Sylvia's murder. I'm not goin' down for you or anyone else—even Rufus Wellington."

"Stop squabbling, both of you," Davenport said. "We can't worry about the police at the moment. Ethan Benson's about to start shooting his story. We gotta come up with a new plan, a new way to contain Rufus and handle the interviews, even you, Janice. This is what I suggest we do."

CHAPTER 29

SARAH WAS LEAFING THROUGH AN *Architectural Digest*, flipping from one page to the next, emotionally distraught, unable to concentrate. She kept peering at the clock, watching the minutes tick by—waiting, hoping, resigned to the fact Ethan wasn't coming. She dropped the magazine on the table and picked up another one, growing more agitated, more unsettled. Then she looked up, and Dr. Schwartz was standing in the door, holding his pen and paper, silently observing her.

"Sarah, where's Ethan?" he said languidly.

"At work. They've moved up his airdate."

"Is he coming?"

"I don't know, Dr. Schwartz," she said, her voice flat. "We've barely said a word since he got home from his survey. It's bad. Very bad."

"Come, Sarah. We'll talk, you and me, while we wait for Ethan."

He led her into his office, closed the blinds, flipped on a standing lamp, and sat down in the high-backed chair across from her. He waited until she composed herself then said gently, "Tell me what happened."

Sarah told him—everything—about the telephone silence while he was away in Boston, about the worried phone calls from his colleagues describing his excessive drinking, about the pimp and the beating and all the blood, and about the frantic ambulance ride to the hospital after he passed out in the psychiatrist's office. Then she broke down and cried, "He doesn't see that he's falling apart and that everyone in the office is figuring it out—all because he won't face what happened to our baby and refuses to get help, even from you, Dr. Schwartz."

"So he's carrying this great weight inside of him."

"And the drinking is making it so much worse." She wiped her eyes with the back of her hand. "He's selfish, thoughtless, irascible. It's pushing him away from me, pushing him to be reckless, to take risks that put him and everyone around him in danger."

"Like the night with the prostitutes."

"Like that night."

"Does he realize he's out of control?"

"He knows."

"Does he care?"

"I don't know, Dr. Schwartz. And that's what scares me."

"What do his colleagues see?" Dr. Schwartz said, skipping back through his notes.

"The people close to him? Everything. I got a call last week from Mindy Herman, his associate producer on the Wellington story."

"Ethan has told me about Ms. Herman."

Sarah wiped her eyes again. "She said he'd been drinking before they confronted the hookers—maybe not a lot, but enough to compromise his judgment and to contribute to what happened. Then the next morning, before he landed in the hospital, she said there was a half-empty bottle of Black Label in his hotel room and that he reeked of Scotch. He tried to hide it when she confronted him, to make excuses, but she knew—everybody knew—even the doctors in the emergency room."

"Did you ask him about it?"

"The moment he got home," she said, angry.

"And?"

"He was in complete denial. Said things weren't that bad. That Mindy must've exaggerated when she called." Sarah grabbed a tissue and wiped her nose. "God, I was so angry I accused him of having an affair with her."

"Is he?"

"Of course not. I just wanted to make him feel bad. It was childish."

"What about Luke? Does he know there's something wrong?"

"He knows Daddy likes Scotch. There's always a glass in Ethan's hand when he's reading Luke a bedtime story. So he thinks that's normal, that you drink when you're having fun."

"Do you tell Luke that's not normal?"

"I try, but he's only six, and he loves Ethan."

"Is he aware anything else is wrong?"

"He saw the gash on Ethan's forehead when he got home from the Quabbin, knows he got into a fight, but he can't process that it's because Daddy drinks too much."

"This could lead to big problems down the road."

"I know. But I can't get Ethan to understand what he's doing to Luke."

"Sarah, this is a difficult question," Dr. Schwartz said, placing the pen and paper in his lap. "Does Luke know about the baby?"

"He's old enough to know," Sarah said, crestfallen. "But Ethan forbids it."

"Why?"

"You'll have to ask Ethan—if he ever shows up—because I don't understand myself what's running through his head."

"Does Ethan know you told me?"

"I told him we talked, the day he got home."

"And what happened?"

"He got hostile and withdrawn," she said, shuddering. "We argued, and I threw him out of the bedroom, made him sleep on the couch in his office." Sarah paused uneasily then said, "And I told him if he didn't stop drinking, I was going to leave him."

"Did you mean it?"

"I was trying to shock him."

"Any attempt at reconciliation?"

"No. We haven't seen each other. He's been leaving for work before I get up and getting home long after I'm asleep. So it's been work, work, work. Hide from Sarah. Hide from his problems—"

"I'm not hiding anymore. I'm here."

~∘≈

Ethan shut the door as he walked into the room and sat down beside Sarah. He'd spent the morning closeted in his office, surrounded by the boxes he still hadn't unpacked—watching the clock, knowing he was at a turning point. As the minutes washed by, he'd grown despondent, torn between guarding his secret and his love for his wife. Then he'd made the decision and dashed out of his office, leaving his story and Peter Sampson and his myriad of producers to fend for themselves.

"I know I'm late," he said apologetically.

"Our session is just about over, Ethan."

"Can we stay a bit longer?" He looked at Sarah propitiously. "I need to clear the air, Dr. Schwartz."

"We can do a double session."

297

Ethan kept his eyes locked on Sarah, "I'm out of control, babe. I'm an alcoholic. And I want to stop."

"I know," she said sanguinely. "But I'm not sure you ever will."

Dr. Schwartz waited a moment then said, "Why, Ethan? Why do you want to stop, now?"

"Because I don't want to lose Sarah, or Luke, or my family, and that's where we're headed."

"So you understand the consequences."

"Yes."

"And you're ready to face your drinking?"

"Yes."

"So why don't you just stop?"

"I can't."

"Progress," Dr. Schwartz said, encouraged. "Are you ready to tell me the reason, beyond everything we've already discussed?"

He dipped his eyes. "Sarah told you why."

"I want to hear it from you."

"About the baby."

"What about the baby?"

"It's hard."

"What's hard?"

"Just is."

"Explain, Ethan."

Ethan stood, paced around the room, then stared aimlessly at the crowds parading through the sheep meadow in Central Park, before sitting back down. He looked up at Dr. Schwartz. "Because I haven't told Sarah the whole truth about that night."

"What are you afraid to tell me, Ethan?" she said pleadingly. "What are you hiding?"

Ethan lit a cigarette, his hands shaking. "What I really did."

"Tell me."

His face grew taut, drawn. "I remember like it was yesterday. You were trying to reach me. My cell phone kept ringing over and over in the edit room." He paused, collecting his thoughts. "My editor knew it was you, knew the baby was due soon, and suggested that after the third or fourth call, I check in—make sure you were okay. But I didn't listen to him. I was too damn busy rewriting script, tinkering with pictures, trying to make a deadline. I laughed each time the phone rang, made a joke about being henpecked, actually turned off my phone so I wouldn't be bothered."

Sarah stared, listening.

"Go on, Ethan," Dr. Schwartz said patiently.

"When I got home, you were sitting there on the floor in our living room—in all that blood—rocking back and forth, cradling our dead baby in your arms, nearly catatonic. And I didn't know what to do, what to say." He tried catching his breath. "But the full implication of my actions rushed through me with a vengeance. If only I'd answered your calls, listened to your pleas for help, maybe our baby girl would have lived and our lives would have been so different." His voice dropped to a whisper, "Instead, Sarah, my selfishness—my obsession with my story, my job, my career, my self-importance—killed our little girl. She's dead. And it's all because of me."

"Why have you never told me?" Sarah said heavily.

"I was too ashamed."

"And you started drinking after the baby's death to smother your shame?" Dr. Schwartz said.

"That was the catalyst."

"Then what happened?"

"The shame turned into guilt and then into other problems."

"Like what, Ethan?"

"Insecurity."

"And?"

"Anxiety."

"What else?"

"Failure. That I wasn't there for Sarah. That I'm never there for Luke."

"So the death of your baby has spilled over into the way you perceive the rest of your life," Dr. Schwartz said, delving deeper.

Ethan nodded painfully.

"And the real reason you feel insecure around Peter Sampson."

"Yes."

"And Paul Lang."

"Yes."

"And why you take so many risks? The hit man on your last story? The pimp on your new story? To show everyone—and yourself—that you're brave, confident, and not a failure."

Ethan lowered his eyes.

"Sarah, is this what you see in Ethan?"

"Yes." She clutched his hand. "You drink, Ethan, because you don't like yourself, because you think you should be a better husband, a better father to Luke, a better man. But, Ethan, you are those things and much, much more. You need to move on. You need to forgive yourself for what happened that night. I forgave you a long time ago."

"Can you do that, Ethan?" Dr. Schwartz said.

"I don't know, Dr. Schwartz." He closed his eyes. "All I see are my flaws and failures."

"Everybody has flaws and failures—me, Peter Sampson, Paul Lang, Sarah, and you, Ethan. But most of us go through life accepting this. We balance the negatives by enjoying the positives—the beauty, happiness, success, and love that are all part of life. You have all those things, Ethan, and always have. You can't change what you did that night. It's time to move forward and accept the fact the baby is gone."

He looked at his watch.

"I know you have a busy week ahead of you, Ethan, but talk to Sarah. Don't shut her out. And, Sarah, be patient with Ethan. He's an alcoholic. And he's not gonna get better overnight."

CHAPTER 30

Janice O'Brien got back to The House of Hope as Ethan was finishing his session with the psychiatrist. She parked her minivan out front, opened her purse, and ogled the envelope Bret Davenport had slipped her upon leaving Nell's Diner.

"Another twenty-five thousand big ones from good old Rufus to keep my mouth shut and play his killing game."

She placed the envelope back in her purse, climbed out of the car, and stared at the unmarked police car sitting a couple of hundred feet down the block, two detectives watching from the front seat, drinking coffee and smoking cigarettes.

Shit, the net is tightening.

The twenty-five thousand would give her a quarter of a million in cash, coupled with the million she'd stashed away in an offshore bank account—more than enough to live in style in some out-of-the-way paradise where the police couldn't find her.

Maybe Rio or Buenos Aires or the Caribbean.

Walking through the rusty gate and up the broken-down steps, she walked into the foyer, ignoring the girls lounging in the parlor watching TV, and headed to her bedroom. She locked the door and went to her dresser, flipping over the top drawer and removing a key taped to the bottom. Then she walked to her closet, pushed a rack of clothes to the side, knelt, and peeled up the carpeting, uncovering a floor safe. After inserting the key, she pulled open the door and stared at the rows of cash.

Pulling one stack out after another, she carried them over to her dresser and added the twenty-five thousand from her purse. Then she grabbed a tote bag from under the bed and ran her hand along an inside seam, carefully searching until she found the false bottom. She placed the cash into the secret compartment, walked back to the safe, and reached for a leather pouch containing a fake passport and fake credit cards she'd purchased on the black market. Then she grabbed her burner and dialed United Airlines.

Which city? Which city? Which city?

When a customer service rep finally answered, there was no hesitation.

"When's your next flight to Rio?" She waited then used her new identity. "My name is Susan Lutz. That's right. Susan Lutz." She waited again. "Tonight at midnight? Perfect. Book me a seat in first class."

After paying with a fake American Express Card, she said good-bye and peered at her watch. Two o'clock. Plenty of time to get ready. Then she crossed the room, pulled a suitcase from the closet, and began to pack. Soon she'd be living the good life in a faraway place with a new name and new papers, where nobody could find her—even Rufus, if the court set him free.

"Ah, good food. Good liquor. And good sex." She smiled. "I'm still young, pretty, and very rich. There'll be lots of men who'll desire me."

Lloyd peered through his binoculars as O'Brien got out of her minivan, looked up and down the street, and walked into The House of Hope. He was parked down the block in his white surveillance van disguised with false logos on both sides announcing that he worked as a lineman for the Dorchester Electric Company. He waited for the front door to close then picked up his cell phone and called Ethan.

"She just got here. Boston PDs been tracking her all day."

"Where was she?"

"Back and forth to Athol. Been there every day this week."

"With Davenport?"

"And McKenzie."

"So now we can place them all together," Ethan said, letting out a deep sigh. "Are they going to bust her soon?"

"Cops are talking to the DA and waiting for an arrest warrant."

"Did they match DNA or fingerprints?"

"Nothin' in the NCIC database."

"So they can't link her directly to the murder."

"No."

"And they don't know who actually killed Sylvia Anderson?"

"Not yet," Lloyd said, continuing to look through the binoculars as O'Brien skulked around her bedroom. "They're hoping to squeeze her and get a name once they bring her in."

"How much time do I have?"

"You better get your ass up here on the next flight if you still want to get her on camera. The door's gonna shut tight once they bust her."

Ethan cursed and immediately called Mindy, "Get David, and come up to the eleventh floor."

"I'm on the phone with Dr. Oliphant, going over logistics for her interview."

"Call her back." He hung up and began packing his briefcase.

Five minutes later, Mindy and David sat down across from him.

"Jeez, Ethan, what gives? I just blew off the shrink. She can't talk to me again until tomorrow morning. She's booked solid until then."

"Couldn't be helped. Just talked to Lloyd. The cops are about to bust Janice O'Brien. We have to get to her first."

"Where you gonna jump her?" she said.

"Outside The House of Hope." He looked from David to Mindy. "You know the drill. Mindy, book me a crew, somebody who's good at shotgun interviews. And, David, call me a car, find me a hotel, and make me a reservation on the shuttle. I'll stop at my apartment and pack then head to the airport. Now do it."

They nodded and hurried out as Ethan grabbed his sports coat and called to Consuela, "Is Peter in his office?"

"Nope. He's at lunch."

"Figures. Tell him I'll brief him when I get to Boston."

"Peter's gonna freak. You have wall-to-wall meetings this afternoon, including a pre-edit with Martin Humphrey to go over the fixes for the Jennifer Lawrence story. Peter specifically told you he wanted you there."

"Reschedule it. I'll call you once I know what I'm doing." On the way to the elevators, he left a message for Sarah then called Monica, "Is he there? I need to talk to him about the Wellington story."

Four hours later, Ethan was sitting in the back of a Chevy Suburban, surrounded by camera equipment, as it pulled to the curb a block from Lloyd's surveillance van. Mindy had booked a crew out of Worcester—a shooter named Hugh Jeremiah and a soundman named Jake Watson. He tapped Jeremiah on the shoulder, told him to sit tight, and slipped out the door. Then he slowly walked down the street, ducking behind parked cars, until he reached the van and climbed into the passenger seat. Lloyd was kneeling in the back, adjusting a camera propped on a tripod that was shooting a wide shot of The House of Hope through a window camouflaged with a black mesh curtain.

"Has she made you?" Ethan said, crouching below the window.

"Don't think so. She hasn't come out since she got back, but I've been watching her pack her bags through the lens of my camera. The cops just got an arrest warrant, so they're gettin' ready to go in. I'm glad you're here. Can't hold them off much longer."

"Where are they?" Ethan said, scanning the neighborhood. "I don't see them anywhere."

"Unmarked car a half block in front of us," he said, gesturing, "another about a block behind, and at least a half dozen patrol cars on the side streets."

"Are they gonna work with us?"

"The head of homicide is an old friend of mine," Lloyd said, "so I called in a marker. He'll try to wait until you get your interview before they take her down."

The front door of The House of Hope opened, and Janice O'Brien—dressed in a gray Armani suit, a black cashmere overcoat, and high-heel shoes—slipped out and headed down the front walk, pulling a large suitcase and carrying the tote bag filled with the cash. She stopped at the front gate and nervously looked up and down the block then turned left and headed toward her minivan. Ethan was hunched in the backseat of the Suburban with his crew.

"Not yet," he said as she walked by Lloyd's surveillance van and stopped one last time to check her surroundings. "Now!" he screamed. "Go. Go. Go!"

The doors flew open, and they spilled out, hurtling toward O'Brien. Ethan was clutching a microphone and shoved it into her face, as Jeremiah circled with a small digital camera mounted on a shoulder harness.

"Ms. O'Brien, Ms. O'Brien, it's Ethan Benson with *The Weekly Reporter*. We met a couple of weeks ago. I'd like to ask you about Heather Starr and Rufus Wellington."

Looking horrified, she shoved her hand in front of the lens and tried to push it away, slowed by her suitcase and the heavy tote bag banging at her side. "I have no comment, Mr. Benson. I changed my mind and don't want to be interviewed." She shoved the camera aside and kept walking—Jeremiah continuing to circle, Watson adjusting the sound levels, as she reached for the driver's door of her minivan.

Ethan stepped in front of her, blocking her path, firing one question after another, "Did you set up Heather Starr on a date with Dr. Wellington?"

"No," she said, shouting.

"Were you prostituting her?"

"Get out of my way."

"Did Wellington pay you for her services?"

"I have no comment."

"Are you working for his attorney, Bret Davenport?"

She stared into the camera but didn't say a word, then let go of the suitcase, and pulled open the door of her minivan, clutching the tote bag with the money, hanging on for dear life.

Ethan continued to ask questions as she fumbled with the car keys, "Ms. O'Brien, what are you hiding?" he said, pushing relentlessly.

"Get that fucking camera out of my face. I have nothing to say to you," she screamed.

"Did you kill Sylvia Anderson because she talked to me?"

O'Brien stopped dead in her tracks and glared at Ethan, stunned into silence.

"She told me you pimped Heather Starr to Dr. Wellington," he said, not missing a beat. "Is that the truth?"

"It's a lie."

"Is that why you killed her?"

"No. No. No."

"Is that why you had your goon try to kill me, to get me to back off my story?"

"No more questions," she said, lunging forward, trying to scratch his face as a half-dozen police cars screeched to a halt and surrounded them.

Pedaling backward, Jeremiah widened the shot and focused on the cops as they wrestled O'Brien to the ground.

"That's mine," she said, clutching her tote bag. "My money. I earned it." Then she turned to Ethan, straining her neck, "You cost me everything, you bastard. So watch your ass, Benson. You slipped through my fingers, but you can't escape Rufus. He's gonna get you when he gets out. You know too much." She laughed crazily, "That's why I was runnin', not from the cops, but from Rufus, 'cause he always gets what he wants. And now he wants you."

Then a detective slapped on handcuffs and pushed her into the back of a patrol car.

"What did she mean, 'Rufus wants you'?" Lloyd said, walking up to Ethan.

"It was a threat to back off," Ethan said unfazed, "and the reason she came after me and killed Sylvia Anderson."

"But why does he want you now?"

"Because I'm getting too close to the truth."

CHAPTER 31

In his nightmare, a wraith dressed in black chased him down a dimly lit side street lined with prostitutes laughing hysterically as he tore by buck naked, running for his life. Janice O'Brien suddenly floated in front of him, pointing a long crooked finger in his face, threatening to kill him. She was about to plunge a six-inch kitchen knife into his chest when his iPhone pinged. He sat up, drenched in cold sweat, the bedcovers bunched at his feet.

His dream seemed so real.

O'Brien's warning must've really gotten to him.

He grabbed his cell phone, but it stopped ringing.

Who called?

Lloyd.

He fumbled for his watch. Shit. Almost ten o'clock. He was late again. Then he dialed Lloyd back. "Sorry I missed your call," he said, his voice raspy.

"Sounds like you had a wild party when you got back to your room."

Ethan reached past the bottle of Scotch for the bottle of Motrin. Why had he gotten drunk? He'd just been to the shrink. He'd just had a heart-to-heart with Sarah, told her the truth about the baby. Why couldn't he control his drinking—not even for one night?

"What's the latest on O'Brien?"

"She lawyered up," Lloyd said. "Won't talk to the cops."

"Do they have enough to hold her?" Ethan said, lighting a cigarette.

"Yeah. She was carrying a fake passport. Definitely about to run."

"What about bail?"

"No bail. She had more than a quarter of a million in cash stashed away in that tote bag she was carrying."

"From Wellington?"

"That's my guess," Lloyd said. "They're trying to track the money trail but may only find out for sure if she tells them."

"Anything else?"

"My source gave me her phone records."

"And?"

"At least one call to Davenport."

"That's all?"

"She had a burner in her purse."

Ethan didn't respond, his head ready to explode.

"Still there, Ethan?"

"Yeah, just thinking. Guess one phone call's better than none."

"When are you leaving for Old Salem?"

"As soon as we're off the phone," Ethan said, climbing out of bed. "Need a couple of days to get the house ready for Sampson. Otherwise, I'm gonna end up spending more of my time dealing with his every complaint than shooting the story."

"Want me to join you?"

"Not yet. Hang in Boston, and keep working your sources on O'Brien, but meet me in Old Salem no later than Wednesday. That's the day I shoot the crime scene with McKenzie. A little muscle might dissuade him from using his deputy to lean on me again. Let's talk when I get there." He hung up, chewed two Motrin, picked up the bottle of Scotch, and emptied it down the toilet. No more drinking. Not for the rest of the shoot. As he was about to hop into the shower, another phone call buzzed into his iPhone.

"I found Virgil Wellington," Mindy said, out of breath. "You gotta get over to his apartment right now. He wants to be interviewed."

An hour later, Ethan walked into the lobby of the Mandarin Oriental, a luxury condominium on the Charles River, and found the concierge desk.

"Ethan Benson from *The Weekly Reporter*. I've got a meeting with Mr. Wellington."

"Your camera crew already arrived," the concierge said as he picked up the house phone. "Oscar, the producer is here. Should I send him up?" He nodded and clicked off. "Please follow me." He led Ethan through a three-story atrium, under a row of Waterford crystal chandeliers, past a wall of Venetian mirrors, and over to a private elevator where he used a key to unlock the door. "Mr. Wellington owns the top two floors of the building. His valet will be waiting for you."

Ethan stepped into the elevator and rode up to the penthouse, the door opening into a lavishly decorated foyer with marble floors, an exquisite Tufft satin love seat sitting under a mountain landscape by Sanford Robinson Gifford.

"Mr. Benson, I'm Oscar. Your crew is setting up cameras in the library."

The valet proceeded up a majestic staircase, past a dining room, a sitting room, a formal living room, and a lavish music room with a Steinway grand piano highlighted by a bright spotlight. At the far end of the floor, he pushed open a hand-carved oak door, sporting the Wellington coat of arms—an American flag decorated with dollar signs—and into a two-story library with walls of first-edition books.

"Mr. Wellington will be here shortly. Can I get you anything while you wait?"

Ethan really wanted a cup of coffee to smooth over his hangover but said instead, "Thank you. I'm fine."

He peered around the room. The crew had created a traditional one-on-one interview setup: two low-backed chairs facing each other, two high-end Sony HD cameras locked on tripods, and a half dozen Keno Flo lights splashing the room with a warm glow. A small Panasonic digital camera was positioned atop an eight-foot ladder to make a wide shot of the entire library with the equipment in the foreground.

"Nice job," Ethan said as he walked up to Hugh Jeremiah, the same cameraman he'd used the day before. "The outdoor light from the wall of windows won't be a problem, will it?"

"Nope," Jeremiah said, adjusting the computer on the back of his camera. "I'm using daylight as the main source of fill light for Wellington, so I need less equipment to build the set."

"Are you almost ready?"

"Just need to tweak the cameras when Wellington gets here."

"Have you seen him?" Ethan said, checking the shots in a bank of monitors.

"Not yet," Jeremiah said, scooting over to a table in the background to shift a lamp a few inches to the right. "That should frame up better behind Wellington."

As he walked back to his camera, Oscar the valet walked into the room leading a small, slightly crooked man with thick white hair, ruddy pockmarked skin, and strong, piercing black eyes. Wearing a custom-made pinstripe suit, a starched pink shirt, and a monocle in his left eye, he was the spitting image of a European aristocrat—a scion of wealth and power, a tyrant used to getting his way.

"You must be Ethan Benson," he said, thrusting out a well-tanned hand. "We need to start the interview right away. I have other meetings this morning and not a lot of time. Where do you want me to sit?"

Ethan walked over to a chair facing the windows. "You're over here," he said. "I'll be here, right across from you." He took his seat and turned to Jake Watson, "Mic us, please."

"Sound's already good to go. I'm using a boom."

Ethan turned to Jeremiah, "Cameras?"

"A-camera is on a tight shot of Mr. Wellington. B-camera is on a lockdown, medium shot of you. Wide shot is rolling. Give me a second to make sure we have speed." A pause, then, "All cameras in sync. You can ask your first question."

Ethan took a deep breath and stared into Wellington's eyes. "You're a tough man to track down, Mr. Wellington. We've been looking for you for weeks."

Wellington's expression remained stoic. "I wasn't sure I wanted to talk to your TV show—that's why I didn't return your phone calls—but now that my son's appeal is about to be heard by the judge, I thought it was the right time to tell your viewers the truth about Rufus."

Ethan hesitated a moment, letting the camera capture the intensity on Wellington's face, then said, "We'll get to the appeal a little later, Mr. Wellington, but why don't we start with the crime? Were you surprised when you heard that your son had been arrested for the murder of Heather Starr?"

"I wasn't surprised at all," he said sharply. "I'd been waiting for years for Rufus to snap."

"What do you mean?"

"Rufus was a train wreck waiting to happen. Even as a little boy, he was peculiar. He had this thing about girls—little girls. But I'm sure you know that already. Everybody knows that. But I'm the only person who knows just how perverted he really is."

"Care to explain?" Ethan said, wondering if Wellington knew about Mary Murphy or, for that matter, Ginger the waitress.

"He hated girls—loathed them. When he was about six, he started cutting out pictures of models—child models—in my wife's fashion magazines and drawing big Xs through their faces with black magic markers."

"Lots of kids do that," Ethan said.

"Yes, they do. But Rufus would hang the pictures on the walls in his bedroom and stick pushpins through their eyes."

"At six?" Ethan said incredulously.

"Maybe even a little younger." Wellington paused and closed his eyes. "Sometimes my wife and I would find him in the garden at our house in Shutesbury playing with dolls—we never discovered how he got them—but he'd hack them into pieces with a butcher knife he'd steal from the kitchen. Then he'd set the pieces on fire, and we'd have to call the fire department so the house wouldn't burn down. It was god-awful."

"Did you get him help?" Ethan said as he thought about the crime scene photos of Heather Starr.

"Of course, all through his childhood," Wellington said, exasperated, "one doctor after another. And at times, he made great progress—especially when he was very young—but his abhorrent behavior always came back, his hatred of women always simmering just below the surface." Wellington leaned forward in his chair. "We hoped moving full time to the country and away from the pressures of Boston would be therapeutic for Rufus, but it didn't make any difference—none whatsoever."

"How old was he when you moved here?"

"He'd just turned seven."

Ethan paused then faced his cameraman, "Are you on a tight shot, Hugh?"

"Right in there on his eyes."

Ethan turned back to Wellington, "So you moved to Shutesbury when Rufus was in, what, second grade?"

"Sounds about right."

"And put him into therapy."

"Yes. But his behavior just got worse, not better. That's when he started killing animals. First it was birds, squirrels, a raccoon here and there, then cats and dogs. I'd find him in the backyard covered in blood, playing with the body parts, as if they were pieces of a stuffed animal he'd taken apart."

"Did you tell anybody? The authorities? His doctors?" Ethan said, quickly glancing at the questions he'd prepared in the cab ride over to Wellington's apartment.

"Of course, we told his doctors. We even discussed institutionalizing him."

"But you didn't."

"No, my wife was afraid we'd never get him back. So we just continued with more therapy at home," Wellington said, his eyes growing misty.

"Do you wish now you'd placed him in a psychiatric facility?"

"I'm not going there, Mr. Benson, and I resent that question." He was suddenly angry. "It's very easy to second-guess yourself, and it's never fruitful. We did the best job we could at the time as his parents. Let's leave it at that."

Ethan waited a moment for Wellington to settle down. "Anything else you want to tell me about Rufus's childhood?"

Wellington sucked in a deep breath, the camera pulling back to a medium shot. "Sometimes I'd find Rufus masturbating on what was left of the animals he'd just butchered. And I'd stand there watching—stunned, horrified, sickened. That's when I knew that killing was a sexual fantasy for Rufus, that we were up against something ingrained in his soul—something that was truly evil, something we might not be able to fix."

Ethan leaned back in his chair. "Are you aware that your son masturbated on Heather Starr after he cut her into pieces and placed her body parts into her grave?"

"I've read Dr. Hosenfeld's psych report. His deviant sexual practices resurfaced when he murdered that girl. I was saddened, but not surprised."

"And your wife? Was she aware that Rufus was exhibiting these perversions as a little boy?"

Wellington sighed. "She didn't live long enough to witness the sexual component to Rufus's problem."

"What do you mean, Mr. Wellington?"

"She died when he was eight."

"What happened?" Ethan said, motioning Jeremiah to lock the camera on a medium shot. "I wasn't aware Rufus lost his mother at such a young age."

"She had a terrible accident," Wellington said, trying to control his emotions. "She fell down a flight of stairs and broke her neck. I was away on a business trip in New York, closing a big textile deal. Rufus was alone with Edith. His nanny had taken the afternoon off to do some shopping. I found her when I got home. She was lying on the floor at the foot of the steps, all twisted and broken. Rufus was hiding in his bedroom, traumatized. He wouldn't come out for days."

"And he was eight at the time?"

"He may have been nine, Mr. Benson. It was a long time ago."

"Did you ever find out what happened?"

"The police pieced it together. They said she must've tripped on a rug at the top of the stairs and missed the banister as she fell. Her head was crushed as she tumbled down the steps, her face a mass of bruises and abrasions and broken bones. You can just imagine what she looked like."

"Did the police talk to Rufus?" Ethan said, wondering why he hadn't read anything about the tragedy in the newspapers.

Mr. Wellington wiped his monocle with a handkerchief and repositioned it in front of his eye as Jeremiah pushed in a little tighter. "They tried, but he never said a word to the police or to me or to his shrinks."

"He won't talk to anybody about Heather Starr either."

"It's all part of the pattern. He crawls into a shell when he's under duress. It's infuriating, simply infuriating."

Ethan paused, trying to decide where to go next, then asked, "Were you close to Rufus at the time of the murder?"

"Not for a long time. We'd drifted apart after he left for college. I only saw him when he needed money and occasionally at family functions. Then, when he got access to his trust fund, we lost touch entirely. I'm afraid we've had no relationship for the past decade."

"And what about his friend, Bret Davenport?"

"I knew Bret. He spent a lot of time at our house when Rufus was growing up."

"And?"

"And he was a bad influence on Rufus," Wellington said sharply. "He was wild and disrespectful, and he was dishonest."

"Dishonest?"

"Very."

"Have you seen him recently?" Ethan said, realizing his own assessment of Bret Davenport was right on the money.

"Not in years. But as I said, I haven't seen Rufus in years either. Why do you ask?"

"Because he still works for your son," Ethan said, staring into Wellington's eyes. "Are you aware of that?"

"Doesn't surprise me. Bret Davenport had his hand in my son's pocket even when they were little. Never liked the kid. Not one bit. He was a schemer. Deviant. A pathological liar. And there was something twisted in their relationship."

"What do you mean?"

"Could never put my finger on it."

"Sexual?"

"Never saw them together, but it wouldn't surprise me." Wellington checked his pocket watch. "Enough about Bret Davenport, Mr. Benson. I'd like to wrap this up. I've got a meeting with an investment adviser in fifteen minutes."

Ethan folded his questions and put them into his coat pocket. "Almost done, Mr. Wellington." He nodded to his crew to keep rolling. "Why didn't you come forward and tell the police about your son's childhood at the time of the murder?"

"They never asked me, Mr. Benson."

"Did you talk to Sheriff McKenzie?"

"Never met the man. After Rufus confessed, the police didn't think his past was important and swept his childhood under the rug." Wellington grew angry, his face contorted. "But now that his appeal is pending and there's a chance he might win and get out, I decided to do everything humanly possible to make sure he stays safely locked behind bars, because Rufus is a disgrace to me and my family and has been ever since he was a little boy, and that, Mr. Benson, is the only reason I'm sitting here today doing this interview." Wellington suddenly stood. "No more questions. I'm done talking about Rufus. He isn't my son anymore. He's a convicted killer who must pay for his crime."

Ethan stood and thanked him then watched as he disappeared down the hallway, proud and defiant. He turned, told his crew to wrap the equipment, and sat down on a camera case.

So Rufus liked killing even when he was a little boy, he thought, *actually got sexual pleasure out of mutilating animals. What the hell does that mean? And how does it play into Heather Starr's murder?* He booted up his iPad and reread the notes from his telephone interview with Dr. Oliphant.

Then a bell went off in his head.

CHAPTER 32

ETHAN PULLED UP TO A modern split-level house on the outskirts of Old Salem. Parking at the end of the driveway, he got out of his rental car, grabbed his luggage, and looked around the property. There was a detached three-car garage where the crew could store equipment, plenty of space out front to park the fleet of cars he was expecting, and a separate wing with its own entrance that would give Peter at least the illusion of privacy.

He walked up the front steps and unlocked the door. The house was enormous, built by a wealthy hedge fund manager who spent his summers in Old Salem and rented the rest of the year. It was clean and luxuriously furnished, with ten bedrooms, ten bathrooms, a living room, dining room, a kitchen with an attached family room, and an entertainment suite with a pool table and an eighty-inch flat-screen TV—plenty of space for the crew to spread out. After dropping his bag in a back bedroom facing the reservoir, he headed to the kitchen. David had hired a housekeeper who'd stocked the refrigerator with enough food to feed an army and enough beer to last for a month.

He'd have to stay away from the beer.

And the Scotch in the liquor cabinet.

He reached for his iPhone. "Just checked out the digs. Nice job, David."

"What do you think of Sampson's wing of the house?"

"He'll find something wrong with it. That's a given."

"But will it work for him?"

"Don't worry. It'll be fine."

"How'd the interview go with Wellington's father?" David said.

"He filled in a lot of the blanks," Ethan said, before giving him a quick rundown.

"Think it's true?"

"Why wouldn't it be? There's no reason for Virgil Wellington to lie."

"Does it change anything?"

"Maybe. But I'm not sure how the pieces fit together. There's definitely a pattern of killing, but we can't prove anything yet. So I'm not ready to draw any concrete conclusions."

"Hey, almost forgot. I shipped you the confession video. Finally got it from Lauren Saperstein. Did the package arrive?"

Ethan scanned the room. There was a FedEx envelope sitting on the kitchen table. He walked over, tore open the top, and shook out a disk. "Did she say why it took her so long to send it to us?"

"Only said they had a tough time finding it."

"Looks like everybody had a tough time finding it," Ethan said sarcastically. "Did you screen it?"

"Made a dub with Joel but only saw pieces. Was in and out of the edit room, doing a million things for our shoot."

"Okay. I'll take a look. When are you getting here?'

"Late tomorrow?"

"And the production crew."

"Same time."

"Good. Call me with updates."

❧

Ethan turned on his laptop, inserted the disk, waited for the first frame to pop into the monitor, then hit *Enter*. The image was remarkably sharp, recorded with a state-of-the-art digital camera mounted on the wall across from Wellington in a small interrogation room. He was sitting alone with his feet propped up on a metal table, unshackled, his hands interlaced and resting on top of his head, a grin on his face. Ethan paused the video. Wellington had been cuffed in the meadow. Why wasn't he cuffed at the sheriff's office? Strange. He hit *Play*, and McKenzie suddenly rumbled into the room, gesturing wildly, his mouth moving a mile a minute.

There was no sound.

That was strange too.

He continued screening, waiting for the sound to kick in, but it didn't.

After a moment, Wellington stood, visibly angry, and shoved McKenzie up against the wall—all three hundred pounds of the sheriff cowering like a church mouse as Wellington railed, his face filled with rage. Then, as suddenly as the outburst had begun, it stopped, the doctor patting the sheriff's cheek, smiling into the camera, and sitting back down. Ethan stopped the video. What the fuck had just happened? He recued the sequence and played it again, just as puzzled the second time. Reaching for his iPad, he wrote a series of new questions for the interviews.

Then he hit *Enter*.

Another two minutes with no sound—McKenzie remaining huddled in the corner, Wellington still smiling like a wild man. Then Bret Davenport strolled into the room. He nodded to McKenzie then leaned over and whispered something into Wellington's ear. Frustrated, Ethan replayed the sequence, several times, trying to read Davenport's lips but unable to make out a word.

He continued watching, stunned by the familiarity in the room.

Then Davenport abruptly left, and McKenzie reached for handcuffs dangling from his belt, attaching one end to a ring bolt in the middle of the table and the other to Wellington's wrists.

Then the sound kicked in.

Right on cue.

And McKenzie began the interrogation.

Ethan followed the interview line by line in a hard copy of the transcript he'd pulled from his briefcase. It matched word for word, nothing unusual there. When it was over, he paused the video, thought a moment, then checked his production notes, realizing he'd just caught the defense attorney in another outright lie: Davenport had met with Wellington before the taped confession, not afterward, as he'd claimed at their dinner meeting. He smiled to himself. It's all a pack of lies with that guy—just as Wellington's father had said. Then he updated the interview questions a second time and called Lauren Saperstein.

"Hey, Ethan," she said, preoccupied, "I'm writing a brief on a drug deal I'm arguing in court tomorrow—"

"I just screened the video of Wellington's confession and found it quite interesting—especially the first couple of minutes."

He could hear her hesitate on the other end.

"There's no sound at the top of the tape. Why's that?" he said, pressing harder.

"Give me a sec, Ethan," Saperstein said quietly. "Lemme find the confession. I wanna take another quick look."

Ethan waited impatiently. Why was the ADA being evasive? She'd sent him the video herself. Hadn't she rescreened it first? She was about to argue the state's case against Wellington's appeal. Wouldn't the missing sound be a red flag?

"I'm back, Ethan," she said, "just looked at the top of the tape."

"And?"

"It's a problem."

"I bet it is," Ethan said forcefully. "There should be sound, right?"

"Yes. That's protocol."

"Did you ask McKenzie why it was turned off?" Ethan said boldly.

"I may have, but I don't remember."

"You don't remember?"

"No. But, Ethan—"

He cut her off, "This is important, Lauren. Did you ask the sheriff what was said in that room before the sound went on? Did he explain his reaction to Wellington's aggressive behavior? He's obviously terrified, but he leaves Wellington unrestrained in the interrogation room. Looks more like he's lounging at home in his living room watching a football game than getting ready to confess to a murder." There was a long silence. "Lauren, are you with me?"

"I'm here, Ethan."

"Shouldn't he have been manacled to the table?"

"Yes. That too is standard protocol in a murder investigation."

"So why wasn't he?"

"I can't answer that."

Ethan didn't believe her.

"Run it down to the point where Davenport walks into the room," he said then waited. "Are you watching?"

"I'm watching, Ethan."

"Do you see where he whispers something to Wellington?" He waited again. Still no response. "What did he tell him?"

"I don't know."

Ethan paused. Either Lauren Saperstein was hiding something, or she was totally incompetent as a prosecutor.

"Have you asked Davenport what he said to his client?"

"Of course," she said defensively.

"Did he tell you?"

"Well—"

"So he didn't tell you."

"No."

"And you didn't pursue it?"

"At the time, I chalked it up to lawyer-client privilege. Then the sound went on and Wellington confessed," she said, irritation creeping into her voice. "So I didn't think it was a problem. Wellington admitted to murdering Heather Starr, waved his right to a trial, was sentenced by the judge, and the case was closed."

"So the missing sound was forgotten."

"Yes."

"But now it's a problem, isn't it?" Ethan said.

There was another pause. "The missing sound has come back to haunt us," she said hollowly. "Davenport is using it as the centerpiece for his appeal. Says it's indicative of the sloppy police work—a breakdown in the so-called chain of evidence, that if the sound was there, it would prove that Wellington was coerced into admitting his guilt."

"But that doesn't make sense," Ethan said, dumbstruck. "McKenzie looks scared, like Wellington threatened him. Then Davenport leaves—before the confession. Shouldn't he have stayed in the room?"

"Absolutely, but he claims the sheriff convinced Rufus to waive his right to an attorney during that gap in the sound then told him to leave the room before he took Wellington's statement and that the sheriff pushed Wellington into making a full confession on tape."

"I don't know, Lauren," Ethan said, "that doesn't seem real to me. I think the sound was deliberately turned off so nobody could hear what they were saying before Rufus gave his confession."

"I agree, and that's what I'm going to argue in court. But it may not be enough."

"Enough for what?"

"To keep Rufus Wellington behind bars."

"How's that possible?" Ethan said, stupefied. "It's just a couple of minutes of missing sound."

"But Bret's going to argue it's part of a pattern—that the sheriff never found the kill site, never found the murder weapon, can't find some of the key forensic evidence—"

"What evidence?"

"The blood DNA is gone."

"So you can't tie Wellington to Heather's body anymore?"

"Nope. And when you couple all this with the fact that Wellington is now recanting his confession, there's a damn good chance the judge is going to side with Bret Davenport and throw out the verdict. If that happens, Rufus Wellington is going to get out of prison, which means he's gonna be back on the street, a free man."

"How come I'm just finding out about this, Lauren?"

"Because the appeal hasn't been argued yet, and I'm not supposed to be discussing it with you."

"Does Davenport know you've sent me the tape?" Ethan said, wondering.

"Heavens, no. He motioned to block its release the day you asked him about it, and the judge agreed and sealed the confession. So it's not part of the public record."

"But you sent it to me anyway."

"I thought you needed to have it."

That was all she'd say and hung up.

Ethan sat a moment and lit a cigarette then grabbed his laptop and e-mailed Mindy, describing his conversation with the ADA. He attached a copy of the video and instructed her to show it to Sampson, adding one last thought to his message:

> The district attorney's office is worried they're going to lose the appeal and that Wellington is going to be released. In light of what I learned this morning from his father, and the fact that Wellington poses a danger to each and every one of us if he walks, we need to refocus our story. Call me after you screen the confession.

He hit *Send* and headed to the kitchen. To hell with his plan to stay sober. The itch was festering, gnawing away at him. It was time for a tumbler of Scotch as he waited for Mindy to call him back.

CHAPTER 33

SHERIFF MCKENZIE ROLLED DOWN MAIN Street just after dusk, lights flashing, and onto the dirt road leading to the rental house. He was worrying about Janice O'Brien, who was sitting in a jail cell, arrested for the murder of Sylvia Anderson. Would she keep her mouth shut? Would she implicate the rest of them? Would she ruin everything? He rubbed the now chronic ache in his chest as he pulled into the driveway, past two crew vans, a grip truck, and three rental cars parked in a neat row on the front lawn. He turned off the engine, got out of the driver's seat, and straightened his tie—his uniform pressed, his shoes polished, his sheriff's badge positioned above his breast pocket. After checking his hair in the side-view mirror, he carefully put on his hat and made sure his sidearm was properly holstered. Then he motioned to Percy Wilkerson to accompany him up the porch steps to the front door. Knocking loudly, he waited for Ethan to answer, his other deputies remaining in their patrol cars, lights still flashing.

"Let me do the talking," he said to Wilkerson. "You just stand there, and keep your mouth shut, unless I tell you to speak."

Wilkerson nodded and adjusted his sunglasses.

McKenzie rapped on the door a second time, growing impatient in the light drizzle blowing in his face. Another moment, and the door opened, and Ethan walked onto the porch, holding a cup of coffee.

"'Evening, Sheriff," he said, glancing a long moment at the deputy.

"'Evenin', Mr. Benson, I think you've met my first deputy, Percy Wilkerson."

"Indeed, I have, on the first day I was in Athol and several times after that," Ethan said, never taking his eyes off the sunglasses. "It's a bit dark to be wearing those things, don't you think, Deputy?"

Wilkerson removed his glasses, stared long and hard at Ethan, then put them back on.

"I've brought a half dozen deputies and three of my best search dogs," McKenzie said. "Tell me what you need us to do."

"Come inside, and I'll give you a rundown of the shots. Then we can head over to Wellington's estate, and you can walk me and my cameras through the crime scene."

McKenzie followed Benson into the house. *I trust you, motherfucker, as far as I can spit,* he thought, pursing his lips. *I'll give you the grand tour all right and show you just what I want you to see.*

Ethan ushered them into the living room then introduced his crew, "This is Herb Glickstein and Bobby Raffalo. They're gonna man two cameras tonight. One will focus on a tight shot of you, Sheriff, and the other on a wide shot of your men and your search dogs. That way, we'll capture—from different angles—just how you searched the property the night of the murder."

"Anybody else joinin' us?" McKenzie said, gesturing around the room.

"My soundmen, Anthony Petulla and Sylvester Jurkins, and David Livingston, my researcher, sitting over there in the corner, organizing the equipment. Say hi to the sheriff, David." David smiled and nodded hello. "And then there's my consultant, Lloyd Howard, sitting on the couch."

"What does he do?" McKenzie said, wiping sweat from his brow with a clean handkerchief.

"He's a private investigator. Got here late this afternoon from Boston, where he's been pulling police records and legal documents for me."

Fuck. He must know about Janice, McKenzie thought, pulling off his hat and running his fingers through his hair. "Why do you need a private investigator to do that kinda stuff for you? Aren't you runnin' the show?"

"I am, Sheriff. But Lloyd can track things down faster than I can because he has the inside scoop and knows lots of people that I don't."

Oh, shit. Shit. He must know everything. He's got to, McKenzie thought, whining to himself. "And why Boston? The crime didn't take place there," he said nervously to Ethan.

"Because that's where Dr. Wellington had his day job at Mass General. Thought the Boston PD might know a few things you guys here at the Quabbin might've missed."

"Did you find anything?"

"We did," Ethan said, goading the sheriff. "Background stuff that's gonna help me tell my story." Ethan paused, trying to decide if he'd hit a nerve.

"Is your private investigator comin' with us on the shoot?"

"Is that a problem?"

"Don't see why you need to bring him, but no, won't be a problem. As long as he stays out of the way of me and my boys," McKenzie said, now completely beside himself.

"You won't get in the way, will you, Lloyd?"

"Fly on the wall, that's all," Lloyd said.

"And why do you need your soundmen?"

"I always record background sound when I'm shooting."

"You ain't gonna ask me no questions tonight, are you?"

"I might ask one or two as we walk the property. Will make the reenactment seem more realistic if you describe what you're doing as we're rolling."

"But you didn't say anything about interviewin' me," McKenzie said suspiciously. "I thought that was tomorrow. You aren't trying to trip me up, are you?"

"Now, why would I do that," Ethan said, placating the sheriff. "The main interview is definitely tomorrow with Peter Sampson, just as we planned, and I promise not to ask you anything difficult tonight. I'm gonna leave those questions for my anchorman."

McKenzie stared at Ethan a long moment, puffing away on a cigarette. "Well, I guess if you only focus on me and my role in the investigation, no harm in askin' a few questions. It'll help show how difficult a job it is for somebody like me to search a crime scene and track down the evidence. No harm in that." He turned to Deputy Wilkerson, "Should make me look pretty good, don't you think, Percy?"

Percy nodded but kept his mouth shut as he'd promised.

Ethan rode in the backseat as McKenzie pulled onto Main Street, Herb Glickstein sitting beside him in the passenger seat, rolling a series of shots of the sheriff looking like a sheriff. Bobby Raffalo followed in a crew van, periodically stopping to make sweeping wide shots of the patrol cars moving along single file on the back roads leading to Wellington's estate. When they arrived at the front gate, Ethan sent David with Bobby and Deputy Wilkerson to photograph the police dogs and the other deputies reenacting their search of the property as they followed an imaginary blood trail down the footpath from the back of the house, through the woods, into the meadow, and over to where they'd discovered Heather's body the night of the murder. Ethan took Herb inside the house to shoot McKenzie as he proceeded up the back staircase, down the central hallway, and into the master bedroom suite—where he cued him to pull his Smith & Wesson handgun and check behind the doors and inside the closets as if he was clearing the room, searching for the killer. He told Herb to vary his camera positions and to make a series of point-of-view shots so the audience would think they were watching the police investigation through the eyes of the sheriff himself.

Ethan was pleased.

The reenactment was turning out better than expected.

"How am I doin'?" McKenzie said.

"Great, Sheriff, but you seem a bit winded. Do you need to take a break?"

"Give me a second," McKenzie said, loosening his tie, sucking in air. "Didn't think it would be so friggin' hot up here."

"You gonna be all right, Sheriff?"

"Be okay in a moment."

"I'll make insert shots while you rest," Ethan said, directing Herb to shoot the overturned furniture, the duvet at the foot of the bed, and the bloodstains on the wallpaper.

"How much more do we have to do?" the sheriff said, rubbing his chest, still out of breath. "I've showed you everything in the house."

"Just a few more shots up here, then we'll link with your deputies out back and make a sequence with you and the search dogs. I know I'll need that for my story."

"Can we call it a night after that?" the sheriff said, restraightening his tie.

"That should do it," Ethan said, turning back to Glickstein. "Herb, lock the camera on a medium shot, and get in front of me and the sheriff. Time to ask Gene a few questions. Lloyd, are you here somewhere?" Lloyd emerged from the shadows. "Guide Herb so he doesn't trip over something as he walks backward and shoots the sequence." He motioned to McKenzie. "Stand to my right, and try to forget the camera. I want this to look as natural as possible, like we're having a conversation. We rolling, Herb?"

"Got speed."

"All set, Anthony?" he said to his soundman.

"All set."

"Okay, let's do it." He looked at McKenzie and started walking. "So this is where Dr. Wellington began to beat Heather?"

"Over there," McKenzie said, pointing toward the bed.

"Could your splatter guys determine from the blood patterns if he beat her with an object?"

"Sure could," McKenzie said, hitching his thumbs to his belt as they walked to a bedside table, Glickstein panning back and forth from McKenzie to Ethan, then over to the table.

"He struck her with this lamp. See the bloodstains on the base? Probably came from her head."

"How do you know that? Did your CSIs test the lamp?"

"Well, sure, that's what they do. They test everythin' so they can reconstruct what happened at the crime scene."

"And they did it right here?" Ethan said, raising both hands in a gesture of surprise.

"Right here," McKenzie said, irritation in his voice. "What you drivin' at, Mr. Benson? I just answered your question."

"You did and quite well. But I was wondering why all the evidence is still sitting here at the crime scene. Why wasn't it logged and bagged and taken to the police lab for additional testing?"

McKenzie stared at Ethan, his upper lip quivering, then lit a cigarette. "Are you questioning the way I ran my investigation, Mr. Benson?"

"No, Sheriff, I'm just curious about why you didn't follow procedure. Aren't you worried you might have overlooked something important by not examining the evidence a little more thoroughly?"

"Fuck, no," McKenzie said, losing his temper. "My guys did a damn good job. Tested everything right here on the spot. I didn't see no need to take any of this shit back to the lab. Besides, Dr. Wellington owned up to the murder the moment I arrested him. That was all the proof I needed. He's guilty—no ifs, ands, or buts."

"But I've been told by a pretty reliable source that Dr. Wellington is now saying he didn't commit the murder."

"Who told you that—"

"And that he's filing an appeal. I'm sure you know all about that."

"Well—"

"And that the basis of the appeal is a breach in the chain of evidence."

McKenzie turned ashen gray. "What are you insinuating, Mr. Benson?"

"I don't know, Sheriff, you tell me," he said, baiting him.

McKenzie sucked rapidly on his cigarette but didn't answer.

"Well, let me ask you my question in a slightly different way," Ethan said, pausing a moment. "Did you fail to follow procedure with the evidence to give your good friend Bret Davenport the ammunition he needs to file an appeal to help free Dr. Wellington?"

"Fuck this," McKenzie said furiously. "You have no basis to make that kind of allegation." The sheriff was now sweating profusely. "We did everything by the book that night, knew plenty about Wellington as soon as we arrested him. That's why we might've gotten a bit sloppy with the evidence. Because we knew right from the beginning he was guilty. End of story."

"But Davenport's using your 'sloppy' police work to get Wellington out of prison."

"I have nothing more to say on the subject."

"But, Gene, you could've learned much more about Wellington's state of mind at the time of the murder if you hadn't been so cavalier with the evidence."

"What does that mean?"

"Just what it implies," Ethan said, pausing so the camera could capture the insipient fear spreading across the sheriff's face as they walked into the hallway. "His father says Wellington enjoyed killing from the time he was a little kid—something you never bothered to investigate—and maybe if you'd done your job more thoroughly, you might've discovered how his troubled childhood played into Heather Starr's murder and why he carved her into pieces."

"I resent that allegation," McKenzie said, exploding. "I'm a fuckin' good sheriff."

"But you never found the kill site, did you?" Ethan said.

"Well—"

"Don't you think it's important?"

"Yeah, it's important."

"So why aren't you still looking?"

"Because the case is long over."

"So it isn't important anymore?"

"Stop trying to trip me up," McKenzie said as they pushed into the kitchen. "Me and my deputies searched every square inch of this place. We spent days lookin' with the search dogs."

"Did you look down in the basement?"

"Of course.'"

"Can you show me?"

Wellington stammered.

"Is that the way down?" Ethan continued, motioning for Lloyd to open the door.

"No," McKenzie said, sweat spreading in deep circles under his arms.

"Open it," Ethan said, motioning to Herb to keep rolling.

Glickstein circled the room and zeroed in on a medium shot as Lloyd jerked open the door and peered down the steps to the basement—McKenzie waving his arms, trying to use his body to block the stairwell.

"Stop," he said, bellowing at the top of his lungs. "That's not where Rufus killed the damn hooker. There's nothin' down there but storage. It's off-limits to your camera."

Suddenly, he clutched his chest, his face twisting into a mask of pain as he gasped for air. Then his eyes rolled into the back of his head, and he collapsed to the floor—his sheriff's hat tumbling off his head, floating end over end through the door and down the steps.

Ethan rushed over and checked for a pulse, placing his head on the sheriff's chest, listening for a heartbeat. "He's alive, but his breathing is shallow. We gotta get him to a hospital right away." He reached for his iPhone. "David, the sheriff just collapsed in the kitchen. I think he's had a heart attack. Call 911. And do it now." He clicked off and turned back to Lloyd, "Shut the door. I don't want anybody to know we were headed to the basement."

"What's down there?" Lloyd said, rolling his eyes questioningly.

"I'll tell you later," Ethan said, turning back to the sheriff. "Help me make him comfortable." As he removed his coat and placed it under McKenzie's head, Percy Wilkerson burst through the door. "Herb, keep shooting," he said, motioning to the deputy.

Glickstein swish-panned across the room.

"What the fuck did you do to him?" Wilkerson screamed, hurling himself at Ethan, lunging for his throat.

Without thinking, Ethan ducked to his left as Lloyd leaped through the air and tackled the deputy, knocking him off his feet. "Take it easy, asshole," he said, pinning the deputy's arms behind his back. "We didn't do anything. The sheriff collapsed out of the blue."

"Fuck that," the deputy said, shrieking. "You must've done something, Benson, you cocksucker. The sheriff doesn't trust you, not one bit. Never has. Thought you were up to no good with your story. I should've taken you out when I had the chance. Shouldn't have left it up to that bitch in Boston."

"What bitch in Boston?" Ethan said. "You talking about Janice O'Brien?"

"I ain't sayin' no more, asshole. And turn off that fucking camera. You have no right to shoot me or the sheriff while he's in this condition." Then he glared at Lloyd. "Take your hands off me, motherfucker, I need to help Gene."

Lloyd backed away and threw up his hands as Ethan stood stock-still, and paramedics rushed in to attend to the sheriff.

CHAPTER 34

Ethan was sitting in the media room, screening the dailies, watching his exchange with McKenzie before he collapsed. After shuttling back and forth several times, he noticed telltale signs all through the footage that something was wrong—grimaces on the sheriff's face, labored breathing, clutching at his chest—the question about the basement the final blow pushing him over the top. He turned to David, "He was panicking we wanted to see for ourselves."

"Think you could've gotten him to tell us what's behind the door in the library?"

Ethan hesitated then rescreened the sequence, watching one frame at a time. He paused the video. "I don't know."

"So now what? We can't put McKenzie on camera tomorrow."

"I've made a request to interview Percy Wilkerson. He's next in line after the sheriff."

"Think he knows?"

"He's too close to the sheriff not to know."

"Will he do it?"

"No, the sheriff's office says they have no comment."

"So we have nobody who worked the police investigation? Nobody who knows what's down in the subbasement."

"We'll use what we shot tonight and explain in the narration why there's no formal interview. I know who to ask about the locked door."

Lloyd had wandered into the room and was staring at a freeze frame of McKenzie sprawled on the kitchen floor. He rewound the video and carefully froze the image after the camera panned from the sheriff to the basement door. "Why'd he freak out when I opened the door?"

There was awkward silence, Ethan striking a cigarette, before glancing at David—who was shaking his head no and mouthing, "Please don't tell him."

Lloyd looked from David to Ethan. "What's goin' on?" he said pointedly. "What's down in the basement?"

Ethan stared at the bottle of Dewars sitting in the liquor cabinet. He longed for a taste of Scotch, to tap down the growing anxiety that he'd never learn what was behind the door or the truth about Wellington. "David and I have been down there."

"When?" Lloyd said. "The day you toured the house with Davenport on your first research trip?"

"Not then," Ethan said.

"I thought we weren't going to tell anybody," David said.

"Can't keep it a secret any longer," he said, shrugging at David. "We need Lloyd's help." He turned back to the PI. "After I was beaten up in Boston, I made a second trip to the Quabbin, remember? You wanted to come with me, but I told you to stay and continue digging on the Sylvia Anderson murder. That was the night we broke into Wellington's house."

"And that was the reason you didn't want me to come with you?"

Ethan smiled. "A little breaking and entering on the side."

"So what's down in the basement?"

Ethan finished his cigarette and stubbed it out in an ashtray. "The usual shit you find in a basement—a lot of junk, mostly. But there was a door leading to a rickety staircase that took you to a subbasement."

Lloyd swiveled back and forth in his chair. "Did you go down?"

"Yeah. There was a library of medical books."

"That's why the sheriff had a heart attack?" Lloyd said, sounding confused. "Because there's a reference library in a subbasement?"

"There's more," Ethan said. "There's a secret door behind one of the bookshelves. I found it when I was searching through the books."

"And you think McKenzie knows about it?"

"Got to. That's why he didn't want us to go down to the basement."

"And what the fuck is behind the door?"

"I don't know. I tried but couldn't open it. But I think it's the real reason Rufus Wellington is bankrolling everybody."

"Any proof of that?"

"Nothing yet."

"Have you told anybody else about this?"

"Now only you, besides David and me. And there's something else." Ethan walked across the room, checked the hallway, then closed the door. He unlocked his briefcase and pulled out the spiral notebook. "I also found this hidden in one of the medical books." He passed it to Lloyd, who thumbed through the pages.

"This is Wellington's?"

Ethan nodded.

"You stole it?"

"I borrowed it."

"And I'm guessing you haven't told anybody about this either?"

"At some point, I have to, but I haven't come up with a way to broach the break-in with Paul and the authorities so it doesn't torpedo me and David and our story."

Lloyd stared long and hard at Ethan then flipped through the pages again. "And you think these drawings and scribblings have something to do with Heather's murder?"

"Only Wellington can answer that question. I can't crack the code."

"Are you going to ask him?"

"Damn straight, I am."

❧

It was nearly midnight when Peter Sampson's stretch limousine pulled into the driveway. His chauffeur, a small Asian man named Felix, hurried out of the car and opened the door for the anchorman. Ethan extended his hand.

"How was the trip, Peter?"

"Long and boring." He waved at the house. "How'd you find this place? Actually looks quite impressive on the outside."

Ethan smiled at the reaction. It was not what he expected. "You've got your own private quarters with a huge bedroom, a formal sitting room, and a master bath, all the way in the back on the second floor. I've left you a basket of fruit and a bottle Remy Martin—the 1988 vintage you like—along with a crystal cognac snifter."

As Ethan grabbed his suitcase, the other back door of the limo swung open, and Consuela climbed out, lugging a briefcase and a shoulder bag stuffed with loose documents. Ethan turned to Sampson, surprised, "You didn't tell me you were bringing Consuela."

"Last-minute decision. Thought I needed my assistant to keep track of my schedule. Hope there's an extra room."

"Not a problem," Ethan said, regaining his composure. Then he said hello to Consuela and led them unceremoniously into the house.

❧

After helping Sampson settle in for the night, Ethan was back in the media room, holding a full production meeting with the crew—Consuela sitting in the corner, taking detailed notes for Peter.

"Did he prep for the interviews on his way here from Boston?" Ethan said, already knowing the answer.

"He asked for the research book, but only glanced at it."

"So I'll have to get him ready first thing in the morning," Ethan said, back timing his day.

"And did you tell Peter about the sheriff?" David asked.

"I told him and got a typical Peter Sampson response," Ethan said. "He was happy he hadn't wasted any time going through McKenzie's section of his research book now that there's no interview."

"And the video we shot?" David said.

"Tried to show him," Ethan said, smiling. "But he waved me off. Said he needed his beauty sleep and that maybe he'd screen it tomorrow." Everybody began to laugh. "Okay. Settle down. All we need is for Peter to hear us joking at his expense." He passed out the new itinerary. "Let's go over the shoot. David, I want you to interview both Ginger and Mary Murphy. I called and told them we were juggling our schedule because of McKenzie and that you'd be doing the interviews."

"Should I take both camera crews?"

"Use Herb to shoot the primary shot and Bobby for a side angle of her face. Lemme show you what I mean." He grabbed a piece of paper and diagrammed the camera positions. "Lock Herb on a medium shot and Bobby on a tight shot so all he sees is her profile. Then we can use his shot as a cutaway and intercut the two images in the edit room. It should look great."

"And after we finish?"

"Head over to Bret Davenport's office, and set up the equipment so we're ready when I get there with Peter."

"What screen direction do you want me to set the interview?" Herb Glickstein said, glancing at the schedule. "We've only budgeted ninety minutes to build the set. I need to know tonight."

"Put the A-camera over Sampson's right shoulder so Davenport is looking screen left. That's Mindy's suggestion. She said it'll cut better with the interviews she's already shot in Boston."

"And what about the two interviews David's doing—Mary Murphy and that hostess from the steak house?"

"Same screen direction," Ethan said, checking his notes. "All the interviews should be shot screen left. And Herb, set up a monitor and a playback machine for Davenport. I want Peter to ask him a series of questions about a video clip we're gonna show him."

"I'll mount a small digital camera on a tripod and make a medium shot of whatever we play back for him."

Ethan paused and looked at the production schedule again. "You know, you're right, Herb. I didn't leave you enough time to get ready for Davenport. The setup's more complicated than I first thought. David, call Ginger and Mary Murphy first thing in the morning and move up their start times an hour. Shouldn't be a problem. They're both eager to do the interviews." He turned back to Herb, "That'll give you ample time for lighting and staging at Davenport's office. So we good to go, folks?"

Nobody said a word.

"Good. Let's get some sleep."

⁓❧

Ethan sat hunched over the desk in his bedroom. There was an ashtray filled with dead cigarettes next to his computer, and a glass of White Label was perched in front of a stack of file folders. It was nearly 3:00 a.m., and his mind was racing, obsessing about the spiral notebook and the door behind the bookshelf. What does it all mean? He sipped his Scotch and rubbed his temples. There were two more days before his interview with Wellington, and he still didn't know the truth behind Heather Starr's murder. It was giving him a headache.

His cell phone rang.

"Hey, it's me, Mindy."

"What are you doing up so late?"

"Same thing you are, worrying about our story," she said. "Thought you might want an update before you go into production with Sampson tomorrow."

"A worthy plan. Start with the court-appointed psychiatrist."

"Hosenfeld comes off as a real asshole—arrogant, condescending, pompous. He stuck to his story. Said Wellington belongs just where he is, locked up in state prison."

"Did Peter ask him my questions about Wellington killing all those animals as a kid?"

"Several times."

"And?"

"He said we were barking up the wrong tree," she said ruefully. "And he wouldn't weigh in on what it meant, no matter how hard Peter pushed him. If you ask me, he didn't know anything about Wellington's childhood."

"Doesn't surprise me," Ethan said. "And did Peter ask Althea Oliphant the same line of questioning?"

"He certainly did, and she was absolutely horrified. Said she'd need to give it some thought, but on the surface, Wellington's history of killing as a child confirms her worst suspicions—that he's completely broken psychologically and that the pending appeal should be stopped before it's argued before the judge, that even the possibility of setting him free is a disaster waiting to happen."

"And you got that on camera?"

"Loud and clear."

"And what did she say about Hosenfeld?" he said eagerly.

"That she'd reread his psych report several times and that he's an absolute charlatan, that Rufus Wellington needs to be transferred out of prison and into a state psychiatric facility where he can be studied, that his penchant for violence and sadism is ingrained in his very being, and that Heather Starr's murder might just be the tip of the iceberg."

"Did she elaborate?" Ethan said, staring at the spiral notebook.

"Said she couldn't, not without spending some one-on-one time with Wellington."

"This is helpful, Mindy. Might shed some light on what all these scribblings mean in this damn notebook."

There was a long pause.

"Jeez, Ethan, what notebook?"

Another pause. "It's a long story, and I should've told you." Then he spent the next fifteen minutes describing the night of the break-in.

"Does Paul know about this?" Mindy said delicately.

"No."

"What about Peter?"

"Not yet."

"They're gonna be pissed when they find out, especially if they hear it from anyone else."

"I know. I know," he said, staring at the empty tumbler of Scotch on his desk. "I'll figure out the best time to drop the bomb on them." He changed the subject. "What about the rest of your shoot?"

"Got the doc at Mass General tomorrow and the ADA on Friday."

"Sounds like you're rolling along. Call me from the hospital after the interview with Rasmussen."

"Will do. And, Ethan, don't forget to tell Paul and Peter about your little escapade at Wellington's."

"I won't, Mom. Talk to you tomorrow."

He clicked off the phone and began to make a plan, deciding then and there just how and when he'd tell them. Then he headed to the media room for the bottle of White Label. He needed to turn off his mind and get some sleep. He'd cope with his drinking problem after his story aired.

That's when he'd get sober.

That's when he'd make things right with Sarah.

CHAPTER 35

THE BLACK LIMO SLOWED, MADE a right turn onto Main Street, and headed west to the redbrick building on the corner of Division Avenue. Felix the driver stopped for a red light and slid open the glass partition to the passenger compartment.

"How much further, Mr. Ethan, please?" he said in a heavy Mandarin accent.

"One more block," Ethan said, pointing to two Econoline vans parked on the left-hand side of the street. "They're the crew cars. Pull up behind them, and let us out there." He began stuffing documents back into his briefcase and turned to his anchorman, "Are you ready, Peter?"

"Give it a rest, Ethan," Sampson said curtly. "I know Davenport's interview by heart for Christ's sake."

Ethan smiled.

Same old Sampson.

They'd been going through the court docket and poring over the documents since they sat down to breakfast. Peter had bitched and moaned unmercifully—arguing story line, demanding proof for each allegation, and tweaking every question in the interview. Ethan had done all he could. Now it was up to Sampson to deliver.

The limousine slowed to a halt, and they all hopped out. A young couple holding hands stopped dead in their tracks as Sampson straightened his tie, nodded a cheerful hello with his anchorman smile, and followed Ethan into the building— Consuela right behind them, laden with two briefcases stuffed with file folders. After trudging up the stairs, they walked to the end of the hall, opened the door, and stepped into the waiting room of Bret Davenport's law office. They were confronted by cables coiled in the corner, video monitors, tripods, sandbags, sound equipment, and cases of light fixtures stacked in neat piles from the floor to the ceiling.

Ethan was pleased.

It looked like a television studio.

The crew was chattering as they worked, putting the finishing touches on the set. Ethan waved then walked up to the lead soundman, Anthony Petulla.

"Is this your mixing station?"

"This is it," Anthony said, continuing to test levels on his sound board. "David thought it would be better to set up my equipment outside the interview room—you know, less distraction for Peter."

"Where's Sylvester?"

"He's hooking up the mics on the set," Anthony said. "He's almost finished."

"And my monitors?"

"Inside Davenport's office, in the left corner. You like to make eye contact with Peter, right?"

"Certainly do," Ethan said, satisfied. "I'm his security blanket. He likes to lean on me if he forgets something. When can I look at the shots?"

"You have to ask, Herb, but maybe another fifteen minutes."

"Excellent," Ethan said, peering at the organized chaos all around him. "Where is he? I don't want to keep Sampson waiting."

"Inside with Bobby, white-balancing the cameras."

"Anybody seen Davenport?"

"Not yet."

Davenport's legal assistant was at her desk, typing a memo on her computer. "'Morning, Ms. Landau. Is Bret on his way?"

"He should've been here an hour ago," she said sullenly.

"Do you know where he is?"

"Beats me. He's not usually late."

"Can you call him? See what's holding him up?" Ethan said impatiently.

"Guess I could do that," she said as she straightened a document on her desk.

Ethan turned and walked over to Sampson, who was staring intently at an original Picasso hanging on the wall.

"This one of his purchases from Wellington's money?" he whispered, turning to Ethan.

"Don't have absolute proof, but I can't imagine it isn't."

"Give me the tax returns and the other financial documents. I want to go over them one more time. Is he here yet?"

"He's due any minute," Ethan said, beginning to worry.

He led Peter into Davenport's office and over to two armchairs facing each other, carefully picking his way around the cameras and light stands. Sampson had forgotten everyone's name, so Ethan dutifully introduced each member of the crew, before motioning to Peter to sit in his chair. Consuela then draped an apron over his suit jacket, opened his makeup kit, and began applying foundation to his face as Peter carefully read the documents Ethan had just handed him. Satisfied his anchorman was occupied—at least for the moment—he searched for David, who was sitting in front of the bank of monitors peering at the output of each camera. He tapped him on the shoulder, "Davenport's not here."

David slipped off his headset. "He's not?"

"No. And Sampson's getting impatient. Go sit on Ms. Landau and make sure she finds him."

David hurried out of the room as Sampson began howling. "Where's my monitor? I wanna look at my shot."

Ethan sighed and nodded to Bobby Raffalo, who grabbed a thirteen-inch TV screen and positioned it front of the anchorman.

"What do you think?" he said. "Do I look okay on camera?"

"We need more fill light to soften your features and more backlight to separate your suit jacket from the bookshelves in the background of the shot," Ethan said forcefully. "Where's Rudy?"

"Right here, boss," said Rudy Finch, the lighting director. "I'll make the adjustments."

Sampson nodded then peered at the laptop computer sitting on a small table in front of him. "Is that where you want me to play back the video during the interview?"

"The disk is on the table. I've isolated the clip I want you to show Davenport."

"Yes. Yes. I remember. I noted the question where I'm supposed to show him the video. I won't forget, and if I do, I'm sure you'll remind me." He looked at his watch. "Okay, I'm ready. Where's Davenport?"

"Should be here any minute," Ethan said, whispering to Rudy to keep adjusting the lights as he headed out of the room. Hopefully, that would keep Sampson busy for at least a few more minutes.

"Is he coming?" he said, sitting in a chair next to Ms. Landau.

"Damned if I know," she said, ignoring his concern.

"You still can't find him?"

"Nope."

"And he knows we're here?"

"Yup."

"And where's my researcher?" he said, now frustrated.

"Went downstairs to wait for Bret on the street."

Peter poked his head out the door. "This is ridiculous. First, no sheriff. Now this? He's got five more minutes, then I'm leaving."

Ethan stood and began to pace. What would he do if Davenport didn't show? He'd be missing his most important interview after Wellington? How would he explain it to Peter? To Paul? How would he tell his story?

Then the door flew open, and Davenport marched in with David at his side. "Worried I was blowing you off?" he said, his eyes piercing. "Came very close to doing just that, after visiting the sheriff at the hospital. You did quite the number on him yesterday. I'm not gonna stand for that kind of treatment."

"Just doing my job, Bret," Ethan said, trying to defuse the growing tension.

"Well, you push me the wrong way, and I'll walk out. You got that?"

Ethan ignored his threat. "Come. Let me introduce you to Peter," he said, extending his hand, as he led him past the equipment and over to Sampson.

After making the introductions, he sat Davenport in the chair opposite Peter and settled in front of his monitors, where he carefully eyeballed each camera—the two tight shots of Peter and

353

Davenport, the medium shot of the computer, and the big wide shot of the room. Then he stared at Davenport. He wasn't talking to Sampson. He wasn't even looking at him. He was just sitting, staring blankly, a stony expression on his face.

"Time to roll," Ethan said, eager to get started. "Quiet on the set. All cell phones off. "

Then he waited for his cameramen.

"I've got speed on Davenport and the monitor shot," Glickstein said, checking focus.

"And I'm good on Peter and the wide shot," Raffalo called out. "Ready when you are, Ethan."

Ethan peered at each shot one last time and put on his headset. "It's all yours, Peter."

Sampson smiled and puffed up his chest. "Thank you for talking to us today, Mr. Davenport. I know you're an old friend of Rufus Wellington as well as his attorney and probably know him better than anyone else. So I'm sure your insights will be invaluable." He frowned as Herb Glickstein scooted around his camera to adjust a key light, causing a kick in the lens of his shot. "No more interruptions," he said gruffly, before turning back to Davenport and smiling. "Let's begin with the sheriff, Eugene McKenzie. Is he feeling any better today?"

"He's still in intensive care but resting comfortably, no thanks to your Mr. Benson," Davenport said hostilely. "The doctors are optimistic, but he needs total bed rest and some time off. Then maybe he'll make a full recovery."

"Unfortunate turn of events last night, but I'm sure Ethan had nothing to do with the sheriff's sudden health crisis."

"Not sure I agree with that," Davenport said, leaning forward, his face stern. "Mr. Benson's actions last night were inexcusable. His line of questioning and his baseless allegations were exactly what caused Gene's heart attack. If you push me the wrong way, Mr. Sampson, I'll take you to court and make you pay big time."

Peter peered into Davenport's eyes. "Why don't we conduct ourselves like gentleman and proceed with the interview. Let's not get off on the wrong foot before we even get started."

"Just giving you fair warning, Mr. Sampson."

"Point well taken." He peered down at his questions then said, "Do you consider yourself a good friend of Sheriff McKenzie?"

"I'm an attorney, and he's the sheriff here in Athol," Davenport said icily, "so we spend a lot of time together."

"Do you know him as well as Dr. Wellington?"

Davenport smirked. "No. I've only known Gene since he became sheriff. I've known Rufus my entire life. He is my best friend."

Ethan stared at his bank of monitors and motioned to Herb to zoom in tighter on the attorney's face. He knew where Peter was heading.

"What was Dr. Wellington like as a kid?" Sampson asked.

"Friendly, inquisitive, funny, maybe a little wild," Davenport said, his mood softening.

"What did you guys like to do together?"

"We played baseball and football, went hiking and fishing down at the Quabbin, a little hunting when we were old enough."

Without a beat, Sampson asked, "Did Rufus like to kill things?"

"I'm ... I'm not sure I understand the question."

"His father says that as a child, he liked to kill things for fun—any animal he could get his hands on—even cats and dogs."

"Cats and dogs?"

355

"That's what his father says. Did you ever see him kill anything?"

"Just when we were hunting, and that's legal," Davenport said sharply.

"And you're sure about that?" Sampson said, pressing.

"Positive. His father must be mistaken."

Peter paused as Herb zoomed even tighter on Davenport's face.

"My producer interviewed Virgil Wellington the other day, and he told us this on camera. Are you saying that his father lied to us?"

"Well, well, well—"

"He should know, shouldn't he, Mr. Davenport? He is Rufus's father."

Davenport pulled a handkerchief from his pocket and wiped his forehead. "I guess he should know. But I don't know anything about that."

"That's not what his father told my producer, and I've got this on camera as well. You watched him kill many animals and also enjoyed the sport of killing," Sampson said, boring into Davenport's eyes. "Didn't we screen that section of the interview this morning, Ethan?"

Ethan nodded.

"So what do you say, Bret? Did you ever see your good friend, Rufus Wellington, torture and kill small animals as a little boy?"

Davenport grabbed a bottle of water sitting under his chair and drained it all at once, the camera picking up the facial tic dancing under his right eye as he searched for a response. Stuttering, he finally said, "I may have seen him kill a mouse or a squirrel or a…a…a…a chipmunk, but never a cat or a dog."

"So you admit you saw him killing animals when you were growing up?"

"Yes."

"Did he enjoy it?"

"How should I know?"

"You were his friend, weren't you? Didn't he tell you how it made him feel when he killed something?" Sampson said, tilting his head.

"No, no, no, never. And I only saw him do it once or twice—and never after he was, maybe, ten."

Ethan stared at his bank of monitors. The facial tic was bouncing like a ping-pong ball. Sampson abruptly changed gears.

"Did your friend like girls when you were going to school here at the Quabbin?"

"Of course," Bret said.

"Did he like boys?"

"What?"

"You know what I mean."

"I certainly don't."

"His father told my producer that, maybe, he liked you more than just as a friend when you were kids."

"Benson insinuated the same thing when we first met," Wellington said angrily. "And I'm gonna tell you the same thing I told him. We were not lovers. We were just best friends."

"No reason to get hostile, Mr. Davenport." He glanced down at his questions. "So Dr. Wellington just liked girls. Did he date much?"

"A little."

"Well, that's not what we've been told. My researcher, David Livingston—he's the man sitting next to Ethan."

"Yes, yes, of course. We know each other."

357

"He interviewed one of Dr. Wellington's neighbors in Old Salem this morning, Mary Murphy. You remember Mary Murphy. You introduced her to us. She went to high school with you and Rufus. She said on camera that he never dated, that he was scary and that all the girls were afraid of him. Was she telling us the truth?"

"Hell, no, she lied to you," Davenport said indignantly.

"But why would she do that?"

"I have no idea. She obviously didn't know him very well and is making up stories about him. I guess she doesn't like him."

"Careful, Mr. Davenport, the cameras are rolling. You don't want to slander Ms. Murphy."

"I'm telling you the truth, and I'm not gonna sit here and answer any more of your questions if you keep trying to put words in my mouth."

"No need to yell," Sampson said soothingly.

Ethan stood, worried Davenport was about to bolt from the room. "Should we take a short break, Bret?"

"No," he said resolutely. "I don't like your line of questioning. It's exactly what I was afraid you'd do, spout a lot of lies and innuendos, but I promised Rufus when we talked this morning that I'd answer all your questions. He won't be pleased if he finds out I walked out in the middle of the interview. But let me warn you, both of you, one last time—I'm not gonna sit here and be abused. So let's get this over with."

"I'll take that into consideration," Sampson said calmly. "We'll try to move this right along, Mr. Davenport."

Ethan held up two fingers, the anchorman nodding and flipping to page 2 of the questions. "Fast-forward to today. Describe your relationship with Dr. Wellington now that he's in prison for the murder of Heather Starr."

"I'm giving him legal advice."

"How so?"

'I'm working on his appeal."

"But didn't he plead guilty?"

"Yes."

"So how can you file an appeal?"

Davenport got aggressive. "We have a very strong case. There were all kinds of lapses in the police work—the crime scene wasn't processed properly, the murder weapon wasn't identified, the sheriff failed to find the kill site, and the DNA blood evidence is missing. So the chain of evidence is tainted."

"So your good friend the sheriff was sloppy and didn't do his job. Is that what you're saying, Mr. Davenport?"

"There you go again, Mr. Sampson. You're twisting the facts."

"No, I'm just repeating what you told me."

"Well, say what you want, but I have a good case," Davenport said, snapping back. "And on top of the botched police work, Rufus was coerced into confessing to the murder."

"It didn't look that way to me when I screened the confession video."

Davenport froze, sweat dripping down his face. "You aren't supposed to have the confession video. The judge ordered it sealed."

"But I do have it," Sampson said forcefully. "Should I describe it to you?"

"Well—"

"I don't think I need to do that, do I, because you were there, Mr. Davenport, weren't you?"

"Well—"

"Even though you told my producer you didn't get to the sheriff's office until after he confessed," Sampson said sarcastically. "Care to tell us what you said to Dr. Wellington when there was no sound at the top of the tape?"

"I ... I ... I—"

"Did you tell him to admit to murdering Heather Starr to shut down the police investigation? Was that your plan, Mr. Davenport? To make your appeal easier now that the time is right?"

"That's preposterous," Davenport said, spittle flying from his mouth. "You can't prove any of that."

"No. I can't, but that's what my producer believes."

"Believe what you want, but my client doesn't belong behind bars."

"Did Dr. Wellington pay you to say that?" Sampson said, turning to Ethan. "Let me have those documents again."

Ethan motioned to his cameramen to keep rolling, walked over to Peter, handed him the folder, and sat back down.

Sampson flipped through the pages. "How much does Dr. Wellington pay you?"

"That's privileged information. I'm not going to answer that."

Sampson pulled out the top sheet and said, "I'd like you to take a look at this." He passed the document to Davenport, Herb Glickstein pulling back to capture Davenport blankly staring at the single sheet of paper.

"It's a summary of your earnings that we pulled together from your tax returns and from dozens of other financial statements obtained from confidential sources. Take a look at the bottom line. What does it say, Mr. Davenport?"

Davenport peered at the document, then at Sampson, then at the camera. His hands were shaking. "This can't be right," he said.

"I can assure you it's accurate. What does it say?"

Davenport continued staring at the document, his eyeballs darting back and forth.

"I'll tell you what it says. Rufus Wellington has paid you almost twenty million dollars over the years. That's a lot of money, Mr. Davenport."

Davenport looked from Sampson to the document and then back to Sampson, speechless.

"And there's another set of financial records I want to show you." He pulled a second sheet of paper from the folder. "This one belongs to Eugene McKenzie. It says right here that he has nearly three million dollars stashed away in his portfolio. How is that possible, Mr. Davenport? He's a county sheriff. Couldn't possibly have made all that money."

The attorney exploded on camera, "I have no idea. You'll have to ask the sheriff that question."

"But I can't do that, can I? He's in the hospital. So I'm asking you instead. How do you think he amassed that fortune?"

"Beats me."

"Did you give it to him?"

"I certainly did not."

"Did Dr. Wellington give him the money?"

"How should I know?"

"I'll tell you how," Sampson said, waving the folder. "It's all in here—bank statements, IRS filings, canceled checks, savings accounts, stock investments—a complete portfolio on you and Sheriff McKenzie." He handed the file to Davenport. "Take a minute, and read through all the documents. I think you'll find them interesting."

Davenport flipped through the pages.

"Well, Mr. Davenport?"

The attorney stared into the camera, his tongue slowly licking his lower lip, then his upper lip.

"I'll tell you what those documents prove," Sampson said forcefully, "that Rufus Wellington was paying off you and the sheriff to do his bidding, to rig the police investigation after the murder so nobody would find out about his past, and then to tamper with the evidence so you could appeal his conviction and set the groundwork to get him out of jail."

"I have no idea what you're talking about," Davenport said, the hairs on the back of his neck standing straight up.

"I think you do, Mr. Davenport. And I think you're hiding something else you're deathly afraid we're going to find out and reveal in our story."

"Enough," Davenport yelled. "You have no proof of any of this—"

"Is it his connection to Janice O'Brien and The House of Hope in Boston?" Sampson said, not backing down. "Yes, we know all about that too. She's a madam, and it's a brothel, and that's where Dr. Wellington met Heather Starr. Is that what he's trying to get you and the sheriff to cover up?"

"That's insane."

"No, it isn't," Sampson said belligerently. "Wellington's also been paying Ms. O'Brien to keep quiet—cash that he's instructed you to give her, cash to hide that he's a pedophile with a taste for teenage hookers."

Davenport started to get up. "I don't have to listen to these lies. You're trying to trip me up, make me look like a fool. Stop the cameras. I'm finished here."

Ethan motioned to his cameramen to keep rolling and leaned over his bank of monitors. "Bret, I know this is difficult, but you don't want our cameras to capture you storming off the set, do you? That'll make you look guilty. Take a deep breath, and sit back down. It'll just be another minute or two."

There was silence as Davenport slumped into his chair.

Sampson shuffled through his questions. "There's still a lot of ground to cover, Ethan. What should I ask?"

Ethan pointed to page 4. "Ask him question 37 and the follow-ups."

Sampson carefully read the question, looked back at Ethan, and said, "We still rolling?"

"Whenever you're ready."

Sampson checked his monitor, smoothed out a wayward clump of hair, then picked up the disk and placed it into the computer. Clearing his throat, he said, "This may be difficult to watch, but my producer thinks it's important." He hit *Play*, and an image filled the screen.

Davenport's eyes were glued to the monitor, and as the camera panned across Rufus Wellington's kitchen, the light from an overhead chandelier cast an ominous shadow. Ethan was facing Sheriff McKenzie and pointing to a door, motioning for Lloyd to open it. As Lloyd reached for the doorknob, the sheriff streaked through the shot, flailing his arms like a wild man, screaming, "Nobody goes down there. That's the basement, and it's off-limits. It has nothing to do with my investigation and nothing to do with the murder." Then his face contorted in pain, and he clutched his chest, staggered backward, and crashed to the floor.

Sampson paused the video and turned to Davenport, "Do you want to see it again?"

He shook his head no as he twisted his hands in his lap.

"Why didn't the sheriff want us to go down to the basement?" Sampson said, his expression sullen.

Davenport's whole body was shaking as he continued to stare at the monitor.

"What's down there, Bret?" Peter said, peering like a laser beam.

"There's nothing down there. It's a basement."

"So why did the sheriff get so upset?"

"How should I know?"

"But there is something in the basement that you and the sheriff don't want us to know about," Sampson said, still pressing. "Is it somehow connected to the murder of Heather Starr?"

"That's preposterous."

"Sure you won't tell me what's down there?"

"Look, Rufus Wellington told me to do this interview over my objections. And I think I've answered enough of your questions without consulting further with my client. If you want to know what's down in his basement, you'll have to ask him. It's his house, not mine." Then he yanked off his microphone, stood, and stormed off the set, stopping and turning when he reached the door. "Now I know why Gene told me not to do the interview this morning. I should've listened to him. Pack your equipment, and get out of my office. I'll see you tomorrow at the prison." Then he straightened his tie and walked out of the room.

"Did you get all that?" Ethan said, pulling off his headset.

"Never stopped rolling," Glickstein said. "The guy turned white when we showed him the video. He knows what's in the basement."

"I know that," Ethan said, walking over to Sampson. "Nice job, Peter."

"The guy was a bit high strung, but we got what we needed," Sampson said, checking the time. "You have nothing else for me this afternoon, right? So I'm gonna head back to the house with Consuela. We'll grab dinner, study the Wellington questions one more time, and then turn in. Tomorrow's a long day, and I'm headed back to New York as soon as we finish. What time we leaving in the morning?"

"Wheels up at eight."

"I'll see you at breakfast."

Ethan watched him march out of the room then turned and addressed the crew, "Peter may be finished, but we still have a full day of scenics to shoot around the reservoir. So let's wrap and get out of here." Plopping down in a chair, he pulled out his iPad and began scanning his notes. His whole story was now riding on the Wellington interview.

It was his last chance to learn the truth.

His last chance to stop the appeal.

And to keep Rufus Wellington behind bars.

CHAPTER 36

THE EARLY MORNING SUNSHINE WAS peeking through the tree-tops as the limousine barreled east on Highway Two toward MCI-Cedar Junction. Ethan had sent David and the crew on ahead to build the set, needing the extra time to work with Sampson. But he'd spent only a few moments prepping his anchorman for the interview, too worried about how to tell him and how he'd react. He was running out of time and couldn't wait any longer. It was now or never.

"Peter, I need to show you something."

Sampson looked up, his reading glasses sliding down his nose. "Can't it wait? My schedule next week is overbooked as usual, and I need Consuela to make a few phone calls and cancel the mayor and the head of the Metropolitan Museum of Art and David Muir, of all people, because you're keeping me too damn busy to meet my other obligations. Plus, I have this damn Jennifer Lawrence story to worry about, no thanks to you."

"But this is for the Wellington interview, Peter, and it's important," Ethan said, trying to remain calm.

"What is it for God's sake?"

Ethan turned to Consuela, who was sitting next to Sampson. "Scoot over so I can sit between the two of you."

He slipped into the plush leather seat and pulled out his laptop. "Before I show you what's on my computer, I need to give you background." Peter still wasn't paying attention as Felix the chauffeur exited Highway Two and headed south on Interstate 495. Ethan decided to pull no punches and dive right in. "I've been in Wellington's basement."

"What do you mean?"

"Just that. I know what's down there."

"But how's that possible?" Sampson said. "The sheriff didn't show you, and Bret Davenport refused to tell us what's in the basement when I showed him the video yesterday. What aren't you telling me, Ethan?"

He took a deep breath, "That I broke into Wellington's house with David on my last trip to the Quabbin."

"You did what?" Sampson said incredulously.

"We went in through a window well and searched the entire crime scene, including the basement."

"But didn't Davenport take you through the house on your first survey trip? You showed me all those damn still pictures David shot when you were trying to convince me to do the story. Why'd you go back and break in? That's a crime."

"Because I didn't trust Davenport and thought he was hiding something for Wellington. And there's something else you need to know."

"What d'you mean by that?" Sampson said.

"I had David document everything we did on a two-chip digital camera. That's what I want to show you."

"So there's a video record of you breaking into Wellington's house?" Sampson said, staring over the top of his reading glasses.

"Yes, and I found something in the basement that could bust this story wide open."

"This better be good," Sampson said testily. "Play it."

Ethan hit *Enter*, and for the next half hour, they watched the footage from beginning to end. Then Ethan handed Peter the spiral notebook.

"Is this what I just watched you steal from the medical library in Wellington's subbasement that you just happened to stumble across?" Sampson said, flipping through the pages. "Well, it looks like gobbledygook to me—a bunch of sketches and indecipherable chicken scratch. What does it mean?"

"Not really sure," Ethan said, dismayed. "Your interview with Rufus Wellington is our only hope to find out."

"And I'm guessing you also want me to ask him what's behind that locked door that's so blatantly prominent in your illegal videotape?" Peter said, scratching his chin. "Have you told Paul about any of this?"

"Not yet. I wanted to run it by you first."

"Well, he needs to know before I talk about any of this on camera." He whipped around to Consuela, "Get him on the phone. Now."

Consuela punched Paul's number into her iPhone and handed it to Peter. "Paul, I'm sitting here with Ethan. He just told me something that may be a problem. Let me put you on speaker." Then they walked him through the notebook and the videotape and listened to him scream.

⁂

An hour later, they passed through the front entrance of the prison and into the waiting room, Ethan still feeling the aftereffects of the tongue-lashing he'd just received from Paul. Standing in front of the security door leading into the bowels of the complex was the warden, Philip Dunkirk, and his director of press relations, Horace Gentry. They shook hands, Peter remaining off to the side, cold and aloof.

"Your crew is finishing up on block 10," Dunkirk said, checking the time. "They're in the visitors' room with all their equipment."

"What's block 10?" Sampson said gruffly.

"It's the maximum-security wing where we house our most violent inmates, like Dr. Wellington," Dunkirk said. He smiled at Consuela. "Are you sure you want to go in there, Ms. Santana?"

"I can handle it," she said pertly. "I live on 125th Street and Broadway in Harlem, can't be more dangerous than that."

"The inmates might make it unpleasant for you," Gentry said, speaking for the first time. "They don't see women too often, especially pretty women."

"She can handle it," Sampson said. "Besides, I don't go anywhere without her."

"Suit yourself," the warden said. "But don't say we didn't warn you."

"Shall we head down to the set?" Ethan said, anxious they were running late. "I'd like to look at the lights and cameras and make sure my guys are ready."

"Horace, go tell Frederick to buzz us in," Dunkirk said commandingly.

The press officer walked over to the glass-enclosed guard station, signaled to the correction officer in charge of the waiting room, and the heavy steel door slowly opened. The warden nodded to Ethan, and they all followed him down the long, musty corridor leading to the first security checkpoint. After emptying their pockets and placing their belongings on the conveyor belt, they walked through an X-ray machine—one by one—collected their things, and proceeded deeper into the prison complex, through the series of secondary checkpoints, and onto block 10. As they walked past a phalanx of heavily armed prison guards patrolling the corridor running the length of the two-tiered cellblock, the inmates began hooting and hollering and yelling obscenities.

Ethan was momentarily unnerved.

All he could think about was the deputy sheriff trying to run him off the road and the pimp with the blackjack.

"Is this the only way to the interview location, past all these unruly criminals?" Sampson said, inflaming the already-volatile atmosphere—the inmates now shaking the bars and screaming at the top of their lungs.

"I'm afraid so," the warden said, unfazed by the chaos around him. "The prison is well over a hundred years old. There's no back entrance to block 10. It was built this way for security."

Ethan leaned over to Consuela and whispered in her ear, "Are you okay?"

"I'm fine, Ethan," she said nervously.

"How much longer?" Ethan said to the warden, beginning to feel bile rise in his gut as he tried to choke down his snowballing paranoia.

"Almost there, Mr. Benson," Dunkirk said calmly. "Just one more checkpoint, another short hallway, and we'll reach the visitors' room."

❧

Within minutes, a prison guard entered a code on a keypad, and Ethan walked through the final security door into a small room—no more than fifteen by twenty feet. The crew had been working for hours, hanging lights, building a sound-mixing station and a control room, and strategically positioning four cameras around the set. They'd also mounted a small digital camera with a wide angle lens on a tripod in the observation room overlooking the makeshift studio where the warden, his staff, and Bret Davenport would watch the interview. In the middle of the room anchored to the floor was a steel chair, draped in straps and chains and padlocks, that was dramatically lit with a beam of light, leaving the rest of the room in near darkness. Ethan gave Rudy Finch the thumbs-up and walked Sampson over to his position.

"Isn't that a bit excessive?" Sampson said, pointing to the steel contraption.

"It's where they plan to restrain Wellington," Herb Glickstein said, his face buried in the computer on the back of his camera.

"It looks like an electric chair," Ethan said, turning to David. "Did you pick this place to do the interview?"

"Wasn't me," David said as he positioned a sandbag at the base of a light stand to anchor it into position. "The warden did. Said Wellington is too unpredictable and that he's got to be locked in that chair."

"What do you think, Peter?" Ethan said, turning to his anchorman.

"I don't care where we do the interview," he said as Consuela began covering the wrinkles around his eyes with a layer of makeup. "But where are my lights? I'm sitting here in the dark. The camera won't see my face."

Ethan turned to Bobby, who threw a switch on a power strip, turning on a bank of Keno Flos. Sampson checked his monitor, swiveling his head back and forth, then said happily, "That'll do just fine."

"Are we close?" Ethan said, turning to Glickstein.

"Just need to tweak the lights when Wellington arrives. Then we can roll."

Ethan walked to his monitors and peered at the five cameras. The set looked like a scene from a big budget Hollywood thriller, the steel chair dominating each shot like a rack in a medieval torture chamber.

He smiled.

It was perfect.

Then he went over to the warden and his press secretary, "Ready to go, Phillip. Let's bring in Dr. Wellington."

CHAPTER 37

THERE WAS SILENCE AS RUFUS Wellington shuffled into the room surrounded by prison guards brandishing rifles and nightsticks. He was wearing a gray jumpsuit with his name printed above his right breast pocket and MCI-Cedar Junction emblazoned in big black letters across his back. He was immaculately clean, his hair combed and his fingernails neatly trimmed. His hands were shackled in front of him, his feet secured with steel leg irons, his body manacled with a heavy chain. A cigarette dangled lazily from his mouth, smoke curling up past his nose and over his head. All five cameras were rolling as the guards pushed him into the steel chair and fastened his hands and feet in the restraints. Then they pulled a leather harness over his shoulders, anchoring his body firmly in place, so all he could move was his head.

Wellington's eyes darted back and forth, before locking onto Consuela, who was sitting next to Ethan behind the bank of monitors. He smiled, a satanic smile, and tried to strain forward then began shrieking, "PRETTY! PRETTY! PRETTY!" He licked his lips, his tongue darting in and out of his mouth like a serpent. "Come here, my sweet pretty, so I can get a closer look at you. You're such a luscious little thing. I'd love to strip you naked and run my tongue all over your body." He sucked in his breath and continued leering then rocked back and forth against the restraints, trying to break free.

Consuela recoiled, unable to speak, abject fear on her face.

The loud speaker crackled, and the warden's voice boomed through the intercom. "It might be better, Ms. Santana, if you watched the interview up here with me and Mr. Davenport. Dr. Wellington seems to have forgotten his manners. I'll send Horace down with a guard to escort you up."

Ethan nodded to the door.

Trembling, she waited for the electronic lock to disengage, stood, and took a wide berth around Wellington—still twisting uncontrollably, his eyes following her every move as she disappeared out the door between the press officer and a well-muscled prison guard. Ethan took a deep breath then pivoted to Wellington, whose piercing glare had shifted menacingly to Sampson.

"Are we ready?" Ethan said, whispering to his two cameramen through his headset.

"Just need another minute," Herb said, hopping out of his chair to adjust a barn door on a fill light to soften the brightness on Wellington's face. "How does it look, Ethan?"

"Much better," he said, eager to roll before Wellington lost control again. "We good to go now?"

"Almost there," Bobby said, glancing at David in the observation room, who was pulling the focus on the digital camera and framing the lens on Bret Davenport.

"All set up here," David said into his headset, motioning to Ethan.

"And sound?"

"Mics are recording loud and clear," Anthony Petulla said, checking the levels on his mixing board. "Can you see the boom in any of the shots?"

"Just the wide shot, and it looks perfect," Ethan said. "Do we have speed?"

"On all five cameras," Herb said, zooming in a little tighter on Wellington.

"Everybody quiet on the set, and turn off your cell phones," Ethan said, peering into the monitors one last time then locking eyes with Sampson, "Anytime you're ready, Peter."

"Have you heard back from Paul?" Sampson said quietly.

"Not yet."

"Well then, we can't use what we discussed in the car," he said, waving his hand dismissively at Ethan before peering at Wellington, "Is that contraption you're bolted into comfortable?"

Wellington sat impassively then spit out his cigarette. "That's a rather innocuous question. Does it look comfortable to you? I was expecting a bit more from the big-network anchorman than how the warden and his guards treat their guests here at this four-star prison for hardened criminals like me."

"Well, I was just wondering—"

"Stop wondering, Mr. Sampson," Wellington said harshly. "I'm a sicko, a sadist, a CONVICTED murderer, and this is how they make sure SUPPOSED killers like me don't wreak havoc in a place like this. They cage me like an animal." He suddenly lunged forward, straining to reach the anchorman.

Ethan stood, alarmed, as the warden's voice boomed over the loudspeaker. "That's enough, Rufus. Any more outbursts, and this interview is over. Do I make myself clear?"

"Perfectly, Phillip," Wellington said, his face turning docile. "I promise to be a good boy from here on out." He eased back and smiled at Sampson, "Next question, Mr. Anchorman."

Ethan pulled off his headset, walked over to Sampson, and knelt in front of him, careful to stay clear of Wellington. "Skip the first page, Peter, and begin on page 2. We've got his father's interview and can narrate whatever's missing about his childhood. It's not important at the moment. Start with Boston and Heather."

"Good idea, Mr. Producer," Wellington said, hissing. "That's why we're here, today, isn't it? To talk about my dear, sweet Heather. We don't need to talk about little boy Rufus, do we?"

Ethan ignored him and sat back down in front of his monitors.

Sampson glanced at his questions then stared into Wellington's eyes, "How did you meet Heather Starr?"

"I think you already know that," Wellington said obstinately. "Bret tells me Mr. Benson visited my good friend Janice O'Brien at The House of Hope and that he knows she set me up on my first date with the beautiful Ms. Starr, such a tasty little thing. I do miss her. Really, I do." He licked his lips and smiled.

Sampson glanced down at his questions again, flustered, then said, "Were you in love with Heather Starr."

"Yes, indeed, I was madly in love with sweet Heather."

"Even though she was a hooker and you were a famous heart surgeon, Dr. Wellington?"

"Might seem a bit strange," he said with a scandalous grin on his face. "But I like hookers. They're so much more adventurous than straight women. And my Heather, well, there wasn't anything she wouldn't do for me. I can still smell her sweet cunt and taste the nectar of her precious little asshole. I loved every square inch of her delicious body."

Ethan shivered and motioned for Herb to zoom in tighter on Wellington's face.

"Then why did you kill her, Dr. Wellington?" Sampson said, trying to regain his composure.

"I didn't kill her, Mr. Sampson. Didn't you hear?" Wellington said, rolling his eyes toward the observation deck. "My good friend Bret Davenport is about to tell the court that my confession was coerced and that I'm innocent of the murder. Isn't that right, Bret?"

Davenport tried to disappear into his chair.

"So did you murder Heather Starr, or didn't you?" Sampson said, confused.

"Ah, is the infamous Dr. Wellington a murderer, or isn't he? That's the big question, and that's why we're sitting here, to see if you're smart enough to figure it all out. So what do you think, Mr. Sampson?"

Sampson turned to Ethan, looking for guidance.

"Go to number 12, middle of page 2."

Sampson quickly read the question and peered at Wellington, "My producer was told by a source that your attorney, Mr. Davenport, is going to claim that there's no proof linking you to the murder and that you were forced by the sheriff, Eugene McKenzie, to falsely confess to killing Heather Starr. Is that correct, Dr. Wellington."

"If that's what Bret says, it must be correct."

"But I'm asking you, Dr. Wellington."

Wellington strained forward, "And I'm telling you, that's our story."

Sampson was flustered, unsure where to go next.

"Question 37, bottom of page 3," Ethan said forcefully.

Sampson glanced at the question then back at Wellington. "But you described in great detail to the court-appointed psychiatrist just how you murdered Heather Starr and dismembered her before you buried her. Were you lying to Dr. Hosenfeld?"

"Ah, you've really done your homework, Mr. Sampson. Or should I say, Mr. Benson has really done his homework."

"Answer my question, Dr. Wellington."

Wellington craned his neck toward the observation deck. Bret Davenport was now pressed up against the glass, frantic. "Let me see. What would Bret want me to say? He'd probably want me to say yes, that I was lying to the shrink."

"To Dr. Hosenfeld?"

"That's what I just said."

"So you didn't murder Heather Starr?"

Ethan leaned forward and stared into Wellington's monitor as Glickstein zoomed into a tight shot of his eyes.

"You're very persistent, Mr. Sampson, very persistent," Wellington said, smiling. "So how should I answer that, Bret? Should I tell them the truth? Any last-minute advice from my learned counselor?" Then he laughed crazily and peered at Sampson. "Yes, indeed, I certainly did murder sweet Heather on that warm moonlit night and sent her off to her Maker in heaven. It was just so beautiful."

"So you did murder Heather Starr?" Sampson said, composing himself. "And your appeal is just a sham."

"Yes, Mr. Sampson, I guess you could say that."

"And you shouldn't be released from prison?"

"Of course not, I'm a killer. The appeal was Bret's idea. The confession was Bret's idea. It's all been Bret's idea."

Ethan sighed, relieved that Peter had just short-circuited the appeal.

"So why did you murder Heather Starr?" Sampson said, leaning forward in his chair.

"Because I had to," Wellington said, his eyes now far away.

"Why?"

"Because she wouldn't accept my unconditional love, so I had no other choice. If I couldn't possess her completely, then I wanted to make sure nobody else could possess her either."

"What do you mean by 'possess her'?" Sampson said, confused again. "She was a young woman, a person like you and me, not a physical object you could put on a shelf and call your own."

"I disagree, Mr. Sampson. I paid a lot of money to keep her mine, and well, when she didn't want me anymore, she just had to go. Simple as that. Poof. No more Heather. Gone for eternity. Except in my mind."

Ethan ran a finger down his list of questions. Wellington was definitely a sociopath and a psychopath, just as Dr. Althea Oliphant had suggested. So why was he here and not under the care of a shrink? Would the court move him to a hospital for the criminally insane after his story made air? Or would it leave him here at Cedar Junction, a homicidal maniac ready to explode at a moment's notice? He checked off the first question on page 4 and made eye contact with Peter, "Ask number 43."

Peter read the question and nodded, "Why did you cut Heather into all those little pieces?"

Wellington smiled. "That's a silly question, Mr. Anchorman. I'm a surgeon. I cut all my patients into little pieces, and more importantly in Heather's case, I needed to know exactly what was inside her. That was the only way I could fully understand what made her unique, what made her so special."

Peter hesitated, his eyes askance. "I don't understand, Dr. Wellington. You're not making any sense."

"Oh, yes, I am. You just don't think the way I do. I neatly sliced and diced her to get closer to her pure essence, to see into her soul. It was the only way I could love her forever. She gave me no other choice when she refused to marry me."

Sampson shuffled his questions then checked with Ethan, "Is he making any sense?"

"Perfect sense, Peter," Ethan said without hesitation, "in light of what the psychiatrist told me."

"Ah, you've talked to a psychiatrist about me," Wellington said, straining to look at Ethan. "Very good. But I hope it was somebody better than that quack Walter Hosenfeld. Such a fool. He didn't understand me at all. Had him wrapped around my little finger the whole time we were together."

Ethan waved to Sampson. "Ask him about the video, Peter, middle of page 4."

"What number, Ethan?"

"Forty-eight."

Sampson read the question and looked up at Wellington. "We've got a copy of your confession, Dr. Wellington."

"The famous video Bret didn't want anybody to see."

"At the beginning, you were sitting in the interrogation room with Sheriff McKenzie, just the two of you, and I must say, he appeared quite terrified."

Sampson smiled. "Yes, indeed, he was."

"Then your attorney, Bret Davenport, walked into the room, put his hand on your shoulder, and whispered something into your ear. But we couldn't hear what he said, Dr. Wellington. In fact, nobody could hear what he said because there was no sound on the disk at that point. Care to tell us what your attorney told you?"

"Ah, it wasn't what Bret told me. It was what I told him and the sheriff," Wellington said, his eyes opening wide like the bores of a double-barrel shotgun. "It upset both of them beyond your wildest imagination."

"Was it about your confession?" Peter said probingly.

"No. No. No, silly boy." Wellington said, laughing hysterically.

Ethan glanced up at the observation deck. Davenport was pressed up against the window again—the camera pointing directly at him—banging on the glass, screaming, trying to get Wellington's attention.

"So if it wasn't about the confession," Sampson said, shuffling his questions, "what was it about?"

"I told them I'd tell the world everything if they didn't do exactly what I said."

"Tell the world everything"? What did that mean? Ethan thought, before scribbling a question on a piece of paper and holding it up for Peter.

Sampson nodded then asked the follow-up, "I'm not sure I understand, Dr. Wellington. Care to explain?"

"Bret says you've already figured out part of it. I was giving them bushels of cash under the table to do lots of things for me."

"What kinds of things?"

"Well, that night, that glorious night I sent Heather to the afterlife, I didn't want an argument from either one of them. You see, Mr. Sampson, I told my two good friends I'd cut off their money if they didn't go along with my plan to cover up my past. And of course, they agreed without blinking an eye. They like my money."

"Let's back up a moment, Dr. Wellington," Sampson said. "You wanted the sheriff and your attorney to cover up your past?"

"That's what I said."

"Enlighten us."

"Why should I do that, Mr. Sampson? Bret and Eugene have worked so very hard all these years, making sure nobody ever finds out. Why should I blow all their hard work and all my money? That doesn't make sense, does it?"

Ethan stared at his monitors. Peter looked unsure where to go next. He glanced at his briefcase and made an instant decision. Grabbing the spiral notebook, he yanked off his headset, Herb and Bobby widening their shots as he moved toward the anchorman.

"Here, Peter, ask him about this."

"Have you heard back from Paul, Ethan? Have our attorneys given us permission to use this in the interview?" he said, waving the small notebook.

Ethan hesitated, but only for an instant. "No, I haven't heard from Paul. But we can't wait any longer. I think Dr. Wellington will answer your last question if you show him the notebook." He sat back down.

"Still rolling," Herb said as he pushed into a medium shot of Wellington.

"Ah, so you found it," Wellington said dismissively.

"In a subbasement of your house, Dr. Wellington."

"Very clever detective work. Very clever. You got into my private library and found my diary. You weren't supposed to go down there. Nobody's supposed to go down there, except me and Bret and sometimes Eugene." He swung his eyes and looked straight at Ethan, "I didn't think you had it in you, Mr. Benson. You see, I broke into your computer and read your personal e-mails, the clever man that I am. I had to know a little about my new number one adversary before I had the pleasure of finally meeting you. So I know you like the taste of good Scotch. I know you like to drink it all day long. I know you're nothing better than a common, everyday drunk. You're a very bad boy, Mr. Benson."

"What's he talking about, Ethan?" Sampson said, surprised.

"Not now, Peter."

Wellington leaned against the restraints, peering up at Davenport, who'd retreated to the door in the back of the observation room. "Looks like the jig's up, Bret. They've got my diary." Then he started howling, his body heaving up and down in waves, his face contorting in a mask of pure evil.

"What's in this diary, Dr. Wellington?" Sampson said, holding up the spiral notebook.

Wellington stopped screaming but didn't answer.

"None of it makes sense," Peter said, fanning through the pages. "What does it mean, Dr. Wellington?"

No answer.

"Are you going to tell me?"

Still no answer.

"What about all these pictures and notations?"

"It's all code to help me remember my experiments," Wellington said suddenly, his eyes sparkling.

"Your experiments? I still don't understand."

"You're not supposed to understand."

"And what about all the numbers?" Sampson said, trying a different tack. "The first page is marked 5-7-9-1." He showed Wellington.

"It's a date," Wellington said, his eyes now ablaze.

"A date?"

"Reverse the numbers."

"One-nine-seven-five. Why's that year important?" Sampson said quizzically.

"It's the year I made my first kill."

"Your first kill?" Sampson said, shocked.

"Yes, my dear old mother, and everything else I wrote on that page explains exactly how I did it."

Ethan leaned forward and stared at Wellington as Herb zoomed into an extreme tight shot.

"You killed your mother?" Sampson said.

"I pushed her down the stairs when I was a little boy," Wellington said proudly.

"Why?"

"Because I wanted to know what it felt like to kill a human being. I'd already killed all these tiny, little animals, and I wanted to know if a person would make me feel the same way. And you know, it felt good. Very good."

"Like Heather?"

"Yes, like Heather and like all the others."

"Hold on, Dr. Wellington. I want to make sure I've got that on camera. Are you saying that you've murdered other people beyond your mother and Heather Starr?"

"Many others, Mr. Sampson, MANY OTHERS. And I cut them all into pieces just like Heather, each and every one of them—except for my dear mother. I was too little back then and afraid Father and the shrinks would find out and think there was something wrong with me. But I longed to cut her up too—to feel the euphoria, the sexual euphoria."

"How many other people have you murdered, Dr. Wellington?"

"How many pages are in my book? Can you count, Mr. Sampson?"

Sampson quickly scanned through the pages, looked at Ethan, and then back at Wellington. "There are twenty-two pages of pictures and notations in here. Are you saying you've committed twenty-two murders? That you're a serial killer?"

His eyes fixed on Sampson like pinpricks. "Yes, that's what I am—a serial killer. I butcher prostitutes—just prostitutes, except for my mother, of course, but I guess she was kind of a prostitute too. She liked to fuck my father. She liked to fuck other men when my father was away on business trips. I used to watch through the keyhole in her bedroom door. I could see everything. EVERYTHING! And oh, it was fun, so much fun. It made me so excited. Watching two people fucking is almost better than doing it yourself." He licked his lips and shrieked, "Would you like to know where I killed Heather and all the other pretty girls in that book? Everybody wants to know where I did my handiwork, don't you, Mr. Sampson?"

Sampson stuttered then said, "Yes, I would, Dr. Wellington."

"Well then, ask Bret. He can show you. He was there the night I killed Heather. He was there when I murdered all my girls—except for my mother. He loved to watch me fuck them. He loved to fuck them too—and to fuck me at the same time— just like when we were little boys and liked to play with each other's little pricks. And Bret, my dear Bret, he also loved to stare into their eyes and see the fear on their faces as I hacked them to pieces. They were always awake, wide awake, but I'm sure you know that, Mr. Sampson, from the autopsy report. You must have seen Heather's autopsy report. There's a whole page on the drug I liked to use. Isn't that right, Bret?"

Ethan looked up at the observation room as Davenport began banging on the door, trying to get out. Everyone was screaming as Lloyd, who was sitting, watching him, leaped from his chair and, in one swift motion, tackled Davenport around the waist, knocking him to the floor. A mad shuffle ensued—fists flying, arms flailing, legs kicking—as prison guards rushed into the melee. David, who'd retreated into the corner next to Consuela, lunged forward and grabbed the digital camera from the tripod then circled the room, bobbing and weaving, capturing the free-for-all as it spilled into the hallway.

"Don't let him get away," the warden said, shouting. "Arrest him."

"Lemme go. I have no idea what Rufus is talking about," Davenport said, wailing. "I didn't do anything. He's lying."

"Take him down to a holding cell until we sort all this out," the warden said as more guards piled on, pinning him to the ground facedown and handcuffing him.

David continued rolling, panning with a seasoned skill, as Davenport—his suit jacket torn, his hair flying every which way—was yanked off the floor and dragged down the hall, the block 10 inmates yelling and screaming and raking the bars of their cells.

Ethan waited for the commotion to die down then whirled to Sampson, who was frantically shuffling through his questions. "Page 5, question 52," he said calmly.

Peter peered at the question then said, "Looks like they just arrested your attorney."

"Guess I won't have to pay him any more money to keep his mouth shut," Wellington said, grinning from ear to ear. "Serves him right. He belongs in a cell right next to me, because he enjoyed the fun and games almost as much as I did."

"Peter, ask question 52. We're running out of time," Ethan said forcefully. "The warden's heading down from the observation deck. I think he's gonna pull the plug on the interview."

Sampson cleared his throat. "My producer found something else besides your diary when he was down in your library—a door hidden behind one of the bookshelves."

"Your producer was a very busy boy when he was snooping around my house. He certainly wasn't drunk that night, must've been stone sober to discover all my secrets."

"What's behind that door?" Sampson said, tilting his head.

"Ah, wouldn't you like to know, Mr. Sampson," Wellington said, bug-eyed. "But no, I'm not going to tell you."

"Is that where you killed Heather Starr?" Sampson said, pressing.

"Not going to tell you."

"And all the other girls you just claimed you murdered?"

"Not another word about it," Wellington sneered. "You're going to have to answer that question on your own. I'm sure the police will reopen their investigation now that I've told you about the diary and all my other lucky victims. Maybe they'll take you along for the ride? Maybe you can even bring your cameras? Then everyone will know what's behind door number one—the magic door. Isn't that a good idea, Mr. Sampson?"

"So you won't tell me, Dr. Wellington?"

"No. No. No! And I'm not gonna answer any more of your questions. We're done here. You've got what you came for, and so have I. Now the world's gonna know exactly who I am, and I can take my place where I belong in the pantheon of madness. That's why I granted you this interview—to set the record straight about me, my good friend Bret Davenport, the sheriff, and even dear, old Ms. O'Brien. We're all guilty—all four of us—of far more than just the murder of the sweet Heather Starr." Then Wellington's eyes glazed over, and his body went limp.

There was silence as Peter snapped his fingers in front of Wellington's face. "Now what, Ethan? He's totally gone, and there's an entire page of questions I haven't asked yet."

Ethan stood as Warden Dunkirk walked through the security door and onto the set. Motioning for his prison guards to follow, he made his way over to Wellington and stared into his eyes.

"He's catatonic again, like he was for all that time before he watched your TV show. We're not gonna get anything else out of him today."

"Can we follow you as you take him back to his cell?" Ethan said, motioning for Herb to grab his camera from the tripod.

"As long as you don't get in the way."

"Shoot everything. I'll need the footage to cover narration in our story."

Glickstein hoisted the big camera onto his shoulder and zeroed in on Wellington as the prison guards unlocked the restraints, reshackled his arms and legs in chains, and escorted him out of the room, followed by the warden and his press secretary.

After the security door slid back into place, Ethan turned to Sampson, "We need to call Paul. The guy just admitted killing twenty-one women, plus his mother, and we've got the only interview with Rufus Wellington."

"And what's Paul gonna say when he finds out we used the diary that you stole when you broke into Wellington's house. And what are the cops gonna say? Well, I'll tell you, Ethan. They're gonna be pissed and throw you into jail—not me, you."

"Let me worry about that," Ethan said with a laconic smile. "We have a much bigger problem than that. Every news organization in the country is gonna be all over our story. We need to crash it to air to stay ahead of the competition." Growing more excited with each passing moment, he spun and faced his crew. "Where's Lloyd? I need him to call his sources. I wanna take cameras and go with the cops when they break down the door in Wellington's library and search the rest of his property for bodies. And I need him to make the call right now!" Then, as all the energy drained from his body, he sat down quietly and placed the call to Paul.

CHAPTER 38

LEADING A CONVOY OF CARS and trucks filled with production equipment, Ethan pulled off the dirt road, went through the front gate, and drove up the long driveway—past the stone pillars and into the front yard of Wellington's estate. It was cold and damp, gusts of wind screaming out of the west as storm clouds darkened the sky. Ethan was tense, his mood mirroring the promise of the threatening deluge. Paul and the network had been furious that he'd broken into Wellington's house and more furious that he'd used the diary without their permission. Paul had threatened to suspend him and kill the story, only relenting after Ethan set up a meeting with federal authorities and handed them a copy of the spiral notebook. The Feds decided not to prosecute in exchange for his cooperation.

His special had been screened by every executive all the way up to the chairman of the board and was scheduled to air later that night. But Ethan still faced one last day of chaos. Lloyd had cashed in a favor with his contacts at the FBI's Elite Serial Crime Unit in Washington and gotten a thumbs-up for Ethan to take his cameras along for the ride as a task force of local, state, and federal officials searched for bodies and opened the secret door in Wellington's library.

It was a Global Broadcasting exclusive—the envy of every other news organization in the country.

The limousine stopped at a police barricade as dozens of cops and crime scene investigators scurried about in a mad frenzy.

He turned to Peter and held up his hand, "Let me scope this out first, then I'll come back and get you when it's time to roll cameras."

Sampson nodded but didn't speak, still half asleep after the six-hour drive from New York. Ethan got out of the car and found Lloyd standing with a young dark-haired FBI agent dressed in navy-blue slacks, a white shirt, hiking boots, and a blue Windbreaker.

"Ethan, this is Special Agent Esther Jackson," Lloyd said, motioning to the tall, good-looking woman. "She's a friend and running the investigation."

"Pleased to meet you," Ethan said, shaking her hand.

"Likewise," Jackson said, a smile on her face. "Any friend of Lloyd's is a friend of mine."

Lloyd cleared his throat. "Esther has a couple of ground rules she wants to discuss before we start shooting."

"No problem," Ethan said, noticing the flood lamps spilling beams of light across the meadow in the back of Wellington's house. It reminded him of the video of the crime scene the night of the murder.

"First off, how are you splitting up your people?" Jackson said as she gestured to a state trooper to remove the yellow police tape cordoning off the back porch. "I can see you brought a big production crew."

"I did, indeed," Ethan said, glancing back at his team. "Me, Lloyd, my anchorman, Peter Sampson, and one of my camera crews—Herb Glickstein and Anthony Petulla—will accompany you and your agents into the house."

Jackson ticked off their names on a clipboard she was holding. "And what about everybody else?"

"My researcher, David Livingston, is directing my second crew—Bobby Raffalo and Sylvester Jurkins. They're going to photograph your agents as they search for bodies on the property. There's also an editor named Joel Zimmerman setting up equipment in our remote truck in case we need to edit another segment for my show. He won't be a bother. Never ventures out except to stretch his legs."

"That should all work as long as you stay clear of my search teams. And please, tell your people this is a crime scene—that we're looking for evidence, for bodies that will prove Rufus Wellington is a serial killer. Make sure they don't interfere with procedure, get in the way of my CSIs, or touch anything. I had to pull a lot of strings to get you out here, so if you compromise even one stitch of evidence, I'm gonna end up twiddling my thumbs in an FBI field office somewhere out in no man's land."

"I'll brief my crew before we start shooting," Ethan said as he noticed a convoy of police cars surrounding what looked like an armored personnel carrier pull up to the police barricade. "What's that?"

"Security for Wellington."

"He's here?" Ethan said, turning back to Special Agent Jackson.

"We had to pull a lot of strings at the Justice Department, but we need him to help us search for bodies. This place is hundreds of acres, mostly dense woods and thick underbrush. He claims to have buried his alleged victims over the course of almost three decades. They could be anywhere. We'll never find them without his help."

"Are we safe?" Ethan said as he watched half a dozen heavily armed security guards surround the back door of the armored vehicle.

"These guys are federal marshals, the best in the business at guarding killers like Wellington. There won't be a problem."

Then the door swung open, and Wellington, shackled in handcuffs and leg irons, stepped out. A burly sheriff's deputy wearing aviator sunglasses and carrying a .45-caliber Glock 21 pressed up against the small of Wellington's back climbed out of the vehicle right behind him.

It was Percy Wilkerson.

"What's he doing here?" Ethan said, alarmed.

"He's the acting sheriff while Eugene McKenzie recuperates," Jackson said. "Only way we could get the Franklin County district attorney to agree to release Wellington into our custody was to let his sheriff's department help guard him. And Percy Wilkerson is their guy."

Ethan nodded and said, unsettled, "Give me fifteen minutes, and my production crew will be ready." He quickly turned and walked straight over to David, "Do you see him?"

"What the hell's Wellington doing here?"

"Long story. And Wilkerson?"

"I see him too."

"Do you want to change our game plan?"

"Nope. You need to see what's behind that door. That's the priority. Then you can join me out here. Plenty of cops guarding Wellington besides that asshole Wilkerson."

"Tell Raffalo to concentrate on Wellington as the CSI search for bodies, and keep me posted on everything that happens. And, David, make sure to stay far away from Wellington. Don't do anything stupid."

Ten minutes later, Ethan was following Special Agent Jackson as she made her way through the kitchen and down the rickety staircase to the basement. Herb Glickstein was getting the shot with a wide-angle lens, and Anthony Petulla was recording sound on a shotgun microphone suspended on a long boom he was holding near the ceiling. Peter was glued to Jackson's side as Ethan directed his team, pointing out different images he wanted to capture as the FBI searched for evidence. When they reached the stairs to the subbasement, Jackson stopped to chat with a crime scene investigator dressed in a light-blue mask and bodysuit, who'd just opened a wooden crate containing hundreds of vials of medicine packed in Styrofoam sleeves.

"What is that?" Peter asked.

Glickstein swung his camera and focused on the anchorman.

"Different kinds of anesthetics," the CSI said as he carefully removed the bottles, dropping them into individual evidence bags.

"Is that what Wellington used to sedate Heather Starr?"

"I have no idea. My field test doesn't recognize the drug. Won't know exactly what's in here until we get back to the lab at Quantico, where I have more sophisticated equipment. My educated guess, though, is it's the same stuff he used to leave her paralyzed but fully awake so she could see and hear everything he was doing as he cut her into pieces. Must've been god-awful."

Ethan whispered into Glickstein's ear.

"Got the whole exchange," the cameraman said, circling Sampson as Ethan told him to zoom into a tight shot and pan across the bottles. Then his iPhone buzzed in his pocket.

"It's sheer insanity out here," David said, out of breath. "There are teams of agents digging all over the property."

"You okay?"

"Fine, Ethan. Just a bit tense."

"What's Wellington doing?" Ethan said, feeling a growing sense of déjà vu, worrying he was making another mistake, putting David in the line of fire—like he did with Mindy in Dorchester.

"He's not saying a word. He's just smiling and pointing, motioning to the CSI where to dig. It's fucking creepy."

"And the federal marshals?"

"All around him."

"Wilkerson?"

"Never leaves his side, his gun permanently shoved into Wellington's back, his other hand clamped on the chains."

"Keep an eye on them," Ethan said, more wary than ever.

"You can bet your ass, I will. And where are you, Ethan?"

"In the basement. FBI agents crawling all over the place, sifting through everything, dusting for fingerprints, and searching for blood smears with infrared lights. Herb's capturing unbelievable footage."

"So is Bobby," David said briskly.

Suddenly, a loud commotion.

Ethan could hear screaming in the background.

"Gotta go," David said, panting. "Agents on the far side of the meadow are waving and shouting about something."

"Keep the line open," Ethan said heatedly. David didn't respond, but Ethan could hear him racing across the field, barking orders at Bobby Raffalo, imploring him to keep rolling. He waited with bated breath, listening to their footsteps crunching on dry leaves and tree branches and to loud shouting off in the distance. "David?"

More waiting.

Agonizing.

Finally, David was back on the line. "They found something," he said, gasping for air.

"What is it?"

"Can't tell yet. They're dusting away loose dirt with a brush." Ethan listened as David continued shouting directions to his cameraman. Another long pause, then David whispered tensely, "Shit. A human skull. Fingers. A leg bone."

"Where's Bobby?"

"Right in there, shooting with the lab techs."

"And Wellington?"

"He's ten feet away, gawking, still smiling—like he's thrilled the cops just unearthed one of his bodies."

Ethan was speechless. Had Wellington really murdered all twenty-one prostitutes he so proudly bragged about during the interview? Christ. A killing field. "What're they doing now?"

"The CSI are still digging, and Wellington's leading another group into the woods, to another location. Call you back."

Ethan put his cell phone into his pocket and followed Sampson and Agent Jackson as they hiked down the stairs and through the door into Wellington's library, the room already filled with FBI agents setting up lights. "Just heard one of your teams found a body."

"Already know." She held out a second spiral notebook.

"What is it?"

Jackson handed Ethan a pair of latex gloves. He slipped them on then flipped through the book. He saw twelve pages with pictures of body parts and coded markings, just like the book he'd found when he broke into the house weeks ago.

"Maybe more victims," she said, reaching for the book and handing it back to the CSI for bagging as an FBI agent walked over to them.

Glickstein backed up and framed a wide shot. "Ready when you are."

Jackson turned to Ethan, "You guys got everything you need in here?"

Ethan checked with his crew and nodded.

"Okay," Jackson said. "Let's see what's behind that fucking door."

They crossed the room—Glickstein letting the camera roll, framing the agent picking the padlock.

"Done," he said, looking back at Agent Jackson. "We can go in."

Jackson pursed her lips then pushed through the door.

A wave of foul air, heavy and stale—like putrefaction in a crypt—hit Ethan. "What's that smell?" he said, gagging.

"Death," Jackson said. "Get some light in here, people. Now."

An agent pushed past Ethan, waving a flood lamp. An operating room table—covered in dry blood and a thick layer of dust—was sitting in the middle of the room next to a stainless steel counter holding a surgical saw, extra blades, an empty syringe, a bottle of anesthesia, and a set of blood-encrusted scalpels. Hanging from the ceiling was a fiber-optic surgical light, and on the floor positioned around the table was a series of drains littered with hair and bone fragments.

"What is this place?" Sampson said, eyes flashing as he turned to Ethan.

"The kill site," Ethan said soberly. "This is why McKenzie had a heart attack when we tried to come down here. He must've known about the operating room and was afraid we might stumble across it."

"Looks like Wellington didn't have time to clean up before he buried Heather Starr," Jackson said, motioning for her CSIs to begin collecting evidence. "I wanna confirm it's her blood and see if there are traces of any other victims down here."

"What do you suppose Wellington used these for?" Ethan said, motioning to a row of grappling hooks suspended from the ceiling.

"To hang body parts," Jackson said, peering at the apparatus. "Test the blood on the hooks too."

Lloyd had drifted off and was inspecting a countertop covered with gauze pads, test tubes, surgical equipment, and more vials of anesthesia. Then he stopped in his tracks and stared at a stainless steel cabinet hanging over a rust-stained metal sink.

"Ethan?"

"What is it?" he said, staring at the cabinet.

"Let's find out," Jackson said, putting on a fresh pair of gloves. "Crack the lock."

An agent unclipped a pouch attached to his service belt, rifled through a series of tools, grabbed a small cylindrical instrument, and after tinkering a moment, popped open the lock. Jackson waved everyone away then pulled open the door, Herb Glickstein rolling off a medium shot. Neatly arranged on a series of shelves were dozens of glass jars filled with a pale yellow liquid, and floating in each jar was a perfectly preserved human thumb.

"What the hell," Sampson said, repulsed.

"Trophies," Jackson said, her eyes poring over the file cabinet. "Same body part from each of his victims."

"The same ... what?" Ethan said, sickened.

Jackson counted the jars. "Thirty-three, and if you add his mother, that gives us thirty-four murders. That matches the total number of victims in the two diaries."

Ethan stared at the cabinet and gestured to Herb to make a tight shot of each bottle. "Get the labels," he said.

Herb could see each one of the girls' names through the viewfinder.

"Do you see Heather Starr?" Sampson said, leaning closer to Ethan.

"There," Ethan said, pointing to the last jar. "The guy's a sick fuck. A real sick fuck."

A lab tech began to bag each specimen.

And Ethan's cell phone rang.

Everybody's cell phone rang.

"What? David?" Ethan could hear gunfire in the background. It sounded like all hell was breaking loose. "What's goin' on?" he shouted as everybody else in the room started shouting.

"Ethan." More gunfire, rapid-fire. *Rat-a-tat-tat.* "He just escaped."

"Wellington?"

"We were headed through the woods, a small group of us." David was out of breath, panting. "He was taking us to another body, far away from the main group of agents. And that fucker Percy Wilkerson unchained him, just like that. Wellington must have bribed him with a pot load of money." The gunfire stopped momentarily then started up again, more intermittent. "And as soon as Wellington was free, he grabbed Wilkerson's service revolver right out of his hand, cracked him in the face—man, there was nothing left of his nose, blood everywhere—then backed up a pace, and shot him through the forehead. Wilkerson was stunned before he went down. Had no idea Wellington was gonna blow his brains out. Then Wellington wheeled around like a robot and killed the three federal marshals and the CSI who was with us. They didn't stand a chance. He was moving so fucking fast."

"Where are you? The crew?"

"Hiding."

"Where's Wellington?"

"I dunno. He tore off through the woods."

"Are you all right?" Ethan said, a sinking feeling in the pit of his stomach.

"We're scared shitless, but nobody's hurt."

"What's all the gunfire I'm hearing?"

"Other agents chasing Wellington."

"Look, David," Ethan said frantically, "stay where you are until you're sure he's gone, then get the hell out of there."

"No shit, and, Ethan, we got the whole bloody thing on tape."

Ethan hung up and, without hesitating, spun, and said, "Herb, Anthony, come with me."

They were out of the lab in an instant, up the stairs, and out the back door—long before Agent Jackson had finished her phone call.

"This way," he said, shouting at his crew as he hurried down the path to the meadow, toward the sound of the gunfire.

"What are we doing?" Herb Glickstein said, yelling.

"Looking for Wellington."

"Are you crazy?"

Ethan didn't answer, just thought cynically, *Maybe I am. Maybe I've got a death wish, that it'd solve all my problems in a nanosecond.*

He kept running—across the meadow, into the forest and thick underbrush, pushing aside tall grasses and prickly thornbushes tearing at his face, shredding his clothes, ripping his skin—always closer to the gunfire now on his left. Changing directions like a tomcat, he followed the sound as it got louder.

"Herb, hang back and use your telephoto lens. Don't want you near the shooting."

"You're gonna get yourself killed, Ethan."

He didn't listen, drawn to the gunfire like a magnet, bent on finding Wellington, determined to capture the moment on tape as the FBI tracked down the escaped maniac.

Then, in a flash, the underbrush cleared, and he ran into a small clearing, surrounded by more dense foliage, and straight into Rufus Wellington—as if their fates were somehow intertwined. Wellington was standing all alone, his clothes ripped and hanging off his body, covered in globs of blood dripping down his arms and onto his hands.

Ethan froze.

Panicked.

"So we meet again, Mr. Benson," Wellington said, his face a sick sneer. "You. Right here before me. Like one of my departed angels. The last piece of the big puzzle finally in place, ready and willing to join all my special friends in heaven. God will be so pleased with my handiwork." He threw back his head and wailed to the crescent moon, peeking through the clouds, illuminating his insanity like a spotlight on a stage. "Are you drunk, Mr. Benson? Have you had a nip at the bottle to get up the courage to face me? That's what you usually do, isn't it, Mr. Benson, to get through your miserable life?"

"You spied on me, asshole."

"Because I'm omnipresent. The black reaper. The devil here on earth."

"You're fucking crazy, Wellington," Ethan said, backing up several steps, his heart pounding, his mind searching for a plan. "Put the gun down. I can hear the cops coming through the woods. You can't get away."

"You think I want to get away, Mr. Benson, when God has delivered you to me on a platter? No. No. No. I don't want to run. What's the fun in that, when I can dispatch you like all the others who came before you. It's destiny, don't you think, Mr. Benson?"

Ethan continued to back up.

There was no reasoning with a madman.

"Now say good-bye. It's time to meet your Maker. YOUR MAKER. YOUR MAKER! And my time to fulfill the last chapter of the prophecy that's guided every single moment of my glorious life."

Then he wailed again, raised the gun, and started advancing—one step, two steps, three steps—Ethan recoiling, but unable to move farther away, as Wellington drew closer, still laughing hysterically, his hair standing on end, spittle dribbling down his chin, snot pouring out of his nose. Ethan could feel the barrel of the gun, pointing directly at him, a black hole ready to suck him in.

"Say good-bye, Mr. Benson," Wellington said, stopping no more than ten feet in front of him, spreading his legs in a shooter's stance, gripping the Glock in both hands, ready to pull the trigger—as a single, deafening shot roared through the air and blew off the top of his head, spilling thousands of specks of blood and brain matter all over the ground.

Ethan fell to his knees—physically shaken, emotionally drained—then turned and saw a plume of smoke drifting from the end of Lloyd Howard's Beretta.

Slowly, Lloyd circled around him toward Wellington, kicking his lifeless body, before placing his hand on Ethan's shoulder and helping him to his feet—just as Special Agent Jackson, a half dozen of her agents, and Peter Sampson raced into the clearing.

"Are you all right?" Lloyd said, holstering his handgun.

Ethan didn't answer.

He just peered around the clearing at all the chaos, the FBI agents forming a protective ring around Rufus Wellington, as David and the two camera crews pulled up and huddled anxiously about him. Finally, he said, very quietly, "I'm okay. Scared. But okay."

Then he looked for Sampson and started shouting in a clear and calm voice, "Listen up, everybody. We have to go back to the remote truck and build a new segment to update the end of the show. We've got three hours before air, and we'll need every second. I'll call the control room and tell Paul's he's gonna have to feed our new spot to the network—*Live to Tape.* There's no other way we'll make it. So let's hustle, people. Can't waste any more time."

EPILOGUE

ETHAN SAT IN THE WAITING room, holding hands with Sarah, gazing out at snowflakes floating through the air and coating the trees in Central Park with a layer of white dust from an early winter storm. His special had rocked law enforcement in the weeks after the broadcast—the justice department launching a formal investigation into the FBI's handling of Rufus Wellington, focusing on the breakdown in procedure that allowed him to escape. Ethan had been called to Washington by the US attorney and questioned about his role in unearthing the evidence that had broken the case, leading to three grand jury indictments against Bret Davenport, Sheriff Eugene McKenzie, and Janice O'Brien for their roles in the murder of Heather Starr and the other prostitutes who had fallen under his knife. The authorities had continued searching for bodies but, without Wellington's help, had only found thirteen of his victims—the remaining twenty prostitutes lost forever in their secret graves on his three hundred acres of land.

The special itself had been lauded by the press—the stark images of Wellington's escape and the gunshot that had brought him down now being touted as a leading contender for Emmy, Dupont-Columbia, and Peabody awards—the most prestigious awards in journalism. Through it all, Ethan had handled the public notoriety with dignity, while privately grappling with the demons he'd been wrestling with for years.

The door to the inner office slowly opened, and Dr. Fred Schwartz walked into the room. "Shall we get started?" he said, smiling at the two of them.

They followed him into his office, the tension between them raw, their marriage still tormented by strife.

"I watched your story, Ethan. Congratulations. You proved everything you've been telling me and much more. Will you be supervising coverage of the aftermath? The fallout's making headlines."

"Peter doesn't do daily news stories," he said. "So that'll be left to the producers in hard news. I'm all but finished with Rufus Wellington."

"Are you?"

"Yes."

"But you can't let go of him, can you, Ethan?"

He pulled out a cigarette, stared at it longingly, then pushed it back into the pack.

"Not smoking today?" Dr. Schwartz said, crinkling his eyes.

"Trying to cut back."

"And what about the Scotch?"

"Still drinking, but much less than before my story aired."

"Your perception, Sarah?"

"He's still hitting the bottle pretty hard, Dr. Schwartz," she said. "But it's out in the open, and we're talking about it."

"Good. Good. That's a first step. And, Ethan, have you told your colleagues at work?"

"Well—"

"He didn't have to," Sarah said, cutting him off gently. "Wellington hacked into our private e-mails, and it all came out

404

during the interview. So Peter Sampson found out and told Paul Lang. Now it's out in the open, all over the office."

"And how does that make you feel, Ethan? Better?"

"Not sure that's the right word."

"Relieved?"

"Maybe a little."

"Embarrassed?"

"Completely."

"Self-conscious?"

"And mostly self-conscious. Because now everybody knows I'm an alcoholic."

"Well, that too is a good start, Ethan. You're no longer hiding your problem. It's out there front and center, so others will now know why you're sometimes out of control, and that should help you confront your drinking head-on." He paused, waiting for Ethan to respond, and when he didn't, said delicately, "Have you told other people about the baby?"

Ethan grabbed a cigarette.

"Guess that answers my question."

"It's still only the two of us," Sarah said softly. "But it's helping me understand, Dr. Schwartz. Ethan tells me what he's thinking, what he's feeling, and what he's hiding from—and how the baby is always there, in the back of his mind, eating away at him. So now I understand—a little better—why he keeps drinking and why he can't stop."

"But he's told nobody else."

"Not yet," she whispered.

"And Luke?"

"I'm trying, really, I am. But he's still just a little kid, and I can't find the right words to tell him he almost had an older sister or what happened to her or why I sometimes act funny, I guess drunk, when I'm with him."

"Just don't wait too long, Ethan. He needs to know from you, and the sooner the better. The last thing you want is to create a problem that will come back and haunt you, because that's what'll happen if he somehow finds out on his own."

"So where do we go from here, Dr. Schwartz?" Sarah said.

"That's up to you and Ethan."

They looked at each other, uncertain, as Dr. Schwartz turned off his tape recorder. "We have a long way to go before Ethan fully understands the consequences of his drinking. It's gonna take time and a lot of work by both of you. Ethan's a functioning alcoholic, and the only way for him to get better is to give up alcohol completely."

"That's what I want, Dr. Schwartz, desperately."

"I know that, Ethan. Can you get away from work and be together as a family?"

"We're headed to the Caribbean on Friday, all three of us, for a couple of weeks of vacation."

"Good. You'll be away from the office, away from Rufus Wellington and away from your story with all the pressures." He gazed kindly from Ethan to Sarah. "Maybe we should plan two sessions a week when you get back. That'll give us more time to talk."

"Sounds like a good plan, Dr. Schwartz," Ethan said, standing. "Thank you for everything."

Then they said their good-byes, walked out of his office, through the empty waiting room, and into the hallway.

Still in love with each other.

But scared of the future.

Not sure they'd find a path to overcome his drinking.

And move forward together as husband and wife and a family.

ACKNOWLEDGMENTS

THIS WORK OF FICTION WOULD not be possible without the help and support of dozens of people who have given me and continue to give me guidance and encouragement. I want to thank Av Westin and the late Jeff Gralnick who taught me everything I know about television production, the incomparable Barbara Walters who drilled into me the fine art of doing an interview, and the countless executives, correspondents, cameramen, soundmen, editors, and lighting directors who helped me polish my creative style and master the nuances of writing, producing, and directing for television.

Special thanks must be given to my friend, colleague, and book editor, Hall Powel, who agonized many sleepless nights over *Live to Tape,* redlined the manuscript, and then spent countless hours on the telephone discussing his criticisms and helping me polish the writing, structuring, and storytelling. This novel would not be the same without his masterful insights.

Of course, I want to thank my loving wife, Amy, always the first to read my manuscripts, and my two sons, Alex and Aaron, who never pull a punch when critiquing any of my works of fiction. Lastly, I want to remember my late father, Vern Diamond, a live television director at CBS News who introduced me to the world of production and helped me embark on a forty year career in television journalism. All of these people have played key roles in my *Ethan Benson Thriller* series. All of these people have been inspirational and supportive as I launch my second career as a murder mystery writer.

AUTHOR BIO

Rob Grien -
Mont Vert Studio.

Jeffrey L. Diamond is an award-winning producer with forty years of experience in television news. His career began in the early 1970s at ABC News where he produced at *Special Events, Weekend News,* and *World News Tonight,* before moving to the weekly newsmagazine, *20/20.* His body of work includes breaking news specials, major newsmaker interviews, entertainment profiles, investigative reports on consumer products, and hundreds of crime stories. During his long career, he collaborated with some of the biggest names in the business—with anchors Barbara Walters, Charles Gibson, and Stone Phillips and correspondents Tom Jarriel, Lynn Sherr, and Deborah Roberts. After taking a break from storytelling in 1991, Mr. Diamond embarked on a decade-long journey as an executive producer—managing broadcast, cable, and syndicated programming. He created *Dateline NBC* in the early 1990s, ran

Martha Stewart Living Television in the mid-1990s, and launched *Judith Regan Television* in the late 1990s. As a show runner, he oversaw million-dollar budgets; supervised hundreds of producers, writers, directors, editors, and camera crews; and planned the creative content of his programming. Mr. Diamond returned to his roots during the final decade of his career, devoting all his creative energies to producing stories, once again, for *20/20*. He's been nominated for dozens of journalism awards and has won six national Emmy Awards, two Dupont-Columbia Awards, one Peabody Award, one National Press Club Consumer Journalism Award, two CINE Golden Eagle Awards, and countless others. Mr. Diamond lives in the Berkshire Mountains of Massachusetts, where he writes the Ethan Benson crime series. A graduate of Lehigh University, he's married, has two sons, a daughter-in-law, two grandchildren, and a golden retriever named Bailey.

CPSIA information can be obtained
at www.ICGtesting.com
Printed in the USA
BVOW09s1152220917
495547BV00021BA/7/P